Nothing to lose

Paul Marco Thrillers, Volume 2

Dominic Fino

Published by Dominic Fino, 2024.

NOTHING TO LOSE

First edition. July 31, 2024.

Copyright © 2024 Dominic Fino.

ISBN: 979-8227262981

Written by Dominic Fino.

Also by Dominic Fino

Paul Marco Thrillers
Lights Out
Nothing to lose
Death Hawaiian Style
Vendetta Vegas Style

Table of Contents

Chapter 1

Paul Marco and his wife, Diana, had opened a small packaging and shipping store with the severance money Paul received from his former employer. The Marcos had operated the store for about a year and were just beginning to show a small profit. The past year had been hard on the Marcos and their marriage. The emotional strain of Paul not being able to find work after his middle management job was eliminated added to the stress levels for him and his wife. Diana tried to help in the store as much as she could, but she still had to take care of the house and all the chores that are a part of owning any home. The Marco bank account was strained to the limit, and they would not be able to hold on much longer if business did not pick up soon. They both knew that they would be OK after Thanksgiving, once the Christmas shipping season officially started. But that was still almost two months away and money was extremely tight.

On October 4, the morning air was cool and the sky was very sunny when Paul entered the store at 8:00 a.m. Diana usually came to work around noon with their lunch and stayed until four or five o'clock. Paul would normally close the store at six and be home around seven o'clock so he and his wife could have dinner together before going over the daily receipts.

After Paul entered the store this morning, he went through his normal routine of putting cash in the register drawer and vacuuming the store so it would look nice for his customers, who usually started to arrive before the 9:00 a.m. store opening. Paul was busy ordering some new mailing envelopes and stationery for the store when he heard the front door open. He quickly looked at his watch and saw that it was only 8:47. Paul also saw that the two male customers standing in the front door opening were in their early twenties and did not remember seeing them before. They were both dressed in jeans, expensive sneakers, and sport coats.

Paul said, "Good morning."

The first young man through the door replied, "Morning. Are you the owner?"

Paul was still completing the order form as he looked up to say, "Sure am. May I help you?"

Paul noticed the second man stood by the front door while the man doing the talking advanced to the counter where Paul was standing. The man said, "Nice store you have here. I suspect you are a fairly new business in the area?"

Paul was becoming a little suspicious of the two strangers as he looked them over before responding. "Yes. We have been at this location just over a year. Is there anything I can do for you?"

The man leaned across the counter to rest his right arm on top while his left hand pointed a handgun at Paul. Paul did not move as he eyed the handgun. He then looked into the stranger's eyes to calmly say, "We only have $100 petty cash. Take it and get out."

The stranger smiled a little while shaking his head from side to side. The other man still at the door was looking at the two of them on opposite sides of the counter and he, too, now began to smile and laugh. The man pointing the gun at Paul said, "My name is Ben and that is my partner Jerry. Get it? Ben and Jerry." Paul was not amused as the man calling himself Ben was now laughing out loud. Ben then said, "We're in the personal protection business. You, as a new business owner, will be billed $500 per month for our security services. Of course, my partner and I will make sure nothing happens to your property so long as you make your payments by the first of each month. Are there any questions?" Paul was getting increasingly angry as the smug punk on the other side of the counter laughed and turned to look at his friend standing guard by the front door. Paul knew he had to act quickly. As Ben turned around to face him again, Paul took the pen he was still holding in his left hand and jabbed it deep into Ben's right eye. Instantly Ben screamed in pain. Paul grabbed the handgun Ben had released so he could use both hands to hold his pen stabbed eye. Jerry had no idea what had just taken place. Before Jerry could draw his weapon, Paul pointed Ben's confiscated

9mm automatic at Jerry and said, "You should take this action as my refusal to hire your personal security services. Now take out your weapon and drop it on the floor very slowly."

Jerry was still awestruck at Paul's quick actions. However, Jerry was obviously not as stupid as he looked, because he did what Paul requested without saying a word. Paul then said, "Now walk toward me and stand by that table."

Paul was pointing to a three-by-six-foot display table that was halfway between the counter, and the front door. When Jerry was in position, Paul walked around to the other side of the counter, keeping the automatic trained on Jerry as he moved. When Paul reached the other side of the counter, he saw Ben lying on the floor still holding his hands over his right eye. The pen was still buried in Ben's eye socket. Paul looked at Ben and very calmly said, "Lesson number one, asshole, is never point a gun at anyone unless you intend to use it."

Ben was obviously still in a great deal of pain but managed to muter, "Fuck you, man. I'm going to lose this eye, you son of a bitch."

Paul looked at Jerry and smiled as he lowered the 9mm to Ben's right knee and squeezed the trigger. Ben's body immediately jerked as he yelled, "Are you crazy?"

Paul said, "Now you are starting to understand, asshole." Paul then pointed the gun at Ben's left knee and squeezed the trigger again. Ben was now screaming with terror and pain. Paul looked at Jerry and said, "You can either take this trash out of my store or I can call the cops and have them do it. It's your call."

Jerry looked as if he had seen a ghost. The screams from his partner lying on the floor were making Jerry very nervous. Without saying a word, Jerry bolted toward the front door and vanished in the parking lot. Paul turned toward Ben and said, "Well, it looks as if it's going to be just you and me. Don't worry; I'm not going to kill you. I want you to spend the rest of your miserable life confined to a wheelchair. However, if you do something stupid like press charges against me for shooting you, I will hunt you down to finish this job."

Ben passed out from the excruciating pain and trauma his body was experiencing. Paul then called 911 to report that a single gunman had tried to hold him up. The police took Paul's statement and did not press any charges against him for shooting the robbery suspect. Several other store owners were now gathering outside Paul's store. As usual, the flashing lights and sirens brought a sight-seeing crowd to the scene. Through the crowd, Diana could be heard crying and yelling, "Is he all right?"

Paul immediately pushed his way through the police and onlookers to grab his wife, saying, "It's OK. I'm all right."

Diana was crying as she held her husband close to her. She whispered, "I saw all the flashing lights and the crowd and thought something had happened to you. I was so scared that you were hurt."

Paul held his wife very tightly as he softly said, "You know I am too damn hardheaded for anything bad to happen to me. Besides, only the good die young. I'll be around until I'm 110."

Diana managed to laugh a little at her husband's sick sense of humor, then asked, "What happened?"

Paul explained the whole sequence of events to Diana as she listened attentively. When Paul was finished talking, Diana said, "Are you crazy? Why didn't you just tell them it was OK, give them the money, and then call the police once they left the store?" Paul looked straight into his wife's eyes and said, "I don't know why it is, but I simply hate it when someone points a gun at me. I know it may sound strange to you, but I figure they are going to kill me anyway, so I might as well take a chance at doing something to stop them. Besides, you know I'm a survivor and always manage to come out of situations like this on my feet."

Diana could see that Paul was pacifying her, so she said, "Yeah, well one of these days maybe your luck is going to run out and I'll be stuck making funeral arrangements."

Paul laughed a little and replied, "Well, when that day comes make sure my hair is combed nice and neat while I'm lying in my coffin. You know how I hate to have my hair messed up. Besides, look at all the publicity the store will now get as a result of this little attempted robbery."

Diana and Paul went about running the store as usual for the rest of the day. From time to time different customers would ask about all the commotion earlier that day and Paul would have to tell the entire story again. By the time the day was through, Paul and Diana must have repeated the same story fifty times or more. That night they had dinner together and were sitting at home watching TV as they went over the day's receipts. Diana asked, "Paul why did you let the second robber go and why didn't you tell the police about him?"

Paul stopped making entries into his laptop computer to look up at Diana and say, "Well, I figured that he was scared enough to go tell whomever they worked for that I was not to be messed with. I didn't want the police to know about him so they couldn't question him about how his partner ended up with two blown-off kneecaps."

Diana persisted, "How did you explain the shooting of the first robber to the police? Surely they could tell he was shot while lying on the floor."

"I told them a single robber came into the store and tried to hold me up. I took advantage of a split-second lapse in his approach and stabbed him with my pen. I then went over the counter after him and we struggled for the gun, which I managed to wrestle away from him. The first shot went off as we struggled for the gun and it just happened to hit the suspect in the knee. Once I had control of the robber's gun, I shot him in the other leg to keep him from running or harming me. Of course, I had to tell the police I feared for my life so I had no choice but to shoot the robber."

"Do you think they bought your story? Suppose the robber decides to tell the police what really happened. You could be in trouble with the law."

Paul laughed a little, then said, "I wouldn't worry too much about the robber talking to the police. He has enough trouble to deal with right now. As for the police, I don't think they believed my account of the incident, but they also did not seem to care. Let's face it, they just as soon I would have killed the son of a bitch so they wouldn't have as much paperwork to complete. Besides, one of the police officers seemed to recognize the crook, because I heard him tell one of the other policemen, 'Looks as if Benny finally met somebody who said no.'"

That night Diana fell asleep quickly. Paul, however, tossed and turned for hours. He kept thinking about how he should have handled the situation in the store. He knew that he was getting soft as the years passed him by. Paul realized that he may have put himself and his wife in jeopardy should Jerry and his partner decide to retaliate. Unfortunately, Paul had forgotten the number one rule in dealing with an enemy. That rule was simply to take no prisoners.

At 6:30 a.m., the alarm clock woke Paul to begin his daily routine. First he would take a shower, then shave and get dressed. Paul then drove to his store, on the way stopping at a local convenience store to pick up a coffee and newspaper. At around eight o'clock Paul would open the doors to begin his normal chores of ordering, stocking, and vacuuming the store. Diana would get up around seven-thirty to do all of her housework before showering and dressing to make it to the store by noon. The Marcos were now set in their routines, and life had taken on a much simpler, more stress-free pace. Had the store been more profitable, they would really have no need to be anxious.

About two months after the attempted robbery, a man entered the store wearing an old olive drab army field jacket, jeans, high-top work boots, and a dark blue stocking cap. It was almost two o'clock and Diana was waiting on a customer. Paul was in the back of the store sorting and stacking a new shipment of packing boxes that had just been delivered that morning. Diana gave the customer her change, then thanked her for coming in and looked up at the man in the army field jacket to ask, "May I help you?" The man looked at Diana, then slowly approached the counter where she was standing. As he moved closer, Diana could see he was in his early thirties, dark-complexioned, as if maybe he worked in some type of outside job, and had a limp. Maybe a carpenter or bricklayer, she thought. The man was now standing at the counter directly in front of Diana.

"Nice place you have here."

"Thank you. Is there something I can help you with today?"

"A couple of friends of mine were in here a few months ago and they were treated rather harshly."

Diana did not know what to make of this mystery man. Her only thought was to get rid of him. Diana replied, "I am sorry to hear that. Now may I get something for you?"

"No. I have something for you." The man pulled a gun out from his jacket pocket and fired two shots directly into Diana's head, at point-blank range.

Paul was still in the back and did not hear the shots from the silenced .22-caliber automatic. Hearing noises in the back room of the store behind the single door that separated the customer area from the storage space, the man slowly walked to the door and listened for a few seconds. It sounded as if someone was moving things around in the back room. He placed his hand on the doorknob and slowly turned the handle as he pushed ever so slowly. The door was open about a half-inch, and the man could just barely see Paul move past his narrow line of sight carrying a cardboard box. As the man was about to burst in on Paul, the telephone rang, startling the man. Immediately after the first ring sounded, a second phone line started ringing. The noise from the two telephones ringing caught Paul's attention. He started to approach the door so he could help Diana by answering one of the phones. As Paul put his hand on the door that separated him from the customer area, a female customer walked in the front door. The man in the army field jacket was now in a bind. He quickly turned to face the approaching customer and fired two quick shots at her chest while racing toward the front door to leave. His element of surprise was gone. Paul opened the storeroom door and immediately saw his wife lying on the floor with blood puddles around her head. The phones were ringing and the limping field jacketed man was just at the front door when he suddenly turned. He quickly fired a shot at Paul, who was already dropping to the floor behind the counter to aid his wife. Paul, now realizing the person wearing the field jacket had just fired a shot at him, crawled to the counter, where he kept a .38-caliber revolver. As he grabbed the handgun, Paul peaked over the top of the counter to see the limping field-jacketed man disappearing onto the parking lot among hundreds of cars, vans, and trucks. Paul also saw the female customer lying on the floor, halfway between the front door and the counter. Paul dropped the gun and hurried to his wife's side. He checked for a carotid pulse but found none. His eyes immediately began to fill with tears as he remembered the awful look and smell of death. Paul gently lowered Diana's head to the floor, then rushed to the female customer on the opposite side of the counter. He felt her neck for a pulse but again found none. Paul's tears were now being replaced with rage and anger. He picked up the phone and dialed 911 to report the incident. He also put the handgun in his belt behind the small of his back while looking out onto the parking lot. Paul scanned the many cars coming and going to see if he could spot the man with the army field jacket. Unfortunately, all Paul saw now were the flashing lights of three police cars racing toward his store.

Homicide detective Theresa McGavin was taking Paul's statement about what had happened. Paul told the detective how quickly things had occurred and that he thought there might be some tie-in to the events that had taken place a few months ago during an attempted robbery. Detective McGavin was copiously taking down notes and asking follow-up questions. Paul had to search his brain for answers. One of the crime scene officers asked Detective McGavin to take a look at something, so she excused herself, telling Paul she would be right back. Paul watched the detective as she left him to his thoughts and grief. Without thinking, Paul lit a cigarette in the store, not caring that the place was crawling with cops. In Maryland they had a very strict law about not being allowed to smoke in public buildings and restaurants.

As Paul was looking for a place to flick his ash, he looked toward the front door and spotted someone he had not seen in a long time. Paul stood up, then headed for the front door. Once he was outside, he flicked his ash and walked toward the plain black car that was definitely a so-called unmarked police cruiser. *The three antennas on the trunk lid are always a dead giveaway,* Paul thought. The man standing outside the driver's door talking to one of the uniformed officers who had first responded to Paul's 911 call was none other than Captain Thiemeyer. Paul caught Captain Thiemeyer's attention as he made his way into the crime scene area, now marked off with the familiar yellow tape. Paul took a drag from his cigarette and smiled as Captain Thiemeyer walked up to him, extending his hand while saying, "Hi, Paul. I'm very sorry to hear about what happened to your wife."

"Thank you, Captain. Long time no see. When was it? Oh, I remember. The last time we met was when you were helping solve the murders at the Baltimore Light Company about two years ago."

"That's right, Paul. It seems that murder is the one thing in this city that will never go out of business. By the way, how have you been since they canned you from the BLC?"

"Well, my wife Diana and I opened this store to try to make it on our own. You know, being our own boss and not having to worry about whether we will have a job each morning. Anyway, we were just starting to make this place work for us when all this happened."

"That's too bad. I see you have Detective McGavin on the case."

Turning to look at the detective as she leaned over the sheet covered body of his wife, Paul said, "Yes. She had been talking to me for about twenty minutes before you arrived. I also told her that I think this shooting may be related to the attempted robbery we had here a few months ago."

"Is that right? Well, you have a real bulldog on the case with McGavin. She is one smart cookie, and I would not be surprised if she doesn't wrap this whole mess up in record time."

"Is that so? She's that good?"

"You better believe it. I trained her!"

Captain Thiemeyer excused himself, then made his way over to where Detective McGavin was talking to the coroner.

"How's it going, Theresa?"

"Hi, Captain. Oh, you know, so-so. I think we have a possible grudge hit on our hands." She pointed to Diana Marco's body. "And it looks as if we have an innocent walk-in over there. Must have caught the triggerman by surprise, and he popped her two times in the chest while making his getaway."

"Theresa, I was talking to Paul outside, and he said there was an attempted robbery here a few months ago. He seems to think the shooting today is related to that case somehow. What's your read?"

"He told me that story, too. I haven't had any time to check it out yet. However, Officer Dunston said he responded to the robbery call back then and he thought there might be more to the story than was originally reported. I'll sort out all the details when I get back downtown. For now, I have to get the family notified for our victim number two over there."

"I know that is the worst part of the job, Theresa. Do you have a make on her yet?"

"Her name is Janet Daymore. She lives about three blocks from here according to her driver's license. We are sending a car over to the house to see if anyone is home now. If that doesn't pan out, we'll track down her husband through some of the information we found in her wallet. It looks as if he works for that big tool manufacturer across Route 30."

"Well, Theresa, it looks as if you're on top of things, as usual. After you get the preliminary report finished, give me a copy so I can brief the commissioner."

"The commissioner! Commissioner Jim Doukup? Why is he being briefed on a simple two-banger like this?"

"Commissioner Doukup knows Paul Marco and his wife Diana personally. I'm sure he is going to take a special interest in how the investigation is handled. So, Theresa, you better cross all your t's and dot all your i's on this one."

Theresa watched Captain Thiemeyer walk over to Paul to offer him some comfort before leaving in his plain unmarked cruiser, then watched Paul reach into his back pocket to retrieve a handkerchief to wipe his eyes as the coroner loaded the body of his deceased wife into the station wagon. There were several other store owners and many curious shoppers gathered around the police yellow tape barrier, watching the sad spectacle unfolding before their eyes. There were also two local TV mobile reporters making sound bites for tonight's six o'clock news.

Paul walked back into the store, where Detective McGavin was waiting for him. She motioned for him to have a seat in the back of the store so they could continue their conversation.

Detective McGavin said, "Listen. Mr. Marco, why don't you close up the place after the crime lab boys are finished, then go home. I understand you know Commissioner Doukup and that he will probably get personally involved with this investigation. Therefore, I see no need for us to hold you up any longer right now. Why don't I come by your place in a couple of days and we can pick up where we left off?"

Paul looked at the young detective with a blank stare. He thought to himself that maybe she looked more like an accountant or, God forbid, a lawyer, as opposed to a police detective working homicide. She simply did not look like a cop, whatever a cop was supposed to look like. Theresa was about five feet, two inches tall, with dirty blond hair and deep blue eyes. Probably 115 pounds soaking wet. She wore a small amount of makeup but really didn't need any. She was wearing a suit made from a wool blend and heels that added almost two inches to her height. Her shoulder length hair was pulled back and French-braided so that it stayed out of her face but at the same time made her look very professional. As Paul was sizing up the detective, he heard her say, "Paul, is that OK with you?"

Paul was shocked back to reality as he said, "Oh, I'm sorry. Sure, come by in a couple of days. That will be fine. I'm really not up to talking anymore right now. I have to make some phone calls to notify family and friends. I guess I also need to make funeral arrangements."

Paul slipped back into a stone-cold stupor. His mind was not able to keep a single thought more than thirty seconds before it raced in another direction.

Later that night, Paul did not remember closing the store and driving home. Everything seemed to just merge into one long daydream. Hunger pains consumed Paul's belly as he remembered that he had not eaten since lunch with Diana. Paul made himself a ham and cheese sandwich and drank the last of the iced tea. He sat in the kitchen and ate while staring at the empty kitchen chair his wife normally occupied. Slowly he finished his small meal and made a few phone calls notifying others about the tragedy. It was almost eight o'clock when Paul finally decided to take a shower. Without realizing it, he had sat on the couch for almost two hours straight, not moving a single muscle. Simply staring out the window into space as he thought about how life was going to be without Diana by his side.

When Paul finished his shower, he put on sweatpants and a long-sleeve sweatshirt, then lay on the bed. He rolled over to where Diana's pillow still carried the scent of her herbal shampoo and cried himself to sleep.

At eleven o'clock the phone rang. Paul reached for it and groggily answered by saying, "Hello."

"Paul, I'm sorry to call you so late, but I wanted to tell you how sorry I am to hear about Diana. She was a lovely person and I will never forget how special you two seemed to be when you were together."

Sitting up now, Paul was trying to place a face with the voice. "Who is this?"

"I'm sorry, Paul. This is Commissioner Doukup."

"Oh, how are you, Commissioner? I didn't recognize your voice. I managed to fall asleep for a few hours and couldn't quite put a face with the voice."

"I understand, Paul. Listen. I'm not going to hold you up right now. I know its been a rough day for you. I just wanted to call and express my condolences and tell you that I will personally look into Diana's murder. Now go back to sleep and I will be talking to you later."

"Thank you, Commissioner. I appreciate your concern and willingness to help. Good night."

Paul lit a cigarette and lay back down on the bed. His mind flashed back to almost two years ago, when Commissioner Jim Doukup, Captain Thiemeyer, and several others had helped solve the murders that had taken place at the BLC. Back then, Diana had been so worried that Paul would be seriously hurt by assisting in the investigation. Now Paul was lying in the same bed without Diana, wondering how things could have gotten so turned around. In just two years, his whole world had changed for the worse. His good-paying job was gone. The best dog he had ever owned had died trying to save him. Now his best friend in the whole world was also gone. Paul looked around the bedroom and saw Diana everywhere. He saw her as she dusted and cleaned the house, in the kitchen cooking, and sitting in her favorite chair reading as the TV sound was turned down so low it was only audible to the dog. He felt her softness, smelled her perfume, and cried as he wished he could turn back the clock so she could be by his side once again.

The night was long and restless. Paul must have smoked a pack of cigarettes in between dozing off and staring out the window into the darkness. His mind would not allow his body to relax. Paul knew he had to make some decisions about what to do next. The funeral, the store, the house, the broken heart.

Chapter 2

The sun peeked above the tree line behind the house. Its brightness focused like a laser beam through the patio doors directly onto Paul's face. His back ached as he tried to raise himself up from the couch in the family room to stretch. His first thought was: *Why did I sleep on the couch in the first place?* Then as his head began to clear he painfully remembered that he could not sleep in *their* bed. Not without Diana next to him. Not last night. Maybe not ever again. Paul looked at the clock sitting on top of the TV, and it read 7:05. Paul thought to himself, *I will make some coffee and get cleaned up before deciding what to do first.*

The coffee machine was dripping into the pot as Paul searched for a cigarette. He could only find a pack of stale cigarettes in one of the kitchen drawers. He turned on the TV to hear the weather report but was not really interested, nor did he care what the talking head was saying. The sun was now up above the trees, and the warm rays filled the homey country kitchen that Diana had kept immaculate over the many years. Paul grabbed a light jacket from the laundry room closet and walked down the long driveway to pick up the newspaper. The air was cold, but at the same time it was also very invigorating and refreshing.

The newspaper was wrapped in its protective yellow plastic bag to keep the dew from soaking through. As Paul started to head back to the house, he saw a couple of deer looking at him from the woods across the road. He watched them for about fifteen seconds, then cleared his throat loudly so he could watch the deer run through the woods to make their getaway. Paul always liked to watch the white-tailed deer that were so common in northern Baltimore County. They were so graceful, with their long strides and high, effortless leaps over the thickets. Little by little their woods were being taken away by housing developers. Paul thought, *How long will it be before the deer have no place left to run?*

Back at the house, Paul made his coffee and sat at the kitchen table trying to read the paper. His mind was still not cooperating with him, making concentration on the simplest task a laborious effort. Eventually Paul gave up on the newspaper and set it aside. He smoked two more stale cigarettes and drank three cups of coffee that was way too strong. *Was it one scoop of coffee per cup or one and one-half scoops per cup? Oh well, time to hit the shower and get this day on a roll,* he thought.

After showering and shaving, Paul put on a suit and tie. Now that he was fully refreshed, he started to feel much better. His first order of business was to stop by the store to place a sign on the door stating that they were closed until further notice due to a death in the family. Paul then called FedEx and UPS to cancel pickups and deliveries until further notice. Finally, Paul stopped at the post office and told them to put a hold on all the mail for the store until further notice. Things were now getting done, and Paul enjoyed his small but necessary accomplishments.

Paul climbed back into his Jeep and headed downtown to make funeral arrangements at Antonio Gino's place on Eastern Avenue. Since Gino's was located in the neighborhood where Paul and Diana grew up, he thought it would be the best location. Besides, it would be less of a hardship on others if the funeral was in town, as opposed to way out in the sticks where Diana and he had lived for the past fifteen years.

The long forty-minute drive to downtown passed rather quickly. Paul had forgotten how long the drive to downtown was, since he had not driven there for over two years, not since he lost his job at the BLC. The traffic was light that time of day, and thankfully there were no disabled vehicles or accidents on southbound Interstate 83, which would turn a forty-minute drive into a two-hour commute from hell. Paul thought, *Yes, I don't miss this long drive to downtown at all.*

Paul reached the Dela Gino Funeral parlor at about noon. He met with Mr. Antonio Gino, the owner of the place for over forty years. Antonio must have buried every soul from the old neighborhood since he first opened his doors so many years ago. Antonio guided Paul through the arrangements, and they decided to have one day for viewing: Wednesday. The funeral would be Thursday morning at ten o'clock, and Diana would be put to rest at Holy Redeemer Cemetery. Paul selected a casket with Antonio's help and decided to have Diana laid out in her favorite blue dress, which she had looked so good in last Christmas. He would bring the dress by Gino's first thing in the morning. Antonio took care of the newspaper obituary announcement and the paperwork required to pick up Diana's body from the coroner.

Paul left Dela Gino's around two o'clock and decided to ride through the old neighborhood to see how things were holding up since he had moved away. To his surprise, the place had not changed all that much. The neat, well-kept row houses looked the same as they did when Paul was a kid riding his bicycle through the alleys and side streets. As he passed by his old house, he decided to park the Jeep and walk down the street for old times sake. Paul had not walked more than half a block when he heard his name being called from behind. Paul turned to look in the direction he had heard his name called.

About thirty yards down the street a man was double-timing up to Paul saying, "Yo, Pauly. It's me, Gary. Gary Roth."

Paul could hardly believe his eyes. He had not seen Gary in almost fifteen years but recognized his familiar smile as soon as he was within fifteen feet of where Paul was standing. Paul said, "Hey, Gary. How in the hell are you?"

"You know. Doing a little of this and a little of that." "Still up to your same old stuff, Gar'?"

Gary extended his hand for Paul to grab. The two men shook hands and smiled as if they each had won the lottery. Gary said, "Yeah, man. You gotta do what you gotta do. Hey, man. I heard about the sad news regarding Diana. Sorry to hear it, man."

"Thanks, Gar.' Sometimes life is damn hard to figure out. Diana was a good person, and I guess they're the ones that go first."

"When's the funeral?"

"I just made the arrangements at Dela Ginos. Viewing on Wednesday, burial on Thursday."

"Listen. I'll be there and I'll also make sure the old gang gets the word. We all knew Diana and would like to pay our respects. You know how this neighborhood is, Pauly. We always stick together when tragedy strikes one of our own. If you need anything, let me know?"

"Well, there is one thing you may be able to help me with." "Name it and it's done."

"You know Diana was shot by an unknown assailant. I want to put some feelers out through the grapevine to see if maybe it was a local punk. You understand what I'm asking, Gar'?"

"Don't say another word, Pauly. I'll see what's shakin' and let you know what I find out. I may have to go see Mikey to get the word out."

"That's great, Gary. Tell Mikey I would consider it a personal favor if he were able to find out anything that may lead to the punk's identity."

The two men shook hands and went their separate ways, Gary off into the neighborhood to do whatever and Paul back to his Jeep to head home. Paul knew that Gary had never held a legitimate job in his life. He would deal in all kinds of stolen goods, such as cigarettes and liquor without state tax stamps, electronic equipment, and a kitchen sink if you wanted one. Whatever anybody wanted, Gary could always get it cheaper than any place in town. Of course, most of his deliveries were done at night.

Mikey, on the other hand, was a legitimate businessman. Michael Weigand was a tavern owner who knew everything that went on, in and around the neighborhood. His network for information was well known to everyone who had a need to know what was coming down, legally or illegally. For example, Mikey would know when the police were planning a raid in a particular part of town. His information services were used by everyone, including the local police department. Of course, all information had a price, and Mikey would make a killing on everything he decided to broker. Mikey was not a snitch, and he was quick to set you straight if you insinuated that he was. Mikey would say he was an information broker with scruples.

As Paul was driving home, depression set in again. He thought about how he was going to carry on without Diana. The house was going to be a steady reminder of Diana, and there was no way to get around the fact that he probably would not be financially able to keep up the mortgage payments. A quick review of his finances in his head indicated that he could hang on for maybe three more months. Not very long, considering it would take time to list the house, sell it, and then close. Also, he had all the furniture to consider. *Maybe I can sell the whole thing, lock, stock, and barrel,* he thought. *Start all over. Make a fresh new start. Why not sell the business, too? After all, it takes two people to run the place, and there's not yet enough profit to allow me to hire part-time help.* The closer he got to home, the more he convinced himself that it was time to make a break with the past and start all over.

A local realtor had offices in the same shopping center where Paul had his store. When he arrived home, he called the realtor and told him he wanted to list his house and store for sale. The contents of both were also to be sold, if possible. The realtor was glad to have the business but told Paul he was sorry to lose him as a neighbor in the shopping center. The realtor added that he would need to come to the house and take measurements and inventory the contents to multiple list the residence. Paul said he would drop off a set of keys for both the house and the store so the realtor could get the ball rolling as soon as possible.

Paul changed into jeans and a sweatshirt. He returned four calls from people who had left messages on his answering machine. They all offered their condolences and said they would see Paul at the funeral. Paul was getting hungry, so he decided to take a ride to the local mall, which was about ten miles from his house. Paul went to the food court and feasted on a cheese steak submarine sandwich with fried onions, lettuce, tomato, and mayonnaise. He had a side order of French fries and a large Coke. As he ate, he watched the shoppers moving in and out of the many stores within the mall. Paul took particular notice of the old couples holding hands as they walked and the young teenagers who also held hands or wrapped their arms around each other's waists. Paul thought, *Why didn't we hold hands more often? We were in love. Why is it that only the very young and the very old show their uninhibited feelings in public?*

After finishing his early dinner, Paul walked around the mall to kill some time. He really had nothing to do at home. Besides, being in the house alone was depressing. Paul looked at several shop windows as he walked, but not really paying any attention to what he was viewing. When he came to the pet store, he went in to look at the puppies. They each looked so cute and cuddly. Paul thought that maybe he could buy another dog to keep him company. But then he thought about how hard it was to have a great pet only to have to go through the terrible grief when it died. *Not now. Maybe after things settle down,* he thought.

Paul left the mall and drove north until he ended up at the Prettyboy Reservoir. He didn't intend to drive to the reservoir but simply had ended up there as he traveled the backcountry roads. The Prettyboy area was a special place for Paul. He always enjoyed coming to the reservoir to listen to the water rumble down the ninety-foot spillway to the bottom, where it fed the Gunpowder River. The entire area was surrounded with full fall-colored trees in all their glory. Paul parked his Jeep facing the west side of reservoir spillway so he could watch the sunset. This time of year, the sun usually set around four-thirty. Paul sat in his Jeep with the radio sound down low as he stared out over the acres of water that backed up to the north side of the dam. Every once in a while, Paul could see a fish jump out of the water. The circular ripples would disturb the glasslike images reflected on the reservoir for a few seconds, and then the water would settle back to its mirror image of the surrounding colorful tree line.

A sudden noise caused Paul to snap his attention to the rear of the Jeep. He looked in the rearview mirror and spotted a young couple walking hand in hand. A large golden retriever happily pranced ten feet in front of them, stopping occasionally to look back at his owners. The dog was chasing falling leaves and barking at jumping fish. The whole time, the couple walked and talked as if they didn't have a care in the world. Paul thought back to when Diana and he would walk around this reservoir with their dog, so many years ago. It was so long ago that they had only dreamed of living out in the area so close to the reservoir. Or could it have been just last year? Paul was lost in his thoughts and feelings.

The sunset was bright red with several shades of blue and violet mixed in as the fireball ducked behind the west tree line. Paul decided it was time to go back home, so he started the Jeep and drove out of the protected reservoir area onto Mount Carmel Road. The ride home would only take about ten minutes, but Paul was going slowly because he didn't want to face the dark, empty house that awaited him.

As he pulled up to his driveway, Paul could not bring himself to make the turn toward the house. He gunned the engine and headed down York Road until he reached the Long Star Tavern in Cockeysville.

Paul went into the smoky bar and stood in the doorway for several seconds as his eyes adjusted to the darkness. The Long Star was an old watering hole that had a bar, two pool tables in the back, and four booths. There were only four windows, which probably had not been washed in this century, down one side of the bar. The neon lights advertised Coors and Budweiser beers. Behind the bar was a man of about sixty. He could have been a former boxer or policeman, judging by the rough look on his wrinkled face. There was one older man sitting at the bar nursing a shot and a beer. In the back there were four loud young men drinking and shooting pool. They looked as if they might be under twenty-one, but nobody really cared as long as the color of their money was green. The jukebox was in the back by the pool tables. It played hard rock crap that, thankfully, wasn't too loud. Paul took a stool at the opposite end of the bar where he could see the exits and he hoped not be bothered by the other patrons.

The bartender was looking at a folded-up newspaper and smoking a cigar stub that had to be burning his lips. There was a TV above the bar showing some soccer game in a foreign country playing for a title that nobody every heard of before. In a gravely voice the bartender asked, "What'll you have?"

"Draft Bud Lite."

The bartender put down the paper and drew a cold beer for Paul, walked to where Paul was sitting, and placed the glass down on a coaster, then picked up the five-dollar bill Paul had fished from his pocket. The bartender made change and placed it on the bar next to Paul's glass. Without saying a word, the bartender walked back to his little corner and picked up the paper and continued reading.

Paul looked at the TV as he drank one beer after another. The soccer game had turned to golf sometime during the night. Paul had no idea how many beers he had consumed. He simply knew that when he finished one beer the bartender was there with another full glass.

Paul had eaten a couple of small bags of peanuts and spent over twenty dollars when he decided it was time to go home. Before he could leave the bar, Paul had to make one more pit stop at the men's room. The small bathroom was clean and smelled like mothballs. When Paul left the bathroom, he noticed the four young men playing pool had now been joined by four young females. He didn't remember when or how they could have walked past him without his noticing. It was not so much that they looked good but that they smelled as women should. Paul could close his eyes and smell Diana's Red Door perfume as he walked past the four young ladies.

Outside the bar, the air was very cold. Paul liked the bite from the chilly air against his face. It helped wake him to a new level of alertness. He would have to be alert to make the drive home through the dark backcountry roads, else be a statistic in tomorrow's paper. Paul climbed into the Jeep and started it up. He left the driver's side window down as he drove home, to help him stay awake.

When Paul arrived at home, he checked his answering machine. There was only one message from a distant uncle. *It's amazing how fast bad news travels*, Paul thought. He called his uncle, and they talked for about ten minutes.

Paul then turned the TV on and lay down on the couch. All of a sudden, he was feeling very tired and sleepy. The sound on the TV was low, and Paul dozed off immediately. He slept for almost an hour before he was forced awake by the ringing telephone.

"Hello."

"Mr. Marco, I wanted to call and introduce myself as—" "Whatever you're selling, pal, I'm not—"

"Mr. Marco, I'm not selling anything. This call is in regard to your late wife."

There was silence on the phone. No one spoke for what seemed like a full minute. Paul finally asked, "Who is this and what do you want?"

"Mr. Marco, I'm the one who had your old lady popped." Silence. "I thought that would get your attention."

Paul was speechless. His emotions were torn between anger and sorrow and every place in between. Finally, he angrily said, "Who are you and what do you want?"

"I want you to know that my partner botched the job at your store. He was supposed to pop you, not your old lady. Apparently, he was interrupted by some bitch who probably wanted to send a package to '*Baldamore.*' Oh, well. It's so hard to get good help these days. I figured your wife would have been an easier mark than you. I guess I'll just have to live with it. Don't you think?"

"You son of a bitch. I'll see you burn in hell—"

"Temper, temper, Mr. Marco. My people made you a proposition for protection and you turned them down. Now, if you had paid for the protection like a good little businessman from *Baldamore,* maybe your wife would still be alive. So listen to me. And listen to me very carefully. I want $100,000 in cash by next week to spare your business and your life. Do we understand each other, Mr. Marco?"

Paul yelled into the phone, "Fuck you!" and slammed the receiver down. His heart felt as if it were beating at twice its normal pace. He could feel the redness in his face as the anger built in his body. Every muscle was as tight as a snare drum. Paul knew he had to calm down, so he began to breathe slowly and deeply, in through the nose and out through his mouth. Paul finally was able to calm himself down to where he could think clearly again. Then the phone rang.

"Hello."

"Mr. Marco don't hang up on me again. The price just went up to $125,000 for your business and life. Every time you try to jerk me around the price will go up. Do you understand me?"

"What is it that you don't understand, asshole? I'm not interested in playing your sick game. I don't give a damn about the business, and I don't have a hell of a lot to live for right now either."

"Well, I know you have a nice insurance policy on your wife that should bring in close to a half-million dollars when the case is settled. Double indemnity and all that."

"Who in the hell are you? And how do you know so much about my personal finances?"

"It's my business to know about my clients. And you will be one of my new *Baldamore* clients before too long. Now, I'll call you in a few days to let you know the details for the payment. I strongly suggest that you keep this our little secret until the deal is done."

"Let me make this as clear as I can. Fuck you," and Paul slammed the phone down again.

Paul now knew why Diana had been murdered and that it had nothing to do with an attempted robbery. A retaliation hit for his refusal to pay protection money to a couple of hoods. Paul now knew what he had to do.

Chapter 3

There was no bright sun peeking above the tree line behind the house this morning. Of course not; it was only four-thirty. Paul had not slept well after receiving the phone calls last night. He decided to get up off the couch and attempt to make some coffee. The newspaper would not be delivered for another two hours. There was much to do today, but Paul did not need to get started this early in the morning. He drank a cup of too-weak coffee and figured that the formula must be one heaping scoop of coffee per cup instead of the one level scoop that he put into the coffee maker. *I'll get it sooner or later*, he thought.

Paul went into the bedroom and opened the doors on Diana's side of the closet. He ran his hands over the many blouses, skirts, and dresses that had been meticulously hung by her own hands. The pretty blue dress he so fondly remembered her wearing was toward the back. After he took the dress out of the closet, he laid it on the bed that he couldn't sleep in now. He retrieved a pair of matching blue shoes from the shoe rack on the floor of the closet, then looked through her jewelry box for her favorite earrings and necklace. The last thing Paul did was go through the picture album that contained a picture of Diana wearing the blue dress from last Christmas. Paul laid everything out on the bed, then sat in the small chair that was in the corner of the room. He held the picture in his hand as he stared at the clothes on the bed, trying to imagine her lying there. That little insignificant moment was the proverbial straw that broke his dry spell. Paul started to weep as if he were a small child lost in a huge mall looking for his mommy. He hurt so much inside. He could not stop crying. The tears flowed from his body, just as the water cascaded over the spillway at Prettyboy Dam. The only difference was Paul would eventually dry up, when no more tears would come, but the hurt would still be there. Over time, the intensity of the pain would probably subside. But for now, the hurt was torturing his very being.

After what seemed to be hours, Paul packed Diana's clothes in a travel carry-on bag for the trip back downtown. Then Paul took a shower, shaved, then put on clean clothes. The sun was up now and the house was starting to feel warmer as the rays filtered in through the south-facing windows. Paul put on a small jacket and went down the driveway to pick up the newspaper. He looked for the deer but only managed to see a couple of gray squirrels chasing each other around a large oak tree by the mailbox. Paul retrieved the paper, then headed back to the house, where he attempted to make another pot of coffee. This time he thought he had the formula right. *Diana always made the coffee and it always tasted great. Why is this task so difficult?* he thought. The moment of truth was only minutes away. When the drip coffee maker stopped, Paul poured a cup, then added cream and sugar. He tasted it, thinking to himself that it didn't taste so bad this time. He would adjust the mixture one more time to see if he could make a simple cup of coffee as good as Diana.

Paul read the paper, listened to the morning news, and drank acceptable cups of coffee until seven-thirty. Paul washed the coffeepot and the few cups and silverware that had accumulated in the sink. There was no reason to run the dishwasher, since he only had a few things dirty, but what was more important, he had no idea how to make the damn thing work. There were about fifty dials and buttons on the front door of the confounded machine. Surely Diana had thrown the manual away years ago because she knew how to make the machine work. Therefore, why keep the manual?

Paul loaded the carry-on bag into the Jeep and headed toward downtown. He arrived at Gino's funeral parlor around eight-fifteen.

Antonio took one look at the photograph Paul gave him and said that the hairdresser and he would do their very best to make Diana look as she had last Christmas. Paul thanked Antonio and told him that he still had some errands to run. "If you need to get in touch with me, call my home number and leave a message. I'll be checking the messages throughout the day."

"Don't worry, Paul. I'll take care of everything."

Paul left Gino's and headed for police headquarters. When he arrived, he asked the receptionist for Detective Theresa McGavin. The receptionist picked up the phone while saying, "I'll check to see if she's in. Who should I say is calling?"

"Just tell her Paul Marco."

The receptionist talked into the receiver as Paul paced in the hall out of earshot. The floor in the headquarters reception area was dingy, white, and cold-looking marble. The walls were marble halfway up to the ceiling, and the rest was plaster painted an ugly shade of dark green. The fluorescent lights in the ceiling made the place feel even colder. On the wall there were wanted posters and tips on how to *take a bite out of crime.* Paul paced the hall while seedy and suspicious-looking characters walked past him or sat on one of the old wooden benches that lined the two sides of the hall.

"Mr. Marco."

Paul turned to see the receptionist looking at him. He approached her station, and she hung up the phone, saying, "Detective McGavin is on her way down to sign you in. Have a seat over there. It will be a few minutes before she actually gets here."

Paul nodded to the receptionist, then took a seat on one of the well-worn benches away from everyone else. As he sat there, he looked at the individuals around him. Most of them were either very young or very old. *The old are probably here to report crimes and the very young are probably there as a result of committing a crime. That's the way life is,* thought Paul. Some bleeding hearts would probably say that the young punks today were victims of their environment. Or maybe their parents were not doing a good enough job teaching them the difference between right and wrong.

That is, if they had two parents. *No matter,* thought Paul. The only criminal he was interested in had called him on the phone last night. *The voice did not sound very young, and it didn't sound all that old either. Probably in his late twenties or early thirties,* thought Paul. *Definitely a white male, with a local Baltimore accent. Only a true local would change the "ti" and make it a "da" when saying "Baldamore."*

Paul stared at the blank wall in front of him for what seemed like thirty minutes. He snapped out of it when he heard Detective McGavin's voice calling his name.

"Mr. Marco, you may come up now!"

Paul stood to shake hands with the detective. "Thanks for seeing me, Detective. I know you said that you would contact me in a couple of days, but I was in the area making funeral arrangements so I decided to stop by to see you instead. I hope that's OK?"

"It's fine, Mr. Marco. I was just talking to the commissioner about your case before you arrived. He is waiting for us upstairs now."

After Paul signed the logbook and went through the metal detector, he and the detective made their way to the elevators. It had been almost two years since Paul had visited the downtown police headquarters building. The sights, the sounds, and even the smell were the same as before. When the elevator stopped, Paul and the detective walked across the room toward the back, where the commissioner's office was located.

"Come on in and have a seat, Paul." The commissioner was holding a cup of coffee in one hand and a stack of papers in the other as he moved toward his office door.

Paul took a seat in front of the commissioner's desk, and Detective McGavin sat next to him in the only other chair not covered with files and stacks of official-looking papers.

"Well, Paul, I understand that Detective McGavin here is pushing ahead with the crime data collected at the scene. The motive we are leaning toward right now is robbery."

Detective McGavin said, "That is, unless you can give us another possible reason for the shootings?"

The commissioner looked at Detective McGavin, then back to Paul. Paul noted, "As a matter of fact, I do know that the motive was not robbery, Detective. However, the details are still a bit sketchy, so let me tell you what I have learned since the shootings."

Paul went through the entire scenario about the phone calls he had received and his impressions as to the age, the race, and the area the killer was native to.

The commissioner said, "Well, Paul, that certainly puts a different slant on things. It's like the Chinese say: *the obvious is not what it appears to be.* Or something like that."

Then the commissioner turned to Detective McGavin and said, "Let's put a tap on his phone immediately. Just in case we can zero in on the extortionists if he's stupid enough to stay on the line. Next, we need to have a surveillance van at the funeral parlor to film everyone who enters or leaves Gino's on Wednesday. Also, schedule the van to be at the cemetery to look over the crowd. You never know when some of these wiseasses will show up. Sometimes they get a kick out of seeing the survivors suffer. The sick bastards."

The commissioner turned to Paul and said, "Don't worry, Paul; you will never know the surveillance van is there. These guys do this stuff all the time, so there will not be any disruptions at either the funeral parlor or the cemetery."

"I appreciate that, Commissioner." Paul turned to Detective McGavin and asked, "Is there anything you can tell me about the crime lab reports?"

Detective McGavin looked at the commissioner, who simply nodded as if to say, "It's OK to tell Paul what you know." Theresa McGavin turned to Paul, then said, "So far we have identified the gun as a .22-caliber. We're running the ballistics test through FBI computers to see if there may be a match with a similar MO. It's highly unlikely that search will turn up anything. These hitters usually use the weapon for one hit, then lose it in the Chesapeake Bay soon thereafter. We also know the same weapon that killed your wife was used to kill the customer, Janet Daymore. From what you told us, we surmised the .22 was silenced, explaining why no noise was heard by you in the back of the store or by the people in the store next to yours. We also suspect that the shooter acted alone, because you saw him head toward the parking lot as if he might be going back to his car. If there were two hitters, one would have been more than likely waiting for the shooter at the front door."

"There's a lot of supposition in your statements, Detective." "That's true, Paul," said the commissioner. "But right now we don't have a lot to go on. I'm hoping that the guy who made the call to you last night will be able to clear this up for us, if we can find him."

Paul hung his head down, as he was feeling very dejected at the realization that the commissioner was right. There really wasn't much to go on. Paul looked up at the commissioner, then said, "I know you're right, Commissioner. I also want you to know that I appreciate everything you and Detective McGavin are doing. Right now, I just feel very depressed with all that has happened."

The commissioner replied, "Don't worry, Paul. With a little luck, we will get the son of a bitch. Now why don't you go home and rest up for tomorrow. Let Detective McGavin and me take care of finding the shooter."

Paul looked at the commissioner and slowly stood to shake his hand. Paul then turned to shake Detective McGavin's hand. As he turned toward the door, Paul said, "You know, Commissioner, I never knew what real pain was until I recently had my heart ripped out of my chest. There is a real sensation of emptiness in my body. Well, I better get going. There are still some things I need to do." The commissioner and Detective McGavin stood there as Paul walked out of the office and headed toward the elevator. The commissioner finally said, "You know, Theresa, I feel sorry for him the way he's hurting right now, I mean."

"I know what you mean, Commissioner. Sometimes I wonder why it is that shit happens to the good people in this world, instead of the scumbags whom we usually have to deal with on a daily basis."

Paul left police headquarters and walked to the parking garage where he had left his Jeep. Leaving the parking garage, Paul drove down Pratt Street to Eastern Avenue and continued east until he turned onto Dundalk Avenue, where he picked up Kane Street. Within a few minutes Paul was parking the Jeep on the parking lot of the *Cell Block Bar and Grill.* Good old Mikey Weigand had named the bar when he first opened it to celebrate where most of his clientele either came from or were going to. Paul entered through the back door and immediately smelled the aroma of stale beer, that very distinctive smell that lingered in just about every bar Paul had ever visited. The *Cell Block* was long and narrow, with several tables on one side and a long bar with maybe forty stools on the other side. The wall behind the bar was plastered with old Baltimore Colt memorabilia, and the opposite wall was filled with Orioles pennants and autographed pictures. This kind of bar was called a *sports bar* long before the yuppies turned the term into one for a loud obnoxious place with ten giant TV screens all showing different sporting events.

Paul walked past the two small bathrooms on his right. There were two old-style phone booths on the left. The wooden phone booths still had folding doors that would drown out the bar sounds if a guy needed privacy when making that all-important call. Paul walked toward the front of the bar, where there were several customers nursing glasses of National Bohemian beer, the local favorite. Paul passed three pinball machines and several tables before he selected a seat at the bar, away from the other patrons. The bartender walked down to where Paul was sitting. The whole time he walked, he managed to keep an eye on the big screen showing a cable telecast of two Mexican middleweights Paul had never heard of before.

"What'll you have, pal?" "How about a National draft."

The bartender poured Paul his beer and set it down on the bar. Paul handed the man a ten spot while asking, "Is Mikey around?"

"Could be. Who's asking?"

"Tell him it's Paul Marco, from the neighborhood."

The bartender gave Paul his change and looked him over a few seconds before saying, "You the one whose old lady was popped a few days ago?"

"That's me. Just tell Mikey I would appreciate a few minutes of his time."

The bartender walked to the back of the bar and exited through the kitchen swinging door. Paul knew the kitchen door led to another door behind which were stairs to a basement office. After about five minutes, the bartender returned and poured Paul another draft. As he set the beer down in front of Paul, he said, "Mikey said to send you down in fifteen minutes. He also said that you already know the way."

Paul drank his second beer as he kept an eye on the clock behind the bar. When the fifteen minutes were up, Paul left a tip for the bartender, then headed toward the kitchen door. No one was there to question his movements, although Paul knew that if he were an undesirable, several people would have been on top of him by now. He entered the kitchen and spotted two cooks who paid him no mind. Paul saw the door marked *PRIVATE* and opened it to descend thirteen steep steps. The steps were covered with linoleum, and the walls were covered in cheap paneling. At the bottom of the stairs there was a small landing and another door. Paul knocked on the door, and it was immediately opened by a giant of a man. Paul was greeted by a huge gorilla like man whose only name was Rocco, one of the many personal protectors for the infamous Michael Weigand. Rocco motioned for Paul to turn around so he could be frisked. Paul turned, spread his legs, then held his arms straight out. Rocco gave him the once-over, then said, "Follow me."

Rocco led Paul through the basement's narrow hall until they came to another door, then knocked once and opened the door for Paul to enter. Paul recognized the great room he had visited only once before. It had happened several years ago when he attended a meeting with Mikey. The great room, as it was called, was spectacular. Supposedly, Mikey had bought the basements of the three businesses next to his and broken through the dividing walls. The room had to be sixty feet long and forty feet wide, lavishly paneled and carpeted with very comfortable furnishings. There was a large mahogany desk at the far end of the room. To get to the desk Paul had to walk over carpets that were at least two inches thick. One long wall was a continuous bookshelf. *There must be a thousand books on the wall*, thought Paul. The opposite wall was covered with expensive works of art. The paintings on that one wall alone could finance a small country for several years. As Paul slowly made his way to the huge desk, he paid more attention to Mikey sitting in the big leather high-back chair. He was talking on one of the three phones that sat on his desk.

Mikey looked up to see Paul approaching and motioned for him to come forward to have a seat. There was a leather sofa and two leather wingback chairs directly in front of the huge desk. Paul selected one of the wingback chairs and sat. Mikey was dressed in an Italian hand-tailored suit. His silk shirt and gold cuff links must have cost the equivalent of a steelworker's weekly pay. Mikey's nails were manicured, and his hair was perfectly groomed. Paul sat there in the leather chair thinking to himself that Mikey looked more like a CEO of a major corporation rather than a kid from the old neighborhood who had done well for himself.

" . . . that's good, Phil. Let's get the deal done and call me when you have all the paperwork ready to go Yeah, that sounds good to me. Let's go with it. OK, fine. I gotta go. See ya."

Mikey stood to extend his hand across the desk to Paul. Paul also stood to shake Mikey's hand. Mikey said, "Pauly, I heard about what happened the other day from Roth. I'm very sorry to hear about your loss. Diana was a good kid."

"Thanks, Mikey. That she was. She is going to be laid out tomorrow and buried Thursday."

"Dela Gino's?"

"Yeah, where else? You know we all end up coming home one way or the other."

Mikey pressed the button on his intercom and said, "Virginia, send a flower arrangement to Gino's tomorrow for Diana Marco." Mikey simply let the intercom switch go and turned back to Paul, saying, "So, you're not here to talk about old times and you certainly didn't come here for the beer we serve upstairs. So, what is it that I can do for you?"

Paul told Mikey about the attempted extortion a few months ago and how he had shot one hood and let the other one go. He then described what had happened at the store when Diana was murdered. It was emotionally draining for Paul to relive the account each time he explained it, but this time it was necessary. Paul said, "Mikey, I'm asking you to find out who's behind this extortion business so I can make things right. I only need the information, nothing else."

"Wow, Pauly. Why do you want to go and get caught up in all this crap before your lovely wife is even in the ground? First thing's first, *mi amigo*. Look. Why don't you attend the funeral tomorrow and the business at the cemetery, while I look into this matter for you. Pauly, you and I had some good times when we were kids, but this ain't no game you're talking about. I'm not going to preach to you about how you can end up in the slammer if you carry out your wishes right now. I know you already know about the consequences. What I want you to do is promise me you will cool off for a few days and let me see what I can come up with. After that, if you want to waste the bastard, so be it. With me, it's only business. With you, however, it's personal, and that can be your biggest weakness right now. Do you understand what I'm saying?"

"I understand completely. You make some good points, Mikey. I'll take care of what needs to be done for now. But I promise you this: I will not let those bastards get away with what they did to my Diana."

"Come with me," said Mikey.

Paul stood up and followed Mikey to the far wall lined with all the books. Mikey reached under one of the shelves to press something, and two of the large bookcases slid open, exposing another room. Mikey walked through the opening created by the sliding bookcases with Paul at his heels. The room was an arsenal of weapons and crates of military ordinance. Paul said, "Jesus. I haven't seen this much hardware since leaving Vietnam."

"This is only a small part of what I can offer you. Pauly, you and me are from the same hood. I trust you like a brother. I'll never forget how you helped me out several years ago when my sister was in trouble. I owe you. Therefore, whatever you need, I'll make sure you get. The only condition is that after today, you never saw this room and our meeting never took place."

"I understand completely. But I don't think I'll need this kind of firepower to do what I have to do."

"Paul, you have no idea what you are up against yet. Let's wait to see what I find out first, and then you can decide what you need. I just wanted you to see that everything I have is at your disposal. No questions asked."

"Thanks, Mikey. I'll never forget you for this."

"Forget it. What do you say we go upstairs to have a beer like in the old days?"

Paul and Mikey went back to the bar to drink a beer together. It was almost impossible for Mikey to sit at the bar without people coming up to him to ask him for favors or to tell him about some guy they knew who knew another guy who had some stuff to sell or needed to buy some stuff. After their drink, Paul and Mikey shook hands. Mikey said, "I'll call you in a couple of days and let you know what I find out." Paul thanked Mikey again, then left the bar using the back door.

Outside the bar, Paul pointed his Jeep toward home. His mind was now racing with the things he needed to do. The long drive home allowed Paul to sort through the details of what had to be done. For the first time, he felt as if he had now laid the foundation for a workable plan. A plan that would eventually even the score.

Chapter 4

Detective McGavin received a call from the FBI about the computer search for the ballistics test. Agent Jack Thompson said their search had turned up nothing for now, but he would keep the file open for thirty days in case something developed later. Detective McGavin thanked Agent Thompson for his efforts, then asked if it was possible to enter the ballistics test results into the computer for future searches that might be requested as a result of this case. Agent Thompson explained that once a ballistics test was received at FBI headquarters it was routinely entered into the central computer system. That way if another ballistics test came in later, it would cross-reference the original test results. Agent Thompson also told Detective McGavin that the local authorities were automatically notified if there was a match due to a cross-referenced file.

Detective McGavin decided to check in with Sgt. Mark Yeager about the phone tap for Paul Marco's house. Sergeant Yeager was one of those tech-heads who loved computers and high-tech gadgets. Detective McGavin went downstairs to where Sergeant Yeager's cubicle was located. The place looked like something out of a sci-fi movie set. There were computers, lights blinking, and reels of magnetic tape swirling around huge machines. The temperature must have been sixty-eight degrees in the computer room, to keep all the fancy machines from overheating.

"Hey, Mark. How's it going?"

Sgt. Mark Yeager turned his attention away from one of the three computer screens he had in front of him, to see Theresa McGavin standing in the open doorway of his cubicle.

"Not bad, Theresa. How about yourself?"

"So-so. Hey, listen. Did you get the phone tap set up for Paul Marco's house yet?"

"Absolutely. That has been done and working for almost an hour."

Mark turned to one of his computer screens and typed in a few instructions on the keyboard. When the screen display had changed he said, "Look here, Theresa."

Theresa moved to where she could look over Mark's shoulder as he pointed to the information on the color monitor.

"See. Here are the phone numbers we are currently tracking. This one is Paul Marco's. When I cursor down to his number and press the *enter* key, the screen changes to show all the calls coming into and going out from his line. See that?"

"That's pretty neat, Mark. It gives you the time, the date, the number and address of where the call came from. Wow, this stuff is pretty remarkable. Does the caller have to stay on the line a set amount of time for the information to be captured by our tap?"

"Yes. Unfortunately, we still need to rely on lady luck with some of this stuff. The good news is the time we need to track a number is getting less and less with newer high-speed communications lines. The other problem is most crooks today know as much about this technology as the authorities. As soon as we get a step ahead of them, they are right behind us finding ways to circumvent the system. Today a lot of crooks use cell phones, and we can only narrow down the cell quadrant from where the call originated. However, every now and then someone gets greedy and stays on a land line too long and we can nab him with this technology."

"Well, thanks for the lesson, Mark. Like you said, maybe we'll get lucky on this one. God knows there isn't much for us to do right now until the bad guys make another move."

Detective McGavin left Mark's cubical and headed to Central Records, which was located two floors above the computer room. She pulled the file on the attempted robbery that took place at Paul's store a couple of months ago. The suspect arrested with multiple gunshot wounds and a pen through his eye was still doing time at the city lockup awaiting trial. The file was thick, with numerous arrest records dating back to his teenage years. His name was, believe it or not, Clark Benjamin Kent. *This has to be a joke,* thought Theresa.

She read the file and made several notes preparing for her scheduled visit to the city jail tomorrow morning at eleven o'clock. She was thinking that there might be a way to bargain with Clark regarding who was issuing his marching orders. After all, the shape he was in now, wheelchair-bound and blind in one eye, would not make him much of a menace to society. Maybe the DA would go for a reduced sentence if they could close two other cases of murder in cold blood.

After writing more notes about Mr. Clark Kent, Theresa went to the operations center to see if they could run a cross-reference check on the name Clark Kent. She wanted to see if he had had any consistent accomplices throughout his long criminal history.

Theresa met her best friend, Pat Dershan, for lunch and spelled out her data request. Theresa and Pat had been working for the Baltimore Police Department for over twelve years. They often brown-bagged lunch together when their workload permitted such a luxury. Sometimes they ate in the cafeteria, but if the weather was nice they would go outside to sit on one of the many benches in the small War Memorial Plaza. That is what they did on this beautiful fall day in downtown Baltimore. The cold October morning had given way to a sunny day with low humidity and afternoon temperatures heading for seventy-two degrees.

Pat said she would run Clark Kent's name through the computer system looking for a pattern of possible accomplices, then jokingly added, "If I turn up a Lois Lane or Jimmy Olsen in the file, I'm never going to let you forget it."

Theresa laughed but knew that if there was a link to other names, Pat would find it.

"When do you need this, Theresa?" "How about yesterday, plus one?"

"No way. I'm up to here with work. The best I can do is Monday."

"Well, I'm going to go see Kent tomorrow at eleven o'clock in the city jail. I guess if the best you can do is Monday, then that is what I'll have to take."

"Don't pull that stuff with me, Theresa. You know I can't drop everything just because you decide to make a request. I have supervisors to answer to, just like you. Besides, tomorrow is probably impossible unless you managed to throw in dinner and drinks at, let's say, T.G.I.F.'s?"

"OK. You're killing me here. It's a deal. You get the computer run to me by tomorrow and Friday's dinner is on me."

Theresa and Pat finished their lunch, then headed back to headquarters. Pat went toward the elevator and back to her office. Theresa decided to leave the office to go to Dela Ginos Funeral Parlor. Upon arriving, she met Mr. Antonio Gino and explained that the police wanted to set up a hidden camera at Diana Marcos's funeral. Antonio showed the detective the room he was preparing for the viewing tomorrow. He had no problem cooperating with the police but still wanted to clear it with Paul before anything was finalized. Theresa asked Antonio to call Paul to see if he could get his verbal approval before two o'clock. She wanted to have the surveillance guys come in between one and two o'clock to set up the camera. Antonio was amenable to the detective's request. Normal viewing hours were three to five o'clock and then again between seven and nine o'clock. So, if the police came in at one and left before three o'clock, no one would be inconvenienced.

Antonio pulled a file card from a small index box he had sitting on his desk. He called Paul Marco's home number and received the answering machine. Antonio left a message for Paul to call him, then told the detective he would call her as soon as he heard back from Paul. Detective McGavin thanked Mr. Gino, then went to her car to go back downtown.

Paul Marco stopped at the local pizza and sub shop to pick up a small pizza for dinner. After picking up the pizza, Paul pulled into his garage and was taking the box into house when he heard a voice from in back of the garage saying, "Don't turn around."

The voice startled Paul to the point where he almost dropped the pizza box. The voice did not sound familiar, as Paul tried to process the sound through the thousands of people's voices he had heard in conversations over his lifetime.

The voice then said, "That's good. I like a person who knows how to follow orders."

Paul could hear the man's voice getting louder as he spoke. Obviously he was moving toward Paul as he talked, but Paul could not hear his footsteps.

Apparently the man was very light on his feet. Paul finally asked, "What do you want?"

The voice was now directly behind Paul, saying, "Oh, you already know what I want. You owe us 125 large, and I'm here to make sure you understand the demands."

"How did you get in here and—"

"Shut up and listen!" the mystery voice yelled. "You don't ask the questions. I do. Now, Thursday you go bury your wife and then take a day to grieve. On Saturday, you will receive a phone call. The person on the other end of the line will give you instructions about how and when to make the drop."

"Saturday! How in the hell do you expect me to get that kind of money by Saturday? Even if I had that kind of cash, the bank is closed on Saturday."

"Then I would say you have a bit of a problem, Mr. Marco. Today is only Tuesday. I'm sure you can get your hands on the money before Saturday. In any event, you must have the money by Saturday or your life is not going to be worth living."

Paul was thinking as the mystery man spoke, *Hell life is not worth living as it is. Maybe I could make a quick move and get the jump on this guy.* Just then Paul felt a sharp stabbing pain in his right shoulder. It felt like a pinprick or a bee sting. He automatically grabbed for the spot where the pain was strongest. Quickly his vision started to blur and he felt a burning sensation traveling through his body. His knees felt week and the pizza box fell to the ground just as Paul blacked out and his body collapsed. Paul turned his head to the side and saw a man with a limp wearing an olive drab field jacket leaving the garage. Paul could not move and lost consciousness immediately thereafter.

Paul woke up in St. Joseph's Hospital. His head hurt and his muscles felt as if he had participated in the iron man contest. He looked around the room and saw a police officer sitting in a chair by the door. The officer was reading a magazine and had not yet seen that Paul had opened his eyes. Paul requested, "May I have some water?"

The young officer almost jumped out of his skin. "Sorry, Mr. Marco, but you scared the hell out of me. Sure I'll get you some water; then I have to call the commissioner."

The officer poured a cup of ice water from a pitcher sitting on the small table next to Paul's bed. His name tag read: *Johnson*. Paul tried to move his arm to grab the cup of water, but it was too painful. Officer Johnson held the cup up to Paul's lips so he could sip some water. Paul said, "Thanks, Officer. Can you tell me how I got here?"

"No, sir. All I know is that I was told to watch you and not let anyone but the doctor and nurses in to see you. I need to call in right now, so why don't you relax for a few minutes."

Paul lay in his hospital bed and tried to work his fingers back and forth to shake out some of the stiffness. Officer Johnson was talking on the phone that was next to the only other bed in the room. Paul could hear the young officer responding to the commissioner's orders: "Yes, sir. . . . Right away, sir. . . . I'll take care of that, sir." Officer Johnson hung up the phone, then said, "The commissioner and a Detective McGavin are on their way over here to see you, Mr. Marco. I'm supposed to call the nurse in here to let her know that you're awake."

Paul just lay there working his fingers, then his elbows, as Officer Johnson pushed the call button on the side of the bed. Within a few seconds, a nurse walked into the room. Her smile was bright as she exposed what looked like a perfect set of teeth. *Her crisp white uniform was very tight and a bit short,* Paul thought. *However, she did have the perfect pair of legs for such a short uniform.* Paul glanced back to the nurse's big smile and managed to smile back at her.

"How are we feeling, Mr. Marco?"

"I don't know yet, Nurse. But you sure have brightened my day by just walking in here."

"Well, I can see you must be feeling better for you to start flirting. Do you have any stiffness in you limbs and joints?"

"I sure do. What happened to me?"

"The doctor is on his way to see you. He will be better able to explain all the details. Can I get you anything to make you more comfortable?"

"I'm very thirsty. Is there any way you could get me some ginger ale, or is that against the rules?"

"If you want ginger ale, sweetheart, then ginger ale it is. I'll be right back, sugar."

The nurse leaned over Paul and fluffed up his pillow. Her heavy breasts were practically in his face. Paul could smell the scent of lilac on her smooth, milky skin. Her name tag simply read: *Cindy*. Paul watched the nurse walk out of the room and then spotted the eyes of Officer Johnson, who was doing the same. Paul said, "She is something, isn't she?"

"You have no idea. I have watched her coming and going for the past four hours. Each time I see those legs walk out of here, I feel like I should arrest her for exposure."

Paul managed to laugh at young Officer Johnson's remarks. When he laughed, his chest hurt a little, but whatever was hurting him seemed to be getting less intense as more time passed.

The door opened and in walked the doctor. Right behind him were the commissioner and Detective McGavin. Officer Johnson stood to go outside the room, so the others could have more room in the small confined space.

"I'm Dr. Fernandez. How are you feeling, Mr. Marco?" The doctor pulled a small flashlight out of his top pocket and flashed it in both of Paul's eyes, placed the ends of his stethoscope into his ears and listened to Paul's heart.

"To tell you the truth, Doc, I ache all over and I'm as thirsty as an Arab crossing the desert."

"That's to be expected, but it is only temporary. Within another hour, you should be your old self again. You were subjected to a strong but not lethal dose of snake venom."

"Snake venom!" said Paul."

"That's right. We were able to analyze it and give you antivenin soon after you were brought into the hospital."

"How did you know it was snake venom?"

Dr. Fernandez looked at Detective McGavin and said, "Because your guardian angel told us when she arrived with the ambulance. I'll let the police explain what happened. I'll check on you in about an hour. If you are feeling all right by then, I'll release you."

Paul had a surprised look on his face but managed to say, "Thanks, Doc. I appreciate you taking care of me."

Dr. Fernandez left the room. The commissioner and Detective McGavin flanked Paul's bedside as if they were coming in for the kill. Paul said, "Well, are you going to explain what happened to me, Detective, or am I supposed to guess?"

"First, why don't you tell us what you remember about going home today?"

Paul told the two officers what had happened when he arrived home and entered the garage. He explained the timetable the mystery man had laid out and that his instructions would be forthcoming on Saturday.

The commissioner said, "Paul, you must have nine lives. I swear to God, I can't figure out how you manage to get into these crazy situations."

"Hey, Commissioner, believe me when I say that I just want to live a quiet life minding my own business. The situation I'm in now has me as baffled as it apparently has you. Now can the detective, my so-called guardian angel, please tell me how I ended up in the hospital?"

"Go ahead, Theresa. Lay it out for him," said the commissioner.

"Well, I went to see Antonio Gino today to ask him if we could put a surveillance camera in the room where your wife is going to be laid out tomorrow. He said it was OK, but he needed your verbal approval first. I told Antonio that I needed an answer by one o'clock. Anyway, Antonio tried to call you but only got the answering machine. He tried several more times throughout the day. When it appeared that he was not going to get in touch with you, he called me to say he was having difficulty finding you. I played a hunch and drove out to your house, only to find you lying on the floor of the garage next to a pepperoni and cheese pizza. With extra cheese, I might add."

"Well, thank you for being concerned enough to look after me, Detective. That still doesn't explain how I ended up here with snake venom in my bloodstream."

"Well, after I saw that you had a pulse and your breathing was weak but present, I called 911. At first I thought you had had a heart attack. You know, a middle-aged male, smoker, who eats pizza with extra cheese. It's not a pretty sight. Anyway, the paramedics get there, as I'm looking around in the garage for some clue as to what could have happened to you."

"What did you find? A snake!"

"No. Nothing that dramatic. Something much simpler. As I said, I was looking around the garage when I saw a vial lying on the floor by the garage doors. The small vial was clearly marked with a picture of a snake, and the label read: *cobra venom*. That coupled with the syringe lying by your body allowed us to make a pretty good guess as to what happened to you."

"Well, that was some pretty fancy work, Detective. Thank you for being my guardian angel."

"You're welcome." Smile.

The commissioner jokingly said, "Are you two through? I'm starting to get sick, for Christ sake. It was no big deal, Paul. Theresa here played a hunch and it paid off. Now if your mystery man wanted you dead, he would not have shot you up with just a small amount of venom. There was enough venom left in the vial to kill you, but then how would he collect money from a dead man?"

"I see what you're saying, Commissioner. My mystery man with the limp wearing the olive drab field jacket was just making sure his getaway was clean."

"Now you're firing on all cylinders. Look. We have the crime lab boys trying to track down the vial of venom. Who knows what may turn up with that? Detective McGavin, aka your guardian angel, will try to trace the syringe to see where that leads. For now, I want you to get yourself together enough so that we can take you to a safe house once the doctor releases you."

"Now hold on, Commissioner. I'm not going to be made a prisoner because some psycho is on the loose firing snake venom into an innocent victim."

"Maybe you forgot, hotshot, but this same psycho was firing a different kind of venom into victims a few days ago. We call it lead poison."

"I know what you are saying, Commissioner, but I need to get Diana taken care of in the next two days and I can't be cooped up in a safe house."

"OK, OK, you got me convinced. I doubt if our field-jacketed friend will try anything until after the burial anyway. You have just bought yourself a few days, but that's all. Come Saturday, I'll have people all around your sorry butt. Is it a deal?"

Paul looked at Detective McGavin and smiled before returning his attention to the commissioner, saying, "It's a deal. Now why don't you two get out of here and catch me a killer with a limp wearing an olive drab field jacket."

The commissioner and Detective McGavin walked toward the door to leave. As the commissioner opened the door, Paul called out, "Detective McGavin!" The commissioner and McGavin stopped and turned toward Paul as he said, "It's OK for you to put surveillance cameras in Diana's room." Paul hesitated a few seconds, then continued by saying, "You really are my guardian angel. Thanks again for being so concerned."

Theresa McGavin smiled and softly replied, "No problem.

Get some rest and I'll see you tomorrow."

Paul was digesting all that had occurred since his day began. The problem was still getting a lead on who was behind the extortion attempts. *Maybe Mikey Weigand will find something out in a couple of days. For now, I need to concentrate on getting through the funeral,* Paul decided.

Chapter 5

Paul had to take a taxi home from the hospital. The doctor told him all the effects from the venom should be out of his system within the next four or five hours. Paul asked the doctor if the hospital kept a supply of antivenin on hand for such a rare occurrence as a cobra bite. The doctor laughed a little, then told Paul that the only place locally that stored antivenin was the Baltimore Zoo. It would not be cost-effective for all the local hospitals to carry antivenin when the zoo was where they really needed it most. As Paul was watching the meter on the cab click past twenty dollars, he thought about what Dr. Fernandez had told him. If the zoo was the only place that carried the antivenin, then that would be the obvious place to start looking. He made a mental note to call Detective McGavin as soon as he got home.

The cabdriver asked Paul for the umpteenth time for directions to his house. Paul sat in the backseat of the cab constantly working his fingers and arms back and forth to keep them loose. As Paul looked out into the darkness of the cold night, he kept running the image of the limping field-jacketed man fleeing from the garage.

"Turn here. At the driveway on your right."

"Thank God we made it. You really live out in the sticks, man."

"Yes, but it's nice and quiet."

Paul paid the thirty-five-dollar tab and threw in an extra ten for a tip, then watched the cabby back out of the driveway to head down the dark country road toward civilization.

Paul looked at his open garage door a few seconds before entering, then slowly made his way to the back and the adjoining kitchen door. He turned on just about every light in the house before checking each room to make sure there were no unwelcome visitors. Paul then saw he had several messages on the answering machine. He sat on the couch and grabbed a pencil and pad of paper to take notes. Four of the messages were from Mr. Antonio Gino, asking if it was OK to allow the police to place a camera at the funeral tomorrow. Another two calls were from Detective McGavin, asking Paul to call her immediately. Since they were early messages, Paul figured they were related to Antonio not being able to locate him. One message was from some salesman selling pool supplies, and two others were from Gary Roth, asking Paul to call him as soon as he gets home.

Paul looked up Gary's number in his little red directory he kept in the kitchen drawer, then dialed.

"Hi, Gar.' It's me, Pauly."

"Hey, Pauly, glad you caught me. I was just heading out the door."

"Well, I had a rough day and just got in. I received your messages. So, what's up?"

"Hey, remember what we talked about a few days ago?" "Sure. You were going to get the word out for me. By the way, I saw our friend Mikey and he said you told him about Diana. Thanks."

"Yeah. Yeah. No problem, man. Listen. I was checking out a few business deals. You know what I mean? Anyway, I'm talking to this dude who says he heard about this other dude that may know where to get some information about the double hit at your store, if the price is right. I told the first dude to get me in touch with this other dude, so I could set up a deal. You know what I mean?"

"What did he say then, Gar'?"

"Well, I'm supposed to meet the first dude later tonight when I pick up some really nice-looking sets of speakers. Are you looking for any sound equipment, man?"

"No. Not right now, Gar,' but thanks for asking. Listen. If you hear any more about this second dude, let me know right away. I'm willing to pay for the information if it's on the level."

"No problem, man. I'll keep an ear to the ground. Hang in there, brother, and I'll see you tomorrow at Gino's."

Paul hung up the phone and thought about the conversation with Gary. If I have to pay every last cent I have for the information I need to get even with mister field jacket, I'll do it.

Next Paul called police headquarters and asked for Detective McGavin. She was not there, but the receptionist transferred Paul to the detective's voice mail. Paul left a message for McGavin to call him no matter what time she received the voice mail. He said he had something very important to talk to her about.

Paul turned on the TV, then went into the kitchen to make himself a sandwich. He could not remember the last time he ate. *I wonder whatever happened to my pizza,* he thought. Paul opened the refrigerator and there it was, bigger than life itself. A small pepperoni and cheese pizza with extra cheese was sitting on the top shelf, still in the box. Paul pulled out the pizza box along with a can of Coors' Light beer and sat at the kitchen table to feast. When he opened the pizza box there was a note attached to the inside lid. The note simply read: '*This stuff will kill you,*' and was signed with two initials: "TM." Paul figured Theresa McGavin was some kind of health nut. She scoffed at his smoking, drinking, and even selecting extra cheese on pizza.

Paul ate two slices of ice-cold pizza and drank two beers. He decided to take a quick shower so he would hopefully be able to relax and get some sleep before his big day tomorrow.

After his shower, Paul looked at himself in the bathroom mirror. The person staring back was not very happy. He was tired, not eating right, depressed, and hurting inside. All he could think about was how nice things used to be just a few days earlier.

Paul was sitting on the couch watching TV when suddenly the phone rang. He looked at the clock on top of the TV before picking up the phone. It was 11:30 p.m.

"Hello."

"Hi, Mr. Marco. This is Detective McGavin returning your voice mail message. I hope this is not too late, but you did say to call no matter what time it was."

"No. No. It's OK. Thanks for getting back to me so quickly, Detective. Were you out on a hot date?"

"As a matter of fact, I was. What can I do for you?"

Paul told Detective McGavin about his conversation with Dr. Fernandez before he left the hospital. He then said, "Does it sound as if the zoo would be a good starting point in figuring out who's the mystery field jacket man?"

"Way ahead of you, Mr. Marco. I called the zoo after I returned to headquarters. It seems that they had a minor break-in a few days ago. As far as they knew, only a couple of microscopes and a computer were missing. I asked them to check their inventory of snake venom, and sure enough, a vial of cobra venom was missing. Apparently, they store over sixty types of venom and antivenin in the lab. The one small missing vial was not discovered at the time of the robbery."

"Then the zoo officials must have reported the break-in when it happened. Right?"

"Sure. The staff herpetologist called the police first thing in the morning, after she opened the lab."

"Detective, what I mean to say is they don't just have sixty vials of snake venom lying around, do they? The stuff must have been locked up, right? So how is it that they didn't know they were missing a vial of cobra venom?"

"Oh. I see what you're saying. If the venom and antivenin are locked in, say, a refrigerator, the broken lock would have tipped them off to inventory their stock."

"Exactly. So how come they didn't notice the vial missing?" "Suppose the locked cabinet was not broken into?" "Detective McGavin, you just lost me."

"Suppose the venom was stolen by someone with a key. That would certainly explain why they didn't know the vial was missing. You know what, Paul? I think I'll pay a little visit to the zoo first thing tomorrow morning. Would you like to come along?"

"Sure. I can meet you there at, say, eight o'clock. That will leave me enough time afterward to come home and change for the first viewing at Dela Ginos."

"OK, Paul. I'll see you in front of the reptile house at eight sharp. Bring coffee. Cream and sugar."

Paul's mind was racing with a hundred ideas since his conversation with Theresa McGavin. He liked the idea that things were now starting to happen with his case. He had Gary Roth as well as Mikey Weigand, looking for information and now he had the police department going after other tangible leads. *Yes,* he thought, *things are starting to happen.*

Paul was exhausted. He did not sleep very much. Either his mind would not let him relax or that damn pepperoni pizza lying in his stomach like a brick kept him awake. At six o'clock, Paul made another attempt at fixing a decent cup of coffee. He turned the coffee maker on, then headed for the shower. After showering and shaving, he got dressed in casual clothes. Paul then went back into the kitchen to pour a cup of coffee. This time, Paul thought, he had gotten the formula right. One level scoop per cup. Paul stirred in some sugar and half-and-half. As soon as the cream hit the coffee, it curdled. Paul looked at the floating white globs in his cup, then at the expiration date on the carton. It was a week past due. Paul poured the cup of coffee down the kitchen sink drain and cleaned out the coffee maker filter. *For some reason he was never going to have a decent cup of coffee again,* he thought.

Paul grabbed a jacket, then went into the garage to start the Jeep. As he headed down the driveway, he picked up the paper and threw it in the backseat. The ride to the downtown area where the zoo was located turned out to be a nightmare. Traffic was heavy and an earlier accident on Interstate 83 was still causing problems with those commuters who felt that it was necessary to rubberneck when they passed an accident scene.

Paul spotted a MacDonald's restaurant about six blocks from the park entrance that housed the zoo. Looking at his watch, he saw that it was only 7:40. He had plenty of time, so he went to the drive-through window and ordered two large coffees. The young girl working the window placed sugars and creams into a small bag along with two stir sticks and some napkins. Paul then drove to the Reptile House entrance and parked his Jeep in the almost empty parking lot. The few cars that were there probably belonged to the staff because the zoo did not open until later.

Paul put sugar and cream into his coffee cup, then opened the newspaper. He sat in the Jeep with the warm rays of the sun filtering through the windshield. Paul looked at his watch to see it was now five minutes past eight o'clock. He lit another cigarette and continued reading the paper. As he was about to turn to the sports section, he saw McGavin pulling up next to his Jeep. She was dressed in a heavy wool blend beige business suit. Her hair was French-braided and lay perfectly on her back between her shoulders.

Theresa got out of her car and opened the door to Paul's Jeep. "Sorry I'm late. Traffic was a real mess this morning."

Paul handed her a cup of coffee, which she gladly accepted.

Theresa started to put cream and sugar into her cup. "I hope it's still hot," said Paul.

"That steam is a pretty good indicator, don't you think."

Paul folded the newspaper and tossed it in the backseat. He could smell the fresh, womanly scent of Theresa's shower and powder. He remembered how Diana used to smell when she would come out of a shower, perfumed and powdered. Not too much, mind you. Just enough to smell fresh and clean.

"Well, Detective, this is the first time I have been to the zoo in almost twenty years. How about you?"

"I was here about two months ago with my niece and nephew. They absolutely loved the polar bear exhibit. You should see how nice the rest of the zoo is, too. A lot of time and money has been funneled into some of these newer exhibits."

"Maybe when we are through with this business, I'll take a walk around the place. Are you about ready to go inside now, or do you want to finish your coffee?"

"No. I'm ready. This fast-food coffee tastes terrible. There is nothing like brewing your own fresh coffee each morning. Don't you think?"

Paul did not answer the detective. He took their cups and exited the Jeep. There was a trash can about ten feet in front of where Paul parked, so he deposited the trash and said, "Lead on, Detective."

The two walked toward the main entrance, where a guard met them saying, "Sorry, folks. The zoo doesn't open to visitors until ten o'clock."

Theresa showed the guard her badge and explained that she was doing a follow-up investigation concerning the break-in a week or so ago. The guard let them through the gate and directed them toward the door that housed the lab and small office for the herpetologist. Paul and Theresa walked up to the door and let themselves in. Paul sarcastically said, "Real tight security."

Theresa agreed. "Yeah. You would think that after they were robbed, they would tighten things up a bit."

Theresa and Paul walked down a narrow hall, then came to a locked door marked: *LAB*. Paul said, "That's better."

Theresa knocked on the door. A female voice on the other side responded, "Who's there?"

"I'm Detective Theresa McGavin and I would—"

The door opened and a woman wearing a white lab coat and holding a monkey in her arms said, "I know who you are. I'm Dr. Dinah Miesman and this cute little girl is Lacy. The guard called ahead to announce that you two were coming. That's why I had the front door unlocked."

Paul and Theresa looked at each other for a brief second, then Theresa said, "Dr. Miesman, this is Mr. Paul Marco. We would like to take a look at where you keep the sneak venom and antivenin."

"Sure, come in. Since we had the break-in, things have been rather hectic around here."

Dr. Miesman walked over to a metal cage and put Lacy inside while saying, "I'll be right back, Lacy. Why don't you play with your toys until I get back?"

Doctor Miesman closed the cage and started walking in another direction. She came to a wooden door, then retrieved a key from her pocket to feed into the lock. She walked through the door with Theresa and Paul following right behind her. Dr. Miesman then said, "That refrigerator over there is where we keep over sixty varieties of snake venom. The refrigerator on the other side of the room is where we keep the antivenin."

Paul and Theresa walked over to the refrigerator where the venom was stored. There was a padlock on the door the size of a man's fist.

Paul asked, "Doctor, is this refrigerator always locked with a padlock?"

"Absolutely. Some of those venoms are extremely dangerous." Theresa asked, "Why is the refrigerator that stores the antivenin not locked like this one?"

"Very simply, if we need to get to the antivenin in a hurry, we can't be running around looking for a set of keys."

"That makes sense," said Theresa.

Paul asked, "How many people have keys to this room and the padlock for the refrigerator containing the venom?"

"Let's see. Oh yes, there are three sets of keys. One set is at the main office at the entrance to the zoo. The zoo director has a set, and I have a set."

Theresa asked, "Then the guards, like the one we met outside, don't have keys to this room or the padlock?"

"No. As I said, there are only three sets of keys."

"I see," said Theresa. "When the break-in occurred, was the door to this room damaged?"

Dr. Miesman put a surprised look on her face, then said, "No. No, it wasn't. And I know I locked the door the night before. I always make sure the padlock is on the refrigerator and the lab door is locked before I leave for the evening. I know I locked them. I'm positive."

Paul asked, "Can you think of any way someone could have gotten one of the sets of keys without you, the zoo director, or the main office knowing about it?"

Dr. Miesman thought for a few seconds, then responded, "My keys are always with me. The zoo director always has his keys with him. The only set of keys that could have been used to open the door and the padlock had to be the set stored in the main office." Theresa said, "Well, thank you for your time, Doctor. You have been most helpful. Our next stop will be the main office building. Can you tell us how we get there from here?"

Dr. Miesman told Theresa and Paul how to locate the main office building. It was a bit of a walk, so they decided to drive over in Paul's Jeep. While going to their destination Theresa muttered, "Something sure is starting to stink around here, and I don't think it's the animals."

At the main office building Theresa introduced Paul to the zoo director, Mr. Michael Bind.

"Have a seat. Now, how may I help you, Officer?" said Bind. Theresa explained the conversation Paul and she had had with Dr. Miesman. Paul looked around the small office while Theresa went on with her explanation as to how they had ended up in the director's office. Paul noticed that the office was very small. In fact, it looked as if it was a very large closet at one time. Behind the little desk where the director sat were several certificates and awards framed in plain black imitation wood. The two chairs Theresa and Paul were sitting in did not match. One chair was green and the other gray. The file cabinets against the one wall were painted olive drab, obviously military surplus or state government issue. Theresa was now summing up her request.

". . . so, can you tell us if you're ever without your keys, Mr. Bind?"

"Never. I have my keys with me at all times. However, the third set of keys you spoke about is hanging over there."

Director Bind was pointing to the wall behind where Paul and Theresa were sitting. There was a large wooden key cutout with eight hooks attached to the plaque. Each hook had a ring of keys hanging by oversize metal rings. Paul stood and took a few steps toward the hanging key rack and saw the third hook had a label that read: LAB & FRIDGE. Paul, looking dejected, said, "Mr. Bind, it looks as if anyone could come in here and get these keys without arousing very much suspicion."

"Well, I guess that's correct. My office door does not have a lock on it, and the front door to the building is open all hours of the night. You see, there really isn't much to steal in this building. The furnishings are old and we are still using electric typewriters for our correspondence. All of the computers and other valuable equipment are located in the labs and hospital."

Theresa thanked Mr. Bind for his time and was about to leave his office when her beeper sounded.

"May I use a telephone to call headquarters, Mr. Bind?" "Surely. Use my phone. I have to go over to the hospital to meet with our visiting hippo veterinarian. We have a bit of a flu bug going around."

Theresa picked up the phone and dialed headquarters. Paul looked around the office some more as he listened to the one-sided conversation McGavin was having.

"Hi, Phil. What do you have for me? . . . I was afraid of that. . . . Anything else? . . . That's just dandy. Thanks, Phil. I owe you one."

After Theresa hung up the phone, Paul asked, "Anything wrong?"

"That was Phil Shultz. I had him check out the syringe the field-jacketed man left in your garage. It turns out that it is a common diabetic-type syringe. There must be tens of thousands of those things floating around. It looks like we hit another dead end."

The news about the syringe was certainly disappointing, but Paul didn't let it get him down. He drove Detective McGavin back to her car, where she said she had to meet with Pat Dershan about a cross-reference file that might lead to something. Paul asked Detective McGavin to call him at home if she came up with anything that could be a positive lead.

Paul pointed the Jeep toward Interstate 83. He stopped to eat at the International House of Pancakes, where he had a large combination breakfast and lunch. After eating, Paul drove home to get ready for the first scheduled viewing at Gino's. As Paul drove home, he thought about how the day had begun with such great promise. Unfortunately, it had fizzled out by noon, with nothing to show for the efforts.

Chapter 6

Paul arrived at Gino's around two o'clock. He wanted to spend some time alone with Diana before the crowd started filing into the viewing room. Antonio greeted Paul with a handshake, then accompanied him to the viewing room. *Antonio knew exactly how to handle such situations,* Paul thought. Antonio slid open the two main doors that led to the viewing room, then motioned for Paul to go inside. Antonio then quietly slid the doors closed before returning to his desk in the front lobby. There was no reason for Antonio to be in the viewing room with the grieving Paul. Through experience, Antonio could sense whether someone would need help to make that lonely walk to the open casket. In this case, he figured Paul could handle things alone.

Paul took a few steps into the viewing room, then suddenly stopped. His eyes scanned the entire room taking in all the floral arrangements that had been nicely arranged by Antonio's staff. His senses were soon overwhelmed by the room. He could smell the aroma of fresh cut flowers and the scent of the very water that filled the many baskets and vases. He could hear the soft hum of the air circulating through the ductwork into the room. The soft lighting where the many chairs had been set up for the mourners quickly changed to bright lights directly over the casket. The casket was draped and surrounded by floral arrangements. Several mass card trees also were positioned close to the casket. Two of the trees were completely filled, and two others were almost at capacity as well. From where he was standing Paul could just barely see the profile of Diana's face lying so peacefully on the silk-covered pillow. He kept his eyes glued to her face as he slowly approached the casket. With each closing step, his eyes began to fill with more tears. Slowly he walked forward until the tears started to freefall over his cheeks and down the front of his shirt. The last few steps were the most difficult and painful. His legs felt as if they were filled with lead as the muscles were steadily weakening. Those shaking, trembling legs barely carried him to a point where he could safely collapse on the small padded kneeler in front of the casket. The tears were flowing nonstop and his chest felt as if someone had yanked ten pounds of flesh away, leaving a gaping cavity exposed for the world to see. Paul lowered his head into his hands and cried until there were no more tears. In his mind he was thinking about how good Diana looked in her beautiful blue dress. Almost good enough that if he could help her out of the confining box in which she lay they could dance around the room among the flowers and soft lights. He remembered some of the great times they had shared together. Most important, he remembered the little insignificant mannerisms and expressions Diana would display at various times: the small friendly smile that accompanied every person she met, the little-girl giggle she made when watching a funny sitcom on TV, those huge laughs she made at one of his lousy jokes that caused her to wipe a tear away from her eye, the soft touch. There were thousands of thoughts racing through Paul's mind. So many, in fact, that his tears now changed to a small smile upon his lips. He knew there would never be another like her in his lifetime, so he decided to reflect on all the joy she had brought him through the years. Upon doing that, there was no reason to cry any longer. From that point forward, when he thought about Diana he would manage to smile. *That's how she would want me to carry on*, thought Paul.

By three o'clock Paul had composed himself and was ready to greet the friendly but engulfing mourners. They came to shake his hand and hug him and they all tried to find those ever-elusive comforting words that simply didn't exist. There had been times when Paul was in the role of the mourner. He knew that no matter how hard one tried to find something to say that would ease the pain of the bereaved, it was useless. Most of the time, it was better to say nothing and just hold the person in pain. Somehow, everyone benefited from those kinds of encounters.

The funeral parlor was now packed with family, friends and acquaintances. The noise from the many ongoing conversations was picking up to an almost disrespectful level. Paul saw Gary Roth over by the far wall signing the guest book and walked over to him, and they embraced. Gary said, "Diana looks nice. I wanted to come over to you sooner, but there were too many people around."

"Yeah. I know, Gar.' Listen. Let's go to the lounge downstairs to take a smoke."

Paul led the way with Gary close by his side. When they entered the small room, there were a half-dozen people smoking and drinking coffee or soft drinks. Paul didn't recognize many of the people, so he suspected they were visiting one of the other three people laid out at Gino's.

Paul found a couple of empty chairs that were out of the way for Gary and him to sit in. They lit their cigarettes, then stared out into space without saying a word. Gary finally broke the silence by saying, "How are you holding up, Paul?"

"OK. I guess. You know, what can I say?"

"Well, let me tell you, man. You look like crap."

Paul let a few seconds pass, then cracked a smile and managed a small laugh, saying, "Thanks, Gar.' I really needed that."

"No problem. Now you sound like your old self. Listen. I know it's tough on you right now, but you'll feel better as time passes. Don't sweat the small stuff. That's what you used to say, right?"

"You're right, Gar.' After all, what can I do about the past anyway."

"That's right. Nothin.' What you need to do is concentrate on today, while you are still here to make a difference."

The two friends sat in the room, each smoking another cigarette without talking. Finally, Gary very awkwardly said, "I don't know if this is the right time to bring this up. But I . . . I"

"You what? Spit it out, Gar.'"

"Paul, I got some information about that dude I told you about."

"Sure. Tell me what you found out."

"Are you sure it's OK to talk about it here? I mean now, with the funeral and all?"

"Gar, if you have information, I need to know about it. So come on, what do you have for me?"

"Well, the dude I was telling you about said that his friend with the information wants five grand for the story. I told him that was OK, but only if the information is legit. Well, he comes back later and asks how we are going to know if the information is legit unless he gives it up. And his buddy ain't giving it up unless we pay. See what I'm saying?"

"Look, Gar. I want that information. Tell this guy I'll pay the five grand. I will give him 2,500 up-front. When I hear what he has to say, and if it's legit, I'll pay him the remaining 2,500. If he jerks me around, I'll cut his throat and he can keep the original 2,500. Got all that?"

"I got you, man. I'll pass the word after I leave here this afternoon. I may have an answer for you by this evening. From what I know about this dude, he is probably skimming some cash off the top. You know, like a broker fee or commission."

"If you find out anything later tonight, let me know. I don't have 2,500 cash on hand right now, but I can get it when the bank opens tomorrow morning."

"Hey, man. No problem. If I can get this dude to cooperate, I'll spot you the money until you can come up with the cash. I don't use no lousy banks to hold my cash. Those kinds of places end up getting robbed. Know what I'm saying?"

"Yeah. Listen. Thanks, Gar. I really appreciate you helping me out on this. I also don't want you becoming involved any more than you already are. Set up the meet, and I'll pay the dude his down payment. If he comes through with the information, I'll make the final payment. This way you can stay in the clear in case something goes wrong."

"It's your game, Pauly. I'll let you know how things turn out later tonight."

Paul and Gary went back to the viewing room. Gary stayed for a few more minutes, then left for places unknown. Paul resumed the handshaking and hugging as new mourners replaced those leaving. The two hours Paul spent greeting people and accepting condolences wore him down. Emotionally he was now officially considered a wreck. Physically, he was not doing much better.

After the last mourner left the room, Paul knelt at the front of the casket to tell Diana he would be back around six-thirty to spend some more quiet time with her. He slowly stood and turned toward the double sliding doors, where Antonio was already waiting for him.

"Mr. Marco, you have a telephone call up front. I told the woman that this may not be such a good time to talk to you, but she said it was important. She has been holding now for about fifteen minutes. I didn't want to disturb you while you were alone with your wife."

"Thank you very much for your consideration, Mr. Gino. However, the call may be important, so I better talk to her. Did she tell you her name?"

"Oh, yes. I'm sorry. She said her name is Theresa. She sounds like the policewoman who was here yesterday."

"Thank you, Mr. Gino. I won't tie up the line very long." "That's OK. Take your time."

Paul went to the front of the funeral parlor, where there was a telephone with four lights. Only one light was blinking. Paul picked up the receiver and pushed the blinking light, saying, "Hello, Detective. I'm sorry you had to wait on hold so long.—"

"No. No. It's OK, Mr. Marco. I'm the one who should apologize for disturbing you at a time like this."

"Well, that's neither here nor there right now. So, what can I do for you?"

"Mr. Marco, are you sure it's OK to talk about this now? If you'd rather wait until another time, I would under—"

"No. It's OK Detective. Everyone must think the world stops when someone is grieving. Listen. I'm fine. I'm a little tired and hungry. But other than that, I'm doing fine."

"Well, Paul, I have an idea. You have to eat and I'm starving, too. Why don't you go over to Smitty's and get us a table and I'll meet you there in less than fifteen minutes. We can both get something to eat, and I can tell you what I found out. How does that sound to you?"

"Well, my daddy told me never argue with a woman when she's making sense. I'll see you at Smitty's."

Smitty's bar and grill was just around the corner from Gino's funeral parlor. The grill was noted for its superb seafood. The specialty of the house was surf and turf. The bar side of the establishment was more a neighborhood hangout than anything else. Paul could remember that on many a Friday night he and his buddies would meet for drinks at Smitty's before heading out to hit the local nightspots. *God, those days seem like they happened centuries ago,* thought Paul.

Paul walked over to Smitty's and asked the maître d' if he could have a table for two. *The maître d' is a short little guy, thought Paul. Maybe five foot tall with his shoes on.* The maître d' looked at the reservation book sitting on top of the podium in front of him, then said, "We can have a table for you in about twenty minutes. Is that OK?"

Paul assured the little man that twenty minutes would be just fine, gave him his name, then walked outside to smoke a cigarette while he waited for Detective McGavin to arrive. Paul wanted to go into the bar to have a drink, but he was concerned that he might miss the detective.

"Is that you, Paul?"

Paul turned around to look at the man who had asked the question. "Well, I'll be. How in the hell have you been, Mark?"

Mark Vanner extended his hand to Paul as he replied, "I have been doing great. What brings you back to the hood, after all this time?"

Paul explained why he was in the area. Mark felt bad that he had not known about Diana and expressed his most sincere condolences to Paul. The two men caught up on fifteen or more years in less than ten minutes. Mark then hurried off to make a call home to tell his wife, Sue, about Diana. *They would make the seven o'clock viewing if it was the last thing they did,* Paul thought.

Detective McGavin walked up behind Paul cheerfully saying, "Did you get us a table?"

Paul turned quickly, clenched his fist, and crouched down as if ready to strike Theresa with a roundhouse left. Theresa backed up a step saying, "Wow! It's me, Paul."

Paul could see the surprised look on McGavin's face, just as she could see the violent look in his eyes. Paul relaxed his fist and stood up straight, saying, "Don't you know it's not smart to sneak up on people?"

Detective McGavin could see that she had upset Paul, but she had had no idea that he was so jumpy. Paul looked at his watch, then said, "Our table should be just about ready."

Paul opened the restaurant door for Detective McGavin and the two walked up to the reservation podium. The maître d' walked toward them and gathered two menus while saying, "Follow me, please."

The restaurant was romantically lit. Each table had a candle burning with a red globe as a centerpiece. The tablecloths were starched bright white with another burgundy cloth placed on top at an angle. The restaurant was very crowded but quiet. Paul pulled the chair out for Detective McGavin, than sat across from her. The maître d' left the menus and a wine list before going off to attend to whatever he did when he was not seating people at a table.

Paul asked, "Would you like some wine with dinner?" "Actually, I would really like to have a beer. That is, if it's OK with you?"

"Beer it is," said Paul.

A young waitress about nineteen came to their table and said her name was Mary. She took their drink order for two Heinekens, then headed to the bar to retrieve the drinks. McGavin said, "Paul, I'm sorry about what happened outside. I wasn't thinking when—"

"It's OK. Forget about it."

"Are you sure it's OK for me to be talking to you at a time like this? I understand that sometimes I get so involved with my cases that I become insensitive to—"

"Please, Detective. It's OK. Really. Let's look at the menu and order some chow because I'm starving."

Theresa smiled slightly, then said, "Me too."

They looked over the menus while Mary brought them their beers in long frosted glasses. She asked if they were ready to order, which they did. Paul picked the first thing he saw, and Theresa selected one entree, then switched her order to something else. Before the waitress left the table, Theresa switched her order back to her original selection. Paul had a slight grin on his face, as the waitress dashed off to place their orders. Theresa said, "What are you grinning about?"

"It's nothing, really. My Diana used to do the same thing when we went out to a restaurant. First she would make one selection; then she would switch two or three times before going back to her original choice."

"My boyfriend gets on me all the time for doing that. I think it has something to do with female genes."

Paul managed to smile again at Theresa's comment. They made small talk while waiting for their entrees to arrive. Over dinner Paul seemed to relax a bit more, then finally said, "Well, what is it that you wanted to talk to me about, Detective?"

"Remember I told you that I was having a cross-reference check computer run prepared on the accomplices of the guy you popped in the store a couple of months ago?"

"Yeah, the infamous Clark Kent, as I recall. Did you come up with anything?"

"Right. Anyway, my friend Pat Dershan at the department rushed the job through for me. She really is a super worker. I would like you to meet her sometime. I know you would appreciate how dedicated she is to getting the job done."

"Are you trying to fix me up, or do you have something to tell me, Detective?"

"Oh. Yeah. Sorry, I get carried away sometimes. Anyway, my friend Pat showed me two names of guys who were arrested with Clark Kent over his long criminal career."

Theresa fished through her pocketbook to retrieve a small spiral notebook. She quickly flipped through some pages until she said, "Here it is. The first guy's name is Brian Ridel. He was arrested with Clark Kent on two separate B and E's [breaking and entering]. They both got off with time served. The second guy's name is Steven Green. He and Clark were also nailed two times while working together as a team. The first time, they were caught dealing drugs. Small-time operation, but they spent a year in the big house for distribution. Soon after they were released, the two of them were picked up for a scam to heist shipments of new washers and dryers from the Port Authority dock in Dundalk. In that caper, a guard was shot and killed. Clark did ten years for that one, and Steven did seven."

Paul was listening to the detective rattle off the litany of crimes these career criminals managed to compile, wondering where it was all leading. The waitress came to clear away the plates and returned with two coffees. The detective kept talking, but Paul was momentarily lost in the aroma and dark rich color swirling in the cup sitting under his nose. *This smells delicious,* he thought. Paul added cream and sugar to his coffee, then took a sip. It was wonderful. A really great cup of coffee, at last.

Detective McGavin stirred in some cream and sugar, then tasted her coffee. She made a bitter-looking face, then asked, "How can you drink that stuff? It must be two hours old."

As Detective McGavin pushed her cup away so she could continue talking, Paul smiled and resumed savoring his cup of coffee. He did not know when he would get the chance to taste great coffee like this again.

Theresa continued talking, saying, "Well, I know it doesn't sound like much, but I went to see our Mr. Kent in jail this morning, after we left the zoo."

"Why did you do that?"

"I wanted to see if he would roll over on his boss. Anyway, I went to see him and offer him a reduced sentence, if he could help us find the triggerman on the double homicide."

"Did he go for it? What did he say?"

The waitress returned to fill Paul's coffee cup. Theresa held her hand over her cup while saying, "None for me, thanks. Could I have another Heineken instead?"

Theresa turned back to Paul, saying, "Well, believe it or not, our Mr. Kent is a real pussycat now that he is tied to that wheelchair for the rest of his life. Thanks to you, I might add. He is very willing to talk if we could get him off with time served. I told him I would run it by the DA to see what he had to say, but that it would probably not fly. I told him that *maybe* we could plea him down to attempted robbery instead of armed robbery. You know, maybe three years. Mr. Kent said no deal. He wants out now, or he isn't talking."

"Then what did you tell him?"

"I told him I would get back to him after I talked to the DA." "Is that it?"

"Hey, Paul. I'm doing the best that I can. I still have to work within the system."

Paul, getting angrier as he thought about that scumbag Kent getting out of jail, looked at Detective McGavin, then said, "You may have to work within the damned system, but I don't. If that scumbag knows who killed my Diana, I'll find a way to get it out of him."

"Hold on, Paul. Don't do anything stupid. We are moving on this thing, and I have a good feeling Clark Kent is going to give us what we want. We just need to be a little more patient."

Paul sat back in his chair, starring at the frosted beer glass the waitress placed in front of Detective McGavin. He thought about all the detective had said, then responded with, "You're right, Detective. I apologize for sounding off. We'll do it by the book for now. Who knows? Maybe that creep Kent will make amends for his lousy life of crime by giving up the triggerman. But to be honest with you, I have my doubts."

Paul paid the bill for dinner, then escorted Detective McGavin to her car. She protested the action, considering she was armed with a 9mm and Paul had nothing but a small pocketknife. Paul insisted on walking Detective McGavin to her car anyway. He explained it by saying, "It's a guy thing."

After Detective McGavin pulled away from the parking lot of Smitty's, Paul walked over to the funeral parlor to talk to Diana. The tears did not come this time, although the hurt was just as intense. It was now 6:45, and the crowd would be coming by within a few minutes. Paul used the quiet time to kneel in front of the casket and conjure up more fond memories of Diana and him walking in the woods with their dog. Going on vacation to the islands, so many years ago, to celebrate their tenth wedding anniversary. *Oh, how the fond memories outnumbered the bad ones,* Paul thought.

At seven o'clock, Antonio opened the double doors to let the viewing begin. Some of the people were the same ones as from the afternoon session, but most were new faces paying their final respects. Paul spotted Mark and Sue Vanner signing the guest book. They approached Paul and said they wanted to volunteer to put the funeral procession together for tomorrow's ride to the cemetery. Paul told them how much he appreciated them helping out, but they were more than happy to do it.

Around eight-thirty, Paul saw Gary Roth coming through the double doors. Gary caught Paul's attention, then held up two fingers to his lips as if he were taking a drag from an imaginary cigarette. Paul knew from that signal that Gary wanted to talk to him in the lounge area. Paul simply shook his head affirmatively, then graciously made his exit through the side door that led to the hall. Gary was sitting in the same seat he was in earlier. There were almost fifteen smokers in the room at one time. Paul came in, lit a cigarette, then offered one to Gary. They sat in silence for almost a full minute before Gary thought it was safe to talk. Gary said, "I talked to the dude and the meet is set." "He went for our terms?"

"Yeah, but he was not too happy about meeting with you instead of me. I convinced him to meet in a nice open public place where both of you could feel relaxed and safe. He went for it. The meet is set up for tomorrow afternoon at two o'clock in the food bazaar at Golden Ring Mall. Are you OK with that?"

"You did fine, Gary. I'll hit the bank tomorrow after the funeral to make a withdrawal. That will give me plenty of time to make the meeting at two."

"Listen. Ask for small bills, tens and twenties, and put the cash in a brown paper bag. He said for you to go by the Boardwalk Fries stall and wait. The dude will be looking for a guy by the fries stall holding a brown paper bag. Remember, he doesn't know what you look like and I have never met this dude's friend that has the information. I think that puts you both at an equal disadvantage." "It will be OK, Gar.' I'll take care of it from here on out.

Listen. I owe you big time, brother."

"Forget it. You would do the same for me. Now, I'm going to be at Golden Ring Mall around the same time as you because I have some shopping to take care of. In other words, you're on your own, but I will be there in case you need some backup. Comprendo?"

Paul smiled at Gary, then stood to shake his hand without saying a word. Gary knew Paul understood that if he set up the meeting, he was going to make damn sure nothing happened to his friend. *Just like in the old days,* thought Paul.

Chapter 7

The long night at the funeral parlor had taken its toll on Paul. He headed home around nine-thirty feeling emotionally and physically drained. Before Paul left, Antonio told him that all the arrangements were in order for tomorrow's ten o'clock funeral procession to Holy Redeemer Cemetery.

As Paul drove north on Interstate 83, he tried to put the day's activities into perspective. His beloved wife was now dead, and he was once again working with the police to solve a crime. A crime that was somehow related to the incident a couple of months ago in his store when two punks tried to shake him down.

Paul quickly pulled off the interstate at the Timonium exit and jumped back on it again. Only this time he was heading in the opposite direction.

Paul took Interstate 83 south to the Baltimore Beltway, where he exited at North Point Boulevard. From there it was a short drive to the *Cell Block Bar and Grill*. Paul parked in the back of the bar once again, then made his way to the bartender who was at the far end serving drinks. The place was very crowded. It usually was on Thursdays, since that was the day the local steel mill paid its employees. The steelworkers would come in to get their paychecks cashed, only to drink half of it away before heading home in a drunken stupor.

The bartender was the same guy Paul saw when he first met with Mikey. The bartender spotted Paul, then held up his index finger to indicate "one minute." Paul sat on one of the stools while the bartender picked up the phone behind the bar. He talked for about ten seconds before hanging up the phone. The bartender poured a draft beer into a glass, then walked over to where Paul was sitting. He placed the beer down in front of Paul while saying, "Mikey said for you to go down in about ten minutes. He's finishing up some urgent business."

Paul placed a five-dollar bill on the bar and told the bartender to keep the change. Paul watched the huge TV screen while finishing the beer. When the ten minutes were up, Paul headed for the kitchen door, just as he had done before. When Paul reached the second door at the bottom of the steps, he was again greeted by Rocco. They went through the frisking ritual; then Paul was led down the hall to the great room.

As Paul walked across the long great room to where Mikey was sitting, he could see that Mikey was still talking on the phone. Paul slowed his pace so he would not come up to the desk while Mikey was still talking.

Mikey waved Paul over to him as he finished his conversation and replaced the receiver. "Hey, Pauly, what brings you back here so soon? As if I don't know!"

"Well, I was in the neighborhood and thought I would drop by to see if you found out anything for me."

"Pauly. You were at Gino's until nine-thirty and were on your way home before you decided to come see me. Right?"

"Yeah. How did you know that?"

"I'm worried about you, Pauly. I had Joey looking after you. You know, in case the guy in the army jacket showed up at the funeral parlor."

"No kidding? Joey. Joey Polucci? I saw him at Gino's but didn't put two and two together. There is no need for Joey to waste his time looking after me. The cops had surveillance cameras inside and outside Gino's place."

"Pauly, I'm surprised at you. The cops! What the hell could they do: take a picture of the guy pumping lead into your butt? I had Joey there to take the son of a bitch out, if he showed up."

"I see what you're saying. Mikey, does that mean you know who Joey should be looking for?"

"No. Not yet anyway. I told Joey to keep an eye out in case he suspected somebody of packing heat. You know, these punks today don't have any respect for something as sacred as a funeral."

"You're right, Mikey. It's not like in your day, when there was still some honor to doing business."

"Pauly, I still operate with honor when doing business. Now, let me tell you what I found out. I had Sal talk to some guys who think they may be able to help you."

"Sal? Who's Sal?"

"You know Salvatore Rosario. For Christ sake, Pauly, you two made your First Communion together."

"Oh sure. Little Sal. I haven't heard from him in years." "Yeah. That's him, little Sal. Only he ain't so little anymore.

Anyway, Sal works at the city lockup as a driver. He picks up and delivers prisoners to court. That kind of stuff, you know. Supposedly, Sal heard there may be a guy who is on the inside with information that may lead us to the triggerman."

"Mikey, I'm ahead of you on this one. The punk's name is Clark Kent."

"You're kidding me, right? Clark Kent? Jesus, these punks can't even come up with original names."

"No. I'm as serious as a heart attack. That's the guy's real name. The one who tried to shake me down a couple of months ago. I put him in a wheelchair for life. He told the police he would give up the information I need, if they turn him loose with a reduced sentence. The cops are working on it with the DA."

"That's interesting, Pauly. I think maybe I could get Sal to see who it is on the inside that might be able to lean on this punk to speed up the process. You know what I mean?"

"Yeah, but tell Sal not to lean to hard on the punk, or he may clam up for good."

"Let me take care of it. As for you, why don't you go home and get some rest? You look like crap."

Paul laughed loudly, then said, "You know what? You're the second person today who has told me that. I guess I better be going. But before I go, there is one thing I need from you Mikey."

"Name it and it's yours."

"I have a meeting with another guy tomorrow afternoon who may have some information for me. I would like to have a cold piece, just in case the meeting doesn't go smoothly."

Mikey smiled, then said, "Follow me."

Mikey took Paul to the room hidden behind the bookcases. Once inside, Mikey opened a locker that was filled with handguns. There were hundreds of them in all makes and models imaginable. Paul picked up a .22 Ruger automatic, then said, "Is this cold?"

"Cold as Alaska in winter, my friend. That's only good for up close and personal work, you know?"

"I know, Mikey. Do you have a silencer for it?"

Mikey opened another smaller cabinet, then said, "Pick one of these."

There must have been twenty silencers in the cabinet, all with different bore sizes. Paul found one that fit and placed it on the Ruger. Mikey handed Paul a box of .22 long rifle hollow-point shells, then closed the cabinet. The two men walked back into the great room, and Mikey closed the bookcases.

"Mikey, I appreciate the hardware and the information." "No problem, Pauly. Now don't get yourself in any trouble with that thing, OK?"

Paul smiled as he separated the silencer from the weapon. He tucked the gun in his waistband by the small of his back, then placed the silencer in his suit breast pocket.

Paul left the *Cell Block* and once again headed for home. As he drove home, Paul was thinking that maybe tomorrow would be a more productive day. The night air was cold enough for Paul to place the heater control on the medium setting. The weather forecast for tomorrow was cool, but thankfully there was no rain or snow expected.

Detective McGavin met with the DA after she had dinner with Paul. The DA was in his thirties and had politics in mind for his future career. His claim to fame was that he was tough on crime, especially crime committed with guns. As an advocate of gun control and bans on assault weapons to the general public he had made many speeches expressing his views. Mostly the female and the elderly populations found him to be a viable candidate for the mayoral seat in the upcoming elections next November. Sidney Milliman was a man who had gone to all the right schools and attended all the right functions. He even made sure his clothes and hairstyles were impeccable for those impromptu sound bites on the six o'clock news. It was rumored that he kept a complete wardrobe in his office just in case he had to be on TV at five o'clock, then again at six. He didn't want to be seen on TV wearing the same clothes twice in a row.

Detective McGavin was sitting in Milliman's office when he returned from his dinner break. Apparently he was working on some hot case that required him to be there so late preparing briefs, etc. "Hello, Detective McGavin. How have you been?"

"Just fine. How about yourself?"

"Can't complain. You know how it goes. What good would it do to complain anyway? Right?"

"That's what they say, all right."

"Well, what can I do for you at this late hour? It must be important or you wouldn't have waited while I grabbed a bite to eat."

Detective McGavin explained that she wanted to make a deal with one Clark Benjamin Kent, so they could possibly solve a double homicide using Kent's information. Sid listened to the detective, then said, "What makes you think this Kent character is going to give up the shooter and his boss? After all, it's like you said, Detective. He is confined to a wheelchair, thereby making him one easy target for retaliation. So, what makes you think he will roll over on these guys?"

"Counselor, I think he just wants to spend the rest of his time out in the free world in his wheelchair, as opposed to be being locked up in prison."

"Well, Detective, you know how I stand on crimes committed with guns. It would be like me going back on my word if I pushed to reduce his sentence."

"Yes, but at the same time it may make it possible for you to put away a murderer and his boss."

"That's right. But the key word in your statement is *possible*. It may be *possible* to put them away. No. I don't like the way this is stacking up. But let me tell you what I'll do. Tomorrow I'll talk it over with my staff, to see what they think. We will also pull the jacket on this Kent character to see what we are dealing with. How does that sound?"

"Counselor, that would be great. I would appreciate you getting back to me as soon as you decide what you are going to do." Theresa left the DA's office and walked the three blocks to police headquarters. The night air was cold, and she wished that she had brought her heavier coat. However, the brisk walk did help her warm up a little.

Before long Theresa was in the elevator pressing the button for the floor where the cafeteria was located. She needed a cup of hot coffee or tea to warm her up inside. As Theresa exited the elevator, she saw the back of Pat Dershan's head making the turn around the corner. She called out, "Hey, Pat!"

Pat turned to look around the hall corner she had just passed and saw Theresa running toward her. "Hey, buddy. What are you doing here so late?"

Theresa said, "I had a late meeting with the DA and just about froze my butt off walking back to headquarters."

"The DA, hm. The cute one that we see on TV all the time.

What's his name? Sidney something?"

"That's the one. Sid Milliman. Do you think he's cute?"

"Of course. Don't you?"

"No. Not really. I mean he's nice-looking and all, but I have seen better."

The two women laughed as they walked to the coffee machine to get something to drink. They sat at one of fifteen or so empty tables in the cafeteria.

Pat sipped her coffee, then asked, "Did that computer run do you any good today? You know, the one I busted my tail to complete for you. Not that I'm complaining or anything."

"OK. OK, thank you for busting your butt. To answer your question, I'm not sure yet."

"What do you mean?"

"Well the names may tie together somehow, but so far, I have not been able to figure it out. I checked the latest data we have for Brian Ridel, and he is serving two to five in Pennsylvania for his part in an auto theft ring. Therefore, he could not have been involved with the attempted robbery at Mr. Marco's store a couple of months ago. And he certainly had nothing to do with the double homicide at the store a week ago."

"That's too bad, Theresa. What about the other guy: Steven Green?"

"He's a different story altogether. He is not in jail and his PO [parole officer] has not seen or heard from him in over five months. Of course, that's a parole violation and he will go back to jail when he is picked up."

"Well, there you go. He was unaccounted for during the time frame of both the robbery and the two homicides. Do you think it's just coincidence?"

Theresa thought for a few seconds then replied, "No. The commissioner taught me to never believe in coincidence. I think there is a good possibility that Green is involved, but we still don't know who he is working for."

Pat drank some more coffee then said, "Well Theresa, you'll figure it out. If not, then maybe you can go meet with the cute DA a few more times to see if he can help you."

"Very funny," said Theresa. "I don't know if the DA is going to fold on his principle of no tolerance for crimes committed with guns. Even if it does mean we could possibly catch a couple of killers."

Paul arrived home, checked the mail, and read the newly placed bright red and yellow *For Sale* sign on his lawn. He then pulled the Jeep into the garage. When he walked into the family room, he saw the answering machine light blinking. He pressed the *play* button while removing his jacket and tie. The realtor's voice said he had placed the *For Sale* sign on the property and had some papers for Paul to sign regarding the sale of the house and the business. He wanted to know if Paul could stop by the office and sign the papers in the next day or two. The realtor had two potential buyers who wanted to see the inside of the house. Paul figured he could shoot over to the real estate office first thing in the morning, before heading to Gino's.

The next message was from Joey Polucci: "Hey, Pauly. It's me, Joey. Ah, I got some bad news for you. Like you haven't had enough trouble already. Ah, anyway, this guy you were interested in, Kent. Well. Ah, he was found stabbed to death in his cell tonight. Sorry, man. I know you were counting on his cooperation. I'll see you tomorrow. Get some sleep."

Paul collapsed on the couch thinking, This can't be happening to me. The one lead I was counting on just blew away like dust in the wind. Who got to Kent? Did they know he was talking about a deal with the DA? Did Detective McGavin place Kent in jeopardy by visiting him in the slammer?

Paul had more questions than answers, of course. As he sat there on the couch trying to piece it together, the phone rang.

"Hello."

"Hi, Mr. Marco. This is Detective McGavin." "How are you, Detective? What's up?"

"Well, I have some bad news, sort of."

Paul knew what she was about to tell him, but he did not let on that he had already heard about Kent. "What do you mean?"

"Well, Clark Kent was killed in his cell tonight. Apparently, he was stabbed by two other inmates in some kind of dispute over cigarettes."

Paul thought, *Sure. Cigarettes, my ass. He was marked for a hit because he was going to talk.* "That's too bad, Detective. I thought we were going to get something from this guy in a trade for his reduced sentence?"

Paul knew his act was not washing with the detective. She played along for a while by telling Paul about her meeting with the DA and how he was going to pursue the reduced sentence, blah, blah, blah. Detective McGavin then said, "Well, this places us back to square one. I still have some more work to do on this Steven Green character. That may turn up something, if we can locate his whereabouts before he also turns up dead."

"That sounds like a good plan, Detective. I guess we will just have to follow every lead, no matter how thin, at this point. After all, what else do we have to go on?"

After Paul hung up the phone, he went to change into sweats. He then pulled out a box from the back of the closet in his small office. It was really a third bedroom, but Diana had always referred to it as his office. Paul brought the small box into the family room and laid it on the coffee table. He then spread some newspaper on the table to protect it from the solvent and oil. The gun cleaning equipment he kept for his hunting guns was still in good shape, even though Paul had not hunted game since he returned from Vietnam, over thirty years ago. There was no longer a thrill in shooting unarmed animals for Paul. The only real hunting he would do had to be for armed men. At least that would make the hunt challenging.

Paul placed the Ruger on the table and carefully disassembled it and inspected, cleaned, and oiled each part. He reassembled the weapon, then loaded the magazine with ten rounds of ammunition. Paul took the silencer out of his suit jacket pocket, cleaned it with solvent, then slid the tapered end over the barrel.

The weapon was in great working condition. It had not been fired very often, by the look of the bolt and barrel.

Paul lit a cigarette, then walked out of the kitchen into the garage. The garage doors were still open. He aimed the Ruger at the woodpile, then squeezed the trigger. The sound of the spent brass shell casing hitting the concrete floor was louder than the noise the weapon made when it fired. Paul was very impressed. He squeezed off more rounds in rapid succession, until the clip was empty. When he was finished test-firing the Ruger, Paul policed up the spent brass and went back into the house to clean and oil the gun again. He loaded the clip with ten new rounds, removed the silencer, then placed the safety in the locked position.

Paul put a new filter in the coffee maker, added two level scoops of grounds, then set the timer for seven o'clock. He then put the cleaning equipment away so he could finally get some sleep. The alarm clock on top of the TV was now ready to wake him at 6:30. Paul was beyond exhaustion, so he lay on the couch, turned off the light, and closed his eyes and mind to the world around him. He thought, *If there is a God, he will allow me to have six or seven hours of uninterrupted sleep.*

Chapter 8

Paul was watching the digital clock changing numbers as he lay on the couch in the dark. When the time reached 6:30, the alarm sounded. Paul got up off the couch to turn off the alarm, then lit a cigarette. He fumbled for the lamp switch, then turned it on as the bright light made him squint as if he were looking directly into the sun. *This was the day to say goodbye to Diana,* he thought. He stumbled toward the bathroom so he could shower and shave. When he was finished, Paul put on his dark navy blue pinstriped suit. As he was dressing, Paul could smell the aroma of the fresh brewed coffee coming from the kitchen. Paul just knew he would have a decent cup of fresh brewed coffee waiting for him this time.

When Paul finished dressing, he gathered the towels and other clothes that needed laundering and carried them to the laundry room. The pile of clothes already there made him realize that the time to do laundry was way overdue. Paul put the clothes in a pile on the floor by the dryer. His attention was then directed at the thirty or so controls, knobs, dials, and buttons on the washer and dryer. His eyes then scanned the shelf that had boxes, bottles, and containers of detergent, softeners, and presoak stuff. Whatever that was. Paul thought for about five seconds, then decided that this job could wait for another day when he had more time.

Paul went into the kitchen to prepare a ceramic mug with cream and sugar. This was going to be his first cup of decent coffee made by his own hands. He picked up the glass pot from the coffee maker, then filled his cup to the brim. He stirred the concoction, then took a long whiff of the aroma before him. It was like the proverbial manna from heaven. Paul took a small sip and thought, *Not bad.* He then took a big drink and almost gagged. His mouth felt as if he had swallowed sand. Paul spit the remaining coffee from his mouth into the sink to try to get rid of the grounds. He poured the reminder of the coffee in his mug down the sink and noticed that it was full of grounds. He looked at the paper filter in the coffee maker and saw that it had folded over somehow when the water flowed through it, causing the grounds to spill over and go into the pot below. Paul cleaned up the mess, then washed out the coffee maker while thinking, *This isn't starting out to be a very good day.*

Paul went to the hall closet to get his overcoat. The temperature was hovering around thirty-five degrees, the sky was gray, and the wind was starting to kick up briskly. Paul took a brown paper bag from the kitchen drawer and wrapped the Ruger and silencer in it for his meeting at the mall later.

Paul pointed the Jeep toward the shopping center where his store and the realtor's office were located. It took Paul about thirty-five minutes to get to the shopping center. His first stop was the drive-through at McDonald's to buy a decent cup of coffee. He tasted it and thought, *How could Detective McGavin not like this stuff?* Then Paul drove to the realtor's office, where he signed his name on what seemed like fifty different pieces of paper. He also left an extra set of keys with the receptionist, telling her it was OK for the realtor to show the house at his convenience; however, Paul would appreciate some advance notice. Paul instructed the receptionist to tell the realtor to leave messages on his machine about appointments, etc., because he would be checking it at various times throughout the day.

Paul headed toward Interstate 83, where he picked up 695 East. The next stop was a small Greek diner on Route 40, where Paul knew he would get a decent breakfast. When he turned onto Route 40, he could see the huge neon sign advertising the diner to all the truckers and passersby. The neon sign read: *LOSMOSKOS*, but everyone called it the Greeks.' The interior of the diner was immaculate. The Greek family that ran the place made sure the food was good, the pricing reasonable, and the coffee rich and hot. Paul found an empty booth and sat so he could see the front door. It was an old habit that he had never been able to break. Paul always wanted to see who was coming in or leaving, just in case. A young waitress, maybe twenty years old, came over to Paul's table with a mug in one hand and a steaming coffeepot in the other, asking, "Coffee?"

"Yes, please," Paul said, as if the waitress were reading his mind.

As the waitress filled his cup, she asked, "Are you ready to order or do you need a few minutes?"

Paul gave her his order for steak and eggs with toast, orange juice, and more coffee. This time of day the diner was crowded with truckers. There were also plenty of utility trucks in the huge parking lot. Paul thought, *They must have had trouble on the system last night for all those workers to be eating at the same time.*

The waitress brought the food and Paul devoured it without really tasting whether it was good. He paid his check, then headed for his Jeep in the parking lot. It was now eight-thirty, so Paul had plenty of time to make it over to the bank and then to Gino's. For no particular reason Paul sat in his Jeep waiting to start the engine. His mind was wandering once again. Next, Paul heard a tap on his window that startled him. Paul looked at the two brawny men outside his door while he lowered the window.

One man with a heavy beard asked, "Are you OK in there, pal?"

"Oh. Yeah, sure. I was just daydreaming. Thanks for asking." The two men looked at Paul as if he were some kind of nut case, then turned away to climb into a huge rig that was heading for parts unknown. Paul thought, *You better pull yourself together and get through these next few hours.*

Paul started the engine, then headed for the bank to make his withdrawal of small bills totaling $2,500. When he had the money, he sat inside the Jeep to take the Ruger and silencer out of the paper bag and put them under the driver's seat. He then placed the cash into the paper bag and slid it under the passenger seat. With that done, Paul headed to Gino's funeral parlor.

Theresa McGavin's day started in the commissioner's office. He was yelling at her, saying, "Damn it, McGavin. What in the hell were you thinking when you went over to the city lockup yesterday? That's something I'd expect a rookie to do, not an experienced detective!"

"Commissioner, I was only trying to lay the groundwork for the plea bargain that I planned to work out with the DA."

"But didn't you think that the prison grapevine would look at a cop visiting an inmate with some suspicion? Where was your head, for Christ sake? You know those animals in there automatically assume the worst. In this case, the worst was probably that Kent was turning snitch."

"I'm sorry, Commissioner. I really didn't think that I was setting him up by visiting him in jail. I should have known better. I don't know what I can do now that Kent is already dead."

The commissioner was calmer now that he had been able to rant and rave about the obvious mistake McGavin had made. He sat in his chair staring at her for a few seconds, then said, "Why don't you bring me up to date on the Marco case, so I can assess where we are now."

Detective McGavin gave the commissioner a synopsis of the case. She also told him that there was still one lead to run down concerning Steven Green. The commissioner listened attentively, then said, "This Steven Green character that you're talking about, do you have his file with you?"

"Sure. I have it right here," said Theresa as she handed the file to the commissioner. The commissioner flipped open the file to read a few lines of one page, then flipped to another page scanning the numerous arrests of Mr. Green. After reviewing the file for about three minutes, the commissioner said, "This guy has some history. I see that he was in on that guard killing down at the Port Authority about ten years ago."

"Yes, that's correct. Kent and he both did time for that one. That's why it's so important that I find him. I have a gut feeling that Green and Kent both worked for the same guy who is running the protection scam."

"What makes you think that, Detective? As I recall, the protection scam this Kent character was trying to pull on Paul Marco was a solo job. Marco popped him a couple of times, thus putting him in the wheelchair. So, how do you tie together Kent and Green's murder rap with the protection scam?"

"Commissioner, I know it's a little shaky right now, but I feel that this Kent character was not alone when he tried to shakedown Mr. Marco a couple of months ago. I think he may have had an accomplice in the parking lot for the getaway, or or—"

"Or what, McGavin? Spit it out."

"Well, sir. I know you and Mr. Marco are friends and all, but I think maybe he is not exactly telling us the whole truth about that shakedown attempt."

"What are you getting at, Theresa? If you have a reason to suspect Marco, then bring his ass in and ask him about it to his face. The fact that we happen to be friends has nothing to do with you doing your job. But I must warn you. I'll have your badge if it turns out that you are pulling any of that woman's intuition crap instead of having hard evidence. Do we understand each other?"

"Yes, sir. That's the main reason I have not pulled Marco in yet. I simply don't have any hard evidence."

The commissioner thought a few seconds, then asked, "Wasn't Captain Thiemeyer on that crime scene when Kent was shot by Paul?"

"Yes, he was. Why?"

"Well, Thiemeyer has a good nose for stuff like this. Why don't you talk to him about your suspicions? You know, to see if he can shed any light on your theory."

Theresa McGavin left the commissioner's office, then headed for her little cubicle one floor below. As Theresa exited the elevator, she heard her name being called: "Hey, Theresa. Where are you going?"

It was Pat Dershan walking down the hall, with her two arms full of case folders.

"Hi, Pat. I'm going to my cubicle to sulk if you must know."

Pat could see by the expression on Theresa's face that she was not having a pleasant morning. Pat asked, "What's wrong?"

"Well, the good news is I lost five pounds. The bad news is how I lost it. I just left the commissioner's office and he chewed five pounds out of my ass."

Pat laughed loudly and snorted, then quickly looked around to see if anyone had heard her uncontrolled outburst. Her face was red and the smile was still on her kisser when she noticed Theresa was also laughing. Pat finally said, "Hey, let me drop these folders off at my desk; then we can meet in the cafeteria, where you can tell me all about your problem over some coffee."

"That's the best offer I have had all day, buddy."

Paul arrived at Gino's funeral parlor at nine-thirty. He walked into Antonio's office to pick up some wallet-size cards that had Diana's death notice on the back side and a picture of the Holy Mary on the front. Antonio also had several copies of the death certificate, which he put into an envelope for Paul. Antonio then had the hard job of taking Paul into the viewing room, where the casket would be closed in his presence. As the two men entered the room, Antonio closed the two sliding doors behind them. One of Antonio's staff was already in the room waiting for them. Antonio and his staff member stood back a comfortable distance as Paul knelt in front of the casket. He said his piece, then slowly stood as the other two men walked up to him.

In a very calm, quiet voice Antonio asked, "Would you like us to remove her jewelry, or would you rather it stay with the departed?"

Paul was surprised at the question but really shouldn't have been. He knew the question would be asked. It always is. It was asked when his father died. It was asked when his brother died. It was asked whenever anyone died. Paul looked at Antonio and said, "Leave it, Mr. Gino. I want God to see how nice she looks."

"As you wish," Antonio replied. Then he and his assistant lowered the casket's half-door and locked it with some odd-looking key that screwed the top in place. Satisfied that the casket was now closed and locked, Antonio opened the sliding doors as people who were going to the cemetery filed into the room to say their last good-byes. Paul could feel the tears coming again but managed to hold them back. There would be plenty of time for crying later. Years, in fact.

Mark and Sue Vanner had done a very nice job of organizing the funeral procession. As Paul entered the limousine, the rain started to fall in cold, sweeping sheets. The wind was blowing the rain against the side tinted window with gusting force. *So much for no rain in the forecast,* thought Paul.

The ride to the cemetery only took about twenty minutes. The rain was mostly a drizzle now, but the wind made the damp, cold air go through Paul's overcoat as if he weren't wearing one at all. The small tent edging that covered the grave site was flapping in the wind, making loud noises as if someone were snapping a towel in a locker room. The priest said his prepared words, but Paul wasn't paying much attention. He looked around and saw maybe forty cold mourners fighting the wind and cold, hoping the priest would not be long-winded. *The priest must have been cold, too, because he was finished in no time at all,* Paul thought.

As the mourners made their way past the casket, they either hugged Paul or shook his hand. He simply stood their numb from the cold or his dead emotions; he couldn't tell which. When the last few mourners paid their respects, Paul touched the casket as the caretaker hit the switch that began lowering the casket into the ground. Paul watched the casket descend into the cavity where the earth would soon surround it, protect it, and signify the burial ceremony was complete. In a month or two a stone would be placed to mark the grave, saying: *"To my loving wife. The only perfect person I have ever known."* Paul turned and walked down the small hill toward the waiting limousine that would take him back to his Jeep.

Gary Roth left the cemetery with the others, to head over to Mark and Sue Vanner's house, where they were serving food and drinks for the mourners. The atmosphere at the Vanners' was joyful. People were talking, eating, drinking, and generally having a good time. Paul arrived around noon. He joined in the festivities, which helped take his mind off the burial that morning. *The wake always has a positive impact on the grieving,* thought Paul. Why that was he didn't know.

Around one o'clock, Paul looked around the house for Gary Roth and found him in front of a large table that had enough food on it to feed a small army. Paul said, "I guess we should make our exit shortly. I don't want to be late for the meeting."

Gary looked at his watch then said, "Yeah. We better start saying our good-byes now. You know how hard it is to get out of one of these places with everyone wanting to hug you. I'll see you later."

Paul managed to smile, then made his way over to Mark and Sue to thank them for laying out such a fine spread for everyone. Of course, everyone there had brought something to eat. But still, the Vanners had taken care of all the details, making the wake very successful and enjoyable for everyone.

It took almost twenty minutes for Paul to actually walk out the front door. He looked at his watch, knowing Gary had made his getaway almost ten minutes ahead of him. Paul started the Jeep, then drove over to the mall. It only took fifteen minutes. Traffic was light since it was a weekday, but to Paul's surprise the parking lot for the mall was packed. He had to work at finding a parking space that was not out in the boonies.

After a few minutes of cruising the parking lot, Paul found a parking spot being vacated by two women in a station wagon. He quickly parked the Jeep, then pulled the Ruger and silencer out from under his seat. Paul connected the silencer, chambered a round in the breech, released the hammer, and flipped on the safety. Now all he would have to do was release the safety and cock the hammer to fire the weapon. Paul placed the weapon in his inside jacket pocket, under his overcoat. Paul then reached under the passenger seat to pull out the paper bag full of money. Assured he was now ready for his meeting, Paul exited the Jeep and walked onto the ground floor of the mall.

The inside of the mall was huge. There were two floors full of a variety of stores. In total, there was maybe 250 stores. On the second floor there was an open-air food bazaar. The bazaar had metal tables and chairs for the patrons to sit and eat a variety of foodstuffs. They served anything from American to Vietnamese food. Paul walked up to one of the many escalators in the mall to make his way to the second level. At the top of the escalator Paul could see the food bazaar about forty yards to his left. He quickly checked his watch to see it was only 1:30. Paul placed the paper bag filled with money inside his overcoat, under his right arm. He did not want the person he was meeting to be able to pick out who he was until the agreed-upon meeting time of two o'clock. Paul walked toward the food bazaar, scanning the Boardwalk Fries stand to see if he could pick out the man he was supposed to meet. Unfortunately, the bazaar was rather crowded and most of the tables were full. Almost all the food stalls had customers waiting in long lines. Paul spotted a couple leaving their table, which was on the opposite side of the bazaar from the Boardwalk Fries stand. He quickly grabbed the table and sat in a position that allowed him to see the Boardwalk Fries stall clearly.

Paul watched customers coming and going for almost ten minutes. At no time did he pick out anyone who seemed to be his meeting contact. He looked at his watch and saw that it was now 1:53. Paul thought, *My contact is probably doing what I'm doing. He is sitting at one of these tables watching the Boardwalk Fries stall for a man holding a paper bag.* Paul gave the surrounding tables a onceover glance, but he couldn't spot the mystery contact. Paul then stood to remove the paper bag from under his overcoat and carried it in plain sight to the Boardwalk Fries stall. As soon as Paul relinquished the table where he was sitting, two young people grabbed it so they could eat their burgers and whatever.

Paul stood by the Boardwalk Fries stall, then looked at his watch again. It was now 1:58. Paul looked around, then heard a voice behind him say, "I'm your two o'clock appointment." She then asked, "Is that bag for me?"

Paul was shocked to hear a female voice. He had been expecting to meet with a man, yet another obvious incorrect assumption on his part. However, he did recall Gary saying the dude had a friend who has some information, but Gary never said whether the friend of the dude was male or female. Paul responded to the woman's voice by saying, "That all depends on what you have to say."

The woman said, "You can turn around, Mr. Marco. I'm not holding a gun on you."

Again, Paul automatically had assumed a gun was pointed at him. He realized that he was way too paranoid for this kind of clandestine work. Paul turned around slowly, to look at his meeting partner. The woman was maybe thirty or thirty-two years old. She was five feet, two or three inches tall and about 120 pounds. Her hair was blond and lightly highlighted. *Not bad looking,* thought Paul. *Not bad at all.* Paul sized up the woman, then asked, "Well, since you already know my name, how about you tell me yours?"

"No problem, Mr. Marco. After all, we're going to be doing business together, so we might as well know each other's names. My name is Karen. Karen Platte."

"Ms. Platte, I have $2,500 in this bag, just as you requested. The money is yours, if you can supply me with the information I need to find the persons responsible for killing my wife. As you know, there is another $2,500 in it for you if the information you have turns out to be legitimate."

"Mr. Marco, I understand the terms of our agreement just fine. You give me the bag of money and I'm going to give you a name and address of a man whom you need to contact. This contact not only has information about the man who killed your wife, but you'll recognize him as soon as you meet him. Now, I'm the one going out on a limb here, because I have to trust that you are good for the rest of the money."

"Ms. Platte, I'm a man of my word. If your information leads me to the son of a bitch that killed my wife, I'll personally make sure the money is delivered to you ASAP."

Karen Platte reached into her pocket to retrieve a piece of paper. She looked around the immediate area a few seconds, then handed the paper to Paul, who simultaneously pocketed the piece of paper and handed Karen the brown paper bag. Karen immediately placed the paper bag into her large pocketbook. Karen then said, "After you talk to the man on that piece of paper and are convinced that the information is worthy of the balance, you may contact me through your friend Gary Roth. Mr. Roth does not actually know me, but the man he does know is the one who can get a message to me. Another meeting will be scheduled for the payoff. Do you understand?"

"Quite clearly, Ms. Platte. However, if the information you have just given me turns out to be bogus, I'll hunt you down. Is that also understood?"

Karen smiled, then said, "Trust me, Mr. Marco. My information is what you need right now. Personally, I hope you find the guy he works for and rid the earth of his existence. However, I must tell you that you are looking for some very nasty people. The type of people that would not think twice about killing you and me."

Karen turned to walk away from Paul, then headed toward one of the many crowded escalators. She headed down to the first level of the mall and disappeared into the crowd.

Paul reached into his pocket to retrieve the piece of paper Karen had given him. He unfolded it to read: "Steven Green, RR 1, Box 721, Hanover Road, Westminster, Maryland." Paul immediately recognized the name Steven Green. He knew that according to Karen Platte he was supposed to recognize Green when they met. Paul tucked the paper back into his pocket, then headed for the escalators.

As Paul made his way to his Jeep, he was thinking about how his meeting with this Steven Green would turn out. Would Green lead him to the person or persons responsible for killing his wife? Was Green the killer? Would Green be waiting for Paul to show up so he could finally finish him? He would soon see.

Chapter 9

Gary Roth was in the parking lot by Paul's Jeep waiting for him to return. Paul approached the parking lot, saw Gary standing there leaning against the Jeep, then said, "Hey, Gar.' You're pretty good at this kind of stuff."

"Well, I saw you talking to that woman by the Boardwalk Fries stand and decided to keep a low profile by watching you from the bookstore across from the food bazaar. To tell you the truth, I was not expecting a woman to be at the meeting."

"I know what you mean, Gary. It surprised me, too. Her name is Karen Platte. Do you know her?"

"Never saw her before. But more importantly, did you get what you needed?"

"She gave me the name and address of a guy who is supposed to have what I'm looking for. I'm heading there now."

"May I ask who it is and where you're going?"

"Are you sure you want to know, Gar'? You're already involved more than you need to be. It may be better if I do this part by myself. That way, if anyone asks you about what I'm up to, you won't have to make up any lies."

"Suit yourself, Pauly. But if you ask me, I think it would be better if I tag along, just in case it's a setup."

"I thought about that, too. But I think I'm going to chance it on my own, just the same. Listen. Why don't I go do what I have to do and give you a call later? That way you will know things are OK."

"Paul, I still don't like it, but it's your call. If I don't hear from you by, let's say, nine o'clock tonight, I'll start the ball rolling to locate you."

"Sounds good. If you don't hear from me by nine o'clock, call my house and punch in code 50 when the answering machine picks up. I'll leave a message as to where I am and who I went to see. I'll leave the message just before I go see this guy, so don't try to track me down earlier than nine o'clock."

"OK, Pauly. You're on your own. It still sounds as if you are taking some unnecessary risks. Do you have anything to cover your ass, or are you going into this flying by the seat of your pants?"

"Gar', I met with Mikey and he fixed me up. Stop worrying.

I've got everything under control."

Paul climbed into his Jeep, waved good-bye to Gary, then headed for the Baltimore Beltway. Once on 695 East, Paul picked up Interstate 83, North, and headed toward home. Before he made a visit to Mr. Green, Paul wanted to change clothes and pick up a few things. The fall day felt more like winter, as the sun set behind a gray cloudy sky and the winds remained brisk.

Paul pulled into his garage, then went into the house through the kitchen door. Once inside the house, he went to the bedroom to take off his suit and put on a pair of black jeans and a black sweatshirt. He chose a pair of dark hiking boots from the closet, then looked in two other closets before he found his dark green goose down parka. Paul went into the basement where he kept his backpacking and hunting gear from days passed. Searching through some of the paraphernalia brought back fond memories for Paul. He recalled how he and his friends would spend four or five days bushwhacking in the mountains. They had hiked areas from Mount Mitchell in North Carolina to Mount Washington in New Hampshire. It was certainly a much better time in Paul's life, as he reflected on the camaraderie they had shared. Especially the good feelings they would experience by just getting away from the city, their jobs, and their wives.

Paul found a small dark blue rucksack and filled it with a flashlight, rope, binoculars, and other assorted items. He then went to the locked gun cabinet and opened the combination. He surprised himself when he actually remembered the numbers with little effort. Inside the cabinet were an assortment of shotguns, rifles, and pistols, all legally registered and in excellent working order. In the back of the cabinet was what Paul was searching for so hastily: a small but deadly accurate crossbow. Paul strung the bow, then set the trigger. He then removed an aluminum-shafted bolt from an unused box of six razor tips and placed it on the bow. He turned and aimed toward the heavy punching bag hanging at the other end of the basement. The heavy bag and weight bench took up the back corner of the basement that Diana wanted to use for a sewing room. Of course, Paul delayed that little job long enough to where it never materialized. Paul fired the crossbow at the center of the heavy bag. The aluminum-shafted bolt buried itself completely in the bag as if it were fired from a shotgun. The main difference between the crossbow and a shotgun was that the crossbow was extremely quiet but just as deadly. Paul broke down the crossbow and added it to the rucksack along with the remaining five razor-tipped bolts from the box Paul knew the general area around Westminster. The small town was surrounded by farms, woods, and some of the best deer and turkey hunting in Maryland. From Paul's house it would take about an hour to reach Main Street, Westminster. At that point, Paul would stop at a convenience store to buy a Carroll County ADC map, which would break down all the back roads in much finer detail.

The last thing Paul did was take the rucksack upstairs to the master bedroom. Paul found Diana's pocketbook where he had left it several days ago, propped in the corner of the closet. Paul dug into the bag to retrieve the small cellular phone he had bought her to use for emergencies. He flipped open the phone to check the battery charge. Its reading was in the good range. Paul placed the cell phone into the rucksack and zipped it shut.

It was now five-thirty and Paul was getting hungry. He decided to make two sandwiches with the remaining lunch meat from the refrigerator. One sandwich he would eat now, and he would put the other along with a can of Coke into the rucksack for later. Paul ate his sandwich and drank a cold can of Coke. As he was eating, he thought, *I need to get some food in this house. Better start making a list. Diana always had a list.*

Paul checked the answering machine and found two messages from his realtor saying that he was bringing a couple of buyers to see the house Sunday afternoon. The last message was from Detective McGavin, asking Paul to call her.

Paul pulled out his wallet to retrieve McGavin's number, then dialed. She was still at police headquarters working on one of the half-dozen cases that the commissioner had assigned to her. "Hello, Detective. This is Paul Marco, returning your call."

"Oh. How are you, Mr. Marco? I mean, are you doing OK, with the services and all?"

"I'm fine. Thank you for asking. What can I do for you?" "Well, I was doing some follow-up work on your case and I think we may have another lead. Although it's slim, I think we should pursue it, nonetheless."

"That's great, Detective. What kind of lead?"

"Well, it goes back to when you were robbed a couple of months ago by the now deceased Clark Kent. We think he was working with an accomplice at the time and that person's name is Steven Green. The same Steven Green I told you about over dinner. Do you remember that?"

Immediately Paul put the pieces together in his mind. Karen Platte had said he would recognize the person when he met him. Well, sure as hell Paul would remember the guy he had let go after the attempted shakedown in his store a couple of months earlier. Paul had told the police then there was only one robber. Now he had to answer Detective McGavin.

"Are you still there Mr. Marco?"

"Oh, yes. I'm sorry. My mind is wandering again. Yes. I remember you said that he and some guy named Ridel were accomplices with Clark Kent or something like that."

"That's right. It's a long story. But to make it short, this guy Steven Green has not been heard from in over five months. In other words, he could have been around when your store was hit and when your wife was murdered. It could all simply be a coincidence or we may actually be onto something."

"Detective, that's some pretty good work you did to piece that together from such minimal data. Do you know where to find this Steven Green?"

"That's the sad part. Right now, it appears he has fallen off the face of the earth. But we will find him soon enough. Guys like him always get in trouble and he will probably show up in some county lockup before the month is over."

"Thanks for the update, Detective. I hope you track him down, so we can get to the bottom of this mess in short order."

Paul replaced the receiver and took several deep breaths to calm himself down. He now had a face to put with the name that Karen Platte had given him. Now he knew what he was up against. The scumbag that he let walk out of his store a few months ago now wanted to sell information to Marco. *He will work for anyone who pays him*, thought Paul.

Paul went into the garage to retrieve a pair of thin rubber gloves he used to mix lawn chemicals and put them into the rucksack. He then tossed the rucksack into the Jeep and headed toward Route 140 North, which would take him into downtown Westminster.

During the drive, Paul was thinking about how he would extract the information he needed from this scumbag Steven Green. He had plenty of experience doing just that over thirty years ago while in Vietnam. Extracting information was easy when death was the only alternative.

The night air was getting much colder. The temperature was only in the thirties, but with the brisk wind the chill factor was now down into the single digits. Paul pushed the Jeep toward Westminster, then spotted a convenience store at the corner of Routes 140 and 97. Paul pulled in to fill the gas tank and to buy a map of Carroll County along with a large coffee and a pack of cigarettes. After paying the clerk, Paul went out into the parking lot, where he sat in the Jeep looking for the best course to Route 721 using the back roads. Paul drank his coffee and smoked a couple of cigarettes while he planned his strategy. When he was sure that he had a workable plan, he started the Jeep and pushed on toward Steven Green.

The back roads were pitch-black. The moon was totally cloud-covered and driving was only safely negotiated by using the high beams.

Paul drove for almost thirty minutes when he saw the Route 721 junction. He turned north toward Pennsylvania, where he now had to keep an eye open for the mailboxes on the side of the road. The closer he got to the Maryland and Pennsylvania border, the more mountainous the terrain became.

After traveling another fifteen minutes down Route 721, Paul stopped to pull the flashlight out of the rucksack so he could read the numbers on the mailbox. It read: 612 *KELLER*. Paul knew that he was getting close. The houses were far apart on Route 721, since most of the people who lived out this far were either horse breeders or farmers of some sort. After meandering down the road another ten minutes, Paul finally saw number 721 on a mailbox. There was no name on the mailbox and the dirt road beside it headed up and into the woods. Paul pulled off to the side of the road, then turned off his headlights. It was extremely dark, making it almost impossible to see. Paul backed up and pointed the Jeep onto the dirt road, still with the headlights off. The trees on each side of the road were his only navigation tool. As Paul slowly eased the Jeep up the steep incline, he scanned the area around him for some kind of light from maybe a porch, kitchen, or even outbuilding. There was none.

Paul had no idea how far the road would take him, so he crept at a three-mile-per hour pace, up the dirt road as it twisted and turned upward. Suddenly, Paul came to a crest on the hill and stopped using the emergency brake handle so the brake lights would not illuminate. He reached up to pull the bulb from the dome light, then pulled opened the rucksack to retrieve the silenced .22

Ruger. Paul left the engine running as he opened the door to step out. He walked the remaining ten feet to the hilltop and gazed down. The road fell off sharply, with a slight turn to the right. Paul could see an outline of a house or cabin down at the bottom of the small valley. It must have been a quarter of a mile away. Paul could see the outline of a pickup truck on the side of the building. Light was shining through two windows on the side of the building, allowing Paul to just barely make out what looked like a discarded washing machine or dryer. The wind was blowing cold, frosty air against Paul's face and hands. *Should have brought gloves and a hat*, he thought.

Paul walked back to the Jeep and backed it down the road about ten feet before turning the steering wheel sharply to the right so the Jeep left the road and entered the woods. He backed off the road through the underbrush and small pines far enough so that if another car came up the dirt road they would not easily see the Jeep. Paul turned off the engine, grabbed the rucksack, and hoofed it down the dirt road toward the house.

If this were thirty years ago, Paul would have never used the road because it would probably have been booby trapped. In this case, however, there was probably little chance of that occurring. The wind was now blowing directly into his face. If Green had a dog, at least Paul was downwind and could sneak up to the house without alarming the animal.

Slowly Paul walked down the dirt road with the Ruger clutched in his now freezing hand. As he approached within twenty yards of the building, he could see it was a cabin and smoke was billowing out of the small stone chimney. *Nice and warm inside,* he thought. *So far, no dog barking, but there still could be a dog inside.* Paul was close enough to see that what he had thought was a washing machine was actually an old kitchen cabinet and sink. Paul ducked behind the cabinet to plot his next move as he blew warm air into his hands with the Ruger tucked under his armpit. The pickup truck was only fifteen feet away, so Paul quickly crouched down and moved to the front of the tuck. He felt the engine hood and found that it was still warm. *Must have just gotten home before I arrived,* thought Paul.

The cabin widow closest to Paul was now only twenty feet away. Paul stayed in a crouch and made his way to the cabin wall, ducking down far enough so his head could not be seen through the window. Paul moved the safety on the Ruger from the safe to the fire position. He then slowly raised himself up so he could peek into the window. The cabin was very small, maybe fifteen feet wide and probably twice as long. The front door was to Paul's right, but he could not tell if there was a back door from his vantage point. The window Paul was standing at was more toward the front half of the cabin. There were no windows in the back half on the side of the cabin Paul was now standing. The furnishings were rustic, but the place looked clean and well kept. The room Paul was viewing seemed to be a combination kitchen and living room. A wall separated the front half of the cabin from the back half. *A single door in the center of the wall probably led to the bedroom and bathroom,* Paul thought. The fireplace was roaring on the other side of the room where the matching window to the one Paul was standing at would have been located.

No sign of a dog or any human, for that matter. Paul was now standing fully upright when he saw the door separating the front half of the cabin from the back half open. A man walked into the lighted portion of the cabin carrying a newspaper. Paul recognized him all right. He had a mustache now, but sure enough, it was the same guy who had come into Paul's store a couple of months ago with Clark Kent.

Paul watched Steven as he walked into the kitchen area, where he took a pot of coffee off the stove to pour himself a cup. Steven Green then walked into the living room area to sit in one of the two comfortable chairs that flanked the fireplace. Steven's back was now facing Paul.

The attack must be one of surprise, thought Paul. He then reached into the rucksack and put on the pair of rubber gloves he had brought from the house. Slowly Paul made his way to the front of the cabin, being very careful not to make any noise that would warn Steven about his presence. Paul was now standing at the front door. He double-checked the safety on the Ruger in his right hand, then put his left hand on the doorknob and turned it lightly. To Paul's surprise, the knob turned easily, meaning it was not locked. As Paul turned the doorknob, he positioned his left shoulder against the door. With one quick motion, he pushed the door open while pointing the Ruger at Steven's shocked face.

"What the hell—"

"Shut up, asshole. Now stand up slowly and face me." Steven was so shocked by the bursting door and the look on Paul's face that he did not move a muscle until Paul yelled, "Now!" Steven stood up with his hands in the air. Paul kicked the door closed behind him as he reached back to set the lock. "You don't remember me, do you, scumbag?"

"What the hell are you doing here? Get the fuck out of my—" "Shut up, asshole," said Paul as he walked over to where Steven was standing. Steven was looking at Paul inquisitively, then, as if a bolt of lighting hit him, said, "Hey, I know who you are! You're the guy who fucked up Kent. Ah, man, what do you want? I ain't got no cash around here. What do you want?"

Paul walked around Steven while inspecting him to see if he had access to any weapons, then replied, "Yeah. That's me. I'm the guy who let you go. Now it's time for you to pay me back."

"Pay you back? With what, man? I ain't got nothin'."

Paul swung the rucksack off his shoulder and unzipped it so he could retrieve the rope. He then pointed next to the fireplace where there was a wooden chair with two high arms. "Bring that chair over here and sit down."

Steven did as he was told. Paul then tied Steven securely in the chair. He tied each arm to one of the wooden arms of the chair. Then he tied each leg securely to the front two legs of the chair. Finally Steven's chest was tied to the back of the chair. Paul was convinced that Steven was not going anywhere soon, so he sat in the chair Steven had been sitting in before Paul burst in on him.

Paul looked into Steven's eyes and very coldly but calmly said, "I'm going to ask you some questions, and you're going to tell me what I want to know. If you tell me what I want to know quickly, I won't hurt you. But, if you want to play hardball, my friend, you're going to experience so much pain that you are going to beg me to kill you. Do you understand?"

"Fuck you. I ain't telling you shit." "Have it your way then," said Paul.

Paul pointed the Ruger at Steven's left knee and squeezed the trigger. Steven immediately yelled with pain. He was tied and could not move, but the nerves around his knee were telling his brain that he was now in big trouble.

Paul said, "Now, my first question is: Who do you and Clark Kent work for?"

"I told you, man. Fuck you. I ain't tellin' you shit. Look what you did to my fucking knee."

Paul went to the kitchen area and opened a few drawers before he found what he was looking for. He then walked back into the room where Steven was tied to the chair. In one swift motion Paul jabbed a large carving fork into and through Steven's left hand. The fork was stuck into the wooden arm of the chair. Steven yelled again in excruciating pain. "You're fucking crazy, man. I ain't telling you nothin,' so why don't you just kill me and get it over with?"

Paul put his face one inch in front of Steven's, then said, "We are just getting started, scumbag. The real pain has not yet begun. Now do you have an answer to my question yet?"

Paul grabbed the fork and wiggled it a little to cause Steven more discomfort. Steven screamed, "Go to hell!"

Paul put the Ruger next to Steven's left calf muscle and fired a round clean through the tissue while saying, "Are you ready to talk yet?"

In a much less convincing voice Steven said, "Go to hell." "OK, Steven. You know, a .22 is an amazing weapon. I can put maybe ten or twelve holes in you without killing you so long as I don't hit any vital organs. Isn't that amazing."

"Go to hell. I'm not telling you anything."

Paul walked over to the fireplace and tossed in another log, then picked up the poker to stir the embers so they could ignite the timber. Paul left the poker in the hot embers as he turned to Steven and said, "You know, they tell me that the fingers are very susceptible to the burning sensation. I guess it's because they are so sensitive to touch. Don't you think?"

Steven was losing consciousness. His head was bobbing as if he was ready to pass out any second. Paul went to the kitchen area to pour a glass of cold water, then returned to where Steven was sitting, and threw the water into Steven's face, reviving him instantly. Paul walked over to the fireplace to retrieve the poker that was now red-hot. He turned toward Steven, who was now wide-eyed with terror. Paul put the poker tip close to Steven's right hand, but he managed to clench it into a tight fist. Paul said, "I guess I'll just have to burn into your fingers from the side." Paul put the tip of the poker in the small circle where Steven's little finger was curled around and pushed it into his fist until the tip appeared at the other end, by his thumb. Steven screamed with pain, then passed out.

Paul went to the refrigerator, where he found a cold beer. He looked at the clock on the kitchen wall to see that it was now 8:45. Paul took the cell phone out of his rucksack and called his house to leave a message on his machine for Gary Roth. Paul basically said he had found Green and everything was fine, so stop worrying.

Paul finished his beer, then opened the front door a little to get rid of the smell of burned flesh. God, how Paul hated the smell of burning flesh. It was one of those smells that you never forgot, once you had a good whiff of it.

As Paul lit a cigarette and stood in the doorway, he watched Steven Green starting to come around. Paul went inside and put his face in front of Steven's face and asked, "Are you ready to talk to me now? If not, I have plenty more ways to make you feel pain."

"No. No more, please. I need some water and I will talk. Please, no more."

Paul went to the kitchen to get a glass of water for Steven, came back to the chair where Green was tied, then sat on the coffee table directly in front of him so he could hold the glass while Steven drank. Steven took a large drink and almost choked swallowing the water so fast. Paul put the glass down beside him then said, "Now, who do you work for?"

Steven could barely hold his head up as he tried to talk. His eyes were glassy and his complexion was very pale. "I work for the Ayatollah."

Paul was furious. "You son of a bitch. I guess you want some more pain. Do you think this is some type of game that—"

"No. No. It's true, man. We call him the Ayatollah. His real name has every letter of the alphabet in it and it's too damn hard to pronounce."

Paul calmed down, then said, "OK, so you call him, Ayatollah. Is he Iranian or Saudi or what?"

"I don't know, man. We call him the Ayatollah. Ismal Ka something or other. Who gives a shit. He's some raghead from the Middle East is all I know."

"OK, where can I find this Ayatollah character?"

Paul, seeing that Steven was weak and on the verge of passing out again, picked up the glass of water and threw it in Steven's face to revive him while saying, "Where can I find this Ayatollah?"

Steven very slowly looked up and managed a little smile as he said, "He is the owner of an Arabian horse farm in Baltimore County." Steven's eyes glazed over; then he passed out.

Paul knew exactly where the Arabian horse farm was located. In fact, he lived maybe thirty miles from the place. Paul stood up and lit a cigarette as he contemplated how he would get to this Ayatollah character.

Suddenly Paul saw a pair of headlights coming toward the cabin. He quickly grabbed the rucksack and Ruger, then looked at Steven Green slumped over in his chair. Paul knew he could not leave a witness, so he fired two rounds behind Steven's left ear, killing him instantly. Paul than dashed out the front door and ran around to the back of the cabin so he could avoid the oncoming headlights.

Chapter 10

Friday morning at eight o'clock sharp, the commissioner had Detective McGavin and Captain Thiemeyer in his office. The commissioner had not been in the best of moods when he summoned the two for the meeting.

The commissioner said, "Detective McGavin, I asked you to talk to Captain Thiemeyer a few days ago regarding the Marco murder. I would like to know what you two have come up with to date."

Detective McGavin said, "Well, I did talk to the captain just as you requested. He agrees with me that maybe Mr. Paul Marco is not telling us the whole truth about what happened in his store a couple of months ago."

The commissioner looked away from McGavin and into the eyes of Thiemeyer. The captain then said, "Yes, sir. I firmly believe that there was more to that shakedown for protection money than Mr. Marco told us about originally. When I talked to Mr. Marco at the crime scene, he was very aloof. I didn't put too much emphasis on it at the time, because he had just been through a terrible ordeal. Besides, we had that Clark Kent character in custody, and by the looks of things it appeared as if Mr. Marco may have already gotten his revenge to settle the score. At least that's what I thought at the time."

The commissioner pondered the situation for a few seconds, then said, "Well, it certainly appears that you two both believe Marco is not leveling with us about the shakedown attempt. That's fine with me. I could care less about this Clark Kent hood. As far as I'm concerned, the world is a better place without him. My problem is he was killed in jail after the detective here paid him a visit, which makes me believe somebody doesn't want him to talk. Somebody who has connections on the inside, if you catch my drift. Now, that leads me to believe that whoever Kent worked for probably wants to remain anonymous. *Why is that?* I ask myself. Do either of you have any theories as to why?"

Detective McGavin looked at Captain Thiemeyer, then turned her attention to the commissioner, saying, "I think it would have been cleared up if we could have had an opportunity to talk to Steven Green. Unfortunately, as you now know, Commissioner, when I arrived at his place in Westminster last night he was already dead."

The commissioner again pondered the situation, then replied, "Yeah, I know. That makes me think all the more somebody wants to remain anonymous regarding what is going on in this case. Why don't you fill us in on what transpired last night so we all can be brought up to speed?"

Detective McGavin opened her purse to pull out a small spiral notebook. She opened it to glance at some notes, then began her summation by saying, "I managed to track down Steven Green by following a trail left by Clark Kent's pickup truck. When we went through the personal effects for Kent after his murder, we found a registration card for a 1996 Dodge Ram pickup truck. The address was an apartment complex in Baltimore County. I took a ride over to his apartment to see what, if anything, I could turn up regarding who he may have worked for or with. You know, routine checks and stuff. Well, I turned up nothing other than the fact that our victim lived like a pig. As I was leaving, I checked the parking lot for the pickup truck but couldn't find it anywhere. Figuring maybe he left it someplace and it was subsequently towed away, I checked with Baltimore County and Baltimore City impound lots and came up with zilch. My last resort was to run the plates through the DMV, where I discovered that a moving violation ticket was issued in Westminster for Clark's pickup while he was in the lockup. That seemed awfully strange to me, so I called the Carroll County police, and they verified that a ticket was written for Clark Kent's pickup outside a bar on Main Street for running a stop sign. I then talked to the officer who wrote the ticket. He remembered that when he asked the driver for his license and registration the driver explained that the truck belonged to his buddy, Clark Kent. The officer wrote the driver's address down on the ticket. Anyway, the man who signed the ticket was none other than Steven Green. That's how I tracked him down to his cabin off Route 721."

The commissioner managed to smile as he said, "Sometimes it's the damndest things that allow crooks to get caught. I give you one thing, Detective, you surely are tenacious in your pursuit of justice. Now tell us what happened last night?"

Detective McGavin flipped to another page in her notebook, then proceeded with her summation by saying, "I drove to the address Steven Green gave the officer who wrote the traffic citation. The place was a bit hard to find because it's way back in the woods, down in a small valley. I pulled up to the cabin, noticing that there were lights on inside and smoke coming out of the chimney. I knocked on the door, but no one answered. So, I walked around to the side of the cabin to look inside the widow and saw a man laying on the floor. I immediately drew my weapon and called for backup. I then announced myself as the police and entered through the unlocked front door. The man on the floor was cut up badly. His throat was slit and his tongue was pulled out through the gash. It was a typical Colombian necktie, but not a very neat job, if you know what I mean. I recognized Green from his DMV photo, and there was no doubt that he was dead. I then did a preliminary search of the premises and found no one else inside or around the cabin. There was no sign of a struggle, nor were there any signs that anything illegal was going on at the cabin."

Captain Thiemeyer listened very attentively to Detective McGavin's report, then said, "Do you think that was a good move, going in there before your backup arrived?"

"I had no choice. At the time, I thought the person lying on the floor may have only been unconscious or in need of medical attention. Anyway, the lab boys and my backup arrived at about the same time. It was over twenty minutes later, because they had difficulty finding the place. We looked the place over pretty well but found nothing of any real significance."

The commissioner said, "What do we know now after several hours have passed since you discovered the body?"

"The coroner said Green died as a result of two small-caliber gunshot wounds behind the ear. An execution-style hit. The weapon used was a .22-caliber. The lack of blood on the floor where Green was lying indicates the Colombian necktie was done after he was shot and killed, according to the coroner. He also said it appears that Green was tortured before he was murdered. His hand was badly burned and he had two other nonlethal gunshot wounds in his body. One gunshot in the left knee and the other in his right calf. The lab report shows no other fingerprints at the crime scene. Apparently, the person wore gloves, not leaving us very much to go on at this time."

The commissioner said, "I see. Why do you think he was tortured? Is it that he had some information that the killer needed? Or maybe the killer was trying to make sure he had not revealed some important information since his partner, Clark Kent, was murdered in the city lockup? What's your read on all this, Captain?"

"You may be right, Commissioner. Maybe our killer or killers wanted to find out just what Green knew. My problem is motive. For example, what could Green know that was so important to someone else that torture and murder were called for? Could it be that our Detective McGavin is right about tying together the Kent and Green murders?"

The commissioner said, "What are you talking about?" Theresa McGavin replied, "I'll tell you what I think. I think Mr. Marco tied Clark Kent and Steven Green together from my phone conversation with him last night. If Marco knew there were two shakedown hoods in his store, as I suspect he did, then I helped him put the name to the face of the second man. If you believe that, then it would not be too far a leap to believe Marco was ahead of us last night, when I paid a visit to Green's cabin."

The commissioner was flustered. He said, "Wait a minute, McGavin. That's not a leap; that's like jumping across the Grand Canyon. How in the hell would Marco be able to figure out where Green was holding out? You said yourself that it was a matter of luck that allowed you to put the pieces together so you could find Green. Now you expect me to believe that Marco did the same thing without the help of the police and DMV information? Besides, that Colombian necktie business would be a bit much, even for Paul. That's assuming he was actually trying to throw us offtrack. I think you are way off base on that one, Detective."

"Hold on, Commissioner," said captain Thiemeyer. "I think McGavin is on to something. Suppose Marco found out where Green lived, I don't know how, but suppose he did. Wouldn't it make sense for him to want to drag information out of Green that would help lead him to the head man responsible for the hit on his wife? As for the Colombian necktie, he could have done that so we would think that there were more people involved. He's no dummy. Think about it."

The commissioner looked somewhat perplexed then said, "OK. OK, you two are going to drive me nuts with your theories. Let's do this. McGavin, I want you to ask Paul to come in to see you. Then I want you and Thiemeyer to lay out what you just told me, so that Paul knows what we suspect. See if he can vouch for his whereabouts last night, etc.; you know the routine. If he's involved with Green's murder, I don't want him to receive any preferential treatment. Is that understood?"

Both Thiemeyer and McGavin nodded their heads affirmatively.

Then the commissioner said, "Off the record, though, if I were Paul in this situation, I would probably do the same goddamned thing. All right, you have work to do and so do I. Now, get the hell out of here and find some answers."

Paul woke up around nine o'clock feeling physically tired but emotionally charged. He had found out last night that the man he needed to talk to was a wealthy horse breeder in northern Baltimore County. Paul knew where the place was located, but he had never actually been on the grounds.

The entrance to the main house of the Arabian horse farm had a ten-foot wall surrounding it and heavy metal gates in front of the long driveway. The gates were probably strong enough to keep out an armored personnel carrier. Before Paul could begin thinking about going into the place, he would have to do some very serious surveillance. There would be plenty of security at the farm, because the horse business in Maryland was colossal. One time, a year or so ago, someone had tried to steal some horse semen from another breeder in the area. That attempted theft caused all the other breeders in the area to become extra careful. Some breeders had closed-circuit TV and heat sensors around the barn and paddock areas to detect intruders. Others actually had hired private security firms to patrol the grounds around their prized thoroughbreds. There were even several attempts in the past two years of thieves actually rustling certain breeds of horses for shipment out of state. In one case, the rustlers actually had several animals loaded onto cargo ships headed for the Middle East. Apparently, horse racing became a Middle East passion as competition among some of the newly founded oil-rich nations increased.

Paul took a shower and shaved, then dressed in jeans and a flannel shirt. The temperature was in the thirties, and the dark skies had the look and feel of snow. Paul took a quick inventory of the refrigerator and kitchen cabinets' contents then headed to the store. He did not make a list but figured he could manage. For Paul, being inside the grocery store was like being in another state. He had no idea where anything was, nor did he have a clue as to what he should do at certain points within the store. He grabbed a cart and started heading down the produce aisle. He did not want to look like a total idiot, so he passed up all the individual fruit, because he didn't know if he was supposed to bag and weigh it or if the clerk did that when he checked out. Paul quickly decided to play it safe by buying a bag of apples and a bunch of very green bananas. Down the next aisle, Paul saw what looked like thirty brands of coffee. He reviewed the choices, made a selection, then moved to the next aisle. *This is not so bad,* he thought. A few cans of soup, some hot dogs, rolls, bread, lunch meat, eggs, soda, frozen dinners, cereal, and milk filled the cart. Down one aisle and up another. Paul picked up some snack food, more half-and-half, and, for good measure, a carton of fresh orange juice. In the checkout line, Paul put the groceries on the moving conveyor and bagged the items as quickly as the clerk could ring them up on the register. Paul then paid the clerk and headed to the Jeep, where he unloaded the bags before returning the cart to the store. As he climbed back into the Jeep to go home, Paul looked at his watch and saw that it only took him thirty-five minutes to go shopping. *Next time,* he thought, *I can do it in under thirty minutes.*

When Paul arrived home, he put the groceries away then made himself a ham and cheese sandwich on toast with a side order of barbecue-flavored potato chips. Deciding that his nutritional intake was not up to par, Paul swallowed two multiple vitamins to even out his daily nutritional intake of whatever the government standard was these days. After cleaning up the kitchen, Paul went into the laundry room to look over the clothes situation. *This was not going to be easy,* he thought. Paul then did the obvious. He started by separating the whites from the colored clothes. He had seen his wife do this a thousand times in the past. There were some items of clothing that could go either way, so Paul tossed them into the white pile. He filled the washer with clothes, read the instruction on the box of concentrated detergent, then added a full scoop of powder to the filling tub. One dial was set to warm wash, cold rinse. Another was set to normal wash, and a third dial was set on large load. It looked OK to Paul, so he closed the lid, pushed the start button, and went back into the kitchen to heat some water on the stove.

The washing machine was doing its thing, and best of all there was no flood of soap pouring out from under the laundry room door. When the water on the stove started to boil, Paul poured it into a cup and added a teaspoon of the instant coffee he had bought at the grocery store. A little sugar, some half-and-half, a quick stir or two, and presto! Paul tasted the coffee and thought, *Hey, this ain't so bad. The flavor was rich, the aroma was good, and best of all, there were no coffee grounds in his cup.*

When the first load of clothes was finished, Paul put them into the dryer and started a second load of wash. The first dryer dial was set on the permanent-press cycle, which looked OK to Paul. He then turned the second dial to automatic drying cycle, dropped in a static cling fabric sheet, and pressed the start button. Both the washer and dryer were humming along nicely. *So far, so good*, thought Paul.

Paul finished his first cup of coffee and decided to make a second. As the water was heating on the stove, the phone rang. "Hello."

"Hi, Mr. Marco. This is Detective McGavin." "Hello, Detective. What's going on?"

"Mr. Marco, I found Steven Green last night and would—" "You . . . found him? Did he say anything about—"

"Hold on, Mr. Marco. I found him, but unfortunately, he's dead. That's one of the reasons for my call. Listen. Would it be possible for you to come down to headquarters today, so we can discuss this case."

"Sure, Detective. What time would be good for you?" "How about 1:30."

"One-thirty is fine. I'll see you then."

Paul thought he was pretty convincing on the phone with Detective McGavin. *She probably doesn't suspect anything, but one can't be too certain. She did say that she found Green last night. I wonder if the headlights coming down the driveway last night were from her car?*

Paul spent the next hour and a half washing and drying clothes.

He hung several shirts on hangers but did not put them away, because they needed ironing. Paul knew how to iron from his army days, so he would get to that task later when he had more time.

As Paul was getting ready to leave for the downtown police headquarters, the phone rang. Paul debated a second or two whether he should answer it, then picked up the receiver. "Yeah. I mean, hello."

"Pauly, it's me, Gary."

"Hey, Gar.' I was just on my way out the door. I have to meet the cop handling Diana's case. She wants to talk about how she found Steven Green last night."

"Listen. Pauly, I heard they found Steven Green in a bad way last night. The word is someone is going around wiping out runners and mules that work for some big shot."

"That could be, Gar.' I now know that Steven Green and Clark Kent worked for the same guy and they are both dead. In fact, the information I received yesterday at the mall proved the connection between Kent and Green."

"Pauly, be really careful. If those two guys worked for who I think they worked for, you may be biting off more than you can chew, if you catch my drift."

"I hear you, pal. Now, I have to get going or I'll be late for my meeting. Is there anything else you wanted to tell me?"

"Yeah. One more thing, pal. I was talking to Mikey last night around eleven o'clock. He wants you to stop by to see him as soon as you can. He didn't tell me anything other than that it was important. You know what I mean?"

"Okay, Gar.' I'll stop by to see him as soon as I'm turned loose by the police. Thanks for the heads up."

Paul took the rucksack out of the Jeep, then walked across the road into the woods where he was sure no one could see him. He was looking for an old felled tree that he used to pass when he walked his dog back there a few years ago. The tree was about ten yards from the trail and directly in line with the front door of his house. The house was about one hundred yards away but clearly visible, since most of the leaves were now off the trees. Paul stuffed the rucksack in the hollow end of the tree, threw in some dried leaves over the opening for good measure, then darted back to the house. Paul looked at his watch and knew he would have to hurry if he did not want to be late for the meeting with Detective McGavin.

Chapter 11

Gary Roth was on his way to meet with a few men who had a hot deal on computers and printers. He was supposed to meet them around noon at the Interstate 95 rest stop between Baltimore and Washington. It was a very busy rest stop, so it would not look out of the ordinary for another tractor and trailer to be parked in the area. Gary took his partner, Johnny Thompson, with him. Gary and J.T., as he was called by everyone who knew him, arrived at the rest stop around eleven forty-five. Gary said, "We're supposed to look for an unmarked trailer attached to a blue tractor cab that has an American flag on the driver's side door."

Gary drove past the rest stop to the next exit, then turned the car around so he could backtrack. Gary and J.T. had done this many times in the past, so it was routine for them to do a drive-by first, to make sure things looked the way they were supposed to before continuing.

On the return trip to the rest stop, Gary slowed down to let J.T. out of the car. Gary went on to the visitor's building, which had several vending machines, bathrooms, and an information booth located inside. Meanwhile, J.T. was walking toward the rigs parked in the large lot behind the visitors' building. Gary parked the car, then went inside the building to get a cup of coffee from one of the vending machines. With coffee in hand, Gary headed back to the car. He looked around the large parking lot where the big rigs were parked and counted thirteen. Six of them had trailers with advertising on the sides, so they were easy to rule out. Four others had tractor cabs that were colors other than blue. That left three possible rigs. They each had plain trailers, and the tractors were some shade of blue. The only way to be certain was for Gary to drive by and look at the driver's side door to make a positive ID. Slowly, Gary made his way out of the visitors' area and headed toward the large parking lot reserved for the big rigs. He saw the rig he was looking for, then parked next to some other cars about fifteen yards from the rigs. Before getting out of the car, he checked the .38-caliber revolver he had strapped to his right ankle. Gary then looked in the rearview mirror where he could see that there were two men inside the blue tractor cab. Evidently, the big diesel engine was idling, as the two exhaust flappers on top of the pipes were doing a fluttering dance between small puffs of black smoke. Gary took another quick look in his sideview mirror and saw J.T. making his way through the tall pine trees that surrounded the entire parking area.

Gary exited his car and walked toward the blue tractor cab with the plain trailer. The driver immediately spotted him and elbowed his sleeping partner awake. Together the driver and his companion opened their doors to climb down and meet Gary. The rig driver asked, "Louie send you?"

"That's right. He said you fellows might have something that I may be interested in brokering."

While Gary was talking to the driver, he noticed the other man circling around him so that he was now at Gary's left side. Gary also spotted J.T. moving out of the pine tree line and toward the back of the trailer.

The driver said, "Well, let's go in the back and I'll show you what we have. Did you bring the money?"

Gary started following the driver to the back of the rig as he said, "Yeah. It's in my trunk. If what you have inside is what I'm looking for, we can make a deal."

The other man jokingly said, "How are you going to get all this stuff in your car, man?"

The driver laughed too, but Gary did not respond. The three men were now in the back of the trailer. The driver said, "Open her up, Phil."

Phil opened the lock, then lifted the lever on one of the big double doors and swung it open. There were cardboard boxes full of computers, monitors, and printers, stacked to the roof. They were lined up on both sides of the trailer, with a small three-foot aisle running down the middle of the trailer. The driver motioned for Gary to climb inside to inspect the goods. Gary climbed inside the trailer to look at several of the boxes containing brand-name equipment. There were different makes and models, but generally all of it was quality stuff. The driver was right behind Gary saying, "Come on up here, Phil, and get out of that cold wind."

Gary walked to the front of the trailer looking and inspecting the equipment on both sides of the aisle for a few more seconds, then said, "I'll give you fifty grand for the entire load."

The driver was not amused. He quickly and angrily said, "Louie told me the deal was for seventy-five grand. What are you trying to pull, man?"

"Well, Louie also told me you had a load of state-of-the-art equipment. Half of this crap does not have Pentium chips, the monitors are only fifteen-inch instead of seventeen inches, and some of these printers are lousy 300 DPI. Now, I might be able to unload this stuff eventually, but it's not the quality merchandise I was expecting to be delivered."

Phil was now angry and nervous. He said, "I don't know shit about Pentium, DPIs, or any other computer mumbo-jumbo. All I know is Louie said the deal was for seventy-five grand and that is what I'm going to walk away with. You got that, man?"

Gary had his back toward the front of the trailer and the driver and Phil were facing him with their backs facing the open double doors. Gary knew J.T. was outside the open door by now. Unfortunately, there was no place for Gary to duck, in case J.T. started shooting.

Gary pondered the situation a second or so, then said, "Well, gentlemen, I guess we won't be doing any business here today. If you two will excuse me, I have another appointment to go to so this day is not a total waste of my time."

Neither the driver nor Phil moved at first. Then Phil reached into his coat and pulled out an automatic pistol while saying, "We're going to do some business today, whether you like it or not. I think we will walk you to your car, where you'll give us seventy-five grand."

Gary did not flinch. He saw J.T. at the open doorway, then said, "If you look behind you, gentlemen, you'll see that my associate has a gun pointed at your heads. I strongly suggest that we call this business transaction a draw and play this little game some other day."

The driver and Phil turned to look at the open door behind them only to see J.T. pointing a silenced 9mm at them. Phil freaked and made a move as if he were going to point his weapon at J.T. Unfortunately for Phil, J.T. fired one round into Phil's chest. The driver tried to catch Phil as he was falling in the narrow aisle but was unsuccessful. Before Phil hit the floor, J.T. fired a second round into the driver's forehead.

Gary had to step over the two dead men to reach the back of the trailer and the open door. He climbed down and helped J.T. swing the back door closed, saying, "You take the rig to the warehouse, have these two canned for shipment, then unload the rig. I'll send Larry and Marcus over to give you a hand."

Johnny Thompson climbed inside the cab of the big rig and pulled out onto Interstate 95 traffic heading north. Gary walked back to his car, where he started the engine, so he could turn on the heat to warm his freezing feet. While he was warming himself, Gary picked up his cell phone to call Louie. Gary's tone was furious while telling Louie that he had waited for over an hour at the rest stop for the load of computers he promised, but nobody showed. He suggested to Louie that maybe his man hit I-95 and kept on going to make some fast cash in New York. Louie was, of course, flustered and upset. He apologized to Gary, saying, "We have done business in the past, so you know I wouldn't rook you, man. I'll check into it and let you know when I have something else coming down. Gary, I'll make it up to you with a special discount, OK?"

Gary knew Louie was ticked off about losing a trailer load of electronics, but he replied, "I don't know. I'll have to think about it. I have better things to do with my time than sitting around a damn rest stop." Gary then hung up feeling pretty good about the haul he had made today.

The drive back to Baltimore went quickly, since traffic was light this time of day. Gary knew he could trust J.T. with the shipment because they had grown up in the same neighborhood and had been in business together for over twenty years. J.T. would take the two bodies and put them into fifty-five-gallon waste oil drums. The oil drums would be stacked outside the warehouse with others that were scheduled for incineration later that month. Of course, the guy who ran the incinerator was an associate of Gary's, so nobody would ever know what happened to the driver and Phil. They would simply disappear without a trace. J.T. would have the rig unloaded and reloaded with some heavy equipment that was stolen from local construction sites in the past few months. There were three air compressors, one bobcat loader, one backhoe, two forklifts, and two concrete mixers ready for shipment back at the warehouse. Gary would then have Larry and Marcus drive the rig to West Virginia later that night. The trailer would be sold, along with its contents of heavy equipment, for a very good price. Heavy equipment all looked alike, and no cops ever stopped at a construction site to check out serial numbers.

Paul arrived downtown around twelve forty-five. He decided to go to Rocky's place for a quick sandwich and beer. Rocky's Bar and Grill was around the corner from police headquarters.

While sitting at the bar eating, Paul looked over at the area where several tables were filled with customers eating or drinking their lunch. He recognized one of the patrons from when they worked together at the BLC a few years ago. Paul picked up his sandwich and beer to walk over to the table as he said, "Is this seat taken, or can anyone sit here?"

Bernie Tallace looked up from his sandwich and managed a huge smile while saying, "Hey, Paul! How in the hell are you doing? Have a seat."

Paul sat down and shook Bernie's hand while saying, "Thanks, Bernie. How are things at the old BLC these days?"

Bernie swallowed his food, then took a drink before saying in a disgusted tone, "The place has gone to hell and nobody gives a shit anymore."

Paul took a drink of his beer, then said, "The merger isn't working out like the big wheels thought it would?"

"Hell no. All the big wheels took golden parachutes and bailed out with fat severance packages. Us peons are left trying to sort out all the mess they left behind. I tell you what, Paul, you did the right thing by getting out when you did."

"I don't know, Bernie. Things have not been all that great with me either."

The two old friends finished their lunch while Paul gave Bernie an update on what had happened to his wife and the whole mess with the robbery attempt at the store. Bernie listened sympathetically, then said, "I'm really sorry to hear about your wife. I had no idea all this stuff had happened to you. We don't get any information at the BLC, unless it has to do with that goddamned merger. I tell you, Paul, I wish I could just pack it in and bail out myself. You know, Paul, they say in Russia the commissars rule your life; in America it's the damn banks and corporations. I think it's a toss-up which is the more abominable dictatorship. You know what I mean?"

They talked for a few more minutes; then Paul looked at his watch and said, "Look Bernie, I have to run or I'll be late for a meeting at police headquarters. It was great seeing you again. Tell the folks at BLC I said hello. OK?"

"Will do, my friend. Listen. If there is something I can do to help you with this investigation, give me a call. I'll be more than happy to help, if I can."

Paul left Rocky's and walked around the corner to police headquarters. The time was 1:29 when Paul asked the receptionist to tell Detective McGavin he was waiting in the lobby. Paul took a seat on one of the wooden benches and thought about what Bernie had said regarding the banks and corporations running their lives. *Did he say they were running or ruining our lives? Did it make any difference?*

It took about ten minutes for Detective McGavin to appear with a big smile on her face, saying, "Mr. Marco, if you will follow me please, we'll be meeting with Captain Thiemeyer up on the third floor. I appreciate you taking the time to come downtown, but I don't think that this will take very long."

The two of them made their way to a small interrogation room on the third floor where Captain Thiemeyer was waiting for them. Captain Thiemeyer stretched out his hand for Paul to shake while saying, "Thanks for coming in, Paul. Have a seat."

Paul sat at the head of the small table with Captain Thiemeyer on his left and McGavin to his right. Thiemeyer asked, "Can I get you a cup of coffee or tea, before we begin? Maybe a soft drink?"

"No, thank you. I just had lunch at Rocky's, so I'm good." Detective McGavin started by telling Paul that she had found Steven Green dead in his cabin located outside the town of Westminster. She gave him the details about how she managed to track him down by way of a moving violation issued on the deceased Clark Kent's pickup truck.

Paul listened to the summation, then said, "You're one hell of a detective, Ms. McGavin. When you found this Steven Green character, you said he was already dead. I suspect it was not by natural causes?"

Captain Thiemeyer asked, "What makes you say that, Paul?" Paul was getting the feeling that he was being questioned instead of brought up to date by the two officers. "No particular reason. I'm just speculating that since Clark Kent was in his late twenties or early thirties, Steven Green was about the same age. Thereby making foul play an obvious conclusion. A little young for, say, a heart attack. Don't you think?"

Detective McGavin said, "That's not bad, Mr. Marco. You're right, of course. Steven Green was tortured, shot, and given a Colombian necktie in order to leave a message. Do you know about Colombian neckties, Mr. Marco?"

Paul was genuinely surprised at what Detective McGavin just told him, and it obviously showed on his face. *What is all this talk about Colombian neckties. Where did that come from?* he thought. Paul managed to finally say, "Yes, I think that's where the throat is slashed and the tongue is pulled out to show the person was a snitch or something like that."

Captain Thiemeyer reached for a briefcase that was sitting on the floor out of Paul's sight and placed it on the table. As he opened the briefcase, he said, "That's close enough, Paul." Thiemeyer pulled out several eight-by-ten-inch color photographs of the crime scene where Steven Green's body was found. As he slid the pictures over to Paul, he said, "It's not a pretty sight, but the message is a strong one to those who work in the nasty underworld business."

Paul reached for the pictures and glanced at each one before placing it in a neat pile in front of him. Paul could see immediately that the body was not tied in the chair as he had left it. He also knew that he did not give Green the Colombian necktie. Everything else seemed to be in place, just as he remembered. Then Paul noticed that the coffee table by the chair was missing the glass that he had used to give Green water. He went through the photographs again looking for the glass but didn't see it in any of the photos. Finally, Detective McGavin said, "Are you looking for something in particular, Mr. Marco?"

Paul realized that he was taking too long to look at the photographs and replied, "No. Not really. I just find it hard to believe that some people have the nerve to do such things as those depicted in the photographs."

Paul's mind was racing. How? Who? Was it the person or persons behind the headlights I saw approaching the cabin when I left?

Captain Thiemeyer said, "Paul, I'm going to level with you on this. We suspect you recognize Steven Green from the shakedown attempt at your store a couple of months ago."

"No. I told you then—"

"Please, let me finish. We also suspect that you tracked down Mr. Green there and had something to do with his demise. Detective McGavin, the commissioner, and I all are on the same sheet of music with this one, Paul. We think you tracked down Green to get even for what he and Clark Kent did to you a couple of months ago, which ultimately led to a retaliation hit on your wife Diana. So why don't you tell us where you were last night, say between eight o'clock and midnight?"

Paul was furious and relieved at the same time. He knew the police had no way to tie him to the Green murder and he sure as hell did not cut Green's throat to leave any message. Paul managed to say, "I was home, of course. And before you ask. Yes. I was alone. Do you honestly believe that I'm responsible for this?" Paul was pointing to the pile of photographs.

Detective McGavin said, "Put yourself in our shoes, Mr. Marco. You had motive, opportunity, and means to take out Steven Green." Paul looked straight into Detective McGavin's eyes, then said, "Yeah, that may be true of me and three thousand others that scumbag had dealings with lately. If you think I feel sorry for him being murdered, you're mistaken. The way I figure it, the air in Baltimore already smells better now that Green is history."

Captain Thiemeyer studied Paul a few seconds to allow him to calm down, then said softly, "Look, Paul. You have to understand that we are just doing our jobs. As a matter of fact, maybe you can help us by telling me who you think wasted Steven Green?"

"I have no idea. If I were you, I would be tracking down known accomplices for Green to try to figure out who the scumbag worked for. At least that way you may be questioning the right people. Now, if you are not charging me with anything, I would like to leave."

Paul angrily looked at Detective McGavin, then said, "Remember, I'm supposed to come up with $125,000 by tomorrow. You do remember, Detective, that I'm a victim in this case. I'm supposed to get a call tomorrow with instructions for making the money drop. Is any of this registering with you?"

Detective McGavin did remember that Saturday was the day Paul was supposed to pay off the person who had attacked him in the garage. She did not respond to Paul's anger.

Captain Thiemeyer responded, "Paul, we know you have been under a lot of stress lately. We have not forgotten about tomorrow. As a matter of fact, Detective McGavin will be at your place beginning at eight o'clock tomorrow morning, standing by for when or if you receive the call."

Detective McGavin said, "That is, if you don't mind me coming over tomorrow, Mr. Marco?"

Paul calmed down and showed an expression of being tired and fatigued. He slowly looked up at Detective McGavin and in a low, calm voice said, "No. I don't mind if you come over tomorrow morning. Just remember, I like cream and sugar in my coffee."

Both Detective McGavin and Paul managed to smile ever so briefly. Captain Thiemeyer stood up to indicate the meeting was now over. Paul shook hands with Thiemeyer and McGavin, then turned to leave the interrogation room. As soon as he got onto the elevator to go down to the ground floor, Paul thought, *Somebody came in behind me to cut up Green. Did they follow me? No way. They must have known where to find him. It must be someone affiliated with the Arabian horse farm. I have to get in there to check out the head man who runs the place.*

Detective McGavin turned to Captain Thiemeyer, asking, "Well, do you believe him?"

"Well, I think he knows more than he is letting on to us. That is, I think he either knew or recognized Green, judging by the expression on his face. However, the fact that he was so surprised when he looked at the crime scene photos makes me think he didn't kill Green. What about you?"

"I think he's one sharp cookie. He may not have killed Green, but he certainly knows more about the murder than he is admitting. I have a sneaky suspicion that we should be keeping a closer eye on Mr. Marco."

Chapter 12

Paul arrived at the *Cell Block* around three o'clock. The bartender was pouring a couple of draft beers into glasses when he acknowledged Paul's presence with a slight nod of his head, as if to say, "Hi." Paul nodded back, then took a seat at the opposite end of the bar from where the bartender was serving drinks. Paul wasn't sure, but it looked as if there were several regulars who were always at the other end of the bar watching the big-screen-TV sporting events. Today's event was horse racing from only God knew where. *There seemed to be more beer commercials than racing going on,* Paul thought. The bartender picked up the phone and talked into the receiver as he had done each time Paul showed up at the bar. After hanging up the receiver, the bartender poured a draft beer and brought it to Paul, saying, "Fifteen minutes." Paul laid a five spot on the bar, then nursed his beer until it was time to go downstairs to meet with Mikey.

When the fifteen minutes had passed, Paul made his way downstairs to go through the routine again with Rocco, the bodyguard, before being allowed into the great room to meet Mikey. Paul entered the great room to find the bookcases open and Mikey not at his regular spot behind the desk talking on the phone.

"In here, Pauly." Paul immediately recognized Mikey's voice coming from inside the hidden room behind the bookcases. He walked over to the hidden entrance, saying, "Gary said you needed to see me."

Mikey was looking at a stack of wooden crates that appeared to be new. In fact, the wood that the crates were made of smelled as if it had been cut recently. One crate was open and Mikey's hands were hidden from Paul's view by the high sides of the crate.

As Mikey pulled his hands out of the crate, he turned toward Paul, saying, "Aren't these beautiful?"

Paul recognized the black plastic stock of the standard military M-16 rifle. "Yeah, they are in excellent condition. Are you outfitting a militia group for a war? There must be twenty M-16s there."

"Thirty, to be exact. And no, I don't sell weapons to militia groups. These babies are going to Florida next week. The drug cartels down there need extra firepower to keep the Cuban and Haitian gangs in line. It's a crazy business, Pauly. One group tries to outgun the other group, so no one can steal what they have already stolen."

Mikey put the M-16 back into its crate, then walked toward Paul stating, "Let's get out of here and go sit at the desk where we can be more comfortable."

Paul followed Mikey as they left the armory, with the bookcase doors closing behind them. Mikey sat behind his desk and Paul sat in the same high-back chair he had used the last time they were together. Paul broke the silence by saying, "What did you want to see me about?"

"Pauly, I had some information for you regarding the partner of Clark Kent, but that is no longer important, is it? Apparently, his partner was found dead last night in his home. From what my sources tell me, he was tortured, killed, and then given a Colombian necktie. Of course, you know all this because you just came from police headquarters."

Paul, never surprised at the grapevine that fed information to Mikey, decided to level with him and tell him the details of what he had done to Green and what he had learned about the Arabian horse farm.

Mikey listened to Paul, then smiled, saying, "You have done well, Pauly. The man you're talking about is Iranian. Ismal Kamal Salam. They call him the Ayatollah because his name is too damn hard to pronounce and he's one ruthless son of a bitch. This guy made his money in illegal arms sales to Iran and Iraq. He plays both sides against each other and will sell his goods to whoever has the cash."

"You mean he is no different from some of our own CIA operations?"

"You could say that, Paul. The main difference is he has legitimized most of his businesses here in the U.S. He breeds Arabian horses for a hobby. He owns several import/export businesses, as well as a shipping line called the *Seascape.* The guy has beaucoup bucks and unlimited resources at his disposal. But, and I do mean but, he has a younger brother who's a big-time punk and usually is not on good terms with the rest of his family. I guess he is the rebel of the clan, if you catch my drift. Anyway, big brother has bailed little brother out dozens of times and will continue to do so because of the blood-is-thicker-than-water crap. For Christ sake, you're Italian. You know what I'm saying?"

"Yeah. So do you think it's the younger brother I should be dealing with instead of number-one son, Ismal Kamal Salam?"

"That's exactly what I'm saying. The problem is big brother will get involved if little brother is hit on too hard. You know what I am saying?"

"I do. My problem is going to escalate to number-one son no matter what I do. What can you tell me about little brother Salam?" "He changed his name to be more Americanized. His new name is William Sharp. Everyone calls him Billy. Anyway, Billy Sharp is into loansharking, numbers, protection rackets, and dope, primarily crack cocaine. From what I hear, he manufactures the crack and has a fairly sophisticated distribution network covering Virginia, Maryland, Delaware, and D.C. When Billy needs muscle to back him up, he usually buys it out of New York. I'm telling you, Pauly, this Billy Sharp can be bad news if you get on the wrong side of him."

"It sounds as if you know him pretty well, Mikey. Does your magic crystal ball have an address where I might find Mr. Sharp?" "Pauly, I can see that no matter what I say, you're going to go see Billy Sharp, so I guess I might as well give you what you want.

The word is Billy Sharp has a condo at Harbor Place in the Inner Harbor area and he has another in Ocean City as well. You can probably find him in one of those places when the weather is good. However, he spends most of his time on a ranch or farm in Virginia. Supposedly he's some kind of nature nut. Hiker, backpacker, mountain climber, and all that outdoor stuff."

Mikey opened one of his desk drawers and pulled out an old newspaper clipping. As he showed it to Paul, he said, "That's Billy Sharp in the middle. He is standing in the winner's circle with his big brother, who is on the left, for some horse show award he won several years ago."

Paul studied the picture a few seconds and burned the image of Billy Sharp into his brain, then asked, "Where in Virginia?"

"I'm not sure, but I can find out and give you a call later." "No. Don't call me at home, Mikey. The cops have a tap on my phone. I'll call you every two hours to see if you have an address for me. Is that OK with you?"

"You underestimate me, my friend. I should have the information within an hour or so. Call me around six o'clock, at my number here. If you decide to go see Billy Sharp down in Virginia, do you want me to send some guys with you?"

"No. That won't be necessary, Mikey. You have done enough for me already. I just want to talk to this guy to see what he knows." "Yeah. Are you going to talk to him like you talked to Steven Green last night!"

Paul managed a smile, then stood up to shake Mikey's hand while stating, "I'll call you at six. Thanks again, Mikey."

The telephone on Mikey's desk rang. As he picked up the receiver he said, "Good luck, my friend."

Paul left the great room feeling that he had most of the information he needed to settle the score with this Billy Sharp character. That is, if he was the one who ordered the hit on Diana.

Paul left the *Cell Block* and headed toward home. As he was driving up Interstate 83, he took the Timonium Road exit so he could stop at the International House of Pancakes for something to eat. He parked the Jeep, then went inside to leave his name with the cashier. There was already a line of people waiting for tables, but the cashier said it would only be about a fifteen-minute wait. Paul sat in the small lobby waiting for his table and thinking about how he would get to meet Billy Sharp. As he was contemplating different options, a blond waitress walked by who caught Paul's eye. She was about thirty-five or so, five feet five or six, and had a great pair of legs. Paul watched the waitress go by a second time, then a third. He thought, *Wow, that is one good-looking, sexy woman.*

The cashier called Paul's name and seated him at one of the smaller booths in the back of the restaurant while saying, "Your waitress will be right with you."

Paul looked at the menu and decided that he would have steak and eggs. It was too late for breakfast and too early for dinner, so he split the difference and figured that he would order something that took both meals into account. He heard a sweet female voice ask, "Do you need more time, or are you ready to order now?"

Paul looked up from the menu and into a beautiful pair of blue eyes attached to the waitress with those great legs. *This has to be my lucky day.* Paul ate and left a hefty tip for the good-looking waitress. He did not make any moves on her because it was not appropriate and besides, for all he knew she was happily married, with three kids, although Paul did not see a ring on her finger. *Oh, well,* he thought, *there will be plenty of time for that kind of stuff later.* Paul knew he was not ready to approach other women yet. He even dreaded the thought of someday having to enter the dating scene after so many years of marriage.

Paul left the restaurant and drove north on York Road to Hunt Valley Mall. It was five forty-five and he wanted to use a pay phone to call Mikey at six o'clock. Paul pulled the Jeep into an empty parking spot by one of the many mall entrances. He went inside and bought two scoops of fudge ripple ice cream in a cup from Friendly's, then sat on one of the benches in the mall. He would eat his dessert until it was time to call Mikey. The pay phones were only twenty feet away from where Paul was sitting, so he knew that making the call on time was not going to be a problem. While Paul was sitting on the bench, his mind was wandering.

He was thinking about some of the possibilities and options he had come up with recently regarding Billy Sharp. His best idea, he thought, was to go to Virginia, surprise Billy Sharp as he had Steven Green, then extract what he wanted to know from him. Unfortunately, Billy Sharp would probably be more prepared than Steven Green was for such a surprise visit to work. This one was going to take some planning, and it might take more time than Paul was willing to dedicate right now. The cops were still suspicious of him being involved with Green's murder. Now if he were to become involved with another low-life punk dealing drugs, it might be the proverbial straw that breaks the camel's back.

At five fifty-five, Paul threw his empty cup of ice cream into the closest trash receptacle, then walked to one of the pay phones. He dialed Mikey's number. It was answered immediately, on the first ring. "What?"

"Mikey, it's me, Paul. What can you tell me?"

"Are you ready, because here it comes. Billy Sharp lives near a place called Harrisonburg, Virginia. It's about 150 miles southwest of Baltimore, down Interstate 81, in the Shenandoah Valley vicinity. Got all that?"

"I not only got it, but I know where you're talking about. It's just north of Roanoke, Virginia. I must have backpacked half the state of Virginia at one time or another. Is there any way to determine when or if Sharp is there as opposed to one of his condos in Maryland?"

"The only thing I can tell you is he likes to spend as much time as he can down in Virginia, especially in the winter during hunting season. My guess is you will probably find him there until the weather breaks in the Spring. His place is called the *Double C*. Probably stands for Crack and Cocaine, if you know what I mean. Anyway, the word is that it's well known down there, so you should not have much trouble finding the place once you hit Harrisonburg."

"Listen. Mikey, I owe you, man. Thanks for the information.

I'll never forget how you have helped me."

"Forget it. You just take care of yourself and call me if I can do anything else for you. Ciao."

Paul hung up the phone, then made his way back to his Jeep. He was only about twenty minutes from home, so he made a beeline there so he could pull out some maps to make sure he had the area correctly etched in his brain.

As Paul pulled up to his driveway, he stopped to pick up the mail, then parked the Jeep in the garage. The mail consisted of the usual bills and junk advertisements, and of course he could be a $10-million winner if only blah, blah, blah. Paul checked the answering machine for messages and there were two. One was from Detective McGavin, saying she would see Paul at eight o'clock in the morning with coffee in hand. The second message was from Gary, asking Paul to call him when he got home. Paul looked up Gary's number and dialed. Gary answered the phone and Paul quickly said, "Listen. Gar,' it's not real clear here, how about where you are?"

At first Gary didn't get it, the weather was great, so he said, "What are—" Then it hit him, Paul was signaling him the line was not clear. Gary said, "I understand, Paul. Listen, buddy. If you're not busy later tonight, why don't you stop by my place for a beer?" "I don't know Gary. I'm kind of beat. It's been a long day. Can we do it some other time?"

"Sure, no problem. Call me when you're up to it." The line then went dead as the two hung up.

Paul was getting the impression that Gary had something important to tell him. So he put on his dark jacket, turned on the front porch light, and headed out through the garage into the woods across the road where he hid the rucksack. In the dark, it was much harder to find the felled tree, but Paul managed with the help of his front porch light as a guide. Paul pulled the rucksack out from the hollowed end of the tree, unzipped it, and retrieved the cell phone. He called Gary saying, "It's me again, Gar.' I'm calling from a cell phone because my house line is being tapped by the cops."

"I figured that's what you were trying to tell me when you said it wasn't clear. Anyway, I wanted to tell you that the word on the street is that some Colombians got rooked on a drug deal that involved this Green character, thus the necktie. I don't believe a word of it, to tell you the truth. I figured someone is trying to lay blame on someone else, if you know what I mean?"

"Yeah. That would make sense. Make it look as if the Colombians did Green in, so others looking to turn on a deal will get the message. I tell you what, Gar', that drug underworld has more angles being played then a championship chess match. They simply seize an opportunity to make others believe what they want them to believe."

"I hear you, Paul. Look. I was thinking that you may not get this call regarding the 125 G's tomorrow, if the one that was supposed to make the call was Green. So maybe your troubles are over. What do you think?"

"No way, Gar.' Green was small potatoes. His boss is to whom I need to get. After I met with Mikey today, he told me where I can find the guy. Does the name William or Billy Sharp mean anything to you?"

"I've heard of him. Rackets, crack, etc. Our paths don't cross because I ain't into that shit. I'm strictly a goods and services man, if you know what I mean."

"I understand what you're saying. I'm going to look up this Sharp character after the cops leave my place tomorrow. He has a place just north of Roanoke in an area called Harrisonburg. Remember we backpacked down that way about fifteen years ago? You, Mark, Chuck, and me."

"Hell yeah, I remember. We had some great times on those trips, didn't we, Pauly?"

"Yeah. Life was simpler back then, I guess. I don't know. Look, Gar.' I have to get going. I'm out in the woods with this cell phone freezing my gonads off. Could you do me a favor and pay that friend of yours the remaining $2,500 from our deal. The information turned out to be good. I'll reimburse you the next time I see you."

"OK, Paul. I'll take care of it right away. I'll also keep an eye and ear open in case something turns up regarding this Sharp dude. If I hear anything, I'll get in touch with you."

Paul put the cell phone back into the rucksack, then placed it in the hollow of the tree just as he had done before. Paul walked back to the house to place a pot of water on the stove so he could make a cup of instant coffee. While the water was heating, he broke out the ironing board and set it up in the kitchen. He then filled the iron with water and plugged it into the outlet. The small TV was on in the kitchen with the sound turned down really low, just like Diana used to do. Paul heard the steam spitting from the iron, so he started ironing one shirt, then another, etc. He took a break to make his cup of coffee and was again pleasantly surprised with how good the instant stuff tasted. Not as good as Diana's coffee, but better than anything he had been able to concoct up to that point. Between sips of coffee and ironing, Paul managed to finish the task in about forty-five minutes. He hung up the newly ironed clothes, then vacuumed the house from stem to stern. Paul noticed dust on top of the coffee table, so he decided to dust every room in the house. As he was dusting, he thought, *How did Diana keep this place so neat and clean? As soon as I finish one task there's another that requires attention.*

Paul finished vacuuming, dusting, and ironing at about ten thirty. He was dead on his feet, and the bathrooms had not yet been touched. *God only knows what has to be done in there,* he thought. *To hell with it! There is always tomorrow.*

Paul went into the master bathroom and took a long hot shower to relieve the aches and pains of tension that had built up during the day. After his shower, Paul went into his small office to pull out the maps he had for Virginia and the surrounding area. He then went into the family room to spread the maps on the nicely Lemon Pledged coffee table. Paul smoked a cigarette while he searched for and found the small town of Harrisonburg. Paul drew a circle around the town and then reviewed the route he would take. From his house he would travel south on Interstate 83 to 695 West. He then would pick up Interstate 70 West, to Interstate 81 South, until he hit Route 33, where he would turn west again. At least 150 or 160 miles, give or take. Paul stared at the map as he thought, *I know exactly where you are, scumbag.* Paul then lay down on the couch to rest, and he hoped to fall asleep. He still had not slept in their bed since Diana was murdered. Paul lit another cigarette to help him relax while he stared up at the ceiling.

The wind outside was kicking up again, and the weatherman said there was a 30 percent chance of snow overnight. Paul pulled the afghan off the back of the couch to cover himself and ward off the chill. He remembered that Diana had crocheted the afghan the first winter they spent in their new house. She said the heat pump always made her feel chilly as it blew cool air around the room.

After Paul put out his cigarette, it must have taken all of about three minutes for him to fall into a deep, sound sleep. Exhaustion was still the best sleeping pill on the market.

Chapter 13

The sound of the doorbell startled Paul to the point where he fell off the couch, entangling his feet in the afghan. The bell sounded again as Paul grumbled, "What the hell," then finally lifted himself up to look at the clock on top of the TV, which read: 8:01 a.m. Paul hurried to the front door, where he saw Detective McGavin standing with two cups of coffee, a newspaper, and a bag of doughnuts. Paul opened the door as the detective's eyes scanned him up and down while she said, "There's no reason for you to get all dressed up just for me, Paul."

Paul scratched his head and wiped the sleep from his eyes, then looked down the front of himself, noticing that he was only wearing jockey shorts and a sweatshirt. Embarrassed, he said, "Jesus Christ. I'm sorry, Detective. I fell asleep late last night and didn't move until you rang that damn doorbell. Please, come in."

Detective McGavin laughed as she eyed Paul's attire, then walked past him to enter the living room. Paul was doing whatever he could to hide the fact that his morning semi-erection was obviously visible to the whole world. Finally he said, embarrassed, "The kitchen is through there, Detective. I'll be right back."

Detective McGavin was still smiling as she laughingly said, "Don't hurry on my part. I know it's sometimes *hard* to be awakened suddenly."

"Very funny, Detective."

Paul went into the bedroom and quickly slipped on a pair of jeans, then washed his face and brushed his teeth. He ran a brush through his hair, but it didn't help very much. Then Paul went into the kitchen, where Detective McGavin had placed two napkins on the table and opened the bag of doughnuts. She was sitting in the chair that normally had been reserved for his wife, but Paul didn't say anything. Paul sat in his regular chair, then said, "Well, Detective. You were late again, as usual. Did you have trouble finding my place?"

"One minute or two doesn't constitute lateness in my book. And no, I didn't have any trouble finding your house because I know how to read a map. Besides that, if you remember, I was here before when I found you on the garage floor shot up with venom, wise ass. Do you want chocolate-covered or honey-dipped?"

"Chocolate-covered, thank you. And whether it's one minute or twenty doesn't really make any difference. Late is late, in my book."

"Well, at least I didn't oversleep. Besides, I'm not the one who greets people at the door half-naked. Not that I minded, you understand. By the way, you have a very nice place here."

Paul and Detective McGavin drank their coffee, and each of them ate two doughnuts. Paul had turned on the morning news so they would not have to make so much conversation. When a commercial came on the TV, Paul asked, "What do you think is going to happen today regarding this long-awaited phone call?"

"I'm not sure, to tell you the truth. Captain Thiemeyer suspects that Green was behind the extortion attempt, thereby eliminating the call entirely, since he's dead. I don't buy it, though. I figure Green was small-time and someone else is pulling the strings. Therefore, we should still get a call."

"I agree with you. I just wish they would call early, so we don't have to hang around here all day and night."

Detective McGavin looked around the kitchen, then leaned her body so she could see out the family room patio doors. She said, "I can think of a lot worse places to spend time, Mr. Marco. The house and the view are absolutely gorgeous. Do you see much wildlife out here?"

Paul realized that the detective was right. The place was very nice, and he should not be complaining. "Oh yes. There are deer, fox, pheasant, and a slew of wild birds that hang around here all the time. It's a very peaceful place to live. Would you like to buy it?"

Detective McGavin stood up to walk into the family room to gaze out through the patio doors, then replied, "If I could afford a place like this, I would buy it in the wink of an eye. Oh, I see you have a pool, too. Do you swim much?"

"No, I rather hate the thing myself. My wife was the swimmer in the family. As a matter of fact, the neighbors down the road use the pool more than I do."

"Mr. Marco, it must me very hard for you to sell this place, with so many fond memories, I mean. But, sometimes it's best to start clean, I guess. You know, a fresh new start and all that stuff people say."

"Perhaps," replied Paul.

"Are you planning to take a trip soon?"

Paul was surprised by the question, then said, "What makes you ask that?"

"Well, I see the maps spread out on the coffee table, and my detective mind automatically starts to fabricate a theory. It's a cop thing."

Paul left the kitchen to enter the family room. He had forgotten about the maps he had been looking at last night, and in all the confusion this morning he had left them out in the open like a fool. Paul said, "To tell you the truth, I'm thinking about taking a backpacking trip to get away for a while. You know, a change of scenery and all that."

"Sounds like a terrific idea. I have done some backpacking myself. It certainly rejuvenates your juices when you are surrounded by Mother Nature."

"Exactly," replied Paul. "Listen, Detective. I'm going to jump into the shower and then shave so I don't look like such a bum. Please, make yourself at home. The bathroom is down the hall, the first door on the right. I'll be using the shower in the master bedroom. If the phone rings, let the answering machine pick it up. I won't be but fifteen or twenty minutes. Relax, read the paper, or just watch TV."

Detective McGavin opened her purse to pull out a cell phone, saying, "I have a few calls to make, so take your time. I doubt if the bad guys are up this early anyway."

Paul took a hot shower, then quickly shaved. He thought that by cleaning up and getting dressed he would feel much better. As he was dressing, he opened the bedroom door to holler down the hall to Detective McGavin, "Did anyone call?"

"No. Not yet."

While dressing, Paul thought he got a whiff of fresh brewed coffee when he opened the bedroom door. *My mind must be playing tricks on me, or maybe it's just wishful thinking,* he thought.

Paul looked into the dresser mirror and decided this was as good as he was going to look today, so he opened the door and headed toward the family room. The closer he got to the family room, the stronger the aroma of fresh brewed coffee loomed. When he stepped into the family room, Detective McGavin was sitting on the couch reading the paper while drinking from a mug of steaming coffee.

Paul said, "I thought I smelled fresh coffee brewing."

"I hope you don't mind? I saw the coffee maker and found the coffee in the refrigerator just as it's supposed to be, so I figured we could use another cup. After all, that stuff I brought over this morning was terrible. This, however, is much more like it. Try a cup; it's rich, hot, and tasty."

Paul replied, "No. I don't mind a bit. I haven't had much luck making decent coffee with that coffee maker, so I have been using instant."

Paul took a mug from the cabinet over the sink and filled it almost to the top. He added sugar and half-and-half and stirred it a second or two. Finally, Paul went for the taste test. It looked like good dark brewed coffee, it smelled like the familiar rich blend he was used to, and it tasted great. The expression on his face told the story.

Detective McGavin smilingly said, "You like it?"

Paul took another sip, then said, "I think I love you, Detective. This is fantastic. It's hard to believe it came out of the same coffee maker that I tried to make coffee with just a few days ago. It must be a woman thing."

They both laughed and settled in to read the paper and drink coffee. The morning news programs were almost over, so Paul turned off the TV and turned on the stereo to a soothing light rock station.

Detective McGavin explained to Paul that he would be wearing a wire in case the call came and they became separated. She said that she would be following his every move and that he should just talk in a normal tone so she would know the caller's instructions. Of course, Paul would not be able to communicate with Detective McGavin, since it was a one-way system only.

After about ten minutes of silence, McGavin said, "It looks as if we are going to have a nice Indian summer day." She then looked at the portable phone and asked, "Mr. Marco, what kind of range do you get with that phone?"

Paul thought a few seconds, then said, "Out here in the country, there's not much interference. I have talked on that phone almost one hundred yards from the house and it sounded just fine. Why?"

"Well, it's such a beautiful day outside, I would like to take a walk around the grounds. If the phone rings we will still hear it, right?"

Paul agreed with Detective McGavin. It was too pretty a day to be cooped up inside. Paul grabbed his jacket and the portable phone and gave McGavin a tour of the three-acre lot. They stopped by the special burial place where the family pets were put to rest. He explained how much he missed his last dog, named Auggie, and how she had saved his life a couple of years ago. They walked to where the family goats and chickens were once housed, now just a distant memory of happier times. Although the pool was covered for the winter, they walked around the brick walkway and patio. Paul explained how he and his friends had laid every single brick on one very long hot summer weekend almost ten years ago. The walk and talk with Detective McGavin were like therapy for Paul. He conjured up all kinds of good memories and freely expressed them to this woman stranger. When the tour was complete, the two of them went back into the house to wait some more.

It was almost noon and Detective McGavin stated, "I have an idea. Why don't we send out for a pizza?"

Paul laughed, then said, "You city folks are funny. Out here in the country, there is no such thing as home delivery."

"You're kidding? How do you survive with no home pizza delivery?"

"It's simple. We drive ten to fifteen miles to the closest pizza carryout and hurry home before it gets cold."

"My God. That's almost inhuman living conditions," said McGavin.

Paul was getting hungry, too, so he said, "I have food in the house. It's not much, but I'm sure I can rustle up something that you could stomach. I'm a terrible cook, but I do have a few frozen TV dinners in the fridge, if that's OK?"

Detective McGavin frowned at the suggestion, then said, "I'm not a bad cook. Let's see what we can put together."

They went into the kitchen, where McGavin surveyed the situation in the refrigerator and storage cabinets. She then said, "Typical bachelor pad. I tell you what, get me a big frying pan, some butter, eggs, a can of mushrooms, bread—"

Paul thought it was like playing twenty questions: "Do you have any onions?" "Do you have any green peppers?" And on and on. When they were through, Paul had set the table and McGavin was filling two plates with an omelet concoction that had everything in it except the leftover pizza in the fridge. And Paul was not so sure she didn't pick the pepperoni off that and toss it into the skillet as well. The coffee maker was dripping, and the food was now ready for consumption. Paul added pepper and catsup to the huge omelet in front of him, then took a small bite. Detective McGavin watched his facial expression, then said worriedly, "Well?"

"Hey, this is good. No. This is really good."

McGavin and Paul feasted on the makeshift omelet and drank coffee. Detective McGavin told Paul about her growing-up years and how she had decided to become a cop when her father was killed in the line of duty fifteen years ago on a routine traffic stop. They ate, drank, and talked until almost two o'clock, when they were interrupted by the phone ringing.

Paul picked up the phone with Detective McGavin on the kitchen extension. "Hello."

"Mr. Marco, this is your lucky day. I suspect that you have the money you owe me and are ready for instructions. I also assume that the phone is tapped, so this is going to be quick. I want you to put the money into a large brown paper bag and drive to Hunt Valley Mall and wait by the pay phone next to the entrance by Sears. I'll call you in exactly twenty minutes, with further instructions."

Paul hung up the phone and Detective McGavin dialed Captain Thiemeyer on her cell phone, letting him know they were on the move.

"Remember, Paul, I'm going to be following you, so after you get the next set of instructions from the caller, repeat them out loud so I'll know where you're going and what you're doing. I'll coordinate the other undercover cops working this case, so we can hopefully nab this bastard."

Paul grabbed a used supermarket brown paper bag from the laundry room and stuffed it with today's crumpled-up newspaper. He threw in an old phone book so the bag had the look and feel of containing something that could possibly be $125,000 in small bills. Paul put the bag into the Jeep and headed for the mall with Detective McGavin following him at a very safe distance.

Paul pulled the Jeep into the parking lot near the Sears entrance. He looked at his watch to see that it had taken him only eighteen minutes to get there. Paul took the paper bag and quickly walked to the entrance where the pay phones were located. He did not look around to see if he could spot Detective McGavin. As he opened the door to the mall entrance he said, "I hope this thing is working, because I'm now standing by the phones."

Paul stood with his back against the wall, as he watched customers coming and going. He looked at his watch and saw it had been exactly twenty minutes since he was first contacted. One of the phones began to ring. Paul spoke into the microphone by his collar: "Here we go."

Paul picked up the receiver, saying, "Marco."

"Very good, Mr. Marco. Now, I want you to drive to Timonium and leave your car at the Metro Park and Ride. Buy a ticket and take the light rail train to downtown and exit at Howard Street. Then walk to the Charles Street subway stop. At the top of the subway stairs, there's another pay phone. I'll call you there in forty minutes."

Paul hung up the phone and headed back to his Jeep. While he was walking, he told Detective McGavin where he was going and what he had been instructed to do next. He only hoped she was receiving the transmission.

Paul arrived at the Timonium Park and Ride, bought a ticket, then boarded the next train to arrive at its scheduled twenty-minute interval. Detective McGavin used her cell phone to call in the Charles Street location to Captain Thiemeyer. The police would have a cop posing as a roving hot-dog vendor next to the Charles Street subway entrance and another two officers nearby in the immediate area.

The light rail train ride was very smooth, Paul thought. He had never used the mass transit system before but found it to be very comfortable. He had an urge to talk into the microphone to detective McGavin but delayed it when a woman sat in the seat next to him. The light rail train ran aboveground from Timonium for about twenty miles to downtown. The Howard Street stop was in the heart of downtown, and Paul was not that happy about that particular neighborhood. The Charles Street subway station was less than four blocks away from the Howard Street stop.

During the entire train ride, Paul kept looking at his watch. The woman who sat next to Paul was not overly attractive, in her thirties and wearing entirely too much perfume. She asked, "Are you late for an appointment?"

Paul, finally realizing the woman was speaking to him, said, "Excuse me?"

"I see that you keep looking at your watch. Are you late for an appointment?"

"Oh. Yeah. I was supposed to meet my wife a half hour ago. She is really going to be upset when I tell her our three kids are home with the sitter and are suffering from some sort of stomach virus."

The woman did not talk to Paul for the rest of the train ride. McGavin laughed and thought to herself, *Well, Paul Marco certainly knows how to turn off a woman on the prowl.*

When the train stopped at Howard and Fayette Streets, Paul exited and started walking quickly so he could make it to Charles Street in time. He looked at his watch and saw he only had five minutes to travel nearly four blocks. The person calling the shots had this route timed very tightly.

Paul was caught in traffic as he tried to cross Charles Street. There was a cop directing traffic at the intersection, so Paul couldn't dart between the oncoming cars. His watch indicated that he had less than thirty seconds. Paul could see the phone booth across the street but was trapped. *The time was up, and the phone was now ringing,* he thought. The traffic light turned red, and the cop waved for the pedestrians to cross the street. Paul ran to the phone thinking, *Don't hang up, you bastard.* Out of breath from his sprint, he picked up the ringing phone, saying, "Marco."

"You shouldn't run like that. A man your age could have a heart attack or worse. Now, walk to Hopkins Plaza and set the paper bag down on the wall that surrounds the fountain. Make sure you place the bag on the wall directly in front of the Federal Building entrance."

Paul now knew the caller must be watching him. How else would he know Paul had run to get to the phone? Hopkins Plaza was only one hundred yards away. Paul started to walk toward the plaza fountain while speaking into the microphone, saying, "Our boy is watching me. He knew I ran to the phone, so he's close. I'm supposed to put the bag on the fountain wall in Hopkins Plaza so it's facing the Federal Building entrance."

Paul approached the plaza, which was crowded with people walking to and from late lunches and the normal everyday office building-to-office-building pedestrian traffic. The fountain was shut down and drained for the winter. Paul walked to the large circular fountain, then stopped when he was directly in front of the Federal Building. He set the bag down on top of the two-foot-high wall that made up the sides of the fountain, then looked around. He did not spot anyone who looked suspicious or out of the ordinary. He had turned to walk away when suddenly a person on a ten-speed bicycle raced by, snatched the paper bag, and headed toward Redwood Street. Paul yelled into the microphone, "A person on a ten-speed just scooped up the bag and is racing toward Redwood Street! The bike is dark blue and the rider is wearing all black. I couldn't tell if it was a man or a woman, or whether the person was black or white. But they sure are quick."

Sirens were now wailing all around Hopkins Plaza. Plainclothes detectives were showing their badges and had their weapons drawn. Detective McGavin was now running up to Paul saying, "Are you all right?"

"Yeah. It all happened so fast. I don't know where that bike rider came from. One second it was pedestrian traffic as usual; then suddenly he or she rode by me and the bag was gone."

Detective McGavin was talking on her two-way radio, saying, "What do you mean, he vanished? He had to come right past you, for Christ sake."

Paul looked at Detective McGavin, then said, "Boy, is that guy going to be pissed at me when he finds out there's no money in the bag."

Detective McGavin managed a smile, then said, "Not as pissed as the man who sent him to pick it up. We had better go over to headquarters, because I'm sure the commissioner is going to want a firsthand account of what happened. The rest of these officers will continue to search for the bicycle bag bandit."

Chapter 14

The commissioner was livid when he heard how things had turned out at Hopkins Plaza. He could not understand how a man or woman on a bike could disappear into thin air without leaving a trace. Detective McGavin tried to explain that the person could have easily picked up the bike and gone into any house or other building surrounding Hopkins Plaza. She even had a theory by which a van might have been waiting for the bag man, so he only had to toss the bike inside and off they went. The commissioner was not impressed with either of the explanations. In fact, he called them excuses, which really ticked off McGavin. Captain Thiemeyer was also reamed out for not having the police helicopter on standby. The captain explained that it was supposed to be a simple bag drop, not an entire police operation involving air support. When the commissioner had his fill of the two officers' excuses/explanations, he dismissed them curtly. That left Paul alone with the agitated commissioner.

"Paul, I apologize for what happened today. We were not very professional in the way this fiasco was handled."

To the contrary, Paul was not all that upset. He figured that there would be another call from the bad guys and they would get a shot at catching them again. He said, "Don't sweat it, Commissioner. To be honest with you, I think you were a little hard on those two. I can't see how they could have done it any better than they did."

The commissioner looked at Paul with a puzzled look for a few seconds, then said, "You still don't get it, do you, Paul. These guys are not just going to call you to say, 'You blew it, Mr. Marco. Do you want to try again, Mr. Marco?' Hell, they are probably so pissed off at you right now that they will take drastic action. It's not the money anymore for these guys. It's personal."

"Commissioner, don't get me wrong. I'm not discounting what these assholes are capable of doing. Remember, I'm the one with the dead wife."

Apologetically the commissioner said, "Paul, I didn't mean to make it sound so cold. I apologize, but you need to understand that the stakes have just been boosted to a whole new level. Your damn life may now be in very real danger. I'm going to assign you protection for—"

"Hold on, Commissioner. I'm not about to become a damn prisoner in my own home or in any so-called safe house you may have in mind. If these guys want to come after me, that's fine with me. That will save me the trouble of looking for them."

"OK, hotshot. Unless you have turned into Rambo recently, I would caution you about doing anything stupid like going after these guys. Hell, we don't even know who they are yet. That is, unless you know something that we don't?"

"No. I don't know any more than you do at this point. I suggest we leave the tap on my phone and wait for them to contact me again. I'm sure they will want to tell me how upset they were to find there was no money in that paper bag. Boy, I bet they're really steaming right about now."

The commissioner smiled at Paul, then replied, "You're having fun with this, aren't you? Look. It's OK, for now. We can keep the tap on your phone and play wait-and-see. But, if I think they are going to make a move on you, I'm sending in the goddamned marines. Do you understand?"

"Thanks, Commissioner. Besides, I'm planning to take a little backpacking trip for a few days to get away from all this crap. That will give the bad guys time to come up with another plan."

"Backpacking? That sounds like work to me. Why don't you go to Florida and lie on the beach for a few days? Soak up some rays. Now that's a vacation."

"Well, to each his own. Listen. Thanks again for working with me on this one. And in the future," Paul said jokingly, "lighten up on Thiemeyer and McGavin. They did the best they could."

Smiling, the commissioner responded, "Get the hell out of here and let me concentrate on my other fifty unsolved murder cases."

Paul left police headquarters without seeing McGavin or Thiemeyer. He walked to the Howard Street light rail station and headed back to Timonium where he had left his Jeep earlier and then headed home. While driving, Paul was thinking of the gear he would need for his three days in the Virginia mountains. He had been backpacking so often, it was like running down a mental checklist: goose down sleeping bag, Optimus cook stove and fuel, dehydrated meals, etc. By the time Paul finished his mental list, he was at the Mount Carmel Road exit on Interstate 83. He pulled off the exit and turned right onto York Road, where the pizza carryout was located. He ordered a cheese steak sub with the works and a side order of onion rings. While the cook was making the sandwich, Paul went next door to the convenience store to buy extra packs of cigarettes, snack foods, plastic knives, forks, spoons, paper plates, and other assorted goodies for his trip.

Paul put the bag of goodies into the Jeep, then went back to the carryout shop to pick up his order. With the Jeep loaded, Paul headed for home to pick up the mail before pulling into the garage. He checked the answering machine and found only one message from Detective McGavin, asking him to call her when he got home. Paul decided instead to eat while the sandwich was still hot. He pulled a cold can of Coors' Light out of the fridge, sat at the kitchen table, then devoured his meal. He looked in the direction of the coffee maker when he finished the meal but quickly decided to heat some water on the stove so he could make instant coffee instead.

While the water was heating, Paul called Detective McGavin at headquarters.

"Detective McGavin speaking. May I help you?" "You rang!"

"Oh! Hi, Mr. Marco. I just wanted you to know that Captain Thiemeyer and I are very sorry things didn't work out this afternoon. Like the commissioner said, we should have done a better job of planning our moves."

"Don't give it another thought, Detective. I told the commissioner that I thought you guys did all that you could, under the circumstances. I'm sure he would never tell you that, but please let Captain Thiemeyer know that I appreciate the efforts. We'll get them next time."

"Thanks. I'll let him know what you said. So, what have you decided to do now?"

"As I told you and the commissioner, I'm taking a few days off to hike through the back country and recharge my batteries. I figure all this other stuff can wait until I get back."

"I hope you have good weather for your trip. Fall can be a tricky time in the mountains, as you well know. When you get back in town, call me so we can figure out what to do about the bicycle bag bandit."

"Will do. I'll call you when I get back."

After hanging up the phone, Paul went into the basement to gather his backpack, sleeping bag, two-man nylon tent, and other assorted paraphernalia. He laid out his gear on the basement floor, as he had done many times before when preparing for a trip. The main difference this time was that he was going alone, so he could not forget anything important.

Warm clothing was an absolute must this time of year in the mountains, so Paul had to pack smart. He checked and rechecked his gear before he was satisfied that it would weigh under fifty pounds when he was through. For some reason, Paul always kept the weight in his pack under fifty pounds, so it would not slow him down too much on the steeper slopes.

Paul went upstairs to grab his jacket, then went out through the kitchen into the garage. He took a quick look around the front of the house, then headed toward the rucksack hidden in the woods. Once there, he retrieved the crossbow and bolts, leaving the rest of the gear in place. Paul went back into the house and down to the basement, where he began placing all the necessary gear into the backpack. It took three attempts to get the load just right, so that the weight was evenly distributed on his back, shoulders, and hips. He took the pack upstairs and set it down on the family room floor, then went to retrieve the bathroom scale. He placed the scale on the floor, then stood on it, reading 180 pounds. Paul then stepped off the scale and strapped on the backpack. He again stepped onto the scale and it now read 227 pounds. Paul smiled as he thought, *Three pounds to spare. You've still got it, old man.*

Paul straightened up around the house before changing into his hiking clothes and boots. He took the maps he had used the night before to plot his course and stuffed them into his pocket, then took one last look around the house, for good measure. Being satisfied that everything was secure, Paul loaded the backpack into the Jeep. Then he walked the trash down to the end of the driveway so it could be picked up on Tuesday morning. Paul figured he would arrive at his starting point in Virginia around midnight, catch some sleep in the Jeep until daybreak, then hit the trail first thing Sunday morning. He would return home Tuesday, if things worked out the way he planned.

Paul headed for the interstate and pointed the Jeep south. He fumbled with the radio dial, which only seemed to clearly pick up late-night talk shows. Finally, he found an easy listening station and turned the volume down low so he could relax and think. *Maybe I'll stop for a hot meal in Virginia before hitting the trail*, thought Paul. *After all, Virginia ham and eggs, with biscuits on the side, makes for one hell of a good breakfast.*

Paul engaged the Jeep's cruise control and let the road hypnotize him as the white lines sped by his window. He was now feeling very tired, but he needed to get a fresh start in the morning, when the weather and daylight were in his favor. Once he was situated, the darkness would be his ultimate ally.

Paul drove through Frederick to Hagerstown, Maryland, where he stopped to fill the gas tank and buy a large coffee. This was the end of the Interstate 70 route for Paul. He would now pick up Interstate 81 south, heading toward Winchester, Virginia, which he figured was roughly the halfway point of the journey. The night air was now getting cold, so Paul would occasionally lower the window so he could revive himself as he drove onward. Many tractor trailers used the interstates at night. Paul stayed in the right lane, going between sixty-five and seventy miles per hour. For the most part, eighteen wheelers passed the little red Jeep as if it were standing still. Each passing truck would send a burst of wind against the side of his vehicle. Paul would then have to tightly hold onto the steering wheel, else he would be pushed onto the shoulder of the road.

Paul continued traveling south until he saw signs for Luray Caverns around New Market, Virginia. Paul pulled into a truck stop to gas up the Jeep, hit the men's room, and drink another large coffee. He walked around to rejuvenate the blood flow in his legs, which were now feeling tingly from sitting so long. He bought a prepaid phone card inside the truck stop, then called his house from one of the pay phones to see if he had any messages. There were none. Paul looked at his watch to see it was now 11:45. He would not make it to Harrisonburg until maybe one o'clock. *Close enough*, he thought. The mountains slowed him down some and added more miles to the trip because of all the up and down driving through the Blue Ridge.

Once he was on the road again, Paul felt fine. His immediate goal was now within reach.

He stopped in Harrisonburg for a big breakfast. The diner was half-empty, but the food and service were very good. Paul finished his meal, then looked at his watch, which now read 2:05. The waitress came over to see if Paul wanted more coffee. Paul was glad to have another hot cup of Java. *She was maybe fifty or a little older. Probably was a waitress most of her adult life*, Paul thought. In a low voice Paul said, "Excuse me, ma'am. Do you all know the best route to the *Double C* ranch? This here is my first haul down this away and I don't want to be late with my delivery, if you know what I'm saying?"

"Sure, darlin'." Big smile. "The *Double C* is right easy to find. Take 33 west until ya come ta Dogwood Road. At Dogwood, hang a left and go about maybe fifteen mile. Can't miss it. Biggest working ranch in these parts."

"Thank ya, ma'am. I appreciate it."

The waitress was all smiles as she headed to another table to offer them more hot coffee. Paul left the diner to find an open convenience store in town, where he bought a local map for the area and one specifically for the George Washington National Park. While still in the store parking lot, he lit a cigarette and studied the maps. He could park at the Swinging Hammock parking area, then hike over two mountaintops to reach the back of the *Double C* property that butted up against the park property. When Paul looked at the topographical map, the terrain did not look all that strenuous, for the most part. Maybe a ten-or twelve-hour day hike in and then swing around for maybe an eight-hour night hike back to the Jeep using the river as a guide.

On the outskirts of town, Paul pointed the Jeep to Route 33 West. He drove into the mountains and through the back roads for almost an hour until he came to a parking area designated for hikers and campers. The small sign read: **Swinging Hammock parking area patrolled by Park Rangers**. *There were a couple of dozen cars and trucks in the area, most, if not all, campers, judging by the hitches on the back bumpers*, Paul thought. The weekend hikers would be coming down the mountain trails later today so they could go back to wherever by Monday. Late fall and winter are not the best time for lengthy mountain backpacking trips, but it never seemed to curtail the campers with their big tents and trailers, because they had heaters.

Paul lowered his seat back as far as it would go and closed his eyes to catch a few hours' sleep before hitting the trail. It didn't take long for Paul to nod off into dreamland.

Around six o'clock, he woke up because he was freezing. He went outside to take a leak and smoke a cigarette. Paul then opened the back door of the Jeep to retrieve an old blanket that was under the bench seat. He climbed back into the driver's seat, covered himself, then nodded off again to catch one more hours sleep.

The sun's bright rays breaking over the horizon woke Paul. He quickly looked at his watch to see that it was now 7:15. Paul lit a cigarette and stepped outside the Jeep, where he could see his breath in the crisp morning mountain air. He took a deep breath, which woke him up completely as the cold rush filled his lungs. Paul stretched his tired, aching back to loosen it up before strapping on his pack. After finishing his cigarette, Paul strapped on his pack. He then took the map of the George Washington Park area and stuffed it into his pocket as he made tracks for *Pickem Trail.*

The first half hour of hiking made Paul's legs ache, and he broke into a good sweat. The sun was now higher in the sky, and the bite was gone from the morning air. Paul put his pack up against a tree so he could remove his goose down vest. He had to control his body temperature and perspiration so he could continue the first climb to the top of Mount Lark. He pulled out the topographical map and looked at what lay ahead. The next two miles were a steady but gradual incline to the summit. After that, it would be downhill for an hour, then back up the steep incline of Mount Robin. Paul picked up his pack and headed for the summit of Mount Lark feeling good to be in the outdoors again.

Paul had to stop every half hour to rest and reached the summit around noon. The view was spectacular and the deep blue sky was clear, with hardly a cloud in sight. Paul had not passed one hiker on the way up Mount Lark. He broke out his Optimus stove, added some white fuel, and stoked it up.

Paul went to the small spring to the left of the trail and filled his large and small aluminum pots with water. When the small stove was raging hot, Paul put on the larger pot of water to bring it to a boil. Paul carried two one-quart canteens of drinking water from home. Since water was available from the spring and he was boiling it, there was no need to use his good drinking water just yet. When the water in the pot came to a boil, Paul removed the pot and immediately placed the smaller pot of spring water on the stove to boil. The first pot of boiling water was for his lunch. Paul opened a bag of dehydrated chicken and noodles, then dumped the contents into the hot water and stirred. He covered the pot with a lid and waited the necessary ten minutes for the chow to be ready. In the meantime, the second, smaller pot of water was now boiling. Paul turned off the stove and poured some instant coffee, sugar, and powdered dairy creamer into the pot. A plastic spoon was all the utensils he would need for this quick hot lunch. Paul took the pot of chicken and noodles and his coffee to a large rock overlooking the Shenandoah Valley below. *It was a very beautiful and peaceful place to have lunch,* he thought.

After the meal was consumed, Paul lay back to smoke a cigarette and finish his coffee. He looked at his watch to see that it was past one o'clock, so he had to saddle up and hit the trail once again. Paul policed up the area where he had cooked and eaten. When all the gear and trash were packed away, the place looked as if no one had been there. The number one rule of the backpacker is: **If you pack it in, pack in out.**

Paul looked at his topographical map again and then followed the blue marked trail down Mount Lark. He would then switch to the white marked trail at the bottom, so he could start his ascent of Mount Robin. The white trail was steep at first but leveled out to a plateau for about a quarter mile before the grade increased drastically. It was now four o'clock and the sun was already starting to set behind the mountainous horizon. Darkness would be upon him in less than an hour. The temperature was starting to drop, so at one of his half-hour rest breaks Paul put his down vest back on to hold in his body heat. An hour later he put on a wool stocking cap to ward off the cold breeze that was now kicking up in the treetops around him.

When Paul reached the top of Mount Robin, it was eight o'clock. The wind was really blowing at the top, and the wind chill factor had to be in the single digits. Paul put on his black wool hooded sweater under his down vest and also put on a pair of warm leather gloves. He pulled out the map so he could reconnoiter his current position. The moon was bright, but he still needed to use a flashlight to see the small trail markings on the map.

His location was exactly where he needed to be for this phase of the trip. Paul walked off the main trail about fifty feet and found a rock cropping where he could later stash his gear. For now, he would be protected from the wind by the large boulders. After almost twelve straight hours of hiking, Paul was exhausted, hungry, and getting colder. He first selected a level spot to pitch his tent. A quick scan and feel around the area with his flashlight allowed him to locate stones and branches, which he tossed out of the area, making for a level, smooth sleeping surface. The next thing to do was unpack the two-man nylon tent, assemble it, and fastened down the corners with aluminum spikes. When the tent was erected, Paul took his flashlight into the surrounding woods to gather wood for a fire. After gathering the wood and twigs, he dug a small fire pit, then started the fire. Immediately the warmth of the fire made Paul feel better. Next, he unpacked his Optimus stove to prepare a hardy dinner of dehydrated spaghetti and meatballs. Dessert was a Snickers bar and a steaming cup of hot chocolate. A couple of after-dinner cigarettes would top off the evening. Around eleven o'clock, with dinner over and the campsite straightened up, Paul gathered more logs for the fire. He would need the additional wood to fight off the cold morning air tomorrow. After all, he had big plans for tomorrow night. The next leg of the trip was not going to be on a blazed trail. Paul would use his compass to take a reading that would allow him to bushwhack his way to the perimeter of the *Double C* ranch, still a little over two miles away. But for now, Paul crawled into the tent and took off his boots. He unrolled his sleeping bag, then took off his down vest, pants, and hooded sweatshirt. He rolled his clothes into a pillow, then zipped himself into his warm sleeping bag. Lying in his bag, Paul thought, *I have to lie around and rest tomorrow during the day, because at night I have to go to work.* It only took Paul about fifteen minutes to fall into a deep uninterrupted sleep.

Chapter 15

Paul woke up at six o'clock because the birds were so noisy it was impossible for him to sleep. He stuck his head outside the warm sleeping bag and was greeted with frosty air that revived him immediately. He finally conjured up the nerve to unzip the bag, crawl out of it, and get dressed as quickly as possible. When he was into his clothes, Paul left the tent to put some wood onto the smoldering embers in the fire pit. At first there was a lot of smoke: then Paul fanned the embers until a flame was catching the wood ablaze. *The heat from the fire felt great on this frosty morning,* Paul thought. There was frost on the tent fly and on the ground surrounding the campsite. Paul put on his boots so he could gather more wood from the surrounding area. When he was done stacking wood, he could relax and make breakfast.

Around seven o'clock, Paul started the Optimus stove to heat water for coffee. While the water was heating, he broke out the plastic container that held six small eggs. He also retrieved a small can of Spam and an aluminum frying pan from his pack. When the flames in the fire pit had died down enough to cook, Paul started breakfast.

The sun was now higher in the sky, and it looked as if it was going to be another beautiful day in the mountains. Paul ate breakfast, drank hot coffee, and relaxed until almost nine o'clock. There was no hurry now, because the cover of darkness was what he needed to accomplish the next phase of his mission. Paul cleaned up the area, then took his canteens and cooking utensils to look for water. According to his map, there should be a spring about one hundred yards down the east side of the mountain. Paul lit a cigarette and started down the steep slope to a point where he spotted two white-tailed deer. They took off immediately when they heard Paul approaching. *They were after the spring water as well,* Paul thought. It took about twenty minutes for Paul to clean the frying pan and pot. He first used dirt and dried leaves as a makeshift Brillo pad to scrap off the heavy soot, then used the spring water to clean them thoroughly. Before leaving the spring, Paul filled his two canteens, and then he made the trip up the steep side of the mountain to his campsite.

Paul put another small pot of water on the stove so he could make hot chocolate. While the stove was heating the water, Paul took out the map to study his route for that evening. He would be traveling light and it was all downhill, so he should make the two miles in less than two hours. However, the darkness could add some time to the trip. The terrain could also be tough in spots, but without a fifty-pound pack on his back it should be a piece of cake.

The hot chocolate hit the spot. Paul smoked another cigarette, then went back inside the tent to lie down. His leg muscles were still a little sore, and Paul was way behind in his beauty sleep. A nap was what he wanted and needed most right now.

Paul woke up at 1:30. He looked at his watch and thought, *Jesus, I must have been tired to sleep that long.* He climbed out of the tent to stretch. Now his back was aching along with his legs. Paul walked it off around the campsite, then checked out his food supply. Lunch and dinner were going to be combined into one big meal. Paul opened a can of chicken noodle soup and set it on the warm embers in the fire pit. He then placed a large pot of water on the stove to boil. His last big dehydrated meal consisted of beef and noodles and apple sauce for dessert. It took an hour or so for the meal to cook and be consumed. Paul looked at the sky directly overhead and noticed that it was starting to cloud over. *Probably a front moving in,* he thought.

Paul policed the area, then broke down the campsite around four o'clock, while there was still some decent daylight. He packed the tent, sleeping bag, and cooking utensils into the backpack, as he kept feeding the fire with the last of his stacked wood. The night was closing in fast, but the fire would keep him warm until he was ready to move out around seven o'clock.

Around six o'clock, Paul started to get ready for the trip down the mountain. He ate several snack foods while looking at the map one more time to review his plan. He squeezed some peanut butter from a backpacking plastic tube onto two slices of white bread and devoured them. He stuffed a couple of Snickers bars into his pocket along with two Hershey bars. Paul then let the fire burn down before dousing it with one full canteen of spring water, then covering the ashes with earth.

Paul inventoried the gear he needed for this leg of the trip. He took the compass, map, flashlight, crossbow and bolts, and one eight-inch-long knife. Paul then cleaned up the area some more and stuffed the backpack into a crevice between two large boulders. He covered the pack with leaves and twigs to conceal its hiding place. Paul then marked the closest tree with a three-inch band by removing its bark using his knife. This maneuver would allow Paul to find this exact spot later that night to begin his escape.

Paul took a compass reading, shot an azimuth, then started walking through the woods. At the top of the mountain there wasn't much foliage due to the high constant winds. The farther down the mountain Paul traveled, the denser the forest became. Without the backpack, Paul made excellent time. He stopped every fifteen minutes or so, to check his compass reading and pick another point to guide him through the woods. Toward the bottom of the valley, the underbrush was very dense. Paul used his knife to hack through some of the thicket but never varied off his course by more than a few feet. He looked at his watch and pressed the backlit button to illuminate the dial. The time was 9:30. He figured that he was about a half hour off his planned timetable, but it didn't matter; the *Double C* was now in front of him, in plain view.

Paul surveyed the area before him and the many outbuildings that made up the huge *Double C* ranch. There were several large mercury vapor lights hanging from poles that illuminated the fronts and backs of some of the larger barns and outbuildings. To the right of those buildings was a huge house. *Obviously the main house*, thought Paul. He climbed over the three-foot-high barbed-wire fence and crossed the open corn field that had long been harvested. The two hundred yards of open field would be dangerous to cross undetected, but no one would be expecting an intruder from this direction. Also, the moon was now being obstructed by some passing clouds, which helped conceal his movements. The closer he came to the main house, the more details Paul was processing in his brain.

Without being detected, Paul made it to the largest outbuilding, which was closest to the main house. He looked around and saw a herd of cattle in a pasture to his right. There was a herd of horses in another pasture to his left. Additionally, there were two cars parked in front of the circular driveway at the main house entrance. Paul skirted along the back of the outbuilding until he came to a single wooden door. He turned the doorknob, which was not locked, and quickly darted inside, making sure the door did not slam shut. The building housed several large tractors and other assorted farm machinery. Paul looked around with his small flashlight and spotted a large silver-painted fuel tank that was clearly labeled: *Diesel Fuel*. Next to that tank was another one labeled: *Gasoline*. Paul needed a diversion, so he searched for and found a ball of baling twine by the huge combine machine. He searched some more and found several burlap bags stacked up in the far corner of the building that had held horse feed at one time. There were also several one-gallon cans of paint thinner, four five-gallon cans of red barn paint, and nine five-gallon buckets of driveway blacktop. He quickly made two long wicks out of the burlap bags, by twisting them like rope and wrapping them with the baling twine. He unscrewed the cap on the diesel fuel tank and shoved in one of the twisted burlap wicks, leaving the last six inches hanging out over the top. He then did the same to the gasoline tank and waited for the two fuels to be soaked up by the burlap wicks. Paul then took a piece of baling twine about twelve inches long and cut it with his knife. He then checked his watch, lit the end of the twine with his lighter, and quickly blew out the flame. The end of the twine was glowing red and would do so until it burned the full twelve-inch length. The twine burned to the end, and Paul again checked his watch. It took four minutes to burn one foot. He then tied baling twine to each burlap wick and cut them to a length of five feet. That would give him about twenty minutes before the fuels ignited. *Of course, that was just a rough estimate, but close enough,* Paul thought.

Paul then retrieved three of the one-gallon cans of paint thinner and placed one can on each of the big farm machinery fuel tanks. He opened the fuel caps of the machinery, set one can of paint thinner next to the opening, and poked a hole in the bottom of the can with his knife. The paint thinner ran down, in, and around the fuel tanks of the three huge pieces of equipment.

Paul went back to the huge fuel tanks to light both baling twine fuses, then quickly blew out the flames. When he was sure both fuses had a nice red glow burning, he checked his watch and left the building the way he had entered. Again, he made sure not to let the door slam shut.

The wind was really starting to blow across the open fields and pastures that surrounded the main house. Paul moved to a place about thirty yards from the main house's front door. There was a small gazebo and wishing well that would give him excellent cover. A sort of flower garden that was well landscaped with shrubs and other plants. In fact, the entire house looked as if it was professionally landscaped. What was more important, though, was that he was at least one hundred yards from the equipment storage outbuilding. Paul put the crossbow together and set the trigger. He then placed a razor-tipped bolt on the rail and waited while he recalled the newspaper clipping of Billy Sharp that Mikey had showed him in the great room. Paul looked at his watch, using only the moonlight, to see that he still had five minutes before the fireworks began.

Paul was expecting the explosion to draw those in the house to the outside, where he could positively identify his target. He looked at his watch again to see that there were two minutes to go. Suddenly there was a tremendous explosion from the equipment outbuilding, followed immediately by another explosion within a few seconds. The explosion and fire even surprised Paul, and he knew it was coming. Within thirty seconds, the front porch lights were being turned on at the main house. People started to come out onto the porch to see what happened. Paul concentrated on the males, to see if he could spot Billy Sharp. Suddenly, two more explosions in rapid succession occurred. There was a five-second pause, then a third explosion rocked the cold night. The entire outbuilding was now engulfed in flames, which were being fanned by the very stiff winds.

Paul saw the people on the porch start to move forward as debris was still falling to the ground from the last explosion. The front part of the house looked as if it were daylight, because the blaze was so intense. Paul still could not find Billy Sharp in the small crowd. Behind him and to the right,

Paul could see two pairs of headlights racing toward the main house. Others obviously had heard the explosion and seen the fire by now and were coming to investigate. Paul waited patiently, but not seeing the intended target began to make him angry. The headlights belonged to two four-wheel-drive pickup trucks with huge knobby tires. They both pulled up to the front of the house and stopped abruptly as the passengers bailed out to ask what was going on. Paul scanned the two occupants from the first truck but didn't see his target. The second truck only had one occupant and Paul didn't recognize him either.

Some of the people standing on the porch were now going back into the house to escape the smoke that was blowing toward them. Paul could hear voices screaming and yelling as to what might have caused the fire and explosion. One person was hollering, "Did you turn off the heaters like you were supposed to? . . . What do mean by that? . . . Never mind him; did you take care of that wiring problem I told you about yesterday?"

The three men standing in a circle were arguing among themselves when they were overtaken by the blowing smoke. They scurried up the front porch steps and into the house. The lone man who had exited one of the pickups was still standing by his open cab door. He then had to duck behind the open door until the smoke cloud passed. Once he thought the air was clear again, he stood up and walked in front of the pickup truck headlights, which were still on. Paul could see that the man was limping and wore an olive drab field jacket. Immediately Paul's adrenaline started pumping faster. He raised the crossbow and took three deep breaths to control his aim. The man wearing the field jacket walked to the truck cab again, as if he had forgotten something. Paul knew it was the same limping bastard that had shot his wife. It had to be. Paul aimed at the man's chest and slowly squeezed the trigger, releasing the aluminum-shafted, razor-tipped bolt like a silent shot. The bolt struck the field-jacketed man in the center of his chest. He immediately grabbed the two inches of bolt still sticking out of his chest with both hands. The look on his face was one of sudden surprise, pain, and shock all rolled up into one expression.

Paul stood up from behind his secure hiding place. In the far distance he could hear sirens heading toward the ranch. The man wearing the field jacket fell to his knees still clutching his chest, as Paul walked up to face him.

The man slowly lifted his head to see who was standing in front of him not offering to help. With a shocked look on his face he managed to say, one word: "You!" The man then fell forward, face first, driving the last two inches of the bolt into his chest. Only the razor tip and blood were visible through the back of his field jacket. Paul was certain that he had just nailed the man who had shot his wife and injected him with snake venom. More importantly though, he was able to look into the victims eyes to watch him die. *Closure at last*, thought Paul.

Suddenly, a voice came from up on the porch saying, "Who in the hell are you?"

Paul ran toward the back of the house. The next thing he heard was voices saying: "Jesus. That's Jack laying there by his truck. . . . Yeah. He's been shot. . . . Is he dead? . . . Yeah, and the guy ran around to the back of the house."

Paul ran around to the other side of the house and headed for the open corn field. He was about one hundred yards across the field when he looked back to see two pairs of headlights coming toward him. They were jumping up and down violently as the vehicles were hitting the uneven rows left by the harvested corn. Paul had about fifty yards to go before reaching the tree line when he heard gunfire behind him. Then the dirt kicked up about ten feet in front of him. Fifteen yards to go. More gunfire. More misses. There was no way for his pursuers to aim steadily as they drove across that corn field. But still, they could get lucky. Paul made it to the barbed-wire fence and jumped over it, heading for the security of the woods. He stopped and turned around so he could locate his pursuers and was surprised to see they were about twenty yards to the left and forty yards behind his position.

Without wasting time, Paul made his way up the mountain face for the two-mile hike back to his campsite. He was still breathing hard from the two-hundred-yard dash and the steep incline that started his climb. After he hiked another five minutes, he stopped to sit on a felled tree trunk. He could barely see the headlights of the two vehicles that were after him, but the fire at the ranch was clearly visible. Paul took out his compass to see where he was in relation to the burning ranch. He took a reading, then started to double-time it up the mountain, satisfied that he was no longer being pursued.

Paul really wanted to smoke a cigarette but fought off the urge until he was well above the valley floor. Another fifteen minutes of steep climbing was reason enough for another short rest. As Paul sat on a large rock, he thought he could hear sounds from the valley below. He listened again more intently and sure enough, he could hear a dog. No. Two dogs. Paul suspected that they were running loose because they were gaining on him too darn fast for a man to be holding onto their leashes. Paul was convinced that the dogs were right on his trail. He looked down the mountain and could just barely see what looked like three lights heading up the mountain. More than likely, they were flashlights. But the lights were far down the mountain and the dogs were getting closer. Paul hated to do what came next, but he had no choice. He looked around and spotted a large rock outcropping and headed for the top. When he was in position, he loaded a bolt into the crossbow and put his knife across his lap. The dogs would have to be taken out if he was to have a chance against the men pursuing him.

Paul waited a few more minutes while listening to the dogs' barks getting louder. Then he heard the leaves rustling to his right. The lead Doberman was trying to scale the rocks. Paul raised the crossbow and squeezed the trigger, hitting the dog in its side. He yelped, fell to the ground, and began whimpering. The second dog was almost on top of Paul when he dropped the crossbow, grabbed the knife, and stood up. He put his right forearm in front of his face and crouched down as the dog jumped and clamped his jaws onto his forearm. With the left hand Paul thrust the knife into the dog's belly as he was knocked backward and to the ground by the weight of the charging Doberman. Paul felt his back slam onto something hard, as he looked to see that the dog was beside him whimpering from the gaping knife wound.

Paul slowly got to his feet to cut the dog's throat, putting him out of his misery, then picked up his crossbow and climbed down the rock outcropping to check the first dog. He was still alive, but barely. Paul looked at the dog and said, "Sorry, pal. But it's you or me." Paul then cut the dog's throat, to finish him off. Looking down the mountain, Paul could see the three lights getting much closer. Their voices were carrying well in the silence of the woods: "I don't hear them anymore. . . ." "I don't hear them either "

"Maybe they lost the scent."

Paul took off up the mountain, trying not to strain his hurting back. When he fell backward off the rock cropping he landed on a flat rock that must have bruised his muscles. He didn't have time to worry about it now. His main objective was to get back to the campsite to gather the rest of his gear, so he could head back to the Jeep. If he were to stop too long, the muscles in his aching back might tighten up even more.

Paul humped up the mountain, stopping every fifteen minutes to check his compass heading. He could not see any more lights heading up the mountain behind him. They must have found the dogs by now and decided that it was not worth trying to continue the search without them.

After another hour and a half, Paul found his campsite. He pulled out the buried backpack and stowed his gear inside so he could start back down the mountain from the other side. The pack only weighed about twenty-five pounds now that the food and water had been used. Unfortunately, each jarring step downhill made his back feel as if someone were punching him in his spine.

Paul lit a cigarette at one of his fifteen-minute scheduled stops to rest his back. He did not take the pack off, because it was too painful. He merely rested his back up against a tree as he pulled out the map and flashlight to see where he would intersect the river below. From his guestimate, it would probably be another half hour. Paul stood up and marched on for another twenty minutes before he heard the sound of the river. He was almost down to the bottom of the mountain, which meant the hike along the river would be more level. No more jarring bounces of the pack on his aching back muscles.

Paul picked up the yellow trail that would lead him back to his Jeep. He lit a cigarette and hiked in the dark as if he hadn't a care in the world. His right forearm was sore from where the dog had clamped onto it, but as far as he could tell there was no puncture wounds thanks to his thick coat. He would check it out better once he got out of the state park. The hiking was now easy compared to what he had done earlier, so much so that Paul only stopped every hour to rest. Paul stopped to get a drink of river water and looked at his watch, which read 4:00. He had another three-hour hike to go, but that was a conservative estimate. He was making great time now that he was on more level ground.

After another hour had passed, Paul walked off the trail about fifty yards to dig a shallow hole in the underbrush. When the hole was about two feet deep, Paul buried the knife, the crossbow, and the three remaining bolts. He did not need them anymore, so there was so reason to take a chance that he could be caught with them. Once the weapons were buried and the brush replaced, it would take an act-of-lottery-type luck for anyone to find them, much less be able to tie them to the murder of the field-jacketed man. Paul hiked back to the main trail to continue on his journey to the parking area.

Paul pushed onward for another hour and a half when he noticed that the trail was widening and the forest up ahead was opening to let in more of the sky, indicating a clearing. He knew the parking area would be coming into view soon.

At the Jeep, Paul put his pack into the back cargo area and stretched his back muscles to relieve some of the tightness. He lit a cigarette, then climbed inside to start the vehicle. He let the engine warm up a little as he pondered what had just transpired. Although Billy Sharp was not taken out as Paul had planned, he knew that there was a sense of accomplishment because he had just evened the score against the bad guys. Paul put the Jeep into gear and headed toward the interstate and home.

Chapter 16

Paul pulled into his garage at noon. He would have been home sooner, but his back muscles kept stiffening. Frequent rest stops were required so he could get out of the Jeep and stretch. He had stopped in Manassas, Virginia, to eat at a fast-food restaurant. He needed access to a drive-through window because he was filthy and unshaven and smelled like something a dog had dragged home.

In the garage, Paul pulled out the backpack, then laid out all the gear on the garage floor. The things that needed washing were placed into one pile, and the rest were stored inside the pack, which Paul took down to the basement.

Paul went into the laundry room and stripped off his filthy clothes. He immediately threw all the dark clothes into the washer and piled the whites on the floor for the second load. He started the washer, then went into the bathroom to take a very hot and steamy shower. As he passed the bathroom mirror, he stopped to look at his face. *I could easily pass for a panhandler on Baltimore Street,* he thought. *Oh well, nothing a little soap and water won't quickly solve.* The hot water hitting Paul's sore back muscles felt great. The shower was just what he needed to begin his recovery. After the shower, Paul shaved, dried his hair, and put on clean jeans and a flannel shirt. He now felt like a million bucks. Paul went to the laundry room, where he put the washed clothes into the dryer, then started a second load of wash for the whites. While the clothes were doing their thing, Paul checked the answering machine and found seven messages. Two were from salespeople. One message was from the realtor, and one was a simple hang-up. One message was from Gary, and the remaining two messages were from Detective McGavin, asking Paul to contact her as soon as possible.

Paul called Gary Roth's number first. The answering machine picked it up, so he left a message for Gary to call him back after eight o'clock. Paul then called police headquarters and asked for Detective McGavin. He was told that she was out on a case, but the desk sergeant said he would leave her a message saying Paul had called.

Paul placed a pot of water on the stove to make a cup of instant coffee. In the refrigerator he found enough food to make a cold-cut sandwich. He added some potato chips and a pickle, then sat down to feast on the meal. When he was finished eating, Paul drank a cup of coffee and smoked a cigarette while staring out the family room patio doors. The sun was bright, the air crisp, and the winds calm. The sound of the dryer buzzer brought him back to reality. Paul took care of switching the clothes from one machine to the other, then went into the bedroom to lie down. He had not been able to lie in the bed that he and Diana shared since her murder. Now he felt that there was some closure to her death, so he tried lying down to see if he could fall asleep. It didn't take Paul very long to find an answer to his question. In less than ten minutes, Paul was out like a light. His back also felt better since he was on a firm mattress, instead of the soft couch. When the dryer buzzer sounded twenty minutes later, he did not budge.

When word reached Billy Sharp that one of his equipment outbuildings and its contents had been destroyed by an intruder, he was very upset. When he was told about his cousin being murdered by an arrow, Billy was enraged. Finally, when he was made aware that the killer had gotten away, he was fit to be tied. Billy Sharp was one upset hombre. He scheduled a meeting at the main house for when he returned from his trip to Florida. Billy was involved with several cartels operating in the Florida Keys area and made frequent trips there to broker or finalize deals. He was in Florida when he first heard that his protection money was not coming in as expected. That was why he had ordered his men to increase their squeeze on strip malls from Philadelphia to Virginia. There were some problems with merchants not paying, but mostly he was doing well with this side business to counter any losses from the crack cocaine business. The increase in state-run lotteries was hurting him, and the new multistate games were a definite drain on his income. Normally the bookie activity, the number rackets, and the protection money were steady income that he could depend on in slow times. When someone interfered with that cash flow, he had to be made an example of in the worst way possible.

Since that one incident in Maryland, when a store owner refused to pay protection money and the messenger was sent to jail in a wheelchair, several other merchants had been bucking the system. Word had traveled to Washington, D.C., and parts of Delaware. It seemed that every week there were more problems for Billy's runners and collectors. The cash flow was down almost 15 percent and getting worse. That's why Billy decided to have his cousin Jack make an example of that damn store owner in Maryland. Even that was botched, when the son of a bitch passed a bag of old newspapers off as the payoff. Billy Sharp now wanted to get some answers regarding this matter, and he wanted them fast. If word got out that he was vulnerable or weak to surprise attacks, he might as well get out of the protection business. There were always sharks and young Turks waiting in the wings to test the current champion.

A limousine was waiting for Billy at the airport. Billy Sharp sat in the back with Leon Acker and John Toby, two of his most trusted men. Billy was tired but wanted to know what they had found out since their call woke him up in Florida. John Toby usually handled the enforcement work when it was needed, and Leon Acker took care of the new business ventures.

With his head hanging halfway down to his chest, John looked at Billy Sharp, then said, "We blew it, Boss. I had Jack set this guy Marco up a couple of weeks ago, and then we went in for the payoff. When it came to the payoff, he ripped us off again. We were making plans to jerk him off the street, to convince him that we meant business, but he disappeared for a few days. Not a sign of him anywhere. Then last night we have the commotion at the ranch. At first, I thought it was just an accident that had occurred, until we found Jack with a goddamned arrow through the heart. Leon got a quick look at the guy standing over Jack's body, and from what he described, it was our boy Marco."

Billy Sharp listened to John's account of what had led them to this point, looked at Leon, then asked, "Are you sure the guy you saw is this Marco character?"

"I'm sure, Boss. He was just standing there looking over Jack's body when I went out onto the front porch. The porch light was on and I got a real good look at his face. It was Marco, all right. I guarantee it, Boss."

Again Billy Sharp listened, but he did not respond for a few seconds as he pondered the situation. He looked out through the tinted limousine window at the Virginia countryside, then asked, "Have we had any more merchants default on payments since this all happened?"

Leon said, "It's too early to tell right now. The hit we took was less than twenty-four hours ago. But I suspect the word is going out through the grapevine, as sure as I'm sitting here. Our collectors will be hitting the Virginia and D.C. areas at the end of the week. By then we will start to hear all types of excuses as to why they can't pay."

John was getting antsy. He said, "That's why we have to move on this Marco character fast. He has to be made an example, or we'll lose all the respect we have built up over the past five years." Billy was thinking the situation over some more. He then asked, "Did we have any TV coverage last night regarding the fire and homicide?"

Neither John nor Leon answered. They both hung their heads down a little as if they were being scolded by a parent. Billy could see that he had struck a nerve, then asked, "Well, what are you two holding back from me? Did we have TV coverage or not?"

John finally cleared his throat, then said, "Boss. That's the worst part. You know how it is down here in the sticks. Somebody blows their nose and it makes the six o'clock news. The local station picked up on the fire and had live helicopter coverage on the eleven o'clock news. They made a big deal out of saying there were several explosions and a possible homicide."

Billy's face was getting red as his anger mounted. He asked, "Do you mean they actually televised the goddamned incident? Jesus Christ. We'll have every punk within one hundred miles trying to take a piece of our action, if they think we are vulnerable. I want that Marco son of bitch dead. I want him taken out in a very public way so everyone knows who wasted him. Is that understood? Do you think you can handle that without screwing it up?"

John knew it was his responsibility to respond. He finally said, "I'll take care of it personally, Boss. Enforcement is my area and Jack had failed to get the job done. I know he was your cousin, but he failed twice."

"Don't worry about Jack. I only took him into the organization as a favor to my family. He would do OK when it came to the small stuff, but this business with Marco should have never gone on as long as it has. If you say you're going to take care of the job, that's good enough for me. Just get it done fast."

As the limousine pulled into the half-mile-long driveway leading to the main house, Billy got a firsthand look at the damage. He could see that the equipment outbuilding was totally destroyed. Two other smaller outbuildings, barely standing, were a total loss. What hurt the most was seeing the main house charred and covered in soot. Fortunately, the firefighters were able to keep the wind-blown flames from destroying the structure. For that, Billy was grateful, but the place looked as bad as he had ever seen it look.

The limousine stopped at the front door where there were still chalk outlines of Jack's body on the asphalt. Yellow crime scene tape was blowing in the wind, and the air smelled like an old barbecue grill. It sickened him to see the place like this. Billy finally said to John, "Get that son of bitch who did this to my house."

The phone rang at five o'clock, waking Paul from his deep sleep. He reached for the phone and groggily said, "Hello."

"Hi, yourself. When did you get back in town?"

"Oh. Hi, Detective. I got home around noon and called you.

Didn't you get my message?"

"I received your message but have been too busy to get back to you. You know, crime never takes a holiday. Did you have a good trip?"

"Yeah, that's what they say. And yeah, my trip was just fine. It was exactly what I needed. The weather was great and the scenery was even better. What did you want to talk to me about? Your messages sounded as if something was urgent."

"That's great to hear, Paul. Well, I found out that our boy Steven Green was not just a two-bit hood working with Clark Kent as a shakedown artist."

"No? Who else did he work for?"

"It appears he has ties with a much bigger fish named William Sharp. Ever hear of him?"

"No. Can't say that I have. Is he from around here?"

"Yes and no. He has business dealings from Philly to Virginia. As a matter of fact, his personal residence had a bit of arson last night and there was also a homicide on the property by means of a crossbow. Can you believe that? A damn crossbow."

"That sure does sound strange. I didn't know they still made those things. Goes to show you what I know."

"Yeah, well whatever. Listen, Paul. I was thinking that when we receive copies of the crime scene photos, you could come in to take a look at them here at headquarters."

"Sure, if you think it will do any good. What does any of this have to do with the murder of my wife, Detective?"

"The man that was found murdered by the crossbow is more than likely the limping field-jacketed person we have been looking for."

Paul had to say something, but what? He finally managed to say, "That's great, Detective. If that's the guy who killed my wife, then this case is closed."

"Perhaps. I don't know if I would go as far as to say the case is closed. We still have someone out there who murdered Steven Green and now Jack McCan. That's his name by the way, Jack McCan." "Well, when you get the pictures let me know and I'll come down to take a look at them, for whatever good it will do."

Paul was a little taken aback by the speed at which the police had put together the Green and Sharp connection. More surprising was how the Jack McCan puzzle was put together so rapidly. *Damn*, he thought. *This Detective McGavin is good.*

After hanging up with Detective McGavin, Paul went into the kitchen to place a pot of water on the stove for coffee. His back was a little stiff from sleeping on it for the past several hours, so he stretched a little and took two aspirins to deaden the pain in his lower back. As the water was heating, he called Gary Roth to see if he was home. To Paul's surprise, Gary picked up the phone on the first ring.

"Hello."

"Hey, Gar.' It's me, Paul. I'm calling from home." *That way Gary will know the line is not clear,* thought Paul.

"Welcome back to the land of the workingman. Listen. I thought you didn't want me to call you until after eight. It's only six o'clock now."

"I know, but I was disturbed from my deep sleep anyway, so I figured I would give you a call. Anyway, I received your message. What's up?"

"Our mutual friend would like to see you when you have some time. I think yesterday would have been too late, if you know what I mean?"

The water was boiling on the stove, so Paul turned off the burner and poured his cup full. He knew Gary was referring to Mikey, and it sounded as if it was rather urgent. Paul said, "I see. Well, I'm going to be tied up here for another hour or so; then I will pay a visit to our friend. Tell him I'll be in to see him between eight and nine o'clock."

"OK. Will do. Take care and I'll see you around, brother." Paul put half-and-half into his cup with one teaspoon of sugar.

As he stirred the coffee, he was trying to think of reasons why Mikey wanted to see him. Only one reason came to mind. It had to be related to the Billy Sharp incident down in Virginia.

Paul smoked a cigarette and finished his coffee as he folded the clothes from the dryer and put them away. He then drew a hot bath to soak his aching back. Hot, moist heat was the best remedy for lower back pain, as he had learned over the years. Besides, it gave him another excuse to sit around and relax some more. With the portable phone close by, an ashtray, cigarettes, and coffee at arm's reach, he was set.

After Paul had been soaking in the tub for about twenty minutes, the phone rang. He was half-asleep when he heard its ugly electronic bell resonate in the small bathroom. He picked up the portable and said, "Hello."

"Mr. Marco, you and I have some unfinished business."

Paul sat up in the tube. His brain was telling him that this was the same voice that had given him the runaround directions for the payoff last Saturday. He then smiled and said, "Don't tell me you spent all that newspaper already?"

"I see we are in a good mood today, Mr. Marco. Well, let me see if I can change that. Your bill is now $250,000 and you have until Friday to deliver."

"Or else what, asshole? You don't seem to be getting the picture here, pal. I'm not going to give you any money. So why don't you go find someone else to play with, like a good little brat."

Paul wanted to slam the phone down, but it was a portable, so the best he could do was punch the little power button. He lit another cigarette, then stepped out of the tub. His back felt much better. Paul stretched a little, then swallowed two more aspirins to keep the edge off the pain.

After dressing in a long-sleeve shirt, sweater, and dark green Dockers, Paul grabbed his coat and headed for the garage. He started the Jeep, then pulled up to the mailbox to retrieve his mail and newspapers that had accumulated over the last few days. He quickly scanned the mail to find that 90 percent of it was junk and the remaining 10 percent was bills. *Just like normal*, thought Paul. Paul turned on the radio and headed downtown to meet with Mikey. As Paul was driving, he kept thinking about the voice on the telephone. *Who could it be? Why was he so insistent on trying to collect money that I don't have? Why was he pushing so hard after what I did to their ranch? Clark Kent, first crippled by me, then murdered by someone else while he was in jail. Steven Green, tortured and murdered by me, then given a Colombian necktie by someone else. Jack McCan, murdered with a crossbow bolt. Last, the infamous Mr. Billy Sharp has his place Zippoed while he was away, according to Detective McGavin.*

Gee, you would think that maybe he would start getting used to the idea that I'm not to be fooled with.

Paul pulled into the parking lot of the Cell Block at eight fifteen. He climbed out of the Jeep into a cold biting wind. Paul looked up at the sky, and the dark gray overhanging clouds made it appear that it might snow. It was certainly cold enough, Paul thought.

Inside the bar, he took a seat in the back as he had done on the previous visits. The bartender nodded at him, then picked up the phone behind the bar. A three-second conversation and then the phone was hung up again. The bartender simply looked at Paul and nodded yes and waved his thumb toward the kitchen. Paul went through the great room entrance routine by someone he did not know. Paul looked at the man and asked, "Is it Rocco's night off?"

The bodyguard who could have made two of Paul, said, "No.

He's taking care of some business for the boss."

Seeing the replacement bodyguard was not a talkative fellow, Paul let the conversation drop.

He entered the great room to see Mikey and Gary by the big desk at the other end of the room. Mikey waved for Paul to come forward. Gary, whose back was toward Paul, turned to look at him, waved, then turned back around to face Mikey.

"Sit down, Pauly. I asked Gary to be here for this meet. I hope you don't mind?"

"Not at all. What's all this about? Gary sounded as if something was hot and you needed to see me like yesterday."

Mikey looked at Gary, then turned his attention to Paul, saying, "Listen. Pauly, it may be time for you to take a little vacation. I don't mean one to Virginia to go backpacking or whatever it is you did the past few days. I'm talking a real vacation until things blow over a little."

Paul, miffed by Mikey's gloomy attitude, responded, "What's the matter with you guys? Did somebody die around here? I feel fine and I certainly don't need a vacation."

Gary turned toward Paul and said, "Listen to what Mikey is saying, Paul. You're in deep shit and it ain't safe for you right now."

"What in the hell are you two talking about?"

Mikey said, "Maybe you haven't heard, but that guy Billy Sharp has put a contract out on your head. He must be really pissed off at you because the hit is for twenty-five grand. Do you have any idea how many guys would pop somebody for twenty-five large? Pauly, you have got to get out of town for a while and lay low."

Paul was surprised to hear about the contract out on him. His face showed it, too.

Gary asked, "I guess you haven't heard about this, until now?" "You got that right," said Paul. "Well, let me level with you guys."

Paul told Mikey and Gary about his backpacking trip to Virginia. When he was through talking, Mikey said, "What in the hell is the matter with you, Pauly? I told you this guy Billy Sharp was one son of a bitch. But did you listen? Hell, no."

Paul was quiet for a few seconds, then said, "Well, I don't give a damn about Billy Sharp, and my goal is to take him down. I want that scumbag taken out for good. I'm not leaving town and I'm not going to run. So both of you might as well get it through your thick heads when I say that I'm in this for the long haul."

Gary looked away from Paul and into Mikey's eyes, saying, "Well, he can't do it alone. I guess we'll have to help him."

Mikey looked at Paul, then said, "If that is your final word, all I need to know is how can we help?"

Paul sat back in his chair and with a big smile on his face said, "I'll need a few things from your back room."

Chapter 17

Paul and Gary left the great room to go upstairs to have a drink. Mikey was already busy on the phone and therefore couldn't join them. At the bar, Gary ordered two draft beers, then asked, "Paul, how are you going to dodge the people out there looking to fulfill the contract?"

"I don't know for sure. I'll change my habits so they can't lie in wait. You know what they say, we're all creatures of habit. Anyway, I won't be able to stay at the house for a while; that's for certain. I guess I can always take a room at one of the downtown hotels."

"You could stay at my place, if you want."

"Thanks. But no way, Gar.' I don't want you or anyone else getting hurt because of the mess I'm in right now."

"Hey, Paul. I have an idea. I know a guy who knows another guy that may have a secluded place where you could hole up for a while. In fact, it's perfect. Do you know where Catoctin Mountain is outside Hagerstown, Maryland?"

"Sure I do. It's about an hour-and-a-half drive due west. As a matter of fact, Hagerstown sits right next to Interstate 81, I believe."

"That's right, Paul. This guy has a hunting cabin on the Catoctin Mountain. Maybe twenty miles on this side of Hagerstown. You don't have to actually go into town to get to this outpost, if you know what I mean. This dude hunts turkey and deer when they're in season up there in the high country. Well, the gun season for both of those type game doesn't open until late November, so the cabin is not in use right now. I was up there several years ago when he first bought the place. It sure is rustic, no phone or TV. He has electricity and running water up there, but not much else in the line of creature comforts. What I'm saying is it ain't no Holiday Inn, but you would probably like it up there just fine."

"That really sounds perfect for me, Gar.' Let me know what he says after you ask him if it's OK for me to use the place for a while."

"There won't be a problem. He owes me a couple of favors, so I'm sure it will be OK. Order me another beer while I use the phone in the back to call him right now. Do you have a pen and paper I can use?"

Paul gave Gary a bar napkin and the pen from his shirt pocket, and Gary went to one of the wooden phone booths located in the back of the bar to make his call. Paul finished his first beer, then ordered them two more while he waited.

About ten minutes passed before Gary returned to the bar saying, "Jesus Christ, this place is way the hell out in the sticks. Everything is set. Here's the directions."

Gary handed Paul the bar napkin on which he had drawn a crude map and took a long drink of his beer while Paul studied the map. Gary then asked, "Does it make sense to you?"

"Sure. I have a very good idea where this place is located." "Good. Now, my friend said that when you pull off Interstate 68 and onto Alternate Route 40, bear to the right. You then drive for twenty miles or so and you will come to a combination gun store, bait shop, and bar. It's called the Angle Inn. I wrote it on the back of the napkin. Anyway, go into the bar and ask for a guy named Lenny. Tell Lenny you're the person renting Tom Yingling's cabin. He will give you the keys with no questions asked. Tom is calling Lenny right now, to let him know that you're coming. Your name is now going to be Danny Nuncie. Got all that?"

Paul was studying the back side of the napkin, then with a smile said, "Danny Nuncie? What made you come up with that name?"

"Hey, I'm just trying to save your ass. I don't know. It was the first thing that popped into my head. So, sue me."

Paul laughed, then mentioned, "Nobody comes up with a name like Nuncie off the top of their head. Smith, Jones, Brown, yes. But Nuncie. I don't think so."

"Pauly, what the hell do you care? A name is a name. Besides, I had a great-uncle named Anthony Nuncieo. Everybody called him Tony Nuncie. What's so funny about that name?"

Now they were both laughing and ordered two more beers.

Gary said, "One more thing. Tom said that the main breaker panel is located in the back of the cabin, inside the bedroom closet. The water shutoff valve is under the sink inside the bathroom. He said it would take about an hour for hot water to be available once you turn on the main water and electric. You may want to let the water run for about fifteen minutes to clear out the pipes, since it has been shut down for over six months. Tom suggested that you still boil all your drinking water, just to be safe."

"Sounds as if this place is just heavenly," laughed Paul. "I appreciate the loan of the place and will take care of it, Gary."

"Yeah, I know you will. Oh, Tom said blankets and cooking utensils are already up there. All you need to do is bring food and clothes. He said something about a supermarket located about five miles from where you turn off the main road to head up the mountain. This guy Lenny at the Angle Inn can give you better directions when you pick up the keys."

Paul and Gary drank one more beer for the road. Then Paul asked Gary for one more favor. He wanted him to pick up his mail and newspapers so it would look as if he were still at home. Paul explained that he didn't want to put a hold on the mail or cancel the paper because it might send up a red flag. Gary said he understood and that he would have it taken care of for as long as Paul needed. They parted company as Gary went out the front door and Paul went out the back to get into his Jeep. He started the vehicle and headed toward home, thinking about all that had happened since he came home from Virginia.

The night air was bitterly cold and Paul had the heater turned up full blast as he traveled northward. The four beers he drank were making him feel sleepy, so he lowered the window a little to revive himself. That did the trick. His back felt surprisingly good, even though he had not taken any more aspirin since he left the house earlier.

Paul was thinking about all the stuff he would need for the stay at the cabin. Warm clothes, his rifle, and the cell phone were at the top of his mental list. He could go food shopping after he settled in at the cabin. Paul thought he'd better take some extra cash just in case he needed it, along with his sleeping bag and a shovel. This time of year, even a four-wheel-drive might need some help in the mountains of Maryland.

Paul pulled the Jeep into the garage and closed the automatic door to keep out the stiff wind. He opened the back cargo door to lower the backseat. That would give him much more room to put his stuff. While he was in the garage, Paul put one five-foot shovel, a pair of strap-on emergency snow chains, and his compact twelve Volt portable air compressor into the Jeep. He then went into the house to check the answering machine. There were no messages. He went into the living room and turned on the front-porch light. Paul then went into the master bedroom and pulled out a four-foot-long zipper-style duffel bag from the back of the closet. He set the canvas bag on the bed and started filling it with clothes and toiletries.

It only took Paul about fifteen minutes to pack what he needed. He went into the basement and opened the gun cabinet to retrieve an old World War II M-1 carbine. It was in excellent condition and was a gift from a longtime friend. He took the four magazines that held twenty rounds each and several boxes of ammo. The M-1 was semiautomatic, light, but very accurate and deadly in the right hands. Paul put the weapon and duffel bag into the Jeep, then raised the garage doors so he could retrieve his cell phone from across the road. He looked around the property wondering if it was still safe for him to be in his own home. There were contract killers looking for him now, so he didn't want to take any unnecessary chances.

Paul walked down the driveway, crossed the road, and went into the woods to find the felled tree with the hidden rucksack. The front-porch light gave him bearings like a searchlight guided ships in the dark. As he was opening the rucksack, he thought that he saw a shadow moving in front of the house. Paul thought maybe it was just a passing cloud playing tricks with the moonlight. He stood up for a better view and saw what looked like two shadows moving around the outside of his house. He immediately reached into the rucksack and pulled out the silenced .22-caliber Ruger. Out of instinct, he ejected the clip to make sure he had plenty of ammo. Then he partially pulled the slide back to make sure a round was in the chamber.

Paul quietly walked out of the woods and came up behind his house using the windbreak made up of tall pine trees as cover. He could now see one man with a weapon in his hand looking into the master bedroom window. With Paul's Jeep in the garage and the lights on in the house, they must have thought he was still inside. Paul figured he had the element of surprise in his favor. They thought he was inside the house and would never expect him to come up from the rear. Paul took off the Ruger's safety, then swiftly but very quietly moved across the lawn in a crouched position. Before the man at the bedroom window knew what was happening, Paul fired two rounds into the base of his skull.

Paul let the man drop to his knees, then helped him slowly fall the rest of the way to the ground so he wouldn't make too much noise. Paul looked around for the second shadow but didn't see him anywhere. Figuring that number two was out front or maybe already in the house, Paul knew the best thing to do was wait. Number two would eventually come out looking for his buddy. Paul lay down flat beside the wooden deck, listening to his heart pounding. After about thirty or forty seconds passed, Paul could hear the second man's voice coming from around the corner of the house where the garage was located. He was calling his buddy, saying in a very low tone, "Ron. Ron!"

Paul's heart began to pound faster. His adrenaline was pumping, but he had to hold his position a little longer. The next time he heard the voice calling Ron, Paul guessed his enemy was about fifteen feet from the other side of the deck. Paul heard the man's foot hit the decking floorboards. Paul knew he was exactly twenty feet from where he was lying in wait. Each step would bring the man about three feet closer. Paul listened for the next footstep, then the next. Suddenly Paul jumped up, firing two quick shots into his enemy's chest. *The man looked more surprised than hurt,* Paul thought. After all, a .22-caliber pistol does not pack much of a punch, but the bullet velocity was extremely high. The man dropped his handgun as he clutched his chest. Paul watched him fall face-first onto the wood decking.

Paul walked up to the man lying on the deck to feel his carotid pulse. There was none to be found. Paul then rolled him onto his back to see if he recognized the man. No such luck. *Probably a contract killer looking for some quick bucks,* thought Paul. Momentarily leaving the man on the deck, Paul walked over to the guy lying by the bedroom window. There was no need to check for his pulse because Paul knew he was dead. He lifted his head by the hair to look at his face but didn't recognize him either. *I guess they were going to split the cash,* thought Paul.

Paul retrieved the two hit men's weapons and put them into his Jeep. Two 9mm Berettas. *Nice weapon, but a bit too messy for close-up work*, thought Paul. He checked their pockets for a wallet or ID and maybe a clue as to who they were but found nothing. Paul then walked back over to the rucksack in the woods to pick up the cell phone. He put the silenced .22 back into the rucksack and stuffed it into the hallowed tree trunk.

While walking back to the house, Paul wondered how the two men arrived at his home. There was no car or truck in the immediate area that he could see. He thought, *Maybe they were dropped off and someone would be coming back for them later.* Paul was trying to decide what to do with the two bodies lying outside his house. At first he thought about dragging them into the woods to rot. But sometimes people rode horses back there making that idea too chancy. He thought about burying them, but that, too, would make it hard to explain if their bodies were found in close proximity to his house. Besides, it would take too long and his back was not in the best condition. *Wait a minute. I don't know these guys. There is no way for anyone to tie the two dead men to me,* thought Paul. *I just need to get rid of them so if or when they are found nobody would know they were killed here on my property.*

Paul went into the garage and emptied the Jeep. He then pulled out a plastic painters' tarpaulin to line the inside of the cargo area. The next part was going to be very difficult for Paul to accomplish with his aching back. Paul took the wheelbarrow from the garage and rolled it to where the body was lying on the deck. He rolled the body until he had it by the edge of the deck. Paul lined up the wheelbarrow and corpse, then rolled the body into it. That was the easy part. Paul wheeled the body into the garage and struggled to get the dead man into the back of the Jeep and onto the plastic. Paul took the wheelbarrow outside to the back bedroom window and had one hell of a time lifting the dead man into it so he could also be moved. Paul's back was holding up fairly well, but for how long? Back inside the garage, he struggled with the corpse to get it next to the other one already lying on the tarpaulin.

Paul closed the Jeep cargo door and headed for the Prettyboy Reservoir Dam. As he drove, Paul scanned both sides of the road leading to his house for a parked car or truck. He didn't see any sign of a parked vehicle anywhere.

Prettyboy was only twenty minutes away from Paul's house. It was a place that was dark, secluded, and very quiet at night. Paul pulled the Jeep next to the spillway, which was dumping tons of water into the Gunpowder River below, backed the Jeep up to the spillway railing, then got out to open the cargo door. A quick look around made Paul feel confident that he was definitely alone. He then climbed inside the Jeep and pushed the first body out the door and through the railing. He watched it free-fall for ninety feet, then splash into the water below. Paul then pushed and rolled body number two out and over the spillway. After Paul saw the second body splash down, he could hardly see the first body, as it was already making its way down the river with the swift current. Paul rolled up the plastic and tossed it over the side as well. He closed the cargo door, then climbed back into the driver's seat. His back didn't feel too bad at this point, but he sure would have liked a couple more aspirins.

On the drive back to his garage, Paul looked for a parked vehicle of some kind that would have been transportation for the two hit men. Again he saw none, and he decided to forget it for now. However, he would keep an eye out for a pickup vehicle cruising the area. Paul went into the house to place a very large pot of water on the stove. He then went into the garage to put his gear back into the Jeep for the trip to the cabin. While the water was heating, Paul checked the answering machine and was relieved to find that no one had called. He took a couple of aspirins and hunted for his good five-cell battery flashlight, which he found in the bottom kitchen junk drawer.

When the water came to a boil, Paul turned on the outside lights for the back deck. He immediately saw a small bloodstain where the second man had fallen. The cold temperature and the small-caliber holes of a .22 did not allow too much blood to escape the corpse. Paul took the boiling water out onto the deck and washed the blood away as best he could. With his flashlight in hand, Paul also checked for blood under the bedroom window and possible splatter spots on the window itself. The grass concealed any outward signs of blood, and the window looked clean. Paul was not too concerned about how things looked, so he went back into the house to smoke a cigarette. While sitting in the kitchen, Paul thought to himself, *Is this how life is going to be? For how long?* Paul grabbed a full bottle of aspirin from the medicine cabinet and stuck it into his jacket pocket. He took a quick look around the house, secured the doors and turned off the lights on his way out to the garage. As he passed the family room to turn off more lights, he looked at the coffee table, thinking, *Where in the world does dust come from? I just dusted that table two days ago.*

Paul headed down Interstate 83 to the Baltimore Beltway. He turned west on Interstate 70 and traveled another fifty or so miles. The gas tank was now running on fumes, so he pulled off the interstate to fill the tank and buy a large hot coffee. His back had stiffened up while he was driving, so Paul stretched and walked around a little before taking two more aspirins washing them down with the hot, stale-tasting coffee. His stomach was telling him it was time to eat something, but there was only junk food at the gas station. Paul asked the attendant if there was a restaurant or diner around where he could get a decent meal. The attendant pointed down the road, saying, "T-bone's Bar & Grill, two miles straight ahead, has good chow and cold beer."

Paul thanked the attendant, then headed for T-bone's. It was now almost midnight. Paul pulled the Jeep into the parking lot, which, to his surprise, was packed with a few cars and many pickup trucks. Paul pulled into an empty spot at the far end of the parking lot. Before he left the Jeep, he grabbed one of the 9mm pistols he took from the hit men and tucked it into his waistband behind his back. His jacket covered the weapon nicely. It was uncomfortable, to say the least, but going into a strange place could mean trouble for an outsider like himself.

The neon sign over the door read: *Open.* Paul walked into the smoke-filled tavern and immediately saw a long bar that was filled with patrons. They hardly gave Paul a second look. To the right was an open doorway, where Paul spotted tables and chairs. *Obviously the grill,* he thought. Paul walked through the door opening and was immediately impressed by the neatness of the place. A young woman came up to him and asked, "Table for one?"

"That's right, darlin.' Just me and myself."

The young waitress seated Paul at a small table along the right side wall. There must have been fifteen little tables in the small cozy place and only a few were empty. Paul ordered the house special, which consisted of T-bone steak, a baked potato, two vegetables, a small salad, and rolls. Add a cold beer or two and Paul was ready to take on the world.

On one of the many trips the waitress made to his table, Paul managed to ask, "How come the place is so crowded this late on a weeknight?"

The waitress looked at Paul rather strangely, then said, "What else are people going to do out here in God's country?"

Paul watched the woman walk away to wait on other tables and noticed that she sure looked good in those tight-fitting jeans. *Nice butt and very shapely legs*, he thought. Paul ordered coffee after his meal and was very satisfied with T-bone's food and hospitality. He paid the tab, left miss nice legs a hefty tip, then headed back to the Jeep.

Paul pulled the 9mm from behind his back and laid it on the seat next to him. He then started the Jeep and went back to the interstate for the final leg of his journey. He should easily be at the Angle Inn before the two o'clock closing time mandated by Maryland law. The moon was now hidden by dense cloud cover. The wind was a brisk twenty miles per hour, and the temperature was hovering in the low teens. Western Maryland already had two snowfalls this year, and it felt as if another might be on the way. The interstate had snow piled high on both sides. Paul continued to push forward and upward in altitude until he saw the sign for Alternate Route 40. Gary had said to bear right and go about twenty miles to find the Angle Inn.

Paul did as he was supposed to do, then pushed the trip meter button so he could tell when he had traveled twenty miles. Route 40 was a two-lane country road. It was dark, curvy, and steadily climbing into the mountains. Paul checked the trip meter to see that he still had ten miles to travel. Every now and then he would catch a glimpse of a house on one side of the road or the other. A few more miles down the road, he saw a closed gas station and grocery store. After traveling two more miles, he actually saw a yellow flashing light in front of the combination volunteer fire department garage and feed store. Another mile farther and the darkness was invaded by a bright sign with neon red letters reading: *Angle Inn*.

Paul pulled into the parking lot next to the only two other cars there. His immediate thought was: *They must not have good food here*. He parked the Jeep, placed the nine millimeter behind his back, and exited the vehicle. He slowly walked up to the front door, opened it, then walked inside. There were three people in the bar area. Two were cleaning up and the other was sitting at a table, adding the nightly receipts, Paul suspected.

Paul could feel the three pairs of eyes staring through him as he said, "I'm looking for Lenny. Is he around?"

One of the men behind the bar wiping beer glasses said, "Depends on who's asking."

"My name's Danny Nuncie. He's expecting me to pick up some keys."

The man sitting at the table rustling with slips of paper said, "I'm Lenny." He motioned for Paul to come forward, then stated, "Have a seat."

Paul sat in the chair opposite Lenny. Paul could still see the other two men in the mirror hanging on the wall behind Lenny's back. Lenny then said, "Joe! Toss me the keys to Yingling's place."

Joe was one of the men behind the bar. He reached under the bar and came up with a set of keys. Paul was watching him closely in the mirror in case he came out from behind the bar with a weapon instead of keys. Joe tossed the keys across the bar, and Lenny snatched them from the air, saying, "Here you go. I won't ask you to show me ID proving who you really are, because I would have to bet you made up a name like Nuncie."

Paul took the keys and laughingly said, "That would be a good bet, Lenny. I understand that my presence at Yingling's cabin will be kept quiet?"

"Forget about Yingling's place. No one has gone up there in at least six months. You will be incognito for as long as you want or until hunting season starts. Whichever comes first."

Lenny told Paul where the supermarket was located and also gave him detailed instructions on how to find Yingling's cabin in the woods. It was so well hidden Lenny didn't think Paul could find it in the dark. Paul tried to convince him that it was OK, but Lenny was very persuasive. Lenny said, "Besides, the supermarket won't open until eight o'clock, so you might as well stay in the back. I have a small office with a couch back there. You can sack out for a few hours, and Mary will wake you when she opens up in the morning."

As much as Paul wanted to get to the cabin, he realized that Lenny was making sense. Paul went out to the Jeep to get his duffel bag. In the back room he lay down on the soft, uncomfortable couch. He covered himself with the old horse blanket Lenny had left for him. After tossing about for a few minutes, Paul placed two couch seat cushions on the floor and covered himself with the blanket. His back felt much better on a solid surface. It was every bit of ten minutes before Paul was sound asleep.

Chapter 18

A farmer's telephone call to the local police department reporting an abandoned car in the woods had no significant meaning at the time. That the car was found about one mile from Paul's house, however, was important. The county police ran a check on the plates and found that they had been stolen a week ago from a 1997 Dodge Neon while it was in a downtown parking garage. The car the plates were now attached to was a stolen 1994 Ford Escort, taken from a Baltimore City neighborhood a few days earlier. The police had the car towed to an impound lot in downtown Baltimore, where it was dusted for prints as a routine procedure. The rightful owner of the car was then notified to come downtown and retrieve his vehicle.

The very next day, a young couple were walking their dogs along the trail that bordered the Gunpowder River. They called police to report that a body was floating in a shallow pool of water about two miles south of the Prettyboy Reservoir Dam. The police investigation showed that the male body had been shot twice in the back of the head. The following day, farther upriver, a couple of kids were playing when they found a second body. The most recent male body had two gunshots in the chest area. The police were becoming concerned that there might be more bodies in the river, so a massive search around the reservoir area was conducted. The six o'clock news sensationalized the entire series of events, because northern Baltimore County was normally an area free of crime. There were interviews with residents living close to the dam who were saying how scared they were now that crimes such as these were showing up in their neighborhood. One woman said that she was going to start locking her doors at night, something she had not done in more than thirty years. Finally a police spokesperson was interviewed, and he said, "At this time we do not know if the two killings are related. Also, preliminary evidence shows the men were probably murdered elsewhere and then dumped at the reservoir site. Therefore, there is really no reason for the citizens living around the reservoir to be overly concerned." The coroner examined the two corpses and ruled them to be homicides. There were no ballistics checks run because the hollow-point .22-caliber slugs were too shattered to perform the test.

Captain Thiemeyer was in his office reviewing the case folder that Detective McGavin had put together. He noted that the fingerprints IDd the two men as Jerry Morgan from New York and Darnel Philips, also from New York. Both men had a history of crime that went back to their juvenile days. According to the report, both men had served time together in Angola State Penitentiary a few years ago for armed robbery and assault, respectively.

Detective McGavin knocked on the captain's door asking, "You wanted to see me, Captain?"

"Yeah. Come in and sit down, Theresa. I was looking over the report you did on the two bodies fished out of the Gunpowder and have a few questions."

"Shoot."

"Well, I see you IDd them and did some background stuff here, but I don't see anything that tells me why they were killed. Do you have any thoughts?"

"Now that you mention it, I do. At first it looked as if these two guys teamed up after being released from Angola back in 1993. They probably got into some drugs, smuggling, or numbers running, whatever, and then crossed the wrong guy."

"Sounds funny to me, Theresa. These two turning up dead at the same time, in the same place, tell my cop gut we should look a little deeper. Did you run their prints through the computer for possible matches with pending cases?"

"Ah, no. I mean, not yet. I ran their prints and IDd them. But since they were already dead, I didn't see any point to rushing to check their prints against pending cases."

"Theresa, I don't expect it to turn up anything. I'm just pulling at straws on this one. It must be my cop mind saying something is odd about these two turning up dead here in Maryland and not in New York."

"Well, I did talk to the NYPD, and they told me the two of them have been clean for the past year. No arrest or trouble and their PO [parole officer] said Jerry was working in the same place for almost six months. He worked in a laundry, I think. As for Darnel, he just started a new job last month as a cook in some restaurant. Before that, he worked at a hotel, in the housekeeping area."

Captain Thiemeyer kept looking at the pictures of the two deceased ex-cons, then said, "Do you see what I'm saying? It doesn't add up. Both of these guys were doing OK until recently, so what could they have done here in Maryland that caused someone to fill them with lead?"

"I'm beginning to see what you mean. I guess I treated this a little too routinely. Maybe I'll do a little more digging to see what I can turn up."

"Sounds good, Theresa. Keep me posted."

"Will do. Say, did I tell you that I talked to Paul Marco a few days ago? I told him that I wanted him to come in to look at the crime scene photos from that arson and murder job down in Virginia."

"Yeah? So what happened?"

"Nothing. I called him again two days ago and left a message, but he never called back. I went out to his house yesterday, but no one was home. The mail was not in the box and no newspapers were lying on the lawn. It's almost as if he has disappeared."

"I wouldn't make too much of it right now. He's probably still trying to get over the death of his wife. Maybe he took another trip or something and a neighbor is bringing in the mail and newspapers."

"I guess. You're probably right. But my cop gut says something may be wrong."

"Forget it for now. We have two more unsolved homicides on our hands, and the commissioner is breathing down my neck because of all the bad press lately."

Theresa McGavin left Thiemeyer's office to go see her friend Pat Dershan. Pat was looking over some printouts when she looked up to see her buddy Theresa walking toward her.

Right away Pat pushed out both of her hands as she smiled, saying, "No! Whatever it is that you want, the answer is definitely no. Do I make myself clear?"

"Hey, what has gotten you so defensive all of a sudden? I came here to see if you wanted to grab some lunch."

Pat, skeptical of her friend's motives, finally put her hands by her side, then quickly said, "No way. No! I'm not falling for that, Theresa. It's freezing outside, so why don't you tell me what you really want?"

"OK, you've got me. I need—"

"Please, don't make the next words out of your mouth be *a favor*."

"I'm sorry, buddy, but it's *very i*mportant this time."

"It's always important with you. Do you see this pile of request forms on my desk? I have enough work here for three people." "Pat, that just goes to show how good you are at this technical crap. Nobody would ask you for data if you weren't any good at delivering."

"That's it. Go ahead. Butter me up with one of those fake warm and fuzzy comments. Yeah, like I give a good rat's behind about compliments. Why don't you tell those damn bean counters upstairs to give me a raise, since I'm so valuable?"

"Pat, if it were up to me, I would give you two raises and a week off with pay. So, what do you say we go get a bite to eat and I'll fill you in on what I need?"

"Sure. Why not? This pile of stuff will still be here tomorrow, the next day, and the day after that."

"There you go, Pat. Now, don't you feel better?"

The dynamic duo left police headquarters to go around the corner to eat at Rocky's Bar and Grill. They ordered cheese steak sub sandwiches, French fries, and, so they wouldn't feel too guilty, two Diet Cokes. While they ate lunch, Theresa told Pat what she needed.

Pat finished her Diet Coke and ordered another before saying, "Is that all you need? Do you want me to run a couple sets of fingerprints through the pending cases file? Why didn't you just say that when you walked into my office? I could have had the damn computer running a search while we ate lunch."

Theresa jokingly replied, "When I walked into your office, you were in no mood for another data request, simple or not."

The two women finished their lunch, then went back to headquarters. When Pat was about to exit the elevator, Theresa said, "Let me know when I can have the data?"

"I'll call you as soon as it's ready. Within two hours, tops."

The elevator doors closed as Theresa leaned back against the handrail. Two more floors passed before the elevator stopped and the doors opened at Theresa's floor. When she was finally sitting behind her desk, she called Paul Marco's house again. His answering machine picked up, so she left another message. She couldn't help think that something might be wrong out at Marco's house.

Paul heard a vacuum cleaner running a few feet from his head. He jumped up off the floor and immediately grabbed his lower back, then painfully asked, "What the hell?"

The woman operating the machine pushed the stop button, then leaned on the handle as she spoke. "I'm Mary. It's damn near nine o'clock. I thought you were going to sleep on the floor all goddamned day."

Paul looked the grouchy old broad up and down a few seconds then decided to be nice to her. Mary was in her late fifties, shoulders like a linebacker, and she had a cigarette dangling from her lips. Paul managed to straighten up a bit, then said, "Sorry. I didn't plan to sleep this long. I was just beat from all the driving last night."

"Something wrong with your back, mister?"

"I pulled or strained it a couple of days ago and it has been aching off and on ever since."

"Let me take a look at it. My ex used to have back problems all the time. We must have spent a small fortune on them there chiropractors. Anyway, I managed to learn a few things over the years."

Mary was now positioning herself behind Paul while putting her powerful arms around his midsection. Paul said, "I don't know about this. Maybe I should just take a—" Pain.

Mary jerked Paul back to her chest while lifting him off the floor at the same time. Paul yelled, "Wow! You're killing me!"

Mary set Paul down, then asked, "How's that feel?"

Paul bent one way, then the other with little or no pain. He bent forward from the waist, then straightened up again, surprised at how good his back actually felt. "It feels fantastic. How did you do that?"

"I told you. My ex and I paid a fortune for someone to do that kind of stuff for years. Hell, I figured if some clown that couldn't make it through medical school to be a real doctor can do it, then so can I. Now, listen. Lenny said you should clear out of here before the regulars start coming in for their morning shots and beer. You can leave using that door over there. It will lead you around the back to where you parked that flashy red Jeep of yours."

"Thanks, Mary. I mean for fixing my back and the advice." Paul reached into his pocket and pulled out two twenty-dollar bills for Mary. He said, "Here you go. That's for your office visit fee and the rest is for your hospitality."

Mary looked at the folded money and quickly stuffed it into her bra while saying, "Weren't nothin'. If you have any more trouble with that sacroiliac, you come and see me. I ain't half as expensive as those doctor want-a-bes."

Paul thanked Mary again, picked up his duffel, and left using the back door. As Paul stepped out into the cold air, he perked up immediately. The sun was bright, but the air had a real bite to it each time the wind gusted. Paul hurried to the Jeep, where he tossed the duffel bag into the back. The 9mm he had put inside the bag last night made a loud clanking noise as it hit against the interior fender well. Paul climbed into the Jeep, started her up, and headed for the supermarket down the road. As he was driving, he could not get over how great his back felt. And all it took was a visit to Mary, the practicing chiropractic cleaning lady.

The supermarket parking lot was practically empty. Paul parked next to the front entrance and went into the store to grab the basic essentials: coffee, sugar, half-and-half, beer, and potato chips and other snack foods. The more advanced staples consisted of several frozen dinners. Without seeing the cabin first, Paul did not know if there was an oven or a microwave in the place. He figured that he couldn't stock up on frozen chow just yet but could always come back later.

It took Paul the better part of an hour to find the cabin. Lenny was right when he told Paul he would not have found the place in the dark. Paul left the main road and turned at the two sawed-off tree stumps as Lenny had instructed. It was then a matter of slowly driving up the steep mountainside for another half-mile to where he was to look for the cabin on the right. The road was more like an old abandoned fire trail. Paul thought, *The Jeep was bouncing in and out of deep ruts as if it was riding on the moon's surface.* After thinking a few seconds, Paul decided the description *moon surface* was too level. This road seemed more like the historic *Burma Road.* As Paul slowly made his way up the mountain, he could not help thinking how much this would have hurt his back if good old Mary hadn't come to his rescue.

Paul was barely going two miles per hour. He couldn't go any faster without losing control of the bouncing steering wheel. The brush and tree limbs had overgrown quite a bit since the road didn't have any traffic on it for over six months. Onward and upward the Jeep climbed until Paul saw the little cabin in a clearing.

He turned into the opening, where he stopped the Jeep by the front door. The place was worn-and weathered-looking but seemed to be in fine shape. Paul turned off the Jeep and walked up to the front door. The birds were chirping as the treetops were swaying with the wind. Paul could hear the wind gust traveling through the evergreens as clumps of dried leaves swirled around the open area in front of the cabin.

Paul opened the door with one of the keys from the set Lenny had given him. His first impression was, *This ain't so bad."* The few pieces of furniture in the living and dining room combination were covered with bedsheets. The wooden oak floor was dusty but in fairly good shape. The fireplace to the left was big and made with the same type of stone that Paul saw on the foundation outside. To the right was a small kitchenette. It had a small refrigerator and freezer combination, a small sink, and even a little microwave oven on the counter. The electric range had two small burners but certainly more than enough for as much as Paul cooked. Paul walked down the three-foot-wide hall to a signal bedroom. The furniture in there was also covered with bed sheets. There was a double bed, a chair, and two night tables with lamps made from deer hooves. He saw the closet in the corner. Paul opened the door, where he saw blankets, pillows, and towels all neatly placed in plastic bags to keep them clean. He also saw the electric panel box, which he opened, located the main breaker and moved it to the *ON* position. Paul closed the closet door, then tried one of the lamps by the bed. It worked. Paul then focused on the opposite side of the room where the bathroom was located. He walked into a small but very usable facility. It had a shower, a sink, a medicine cabinet, and a toilet. It was small, compact, and very efficiently designed. Paul looked under the sink and saw the hot and cold water valves for the faucets. Next to them, he found a single valve with a paper tag labeled: *MAIN*. Paul cranked the valve to the full open position and immediately heard rumbling air and water gushing through the cabin pipes. He opened the sink faucets to bleed off the excess air in the lines; then, like magic, water started to pulse forward.

Slowly at first, then the pressure began to build. Paul heard the toilet tank filling with water so he gave the handle a pull and it flushed just like the one at home. Paul left the sink faucets running and returned to the kitchenette to turn on the water in that sink. The pipes rattled and made plenty of noise until water began flowing at a steady rate. There still was no hot water, but that would take a while longer.

Generally speaking, the place was very nice. Paul looked out through one of the two bedroom windows to view the perimeter. It was clear-cut for about thirty feet around the cabin, then it was all dense woods. *Not much of a safety zone*, he thought.

Paul checked the refrigerator to see if it was getting cold. It was working just fine, so he went out to the Jeep to bring in the groceries and put them away. The thing he needed to do first was take off the sheets covering the furniture and dust out the place. Dust seemed to just follow Paul around. He opened the front door and the windows in the bedroom to get a stiff cross-ventilation effect going. As a result, it did not take very long for the musty closed-up smell to disappear from the cabin. Paul went outside to check the firewood supply. There was about a half-cord of hardwood stacked along the side of the cabin. He would cut some more tomorrow if he could find an ax.

It was noon when Paul stopped to take a rest break. The cabin was still airing out, and he had swept, dusted, and wiped down the entire place. He could not believe how easy it was to clean the place from stem to stern while his house seemed to take forever. Paul located a small toolshed behind the cabin. The key ring Lenny had given Paul also had the key for the shed padlock. Inside the shed there were brooms, dust mops, buckets, and all kinds of other cleaning utensils. The important thing was that Paul found a fourteen-inch chain saw, two splitting axes, a couple of steel wedges, and two bow saws. All the necessary tools for cutting and splitting firewood.

Paul gathered some kindling while it was still light out and filled the wooden tinder box by the front door of the cabin. He then carried some firewood into the cabin to stack it by the fireplace. He made sure not to carry too much at one time, because he didn't know if his back could take a heavy strain yet.

Around one-thirty, Paul went into the cabin and closed the windows in the bedroom because it was starting to get cold outside. He located the thermostat in the hall and turned on the electric baseboard heat. At first there was the smell of old dust being cooked, but that soon changed and the temperature gradually began to rise. Paul found a pot under the sink and put on some water to boil. While the water was getting hot, he made a cold-cut sandwich with chips and a cold beer on the side. After eating, Paul felt very relaxed as he located the coffee mugs in one of the small cabinets in the kitchenette. He washed them in the sink, then made a cup of instant coffee.

Paul decided to sit by the window in the living room while looking out toward the front of the cabin. The wind was kicking up, and snow flurries were bouncing off the Jeep. Paul lit a cigarette and rested while he finished his coffee. He took out the cell phone to see if it would work this far from home. When he turned the phone on, the low-battery indicator immediately started blinking. *It was probably due to it sitting out in the rucksack for almost two weeks*, Paul thought. He flipped the phone over and pulled out the charger prongs, then plugged the phone into an outlet to start the charger. That would take several hours, so Paul decided that he would try it again tomorrow.

It was only three o'clock, and Paul was already tired. He went into the bedroom to make up the bed with clean sheets and blankets. He put his shaving gear in the bathroom and took two towels from the closet to place on the rack behind the bathroom door. Paul checked the hot water in the sink, and it was working just fine. He decided to shower and shave, then maybe go down to the main road to look for a place that served a good home-cooked meal.

As Paul was shaving, he decided not to go to the Angle Inn for dinner. The vacant parking lot last night still loomed in his mind. He would head toward the supermarket he was at earlier to see if there was another place to eat.

Paul put on a clean pair of jeans, a dark green flannel shirt, and a green sweatshirt. It was getting colder with each passing hour, so Paul pulled out the big down parka and his gloves from the duffel bag. The last thing he did was put the 9mm in one of the many inside pockets of the fluffy jacket. *No sense walking around with the damn thing stuck in my back,* he thought.

Paul put the rest of his clothes in the closet and turned the thermostat down to sixty degrees. There was no sense in running up a big electric bill, especially since he was not going to be there to enjoy the heat. Paul locked the cabin door, then climbed into the Jeep. He slowly pulled out of the clearing onto the *Burma Road* and held onto the steering wheel with both hands as he made his way down to the main road. Once he was on a solid, flat surface, he kicked the Jeep into high gear and sailed down the country road. The radio selections were country music or more country music. Paul decided to listen to country music, for the first time in his life. It seemed as if every song was about somebody leaving somebody or somebody's dog dying. Paul turned off the radio and concentrated on the road in front of him.

About ten miles had passed when Paul noticed a group of bright lights straight ahead. It was a town with stores, gas stations, and restaurants. The sign read: *Welcome To Small Town. Population 335*. Paul looked like a tourist with his head turning this way and that trying to read all the signs on the storefronts. Finally, he saw a place named Libby's Steak House. Paul didn't hesitate for a second. He pulled the Jeep over to the side of the road and parked twenty feet from the front door. When he walked inside the place there were people already waiting for tables. *That was a good sign*, he thought. He left his name at the desk and was told it would be about twenty minutes before a table was available.

Paul told the woman that was fine, then asked if they had a pay phone. She pointed to the rear where the restrooms were located. Paul thanked her and made his way to one of the vacant telephones. He pulled out the calling card from his wallet and dialed his house to listen to his messages. Nothing happened. A recording came on saying the number was no longer in service. Paul's first thought was that he had miscalled, so he tried the number again, with the same result.

That's odd. Why would the phone company say the number was no longer in service? I paid the bill only two weeks ago. Something isn't right.

Paul tried to call Gary and his answering machine picked up. Paul didn't leave a message because after dinner he would try Gary again to see if he knew what was going on at Paul's house.

The meal at Libby's Steak House was absolutely outstanding. The steak was tender and juicy, cooked to a light pink on the inside, surrounded by mushrooms, and covered with fried onions. The stewed tomatoes were zesty, the mashed potatoes soft and fluffy, and the bread served warm with lots of country fresh butter. Paul never touched the salad in front of him because there was no place in his stomach for more food. While Paul was drinking his second cup of coffee, the waitress placed the tossed salad into a plastic container so he could take it home. Paul paid his bill, then tried Gary's number one more time.

Gary picked up the phone on the second ring, saying, "Hello." "Gary, it's me, Paul. I was trying—"

"Don't talk. Just listen. Your place has been torched, man. I mean it was burned to the ground early this morning. I went out there to get your mail and newspaper like you asked and ran into about five fire trucks. It was arson, man. I hate to be the one to tell you about it, buddy. I tried to get a message to Lenny, so he could have you call me. But he wasn't around and I didn't want anyone else to know where or who you were. I was going to try again later."

Paul was in shock. *My house? It's gone?* "No. It's OK, Gar.' I understand. You said that it was arson?"

"Yeah. That's what the fire marshal was saying. Some kind of flammable liquid poured on the living room rug. Listen. The cops are looking for you, too. Some broad named Davin or—"

"Detective Theresa McGavin."

"Yeah. That's the one. She was asking if anybody has seen you in the past few days and all kinds of stuff like that. You know what I mean?"

"Yeah. OK. Listen, Gary. Do me a favor. Call police headquarters and ask to speak to Detective Theresa McGavin. Tell her that I contacted you and I'm fine. I'll call her in a few days to talk about all that has gone down. Don't tell her where I am, and don't talk to anyone else but Detective McGavin."

"I got it, buddy. Listen. Take care of yourself and call me, day or night, if you need anything."

"Gary, I'll call you each night at eight o'clock sharp. Your phone may be tapped, so I'll call the phone booth where we last had a beer. If I don't call you, take that as a signal that I need help."

Gary knew Paul was talking about the phone booths at the *Cell Block*. He responded, "I hear you, man."

Paul hung up the phone and walked out of the restaurant, leaving his salad by the phone. His mind was all jumbled. First they kill my wife. Then they torch the place where we had fond memories. What in the hell is going on with my life?

Chapter 19

Billy Sharp was very pleased to hear about the torching of Paul Marco's house from his main enforcer, John Toby. Sharp's only regret was that Paul was not in the house at the time of the fire. Of course, this by no means began to even the score. Sharp was still fuming over the destruction at his Virginia ranch. Luckily, the main equipment outbuilding fire did not make it to the underground communications vault. The old barn floor with its four feet of earth on top protected the twenty-foot-square buried concrete communications center. Inside the center there were computers, phones, faxes, and satellite feed. The Vegas betting line was telecast on a huge four-foot flat liquid crystal screen. From the communications center Billy Sharp conducted all his bookie operations that spanned up and down the East Coast. He also used scrambled satellite signals to keep his network of deals in drugs and guns from being discovered by the feds. Billy affectionately called the huge secured room his *bunker*.

After the fire at his ranch, Billy Sharp had to shut down the bunker for a few days. There were too many police, newspeople, and fire marshals around for him to comfortably keep the operation up and running. Besides, a lot of debris had to be moved so the auxiliary generators could be activated to supply electrical power to the bunker. Normally, the power for the bunker came from an underground feed at the main house. Unfortunately, the buried electric lines ran directly under the two main fuel tanks that exploded. The explosion damaged the main power feeder lines, and only the auxiliary generators could keep the bunker running for now. The way things were, Billy didn't need anyone asking a bunch of questions about why he needed the generators running when power was on in the main house.

The bunker was reserved for only a select few in Billy Sharp's cadre. Although Sharp was a shrewd businessman, he never fully trusted anyone, except for Leon Acker and John Toby. The main house staff, which consisted of a live-in maid and cook, had never been to the bunker. The regular technical staff consisted of two men and one woman. The tech-heads, as Billy referred to them, would keep all the systems up and running in eight-hour shifts. The tech-heads did not live in the main house. They had regular lives outside the corrupt world of Billy Sharp. The tech-heads only took care of his computer equipment and knew very little about what Billy actually did for a living. However, they knew enough to put Billy away if they ever decided to talk to the feds. Billy knew that and paid them extremely well. Not just for their technical expertise, but also for their silence. Besides, they knew enough about Billy Sharp to realize that he was not a person one wanted to cross.

John Toby was in the bunker when Billy came down the steep set of steel steps that led to the concrete structure. Billy looked up at the big liquid crystal screen, then scanned several computer monitors that were flashing statistics, wagers, and late scratches from the many racetracks around the United States. The fluorescent lighting and the many color monitors around the room gave the place a greenish hue. Billy asked, "What's the action look like today, John?"

"Not bad, considering it's still early. The tracks in California won't be open for another two hours, so things will pick up soon."

"OK. Say, I hear our boy Marco might be on the run?"

"I know, Billy. The boys I paid to Zippo his place said they couldn't find him anywhere. The word in town is that he may have taken off on an extended vacation. Boy, is he going to be surprised when he gets home."

"John, I still want that bastard dead. Better yet, I would like him delivered to me alive, so I can pop him."

"I know, Boss. I'm working on it. I thought we had two good hitters last week, but they both ended up floating down some damn river belly-up. The contract is still in force, and there are plenty of takers, itching to grab at the silver ring. Besides, our boy Marco still has a store, remember? Well, that is being torched as we speak. I'm hoping we can smoke the bastard out into the open."

Billy was staring at one of the computer monitors when the red phone rang. That meant it was a call from the main house. Billy picked up the phone, and it was his wife. "Yeah, I know. . . . Sure, babe. . . . I'm on my way now."

"I have to go, John. The old lady wants me to go with her to some goddamned charity function. God, I hate those things. It's a bunch of do-gooders sitting around begging for money for some useless group of people that can't or won't work to support themselves."

"Hey, Boss. Better you than me."

Billy managed to laugh along with John as he headed to the steps to climb out of the bunker. Before he took the first step, Billy turned and said, "By the way, the cable from the main house is supposed to be fixed tomorrow so we won't have to hear those damn noisy generators running anymore."

John simply nodded his head affirmatively as he concentrated on the new information coming up on one of the computer monitors. Billy Sharp walked to the main house and into the kitchen, where the cook was busy doing whatever she did. Billy didn't talk to the domestic help very much. Today, without stopping, as he passed the cook he managed to say, "How are you, Maria?"

"Fine, Mr. Sharp," she replied without looking up from the big pot of string beans she was fixing.

Billy left the kitchen and walked through the dining room and living room to the huge staircase that led to the second story. The house had six bedrooms and eight bathrooms. The kitchen was the size of most people's house, with walk-in freezers and cookstoves that would make most restaurant chefs envious. The upstairs master bedroom was large enough to play indoor tennis.

Billy found his wife at the massive walk-in closet trying to pick out a dress for the charity event. He sat on the oversize king-sized bed, then asked, "Do I really have to go to this banquet tonight?"

Lucy came out of the closet holding two dresses saying, "Yes, you have to go, silly. You're donating a quarter of a million dollars to this cause, and the people running it want to give us an award. Now, which of these do you think I should wear?"

Lucinda Parker Sharp was about five feet, two inches tall in her heels. She probably weighed close to 105 pounds and was as meanspirited as she was petite. Her dark black hair against her milky complexion made her look as if she were a member of the walking dead.

For a few seconds Billy looked at the two dresses Lucy was holding up, then said, "The one on your left."

Lucy looked at both dresses again and selected the one in her right hand. She walked back into the closet and returned a minute later wearing the dress, asking, "Are you sure this looks OK? It's a formal event, you know, so I suggest that you get moving or we'll be late."

Billy didn't say a word to Lucy. He simply went into his private bathroom to the left of the huge bedroom to shower and shave. When he was through, he went back into the bedroom, where Lucy had laid out a black tuxedo for him to wear. As he dressed, he could hear the generators running outside. Lucy was already upset at him for taking so long to get the bunker electric lines fixed. She would gripe about it every night, saying how she couldn't sleep because of the noise. Billy actually didn't mind the noise since Lucy decided to sleep in another room at the other end of the house until it was quiet again. Also, it took a little longer for Billy to find a contractor to come way out to his ranch that could also keep his mouth shut.

Lupo Electric, Inc., was a small contractor who had been contacted by Leon Acker about doing a special job in a hurry. Vinny Lupo didn't care what the job consisted of, so long as he was paid with cash. Besides, Leon had promised him a fat cash bonus if he finished the job in two days or less.

Around five o'clock, the Sharps were picked up by a chauffeured limousine in front of the main house. It would take almost an hour for them to drive the fifty miles to the charity banquet. As the limo pushed ahead, Lucy managed to take a nap while Billy watched the countryside slip past his window. Every now and then he would look over at Lucy as she slept. She was such a beautiful woman and could be so loving at times that he would tolerate just about all of her shenanigans. Unfortunately, there were times when he would just as soon put a bullet in her head to shut her up. Especially when she was ranting and raving about some insignificant matter regarding his business, about which she knew very little.

The limousine pulled up to the Mariott Hotel in full view of the local press and ogling onlookers. Billy and Lucy Sharp made their elegant entrance to the banquet room to the cheers and accolades of others as their name was announced over the address system. They were escorted to the head table, which was reserved for all the big contributors. Lawyers and doctors mostly and one snot-nosed kid from the deep hills of Virginia who could buy and sell them all many times over.

Paul drove back to the *Burma Road* leading to the cabin. He made the turn at the two tree stumps, then started the slow, steady climb to the top. At the clearing, he pulled the Jeep next to the front door. The wind was gusting over thirty miles per hour, and the temperature was now in single digits. Paul unlocked the front door and relocked it when he was safely inside. The first thing he needed to do was get the electric heat going. He turned the thermostat dial to seventy degrees. It was still too cold in the cabin to remove his coat, so Paul left it on as he went over to the fireplace to get a fire started. He set a few pieces of wood on top of some kindling and balled-up paper he had saved from the grocery bags.

The flame started immediately, and the smoke was quickly sucked up the chimney. With the stiff wind outside, the chimney was probably drawing more heat outside then the fire was radiating inside. After a few minutes, Paul placed a few logs into the fire and felt that it was now warm enough to remove his jacket.

Paul went into the kitchenette and placed a pot of water on the stove so he could make coffee. While the water was heating, he took the 9mm out of his coat and placed it behind the stacked wood by the fireplace. He then went into the bedroom closet to remove the second 9mm from the duffel bag, and he placed it under his pillow. The M-1 carbine was safe in the closet for now. Paul could not get the image of his house burning down to the ground out of his mind. He and Diana had carefully selected the land, the house, and even the trees that surrounded the place. It seemed as if it was only last week that they had planted a new bush along the wooden fence. Now it was all gone. Up in smoke. For what?

Paul made a cup of coffee and sat by the crackling fire to sip it while his mind wandered. He must have sat there staring at the fire for over an hour without moving. He was desperately trying to think of what he should do next. He looked at his watch and saw that it was now seven o'clock. He decided that tomorrow he would cut some firewood to help work out his frustrations. There was nothing like bashing a splitting ax into some hardwood to release internal pressure.

Paul allowed the fire to burn down, then cleaned up the kitchenette. He then looked at the cell phone charging in the wall socket. He took the phone out of the wall socket to dial Mikey's number. He heard the phone ringing, which was a good sign.

"What?"

"Mikey. It's me, Pauly. Can you hear me OK?"

"Jesus Christ, Pauly, you must be psychic. I was just talking to Gary about you and I'm afraid I have some bad news."

"Yeah. I know all about it, Mikey. Listen. I'm going to need a few things from your back room, buddy. Would it be OK for me to come down there later tonight?"

"Sure. Just you be damn careful. I'll be here until midnight." "That's plenty of time, Mikey. I'll leave now and can be at your place in less than three hours."

"OK, I'll be keeping an eye out for you. And listen, Paul. I'm sorry about your business."

Paul didn't know what Mikey was talking about as he asked, "My business? What does that have to do with anything?"

"I thought you said that you knew all about the bad news?"

"Yeah. Gary told me earlier today my house had been torched.

What's this about my business?"

"Ah shit, Pauly. I hate this crap. Look, pal. Your business was torched tonight. Happened about two hours ago. I thought you knew."

Paul was silent at the other end of the line. Finally he said, "That's it, Mikey. It's time to play hardball. I have nothing left to lose."

"I hear you, Pauly, but you're pissed off right now. Don't go off half-cocked, you hotheaded guinea. When you get here, we can come up with a plan of attack. These bastards have gone as far as they can for now."

"I know what you're saying, Mikey. I'll take care of this business in my own way. After all, it's my fight. I just need a little backup support from my friends if you know what I mean."

"You name it, and it's yours. See you soon and be doubly careful."

Paul turned off the cell phone and stuffed it in his jacket pocket. He then took the 9mm from under the bedroom pillow and stuffed it into another pocket. Paul turned down the thermostat and locked the cabin before he climbed into the Jeep. He was fuming mad right now and knew it was a good thing that he could not react instantly. If he did, he might make a stupid error. It was always better to be prepared for battle. Cool head, steady aim, and quick execution. Nothing short of precise execution would do now.

Paul started down the *Burma Road,* then out to the interstate, where he would gas up the Jeep. The night was pitch-dark and the air was freezing cold. Paul was driving as if on automatic pilot. His mind was laying out his plan for retaliation. What he needed most right now was information. Between Gary and Mikey that should be easy to obtain. Paul needed to know where he could find Billy Sharp at any given time and also needed to know what he loved most, so Paul could take it away, preferably while Billy was alive to experience the pain of the loss. Paul wanted Billy Sharp to suffer, as he was suffering. People like Billy Sharp needed to be killed. The world would be a better place after the deed was done.

Paul dove toward downtown Baltimore as his mind planned and schemed. He sorted through details and played out some scenarios in the back of his mind as he pushed forward.

A half-pack of cigarettes later, he was pulling the Jeep onto the back parking lot of the *Cell Block.* Through the bar and down the kitchen steps he went. Rocco was back on duty, and Paul handed him the 9mm before he was frisked. Rocco looked at the weapon, then said, "Nice piece. You can pick it up on your way out."

Rocco led the way to the great room entrance, where he left Paul on his own. Paul looked at his watch to see that it was almost nine-thirty. He opened the great room door to see Mikey at his desk. Paul started to walk forward as Mikey stood up to meet him halfway. They shook hands, and then Mikey said, "I'm really sorry the way things are working out for you, Pauly. I know I can't make things the way they were, but I can sure help you make things right. Come and sit at the desk and we can have a drink while we talk."

Paul and Mikey each drank a shot of tequila and sipped at a cold beer while they discussed how Paul could even the score. Paul laid out his tentative plan of attack but needed some information to make it all work.

Mikey listened to Paul talk, then said, "You have a good head for this stuff, Pauly. I sure am glad I'm not the one you're after. Now, what you're asking me to get is going to be difficult, but not impossible. How can I get word to you when I find out something?"

Paul explained the arrangement he had set up with Gary. Paul would call the phone booth upstairs each night, starting tomorrow, at exactly eight o'clock. "If I don't call, then I'm either dead or in deep trouble."

"OK. That sounds like a good plan. Now, let's see what we have for you in the back. Since we don't know exactly what you will need, we may have to go overboard a little."

Paul and Mikey went into the hidden back room, where Paul picked out several pieces of equipment that he would need. He chose a pair of night-vision goggles and several pounds of C-4 plastic explosives with timer detonators. In a wood box the size of a milk crate he loaded a dozen fragmentation grenades and three claymore mines with detonators. Mikey took another box and filled it with ammunition, a sawed-off riot shotgun, and several incendiary grenades. It required Paul, Mikey, and Rocco to load the Jeep with all the ordnance.

Rocco returned Paul's 9mm then left the two men alone by the Jeep. Paul thanked Mikey one more time, then said good-bye. Mikey's parting advice was, "Drive the speed limit, buddy. If you are pulled over, you're going to have a lot of explaining to do."

Paul laughed, then waved as he pulled out of the parking lot heading for the Beltway. Paul drove until he hit the interstate, where he gassed up the Jeep and bought a coffee. Since he was still close to Baltimore, he used his bank card to withdraw some more cash. Paul did not want the police to know where he was, so he only used cash while out at the cabin. The problem was he could only withdraw $400, because the bank machine had a withdraw limit for security reasons. That would not be enough money to sustain Paul very long. He would have to make some other arrangements if he stayed out at the cabin for an extended period.

The ride back to the cabin would take another hour, so he listened to an oldies radio station and thought about how things were starting to come together. Suddenly, a song came on the radio that put it all in perspective. Janis Joplin was signing the chorus from "Me and Bobby McGee": *"Freedom's just another word for nothin' left to lose."* Paul thought, *That's me." I'm now finally free because I have nothin' left to lose. No wife, no house, no more business. That also means I'm also the most dangerous because I have everything to gain and absolutely nothin' to lose.*

Chapter 20

Detective McGavin picked up the computer printout from Pat Dershan when it was ready. The computer run matched the fingerprints of Jerry Morgan and Darnel Philips to those taken from a stolen vehicle that was located less than one mile from Paul Marco's house. After she reviewed the data, a few pieces of the puzzle fell into place for her. Theresa called the Baltimore County Police barracks in Timonium to talk to the officer who had prepared the stolen-vehicle report. Officer Garcia, however, was not very helpful. He told McGavin that he had responded to a farmer's complaint that a vehicle was abandoned in the woods by his corn field. At first, the farmer thought the car belonged to a squirrel or rabbit hunter. When he saw the car in the same place for two consecutive days, he called police headquarters. Garcia said their routine investigation showed that there were stolen plates involved and the rest of the story was history. Officer Garcia asked, "Why all the interest in this small-time case, Detective?"

"The prints your lab boys lifted from the stolen car matched those of the two men fished out of the Gunpowder River a few days after you filed the stolen vehicle report."

"Well, Detective, I'm no hotshot big-city cop, but that is a long way to park if you want to go swimming at Prettyboy."

"How far is it from where you found the car to the reservoir?" "I would say at least twenty miles, give or take a mile. So that means either someone popped your two water rats, then ditched the car in the old farmer's corn field, or you have one hell of a mystery to solve."

"Thanks for your help, Officer Garcia. I appreciate your time.

Unfortunately, I have a mystery to solve, and I don't like the way things are starting to stack up at this point."

Detective McGavin hung up the phone and pondered what Officer Garcia had said. It could be possible for someone to dump the car in the corn field, as he said, but it was too much of a coincidence that the car was found so close to Paul Marco's house. After all, the commissioner had taught her not to believe in coincidence. Somehow, the two bodies from the river were tied to Marco. But how?

Theresa called Captain Thiemeyer to let him know what she had discovered. Thiemeyer was very interested in the latest findings, so he asked her to come up to his office immediately. Theresa laid out the chain of events for Thiemeyer, then asked, "Well, what do you think went on out there in the country?"

Captain Thiemeyer was very intrigued with the entire scenario. He steadily bounced a wooden pencil on the top of his desk, then said, "Try this on for size. Suppose the two bad guys go see Marco and he doesn't like what they have to say. He pops them both, dumps the bodies into the reservoir, then stashes their car in the corn field later."

"Why would he stash the car less than a mile away from his house? I agree that would certainly make it easy for him to walk home afterwards, but come on, Captain. Nobody is that dumb. It would be better if he just left a sign on the stolen car's windshield that read *Murderer lives up the road.*"

"OK. OK, I know it's shaky, but it's the best I can do for right now."

Theresa said, "You know what? Maybe the bad guys left the car in the corn field, then sneaked up on Marco at his house."

Captain Thiemeyer thought a few seconds, then replied, "You may have something there, Theresa. Suppose you're right. I mean, the two ex-cons figure they could hide the car, then visit Marco to make him pay the extortion money."

"Then, something goes wrong. Marco does his Rambo thing, and now we have two stiffs floating down the Gunpowder River."

"That's good, Theresa. Now let's say Marco dumps the bodies in the reservoir, but either he can't find the car or he takes off running before he has a chance to take care of it. You did say he has not been seen or heard from in several days, right?"

Theresa's face quickly went from happy to dejected. Captain Thiemeyer asked, "What's wrong?"

"I thought we had this thing figured out, until you said that about no one hearing from Marco."

"What do mean, Theresa?"

I received a call from some guy who calls himself a friend of Paul Marco's. The guy said he was instructed to call me and say that Paul is OK and will call me in a few days to fill me in on what he has been up to recently."

"That's it? That's all this so-called friend said?"

"I'm afraid so, Captain. So, you see, that puts a hole in our theory. Wouldn't you say?"

Captain Thiemeyer was tapping the pencil on the desk again. Suddenly he said, "No. No, it makes the theory work better. Look. Marco is being dogged by somebody who wants extortion money, right? He sends a couple of ex-cons to collect, and they get wasted. Marco takes off and leaves the car in the corn field, and now he is going to tell us all about it when he calls you. You see. It all fits." Theresa was not becoming excited over the summary by Thiemeyer. Finally she said, "Unfortunately, we can't prove a damn word of it, one way or the other. And Marco's house may have held a clue to tie it all together, but now that is gone as well."

Thiemeyer said, "You don't think he torched his own house to cover up evidence, do you?"

"No way, Cap.' I saw the way he touched things in that house and how he was so careful not to move anything his wife may have touched. I would bet my badge that he didn't torch his own house. Too many good memories there, for one thing. Besides that, it would follow then that he also torched his business. I just don't buy it. Too nice and neat a package if you know what I mean?"

"You're probably right, Theresa. I guess all we can do now is wait for him to contact us so we can try to put the puzzle together. I still think he is our number-one suspect in the murders of Morgan and Philips."

"The way I see it, Captain. He's our only suspect."

Theresa left Captain Thiemeyer's office to go back to her desk. The whole time she was walking, she couldn't help from thinking how easy it is for good people to turn bad when their backs were up against the wall.

The Sharps returned to the main house around midnight. The charity banquet had been a huge success, with over $4 million being donated. During the limousine ride home, both Billy and Lucy slept without as much as two sentences being spoken between them. Apparently, Lucy was upset at her husband for the way he would always try to one-up the person telling a story. *It was one of his many faults*, she thought.

Billy, of course, had tried to get the evening over with as soon as possible before being bored out of his skull. There were plenty of politicians and political want-to-bes at the banquet. One old master of the back-scratching set managed to pull Billy onto the side for a few minutes of private conversation. Former state senator Lucius Jackson wanted to introduce Billy to a friend of a friend. The senator said, "Billy Sharp, I would like you to meet the CEO of Walker Construction, Mr. Jack Walker."

The two men shook hands and made small talk for a few minutes before the senator excused himself so Billy and Jack could talk some business. Jack Walker ran a large construction company that did a tremendous amount of work for the state of Virginia. Some said he had inside information when it came to winning the so-called sealed bids for lucrative jobs around the state. Anyway, it seemed that Jack Walker had accumulated excess inventory of heavy equipment and wanted to know if Billy knew anyone who might be in the market for such goods. Billy said, "I know several contractors that may be interested in making some purchases. Would there be any problem if the delivery was to be, say, to the Las Vegas area?"

"No. Not at all, Billy. I understand there is a tremendous building surge out in Nevada right now, and the kind of equipment I have in my inventory could be trucked there within, say, five or six days after settlement."

Billy Sharp did not like to fool around when it came to business dealings. He liked things to be up-front and out in the open. Billy said, "What do you have and how many?"

"Well, Mr. Sharp, you certainly get to the point. I like that when I'm doing business. I have three front-end loaders, two backhoes, one grader, six air compressors, two gradall cranes, etc." Jack Walker sounded like a damn recording, rattling off the inventory as if it were tattooed on the backs of his eyelids.

"OK, here's my deal. I'll buy your excess inventory and pay half up front, in cash, of course. You ship the equipment to a warehouse in Vegas, at your cost. Final payment will be made at the warehouse, in cash, of course. Do we have a deal?"

"We have a deal, sir, if you can come up with three-quarters of a million dollars in two days. In cash, of course."

Billy smiled, then asked, "Do you want it in large or small bills?"

The two men shook hands and finalized the deal with a drink at the bar. Billy gave Jack his business card, then said, "Call me tomorrow and we can make the final arrangements for the down payment and delivery."

As the limousine dropped the Sharps off at the main house, Billy was thinking about how he hated to attend charity banquets. That is, unless he had an opportunity to make a few deals on the side.

Paul Marco arrived at the cabin a little after eleven o'clock. Snow was falling, and there was already a light dusting on the ground. Paul backed the Jeep up to the cabin door so he could unload the ordnance he picked up from Mikey.

Paul unlocked the door and immediately went to the thermostat to crank it up to seventy degrees. He made a quick check of the embers in the fireplace hearth to find that there were plenty of hot pieces still smoldering. He grabbed a handful of kindling from the tinder box out by the front door and tossed them onto the hot embers. He had to blow on the embers a few seconds before the dried kindling ignited. When he thought the fire was burning hot enough, he tossed in a few small logs so they could catch fire.

Paul unloaded the Jeep and laid everything out on the living room floor. The room was now warm enough so he could remove his jacket and light a cigarette. Paul took the 9mm out of his jacket and placed it on the sofa. He then took the cell phone and plugged it into the wall outlet so it could continue recharging.

As Paul checked out the ordnance, he imagined that it would be possible for him to take out a small army with all that lay on the floor. The big questions were when and where. He needed information from Mikey and Gary so he could finalize his plan of attack. Paul took the twelve-gauge sawed-off riot shotgun and loaded six double-aught buck shells into the slide. He needed to make sure that there was a weapon available to him no matter what room he happened to be in at the time. The folks who wanted to fulfill the contract on him could find the cabin somehow, and then it would be a real challenge to survive if he was not ready. Paul set the twelve-gauge by the refrigerator, then took the 9mm off the sofa and placed it back under his pillow in the bedroom.

After thinking about all that had happened that day, Paul decided it was time to get some sleep. The chances that someone would find him tonight were slim, so he decided to sleep in the bed. Tomorrow, however, he might have to change his sleeping arrangements. Paul took off his clothes and climbed into bed. He could see through the bedroom window that it was now snowing much harder. Paul closed his eyes to think about how much his life had changed in the past few years. It had been one steady spiral downward. Now, however, he had something very important to do for the first time in almost three years. Something that only he could do. But right now, what he needed most was sleep.

Gary Roth was lining up another load of stolen construction equipment for shipment to Virginia. His Cousin who lived just outside Culpeper, Virginia, was his contact for sales, storage, and distribution of stolen construction equipment. His Cousin's name was Holland Willis. He was related to Gary on his mother's side of the family. Holland and Gary would talk every two weeks to compare inventory and discuss routine business needs. On this particular occasion, Gary told his Cousin that he was looking for some information about the owner of a place called the *Double C* ranch. Holland said, "Yo, Gary, my man. Stay away from that dude, 'cause he is bad news. Ya know what I'm saying?"

Gary assured his Cousin that he did, in fact, know about the reputation of Billy Sharp, then said, "Hol,' do you know anybody you can trust who may be interested in seeing Sharp taken out of the picture?"

"Oh, I see. Yeah, come to think of it there was some talk a month or so ago. One of his employees was really upset with the way things were run out at the *Double C* and wanted to quit. Well, nobody, and I do mean nobody, quits working for the man. Ya know what I mean? Anyway, my buddy heard this dude talking about getting out from under Sharp's thumb while he was drinking at the local gin mill. I can talk to my man to see if he can set up a meet down here if you want."

"OK, Cous.' But I need this information like yesterday. You know what I mean?"

"Let me call my man, and I'll get back to you ASAP."

Gary hung up the phone and thought about what his Cousin was trying to do for him. Holland could get into real trouble, especially if the guy he talked to decided to sell him out to Billy Sharp. Gary knew he was between a rock and a hard place, because he had a friend that needed information and another who might be able to help. Unfortunately, one or the other or both could be hurt if things don't go smoothly.

Around midnight Gary's phone rang. "Hello."

"Hey, Cous.' It's Holland. I got something for you. My man talked to the dude that was doing all the complaining at the gin mill."

"Yeah. What's the scoop, Cous'?"

"The dude works in this underground concrete information center at the *Double C.* Computers and all like that. Anyway, he wants out of there so bad he is willing to sell out this dude Sharp, with no strings attached. The problem is he works there, in this underground center, every day on the three-to-eleven shift. He doesn't want anything coming down while he's around. Got it?"

"So far, Cous,' you're doing fine. Tell me more."

"The dude drew a map of the place, and it has all kinds of shit written on it, like where the air ducts are and electric lines and stuff like that. He must be some kind of engineer or something, man. The dude also said the place was built like a bunker. Solid concrete and stuff like that. As a matter of fact, he said the place is located under an equipment barn that burned down a little while ago, and this hidden room wasn't even singed. This Sharp character must be one paranoid son of a bitch. Listen. I'll fax you this paper, as soon as I hang up. Is that cool with you?"

"Yeah, fax away, Cous.' I owe you large, on this one."

"Don't sweat it, Cous.' It weren't nothin' to get this stuff. The dude must really have it in for his boss. I guess that's why I'm such a nice boss to my men. Right, Cous'?"

"You got it, Holland. Thanks again for the quick turnaround on this. If it wasn't for a really good friend of mine, I wouldn't have asked."

"I hear you, Cous.' Talk to you in two, man."

Gary hung up the phone and switched the phone line over to the fax machine. Within fifteen seconds the machine was humming and a piece of paper was entering the tray. Gary looked at the map with all its detail, then thought about how happy Paul was going to be when he got this little gem in his hands.

Mikey was busy working the phones from his end. He was doing his best to come up with some information for his neighborhood buddy, Pauly. The trouble was Mikey didn't do very much business in the Virginia area as a rule. His contacts were mostly in New York and New Jersey. On a hunch, Mikey called a friend of his in Jersey who had run a large bookie operation for many years. Mikey never got into the bookie business because it required too many people to make an operation profitable. There were runners, collectors, and enforcers, and every now and then you had to be able to lay off some big money in a hurry. Especially when big sporting events like the Super Bowl and the Derby were in season.

Tony Donello was someone Mikey had done a few favors for in the past, and he thought it might not be a bad idea to see if Tony could help. He was a hard man to get hold of, so Mikey left messages for Tony to call him in three places. If Tony was up to his usual routine of checking all the football spreads this time of year, he would be calling back very soon.

About an hour after Mikey left the last message for Tony, he returned the call. "Hey, Mikey. When are you coming up to Atlantic City again so we can have some fun?"

"I tell you Tony, I have been so damn busy that it would be tough for me to get away right now."

"I know what you mean, Mikey. When business is good, you have to roll with it. So, I got the word you have been looking for me. What's up?"

Mikey laid out the information he wanted, then asked Tony if he could help him help an old friend. Tony said, "I know the son of a bitch you're talking about. Billy Sharp dabbles in Jersey some, but more so in New York with his string of betting parlors. I can get something for you, but it may take a day or so."

"Tony, I don't have that much time because something may be coming down on this guy Sharp very soon."

"OK. Let me make a few calls and I'll get back to you in a few hours to let you know what I find out."

Mikey knew that Tony would have all the information about the bookies operating in and around his turf. From the sound in Tony's voice he would appreciate someone eliminating a little of his competition.

Chapter 21

Paul slept like a baby. He woke up around seven-thirty to a bright sun, which was shining through the bedroom window. He got up to look out the window and saw two to three inches of fresh snow blanketing the ground. It was a beautiful sight. The snow was the wet, sticky kind that stuck to all the trees and branches. *It looked almost like the proverbial Christmas card scene variety*, Paul thought. Paul walked down the small narrow hall to turn up the thermostat. He then quickly ran into the bathroom to jump into a hot shower to warm up while the cabin did the same. After showering and shaving, Paul got dressed in jeans, a flannel shirt, and a sweatshirt. He put on two pairs of socks, because he would be cutting firewood today and his steel-toe work boots were not the insulated variety. Once he was dressed, Paul decided to make himself breakfast. First he placed a pot of water on the stove for coffee. Then he hunted for a frying pan so he could scramble some eggs. Paul eventually found what he needed, cooked his breakfast, and was a bit surprised at how good the meal actually tasted. Of course, when you're hungry everything tastes good. Besides, Paul managed to scramble six eggs without ruining the frying pan. He also had four pieces of toast, very well done, of course. But a little scrape here and another there made the toast edible. Additionally, Paul had two cups of instant coffee and a Snickers candy bar to top off the hungry man's breakfast.

Paul cleaned up the kitchenette, then retrieved the 9mm that was behind the wood stacked next to the fireplace. He stuffed the gun into his coat pocket, then went outside to look for a felled tree or two to cut up for firewood. It didn't take long for Paul to find a large hardwood tree lying on the forest floor. In fact, the tree was only about ten yards into the tree line. Paul went back to the toolshed behind the cabin to check the chain saw for fuel. It took an oil and gasoline mix to operate the two-cycle engine. Paul found an empty one-gallon gas can in the shed, so he continued looking around and found a small siphon hose. He used the hose to take some gasoline out of his Jeep gas tank. After partially filling the gas can with fuel, Paul added a pint of two-cycle engine oil that he also found in the shed. When the fuel and oil were mixed thoroughly, Paul filled the chain saw gas tank. He put the choke on, then pulled the starter cord a few times before the engine finally sputtered. The next pull of the starter cord fired the saw up, and it began to run at its normal operating RPMs. Paul turned the chain saw off, then took it along with the gas can of mixed fuel into the woods to start cutting up the big fallen oak tree.

After an hour of cutting the trunk and limbs into smaller pieces, Paul took the saw and gas can back to the shed. He then took the two steel wedges and one of the splitting axes back to the felled tree site. It was a clear, cold day with very little wind. Paul knew that he would work up a sweat splitting wood, so he removed his jacket. He then set up one of the larger tree-trunk pieces of wood to use as a makeshift chopping block. It took a little maneuvering on his part, but soon Paul was splitting the dry wood into pieces that would fit nicely into the fireplace. With each swing of the ax he would envision Billy Sharp's head being on the chopping block. Within fifteen minutes, Paul had accumulated a fairly good-sized pile of split hardwood. He was also sweating as if he had just run five miles in the dead heat of July.

Paul took a smoke break while he sat on the chopping block. His watch and stomach were beginning to tell him that it was almost noon. He ate a Hershey bar to curb his hunger and split wood for another half hour. After that, Paul started carrying the split pieces of wood up to the cabin for stacking.

It was almost two o'clock before Paul finished his many chores. There was still plenty of wood to be split, but he had enough for the next few days if he didn't go overboard with his use of the fireplace.

Paul went inside the cabin to retrieve the three claymore mines that he had left on the living room floor last night. He then went outside to set one mine up in the back and one more on each side of the cabin. He placed the back of the mines up against the cabin's logged walls, then fished the detonator wires around to the window on the living room side of the cabin. Paul ran the wires up the cabin wall and under the window so that he had fifteen feet of wire inside the cabin for each of the three mines. Paul stacked firewood against the cabin wall to conceal the wires, and the snow covered those around the perimeter. The mines were then covered with some evergreen brush that Paul cut from the surrounding woods. They were fairly well concealed in the daylight, but they would be almost impossible to see at night. Inside the cabin, Paul attached the detonator plungers to the three sets of wires that led to the mines. He placed them so that the middle plunger was for the claymore in the back of the cabin and the one on the left was for the left side of the cabin, etc. That way he could detonate the correct claymore by feel, even if he was in total darkness.

After the mines were set up, Paul took the fragmentation and incendiary grenades and put them into a white plastic kitchen trash bag. He then took the C-4 with timed detonators and placed them into another white trash bag. Paul took the two trash bags of explosives into the woods where he had split the firewood. He moved the large log he used as a chopping block about two feet to the side. Then Paul dug a shallow hole so he could bury the two white trash bags. He then covered the bags with earth before sliding the chopping block over the top of them to mark the spot.

Back at the cabin, the only ordnance-related item left on the floor was the night-vision goggles. Paul checked the batteries to make sure they were good before sliding the goggles under the couch.

It was now four o'clock, and Paul was really getting hungry. He decided to take another hot shower to wash off the dried sweat and body odor. Paul put on the last of his clean clothes when he was finished. He looked in the corner of the bedroom and saw that the dirty clothes were starting to mount. Since there was no washer or dryer in the cabin, Paul placed all the dirty clothes into one of the pillowcases so he could do laundry in Small Town.

Paul loaded the laundry into the Jeep, checked to make sure he had the 9mm in his jacket, then headed down the *Burma Road*. It was almost six o'clock when Paul drove into Small Town to locate a Laundromat. As luck would have it, there was a Suds and Wash across the road and maybe two blocks south of Libby's Steak House. For Paul, there was no question that this was a sign from God to eat at Libby's again. Paul pulled over to the side of the road to park the Jeep.

The temperature was definitely dropping, so Paul hurried inside the restaurant where it was warm. The hostess was not the same one who had greeted him last night. This woman was maybe thirty-eight and looked as if a beauty queen trophy could have been on her mantel from years gone past. She was wearing a western-style white blouse and a short, full-cut black skirt. Paul smiled at the woman, who was sporting a name tag announcing to the world that her name was Jill.

Paul said, "Hi, Jill. Table for one, please."

Jill smiled at Paul with a set of pearly whites that must have cost her parents a fortune. Her smile was absolutely beautiful. Jill also had the hourglass figure that Paul usually only saw on women in magazines. She asked in a very high-pitched voice, "Only one, sweety? A good-lookin' feller like you shouldn't be eatin' alone."

Paul was turned off by her voice and hillbillylike grammar. The only thing he could manage to say was, "Well, my wife and kids are going to meet me later in Roanoke."

The hostess's smile turned to a frown as she said, "This way, sir."

Paul followed the hostess to a table in the back of the restaurant. *The place was only half-full because it was still early for dinner*, Paul thought. As he followed the hostess he checked out her legs, which he thought were her least impressive feature. *Jill lacked defined ankles and shapely calves*, he thought.

Once Paul was seated, a waitress came over to take his order. Paul didn't need to look at the menu. He simply said, "I'll have the house special, medium well done, and a cold draft."

The waitress dashed off to place the order and bring Paul his beer. The atmosphere was very nice and peaceful at Libby's. Paul thought about how much Diana would have enjoyed coming here for dinner. His mind wandered about in the past until the waitress broke his trance by placing a sizzling plate down in front of him. Paul ate his meal, followed by two cups of excellent coffee, then waited for the check. The restaurant was now full of hungry customers, and a line for tables was starting to form by the front desk. Paul looked at his watch to see that it was now seven o'clock.

He left the restaurant and headed for the Laundromat to take care of his dirty clothes. Inside the Laundromat, there were a dozen or so washers and six huge dryers. There was only one other person in the Laundromat. A woman, maybe fifty or so years old, was sitting in the corner on a metal folding chair reading a paperback book. Paul split his dirty clothes into two loads, added detergent he had purchased from a vending machine, then started two machines with his remaining quarters. After about twenty-five minutes, he took both loads of wash and placed them into one of the huge dryers. Again he added more quarters, which he had to get out of the change machine from hell. He would put in a dollar bill, and the machine would instantly spit it back out. He did this two more times, then tried three other one-dollar bills with the same frustrating result. Finally the woman who was sitting in the corner came over and smacked the change machine on the side, saying, "Sometimes you got to get its attention first."

Paul put the wrinkled old dollar bill into the machine, and out came three quarters, two dimes, and a nickel. He looked at the woman savior and said, "Thank you very much, miss."

The woman looked at Paul, nodded affirmatively, then went back to her corner of the Laundromat to finish reading her novel.

When the dryer stopped tumbling, Paul pulled the pillowcase out first, then filled it with the rest of his laundry, which was extremely hot to the touch. Paul looked at his watch and saw that it was almost eight o'clock. He quickly went outside to put the laundry into the Jeep, then took out his prepaid phone card to call Gary at the *Cell Block*. The pay phone on the wall outside the Suds and Wash was dirty, but at least it worked. Paul called the *Cell Block* at exactly eight o'clock.

After the second ring, a voice said, "Who's this?" "Paul. Who's this?"

"Hey, Paul. It's me, Gary."

"Gary, do you have anything for me, buddy?" "Oh yeah. Are you ready?"

Paul took out a folded paper napkin from Libby's and a pen from his coat pocket while saying, "Go ahead."

Gary filled Paul in on the details his cousin in Culpeper had discovered. Then Gary told Paul what Mikey had found out from some bookie in Jersey. Gary added, "Listen. Mikey told me to tell you that this guy Sharp comes to Atlantic City every Wednesday to check on his betting operations. He stays overnight and then returns to the main house the very next day. Usually he flies by a private plane that takes off from Hickman Field in Charlottesville, Virginia, just off of Interstate 64. It's about a thirty-minute drive from the main house to the airport. Mikey also said to tell you this dude Sharp never misses the run to Atlantic City. If the weather is bad, he travels by limousine. Apparently, he picks up some heavy duty cash, because he takes his main enforcer along for the ride. Some guy named John Toby. Did you get all that?"

Paul's mind was going in thirty directions at once. He jotted down a few notes, then said, "Yeah. You and Mikey do really good work. I appreciate the information, and I don't care how you got it either. Listen, Gary. Make sure you thank Mikey and your cousin Holland for the fast turnaround. I owe all of you a big thick, juicy steak."

"Don't sweat it, Pauly. We're all more than happy to help.

Now, how am I going to get a copy of this map to you? You know, the one that dude drew showing the hidden communications center?"

Paul looked around the area and spotted a convenience store across the street that had a sign in the window advertising services that read: *Copies Made Here*, and another read: *Fax It Here*. Paul said, "Gary, I'm going to hang up so I can go across the street to get the fax number to the convenience store here. I'll call you back in five minutes with the number; then you go downstairs and ask Mikey to fax me the map."

Paul ran across the street to ask the proprietor for his fax number. Paul then ran back to the pay phone and called Gary. Paul thanked Gary one more time before saying, "Remember, I'll call you again tomorrow at eight o'clock sharp."

Gary couldn't help laugh, then said, "That's good, Paul. Sharp, as in Billy Sharp. Now, are you sure that you don't need some help? Remember, I have kinfolk down there in Virginia, who would love to get in on the action."

Paul said, "You have already done enough, my friend. The rest of this little project is purely personal."

Paul hung up the phone and went back into the convenience store. While he was waiting for the fax to arrive, he bought some cigarettes, a local newspaper, and more snack foods. He also bought two nine-volt batteries and a roll of electric tape. He poured himself a large coffee, as the fax machine started rumbling. The sixty-year-old man behind the counter never looked up at Paul other than when he took Paul's money for the purchases. The man was looking at one of the *Penthouse* magazines he kept behind the counter and had the centerfold picture lying wide open on the small table behind the customer counter. As Paul was paying the man, he couldn't help but look at the centerfold. She was absolutely gorgeous, with a pair of legs that were out of this world. Paul picked up the fax and his other purchases, then headed back to the Jeep. While he was walking, it started snowing again. Paul started the Jeep to get the heater going and turned on the overhead dome light. He studied the map Gary faxed to him and was impressed with its level of detail.

Paul lit a cigarette and studied the map some more. When he realized how close he recently was to the hidden bunker, it upset him. He was standing right on top of the place when he rigged the two fuel tanks to explode. Paul turned off the dome light and headed for the gas station at the end of the street, to fill his tank. While Paul was filling the Jeep, he was thinking about how he would take care of Billy Sharp's hidden fortress. He already had a few ideas in mind as he walked into the garage part of the station to pay the attendant for the gas. The station attendant was in his late seventies but obviously still capable of working on vehicles.

He was under the hood of a fairly new pickup truck when Paul approached.

"Howdy. I got fifteen dollars' worth of regular gas."

The old man slipped his head out from under the hood of the pickup, saying, "Just lay it on the desk in there, pal."

Paul put the money on the desk, then asked, "Excuse me; do you sell one-gallon gas cans, by any chance?"

The old man stuck his head out from behind the pickup, saying, "I have the metal type, not them damn new plastic contraptions."

"That's exactly what I'm looking for. I need four of 'em, if you have 'em?"

The old man scratched his gray-whiskered face, thinking a few seconds, then said, "Look over there by those grease barrels. I think there are a half-dozen one-gallon cans in a cardboard box sitting back in the corner."

Paul looked at the spot where the old man was pointing and walked over to look in the corner. Sure enough, there were new one-gallon gas cans inside a box. Paul took four cans out and asked, "How much do I owe you?"

"Add another six dollars to the gas money, and we'll call her even."

Paul dug out the extra cash and placed it on top of the fifteen dollars he had already placed on the desk. As Paul was walking out of the garage, the old man asked, "Say, fella, what ya need four of them cans fer?"

Paul knew he couldn't fool an old-timer like this, so he said, "I have to keep one for my tractor, one for my kerosene heater, and two are separate fuel and oil mixes for two cycle engines."

The old man scratched his gray bristles again. Apparently accepting the explanation, he nodded affirmatively and ducked his head back under the hood of the pickup truck.

Paul loaded the four gas cans into the Jeep and headed toward the cabin. The snow was coming down harder now, but Paul had no idea what the forecast was for the night. He tried to find a noncountry radio station on the Jeep radio, but that was damn near impossible in these mountains. He drove to the entrance of the *Burma Road* and turned to begin his steep, steady climb. The fresh snow had covered the tire tracks he made earlier when he came down the mountain.

At the clearing, Paul turned in and parked the Jeep by the front door. He looked around and could not see any fresh footprints in the snow, so he figured it was safe to go inside. Paul took the four gas cans and his laundry inside the cabin. He immediately turned up the thermostat and started the kindling he had placed in the fireplace earlier.

After Paul was satisfied the temperature was acceptable to shed his coat, he did so. He put the 9mm back behind the wood piled next to the fireplace. Paul also put the laundry away and started a pot of water on the stove so he could make some hot chocolate.

As the water was heating, Paul took the night-vision goggles from under the couch to see how well they worked. He turned the goggles on and immediately heard the whine of the tiny compact electronic package starting to power up. Paul went into the dark bedroom to look through the goggles. It was as if he were looking at a room filled with green light. Paul was very impressed with the clarity the goggles afforded him. He then looked out the bedroom window to see what kind of range they offered. He could clearly see all the way to the tree line and maybe another ten feet or so before the images of the trees darkened. Again Paul was impressed with the quality and clarity of the equipment. He turned off the power supply and returned the goggles to their hiding place under the couch.

When the water was ready, Paul made a cup of hot chocolate, then sat on the couch in front of the blazing fireplace. He now had a good burn going in the hearth and could feel the heat radiating around the small room. Paul turned on the lamp by the couch, lit a cigarette, then took out the map Gary had faxed him to study it some more. He would again need a diversion to draw the people out of the main house. This time it would be farther down the road, so he could set his charges properly. He took his pen and made some notes on the map. He figured out the places where the C-4 would be most effective and marked other places where the fragmentation grenades could be placed. He then made other markings that allowed him an escape path or two with appropriate booby traps in place to take care of anyone who dared follow.

It was almost midnight before Paul had finalized his plan. In his mind, it was all worked out and it only needed to be executed properly. *It would be better to have a two-man team,* he thought. *But right now he was all alone.* Being alone made the plan a bit more difficult, but still very doable. The weather would also be an important factor, so Paul had to know what the forecast was for tomorrow night. That was when he planned to sneak onto the *Double C* ranch to set up the fireworks.

Chapter 22

Gary Roth was feeling pretty good about how things had worked out so far with Paul. However, Gary was not very happy about the idea that Paul was going to make a solo run at the *Double C* ranch. Gary really wanted to offer his friend some backup, just in case there was trouble. After Gary faxed the map to Paul from Mikey's office, the two men sat and talked about how hard it was to just wait around for something to happen. Mikey was in no shape to go on a night mission down in Virginia, but Gary certainly could handle it easily. Mickey told Gary that Paul would probably become very upset if he showed up uninvited. In fact, judging from all the ordnance Paul had taken with him, it might not be a good idea for Gary, or anyone else to try to see Paul without giving advance notice.

A few drinks later, Mikey finally came up with a workable plan for action. He said, "Gary, here's what we can do. You head down to the Angle Inn tomorrow so that you are there by eight o'clock in the evening. When Paul calls here tomorrow night, I'll tell him where you are. That way, he has one of three choices to make. He can come get you, if he wants your help. Or he can leave you there to sulk in your beer if he'd rather go it alone. The last option is he could join you for a beer, then send your butt back to Baltimore."

"Sounds like a good plan, Mikey. At least I wouldn't have to take a chance of getting my head taken off accidentally. Let's face it, he's a little trigger-happy right now, so I don't want to be driving directly to the cabin unexpected."

"How about another beer before you leave?"

"Sure. Why not? I'll also need to take a little insurance with me, Mikey, if you know what I mean?"

"Sure. We can pick something out for you in the back room before you leave here tonight."

Detective McGavin was working in her office late because the homicide rate in Baltimore seemed to be on a never-ending upward spiral. It was almost ten o'clock when she started to wrap up the paperwork for two homicide cases on which she was working. On his way out, the commissioner walked up to her desk, saying, "I see we're both burning the midnight oil tonight, Detective."

"Well, Commissioner, look around. We're obviously not the only ones. Have a seat."

"Theresa, how's it going with the Marco case these days?"

Detective McGavin gave the commissioner the latest rundown on what was happening and shared some of the theories Captain Thiemeyer and she had been working on together. She then said, "So, as you can tell, we are up against a brick wall right now until something else happens or someone comes forward with a new angle."

The commissioner, looking very tired, rubbed his face with his hands, then said, "I suppose you have ruled out coincidence regarding the stolen car being so close to Marco's house?"

"Absolutely. There has to be a link there somewhere. Unfortunately, any evidence that could tie the two pieces of evidence together probably was destroyed by the fire."

"You may be right, Theresa. Why don't you take the lab and arson guys to Marco's and have them snoop around the ashes? They're pretty good at finding a needle in the haystack. Who knows? They may be able to turn up something, or at least rule out some of your suspicions. Besides, you don't have anything else going on with the case anyway."

"I guess it couldn't hurt, Commissioner. I'll talk to them tomorrow to see if we can't go out to Marco's house to find that ever illusive smoking gun."

Commissioner Doukup left police headquarters thinking about the chain of events that had led up to Paul Marco being considered as a prime suspect for the murder of two ex-cons. It didn't sit right in his stomach, but then, as police commissioner, he had seen many things that didn't make much sense. *A man will do some strange things if given the opportunity or if pushed to his mental limit,* he thought.

Detective McGavin left police headquarters to get something to eat at a local restaurant close to her apartment building in Bel Air. It was almost midnight when she picked up her mail on the first floor of her building. On the elevator ride to the seventh floor she looked at the stack consisting of bills, more bills, and junk mail. They were more than she wanted to deal with right at the moment. Inside her apartment, she pressed the answering machine button to listen to the messages while she got undressed. There was a call from her married older sister inviting her to Thanksgiving dinner this year. Of course, Theresa's sister was going to invite a male friend, but she was not really trying to help fix her up or anything. There was also a call from her mother asking, no begging, her to come to Thanksgiving dinner this year to meet a dear friend's son. He had a job and everything, her mother gloated.

Theresa filled the tub with hot water, splashed in some scented oil, and soaked in the warmth with a glass of chilled red wine. After a long day, Theresa McGavin found that a hot bath and a glass of wine would put her to sleep in record time. She was about halfway through her glass of wine when the phone started ringing. Theresa was startled and surprised that someone would actually be calling her this late at night. She lay back in the warm water, deciding to let the answering machine pick it up. After the fourth ring, the machine clicked on and Theresa could just hear the caller's voice.

"Hi, Detective McGavin. I guess you're out catching bad guys this late at night. I was calling to tell you that I should be back in town in a couple of days. I'll call you as soon as I get back so I can fill you in on all the details of the past week. I'll talk to you later. Bye."

Theresa, realizing that it was Paul's voice on the phone, jumped out of the tub, grabbed a towel, then slipped on the steamy bathroom floor. She could still hear Paul's voice leaving the message, but by the time she got to her feet and to the phone, he had already hung up. She was livid. First she was angry that someone had called so late at night. Second, she was angrier that it was her only suspect in a double homicide case. Yet she was sorry that she had missed Paul's call. Theresa really wanted to talk to Paul to see if she could help. He seemed to be a very sensible guy who may have simply made one big mistake in life. She knew that if she could talk to him, she could stop him from doing something else that might jeopardize his freedom.

Billy Sharp was in the bunker talking to John Toby. John was checking the receipts from that day's delivery. The cash from some of the more remote operations up and down the coast came to the *Double C* ranch by way of UPS. The boxes of cash were immediately opened, and John's job was to compare the computerized tally sheets to the actual cash that was shipped. Although it was not recommended to ship large quantities of cash through UPS, most people did not bother looking into boxes marked: *medical specimens* destined for a horse breeder. The regular UPS delivery personnel had no idea what they were carrying and didn't much care so long as they met their tight delivery schedule. Their annual bonus depended on them making timely deliveries, not legal or ethical ones.

Billy asked John how the collection business was going in general.

John was not happy about giving his report to the boss. He said, "You're not going to like it, Boss. Several merchants in the Maryland and Delaware areas didn't pay their protection money when we sent out the collectors. Worst yet was what happened in Washington, D.C. A competitor has been making visits to shopping center merchants, selling their services for 15 percent less than our going rate. Supposedly, the new kid in town is offering to take care of our enforcers if they come around, at no extra charge. We are looking into it now, Boss, but it appears that the Jamaicans are making a move into our turf."

Billy's face was getting blood red from rage. All he could say was, "That goddamned Marco," as he punched a cardboard box filled with money off the table, sending bills everywhere. Billy yelled, "I thought you told me that you were taking care of that son of a bitch! No! You said that you were personally going to handle it! Didn't you, John?"

"Yeah, I'm working on it, Boss, but—"

"No more buts, damn it. I have had enough of this Marco bastard screwing up my business. I want him taken out. Do you hear me?"

"Boss, I have a possible lead on him."

Billy was quiet for a few seconds as he caught his breath and allowed his blood pressure to come down. "You say that you have a lead? Tell me more."

"I have a guy who has some back problems, and every now and then he needs an adjustment. Anyway, he goes to see this old broad at the Angle Inn who works some magic on his back. He pays the old broad ten dollars for about three seconds' work, but he walks out of her place a new man."

Billy was getting restless listening to the long-winded tail of some guy's backache. "Is this going anywhere, or are you going to bore me to death with this old-broad story?"

"No, it gets better, Boss. Anyway, this guy is talking to the old broad, and she says that she worked on a big-city guy's backache a couple of days ago. He spent the night in the back of the bar, then slipped out the next morning driving a fancy red Jeep. Well, Paul Marco has a red Jeep. So on a hunch, I go down to talk to this old broad. I paid her a few bucks and got a description of the big-city guy she worked on and it fits our boy Marco to a T."

Now Billy's eyes were starting to brighten. He said, "Well, where is he? Marco, where's Marco now?"

"I talked to one of the bartenders that works days, and he didn't know anything about the guy who spent the night there. I'm going back later tonight to talk to the night bartender, to see what he can tell me."

"Bullshit! You go down there tonight after you finish here and bust some heads if you have to. I want that son of a bitch Marco dead, yesterday. Understand?"

John Toby finished up his shift in the bunker counting and verifying receipts a little before eleven o'clock. Billy Sharp stormed out of the bunker into the night so he could inspect the construction work going on aboveground. The burned outbuildings were now demolished and had been hauled away. Steel beams and girders were being erected in their place so that the new outbuildings could be made bigger and better. The backup generators were finally silent after the electrician finished his job earlier in the day. The trench he dug from the main house to the bunker was backfilled and graded. In the spring, new sod would be laid down to make the grounds more aesthetically pleasing. The power washers and painters still had scaffolding erected on two sides of the main house. They were washing off the soot from the fire and repainting areas that were actually blistered by the intense heat generated by the fire.

Billy Sharp took a look around his ranch in the cold night air and was rather pleased with the way things were starting to shape up. Things were just going to get better now that John, the enforcer, had finally gotten a line on Mr. Paul Marco. *Once the Marco business was taken care of, things would get back to normal,* Billy thought.

Paul put on the night-vision goggles and scanned the perimeter before turning in for the night. He had a big job to do tomorrow night, so he needed to get plenty of rest. The perimeter was secure, all of his weapons were in their proper place, and the detonators for the claymore mines were hidden under an overstuffed chair that Paul had moved by the living room window. He lit a cigarette as he lay on the couch to watch the fire burn down. The last thing Paul remembered was throwing his cigarette butt into the fireplace around one o'clock in the morning. His wood cutting and splitting earlier in the day must have taken a lot out of him. He was dead tired and never actually made it into the bedroom.

All was well until around five o'clock in the morning, when Paul thought that he heard a noise outside. He sat up and listened more intently. He was now sure he heard footprints crunching in the frozen snow outside the cabin. Quickly Paul went to get the 9mm behind the stacked wood by the fireplace. He chambered a round and took off the safety as he picked up the night-vision goggles that were sitting on the coffee table. The whole time, he heard the snow being crunched outside. This time it sounded as if the noise was coming from below the living room window. Paul crawled over to the kitchenette to grab the twelve-gauge shotgun. He put the night-vision goggles on and flipped the power switch. With the goggles on, the 9mm tucked in his waistband, and the twelve-gauge at the ready, Paul crossed the living room floor, hearing glass being broken in the bedroom. Paul did not wait for another sign. He reached under the overstuffed chair and pumped the right claymore mine plunger three times fast. The explosion rocked the small cabin and shattered the quiet night for at least a one-mile radius. Paul then heard more voices outside. Only this time they were coming from the living room side of the cabin. Paul pumped the left claymore detonator plunger three times and the house rocked again, as the explosion pierced the frigid darkness.

Paul looked out through the living room window and saw two bodies staining the white snow with fresh steaming blood. A claymore mine fires hundreds of steel balls that are a little smaller than a child's marble. The kill zone is very wide and extremely accurate. Paul rushed to the back of the cabin, where he looked out through the broken bedroom window. There were only parts of what could have been one or maybe two bodies lying on the blood-covered snow. *They must have taken the full brunt of the blast*, thought Paul.

Paul went into the small hall to listen in both directions from the cabin. He did not hear any more footsteps crunching the frozen snow. He listened for almost two minutes but did not hear any voices or vehicles. *They must have parked down the Burma Road and walked up to the cabin,* he thought. He waited another two minutes, then climbed out of the bedroom window. He did not want to use the front door in case someone was waiting for him on the other side.

The night-vision goggles were fantastic. Paul scanned the right side of the cabin, then walked to the back, looking for more footprints in the snow, but found none. He continued moving around the back until he was on the other side of the cabin. Paul scanned the area with his goggles as he slowly moved around the cabin hugging its walls. His only objective was to make his way to the front of the cabin. The goggles allowed Paul to see five or six sets of footprints approaching the cabin from the direction of the *Burma Road*. With two dead on the living room side and one or maybe two more dead on the bedroom side of the cabin, Paul figured that left one or two escapees. Paul dashed across the clearing onto the *Burma Road,* where he confirmed that six sets of footprints led up to the cabin, but only two sets were headed in the opposite direction. Paul went back to check the two bodies on the living room side of the cabin for ID. They had none. No wallet or papers whatsoever. Paul did observe, however, that they each carried expensive machine pistols. That could only mean that they weren't coming to see him for a neighborly visit. The two bodies on the other side of the cabin were too messy for Paul to go through their pockets.

Paul knew he had to get away from the cabin fast. He took off the goggles and placed them into the Jeep along with the twelve gauge. He went inside the cabin to gather all his belongings, clothes, cell phone, weapons, gas cans, etc. Paul retrieved the grenades and C-4 he had buried under the stump and the one remaining claymore from behind the cabin. He thought about wiping down the cabin to hide his fingerprints, but didn't want to spend any more time there than he already had. Paul took two of the incendiary grenades and wrapped a separate piece of twine around each of the handles and canisters. He tied them securely, leaving a four-foot piece of string as a tail, then pulled the pins. He placed one of the incendiary grenades on the kitchenette counter. He lit the end of the string and blew out the flame immediately. In an hour or so the string would burn to the knot releasing the handle, thus starting the inferno. Paul put the second incendiary grenade in the small toolshed. His prints were on many of the tools, so everything had to be torched. Paul lit the string just as he had in the kitchenette, then blew out the flame.

It took Paul less than fifteen minutes to pack up his gear and head down the mountain. The whole time he was packing, he was trying to figure out who the men were and how they knew where to find him. In roughly forty-five minutes he would not have to worry about anyone tying him to the cabin. The only people who could possibly do that were, Gary and the Angle Inn employees he had met on the first night when he picked up the keys.

On the way down the *Burma Road*, Paul stopped to inspect the vehicle tracks that appeared in the fresh snow about fifteen feet from the main road. The bad guys definitely had two vehicles with knobby tires, the big knobby tires that were more for recreation and sport instead of street use. Paul saw a piece of red plastic taillight lens lying on the top of the snow. The tire tracks showed that the truck had backed up to turn around and the driver must have struck the small tree in his haste, breaking the taillight. The tracks also told Paul that it was the left taillight. Paul then put the piece of lens in his pocket as he looked at his watch to see that it was almost seven o'clock. *Too early to pay a visit to the Angle Inn and have a talk with the proprietor,* he thought. Paul turned onto the main road and headed for Small Town to eat breakfast. All of a sudden he was very hungry, and his appetite for Billy Sharp was growing stronger by the minute.

Chapter 23

Gary Roth telephoned one of his cousins who lived in Frederick, Maryland, to tell him that he was going to drive over for a visit. Gary planned to spend several hours with his cousin, then drive over to the Angle Inn just before the eight o'clock call came into the *Cell Block* from Paul.

Gary left Baltimore at 9:00 a.m. with a beautiful day forecast for the downtown and surrounding areas. The temperature was already fifty degrees, the winds were calm, and the sunshine was that extremely warm, bright kind that only fall could bring. The drive to Frederick was absolutely gorgeous, and traffic was moving at a fast, steady pace. If things held constant, Gary would be pulling up to his cousin's front porch by ten o'clock. Gary's cousin only lived an hour away from Baltimore, but they hardly ever saw each other except at funerals and weddings. His cousin was very surprised that Gary was coming and was busy making plans for them to do a little fly fishing after his arrival. Fly fishing was something they used to do as kids every summer while Gary stayed at his cousin's parents' farm.

John Toby did not want to wake the boss to give him bad news about his men missing an opportunity to take out Marco again. The body count was starting to mount, and John had nothing to show for it so far. *This Marco character must be the luckiest son of a bitch alive,* thought John.

Around nine-thirty John Toby went into the main house, where Billy was finishing his breakfast. Billy was sitting in the kitchen by himself reading the paper as he ate. Billy finally looked up, folded the paper to set it down on the table, then observed John's pitiful facial expression. Billy said, "Come on in and sit down. Do you want some coffee?"

"No, thanks. I have—"

"By the look on your face, John, you must have bad news to tell me. I told you I wanted this Marco business finished. Please, tell me you have completed the job?"

John was now starting to get angry with Billy. He was trying his best, but that was not good enough just yet. "Look, Boss. I sent a couple of hitters to take care of this business at Marco's house, and they ended up dead. I sent Joey with five other men to take him out after we found out he was holed up at some cabin in the mountains. Now I hear he took out four of them, in a very messy fashion. Joey said the cabin was booby trapped with explosives. He had never seen anything like it before. I'm running out of men and ideas. So, if you have a way to take Marco out, then I'm all ears."

Billy listened to John rant and rave until he felt that it was now quiet enough for calmer heads to prevail. Billy said, "You know, John, you surprise me."

"Yeah? How's that?"

"Well, you are obviously dealing with idiots. All this time you have been trying to take out Marco on his turf. What you need to do is tilt the playing field in your favor a little. In other words, make him come to you for a change. On your turf, where you can set the traps. Do you follow me?"

Before John could reply, his beeper sounded. John looked at the number, then said, "I need to use a phone."

Billy pointed to the phone on the kitchen wall, then poured himself more coffee as John dialed. "What's up? . . . You're kidding! . . . That son of a bitch. OK, I'll get back to you later."

John slammed the receiver down on the switch hook.

Billy put down his coffee cup and asked, "What was that all about?"

"You're not going to believe what happened to the last two men I sent after Marco."

Paul stopped for breakfast at a small greasy spoon he found at the other end of Small Town. The place was really an old railroad car that the owner had turned into a diner. The parking lot was large and practically filled with tractor trailers idling to keep the cabs warm while the drivers were inside eating.

The diner counter had fifteen stools, and to the left there were eight booths that could each hold four people or two adults comfortably. Almost all the counter stools were taken up by the big-rig drivers. They had that brawny look about them and more than likely couldn't fit in the booths due to their sheer bulk. Paul sat in one of the booths overlooking the front parking lot that faced the street. A waitress came to the table with a mug and started filing it with coffee before Paul could say a word. The waitress was in her forties, trim, and, judging by her body language, not in the mood for small talk. She placed the coffeepot on the table and took out her ordering pad, asking, "What'll you have?"

Paul looked up over top of the counter where the menu was displayed, saying, "Steak and eggs. Over easy on the eggs and medium well on the steak. I would also like a large glass of orange juice and a side order of white toast with butter."

"That it?"

"Yep."

The waitress tucked her order pad into the front of her apron, shoved the pencil behind her ear, grabbed the coffeepot, and left. Paul was obviously not in the mood for small talk either.

Paul sipped his coffee and stared out the window. Suddenly he heard sirens screaming through the town. First there was a huge fire truck, then two smaller ones following close behind. Paul thought, *Someone must have reported the fire at the cabin.*

One of the patrons sitting at the counter stood up to look out the front door and watch the action. He opened the door and yelled something to the owner of the store next to the diner. When the patron came back inside the diner, he said in a loud voice as if making an announcement, "Milt said he heard on the scanner that Yingling's place is on fire."

Another patron sitting at the counter replied, "I didn't think Tom used that place until huntin' season started."

Paul finished his coffee and eavesdropped on the conversations going on all around him. Apparently, in Small Town a fire was big news. After a few more minutes of chatter the topic changed to the weather and road conditions heading north and west.

The waitress brought Paul his meal and juice in one spectacular balancing act. She had plates up her arm and a glass and silverware in one hand and a coffeepot in the other. Somehow she managed to set it all down in front of Paul without dropping a morsel of food or spilling a drop of coffee. Paul added some pepper to the steak and eggs, then chowed down. He was very hungry and the hot breakfast was just what he needed to pick him up. The food was steaming hot and tasted outstanding. The eggs were cooked to perfection, and the steak was just how he liked it prepared. After Paul finished eating, the waitress cleared the plates and filled his coffee mug as she placed the check on the table. The tab was a whopping $5.50. Paul looked again at the total and could not believe his eyes. For a meal that good he would have paid twice that amount.

Paul went to the front of the diner to pay his tab. The waitress obviously had to pull double duty, because she met him at the cash register to take his money. Paul gave her eight dollars and left the diner as he heard her say, "Thanks."

Outside, Paul went to his Jeep and started the engine so he could turn on the heater. The air outside was cold and crisp. The temperature was only in the thirties, and another threat of snow was forecast for the mountain region. Paul looked at his watch to see that it was only nine o'clock. He had to find a place to get a few hour's sleep, so he pulled out a road map from the glove box to see what was in the immediate area. The big town of Hagerstown was only about twenty miles away. Paul figured he could get lost in one of the many motels around there for several hours easily. Paul put the Jeep into gear and was about to pull away when he saw a raised pickup truck pulling into the parking lot. Behind that truck was a second raised pickup. Both trucks had big knobby tires on all four wheels. They parked on the other side of the diner, so they could not easily see Paul's Jeep parked among the big rigs. Paul watched as the two drivers left their trucks and went inside the diner. Paul's mind was racing. *Could it be the two trucks that visited me early in the morning? How could I be sure it was them without an actual confrontation? Maybe there are hundreds of raised pickup trucks with knobby tires on all four wheels.* Paul reached into his pocket and pulled out the small piece of lens from the broken taillight he had found at the bottom of the *Burma Road*. He turned off the engine, put on his gloves, then got out to walk to the back cargo door of the Jeep. From inside the Jeep Paul took two fragmentation grenades, then wiped them clean of fingerprints. He also cut four pieces of string about eighteen inches long. He put all the materials into his pockets, then walked around to the back of the diner. Keeping his body close to the several dumpsters and discarded boxes and pallets stacked behind the diner, Paul made his way to its side, where the two pickup trucks were parked. They were parked so the fronts of the vehicles were facing the diner. Paul ducked down beside one of the trucks and slowly made his way to the rear of the vehicle. Both red portions of the taillights were intact. He quickly checked the second truck to find that the left taillight was broken. Paul reached into his pocket to pull out the piece of plastic lens, then held it up to the taillight. There was now no doubt in his mind that this truck had been at the cabin earlier today. Paul put the piece of lens back into his pocket as he looked around to make sure no one was coming. Paul thought, *The beauty of these raised trucks with huge tires is that getting underneath them is a piece of cake.* Paul took one fragmentation grenade and tied it to the underside of the truck with a piece of string. He then tied one end of another piece of string to the pull pin. When that was done, Paul securely wrapped the other end of the string around the drive shaft. When the drive shaft started turning, it would wind up the string, which would remove the grenade pull pin. Exactly seven seconds later there would be no more driver or truck. Although Paul was not absolutely sure the second pickup had been at the cabin, he was now pronouncing it guilty by association. Paul scooted under the second pickup truck and secured a frag to the underside, just as he had done to the first truck.

Paul went back to his Jeep feeling that he would now be able to rest, knowing that all those who had tried to kill him earlier had been neutralized. That would leave him a clear slate when it came time to dealing with Billy Sharp.

There was no need for Paul to hang around the diner any longer. He was confident that the booby traps would work. However, there was always something of a thrill in actually knowing that things worked the way they were planned. Paul started the Jeep and pulled down the road to the convenience store a few blocks away to buy a coffee and newspaper. There were several other customers in the store, but Paul really was in no hurry. The same man who had received the fax from Gary was working behind the meat case cutting some lunch meat for one of the customers. Paul fixed his coffee and browsed through the newspaper while he waited. He looked at his watch to see that the two knobby-tired truck drivers had been in the diner for almost forty-five minutes. *It won't be long now,* he thought.

The man behind the counter rang up the sale for the lunch meat, then sold several lottery tickets to a couple of other customers before it was Paul's turn to pay. The man behind the counter said, "That'll be a dollar forty-three."

Paul handed the man two dollars, and suddenly a loud explosion sounded. It was quickly followed by another explosion a few seconds later. Paul asked, "What was that?"

The old man looked up and gave Paul his change, then hurried to the front door and looked down the street. As Paul exited the store, he passed the old man as he was saying, "Looks like a car exploded right there in the middle of the street, in front of the diner."

Paul could see the black smoke climbing into the sky and then heard the sounds of sirens rushing firefighters to earn their pay once again. While half the town was outside looking toward the smoky mess, the old man said, "Damn, this is more excitement then we have had around here in years. First a fire, now this."

Paul climbed back into his Jeep and headed toward the explosion. He would have to go past the debris on his way to Hagerstown. When he passed the site, there wasn't much to look at: two burning pickup trucks lying on their sides with a couple of firefighters spraying water on the flames. Paul could see that two bodies were covered with white sheets over by the far curb. There were several men with brooms sweeping up broken glass and truck parts so traffic could negotiate around the site. Paul continued past the diner to a small roadside motel just outside the town limits of Hagerstown. He registered at the desk using the name William Sharp, then took the key from the *"I'm not interested in who you really are"* clerk. Paul pulled the Jeep in front of his unit and went inside. The room was small but clean. Paul went back out to the Jeep to get his clothes, shaving gear, and one 9mm. Back inside, he took a steaming hot shower, then crawled into bed to get some much-needed sleep. It was only eleven-thirty, so he had plenty of time before he had to make the call to the *Cell Block*.

Gary pulled up to his cousin's house trailer and was immediately greeted with hugs, kisses, and smiles. Cousin Sam and his wife, Doris, followed by their three kids, ages eleven, ten, and eight, were hovering around Gary as if he were some rock star. Gary went to the back of the car and opened the trunk to take out the presents he had brought. There were games for the kids, two dolls for the girls, and a bat, ball, and glove for little Sammy junior. The kids were so grateful for the gifts they nearly strangled Gary with hugs and kisses.

Sam and Doris didn't have much when it came to worldly possessions, but they had a loving family that appreciated any good fortune that came their way. The smiles on Sam's and Doris's faces, as they watched their kids being so happy, made Gary feel warm all over. He then said, "Hey, I didn't forget you guys."

Gary pulled out a huge gift-wrapped box and gave it to Doris. Her eyes were twinkling as she looked at the beautiful box. Her excitement finally got the best of her as she ripped the paper to shreds. All eyes were on her as she opened the box to find a bolt of fabric. She was stunned at how beautiful the cloth looked and felt. Gary said, "I figured you could put that to good use."

"It's gorgeous, Gary. Come look, Sam. I can make curtains for the whole house with this material."

Gary said, "Look underneath, Doris."

Doris lifted the bolt of fabric to find a clothes catalog, with a $500 gift certificate attached. Her eyes were as big as saucers. Gary said, "You didn't think I would only get you some lousy material to play with, did you?" Doris had tears in her eyes as she hugged Gary around the neck. Gary said, "You buy yourself something really nice. Splurge a little, Doris."

Sam was watching his family and couldn't help but feel proud of his cousin for lifting their spirits so high. Sam finally said, "Hey, Doris made us some sandwiches, so what do you say we go catch some trout for dinner?"

"Sounds great. I have a six-pack on ice in the trunk. I'll grab it and you get the rods."

"I already have everything in the pickup, Gary. Let's go."

Gary and Sam drove to a stream located about ten minutes down the road from the trailer. They were drinking cold beer while they talked about the things they use to do together as kids. It was good for Gary to get away from the city every now and again so he could restore his faith in the human race. His cousin Sam was a hard worker who took care of his family. He only had an eighth-grade education but, had managed to hold a job with the local lumber yard for over twenty years as a forklift driver and foreman. After Sam caught the first rainbow trout and taunted Gary with it for what seemed to be an hour or so, he asked, "What really brings you way out here, Gary?"

Gary sat on the riverbank with his cousin to lay out what was going on with him and his friend Marco. Sam listened to the story, then said, "Anyhow, you're going to go team up with him, then go down to this ranch and blow the guy away, right?"

"That's about the size of it. That is, if he lets me go along. He may tell me to stay out of his business; you never know."

"That may be some good advice, Gary. You're no damn hero. What makes you think you can go down to this ranch and pull this thing off? I mean it sounds as if you guys may be going into a lions' den to pick a fight."

"I know what you mean, Sam. However, sometimes you have to take the fight to the bull. This guy at the ranch is not the kind that fights his own battles. He pays folks to do that stuff for him." "I got the picture. Man, I hate guys like that." The two fished a while longer; then Sam said, "You want me to tag along with you for some additional backup?"

Gary hooked a trout and played it while Sam shouted instructions and suggestions. Finally Gary yelled, "Just hold the damn net!"

After they landed the three-pound beast, Gary said, "No way are you coming with me, Sam. You have a family to look after, and they can't go it alone. However, I do want you to do something for me."

"Name it, Gary."

"When we get back to the house, I have a box in the truck of my car I want you to hold for me. If something happens to me down in Virginia, you take that box and put it to good use. There is cash in there for you and the family to spend as you see fit. There is also information about my business dealings with Cousin Holland. You can either sell off the business to Holland or you can work it yourself. Either way. It's your call. If you decide to sell it to Holland, he'll give you a fair price. Just show him the letter in the box where I lay out what I think it's worth. Do you have all that?" "I promise to take care of it just as you ask, Gary. But please don't let Doris know anything about this for now. You know how much she worries."

Gary put out his hand to shake Sam's hand, saying, "It's a deal."

They fished for another hour and landed a total of six decent sized trout. Doris would fix up a big meal for them when they got home and the trout would be as tasty as if they were cooked in one of the world's best restaurants.

Chapter 24

Detective McGavin was watching the crime lab and arson guys sift through the charred remains that were once Paul Marco's house. For her, it was about as exciting as watching grass grow. They had been at it now for almost three hours when a U.S. Mail truck pulled into Marco's long driveway. Theresa walked up to the postman as he leaned out of his vehicle to ask, "Is this your place?"

"No." Theresa flashed her badge. "We're investigating the cause of the fire. Is there something I can do for you?"

"Oh, yeah. Look. I have a bunch of mail for a Mr. and Mrs. Paul Marco here and their mailbox at the end of the driveway is full. Do you know when they will be picking up their mail?"

"Mr. Marco is away for a few days, but I'll be seeing him as soon as he returns and let him know you stopped by."

"Tell him I can't put any more mail into the mailbox. I'll be taking today's mail back to the post office with me and place a hold on future deliveries until he stops in the PO."

"I'll make sure he gets the message as soon as he returns." The mailman backed out of the driveway to continue his appointed rounds. Theresa waited until he was out of sight, then walked down to the end of the driveway to look inside the mailbox. The mail was packed inside so tightly that she had to really pull and tug to break some loose. Once she had a few pieces of mail in her hand, the rest came out easily. There were circulars, advertisements, and assorted junk mail among several bills. There were bills from the telephone company, the gas and electric company, and several credit card companies. Theresa saw a second telephone bill with only Diana's name on it, which struck her as being a little odd. Theresa then held onto the two phone bills and jammed the rest of the mail back inside the mailbox. She walked back to her car to sit inside while she fished a nail file from out of her purse. Theresa very carefully opened the phone bill that was in Paul's name. The list of numbers he called, the dates, and the times all seemed reasonable. Theresa copied down several numbers into her notebook that seemed to be repeat calls. She then placed the pages of the bill back into the envelope. She used a little dab of clear nail polish as glue to reseal the envelope. Next, she opened the phone bill that was in Diana's name. It was a phone bill for a cell phone. The interesting thing about the calling pattern was that she was making calls after her death. Theresa looked at the three-digit area code for the last four calls and recognized it as being for Virginia. To substantiate her suspicions that Paul was the one using the cell phone, she saw a call made to her home in the late-evening hours. The same night that Paul left the message on her answering machine while she was in the tub relaxing. Theresa stuffed the billing pages back into the envelope, then sealed it using the nail polish.

McGavin now knew that Paul was somewhere in Virginia, and with a little luck the telephone company could tell her from where his call had generated. That would help her nail down where Paul Marco was now holed up. The reason he was calling from Virginia was still a mystery, however.

The crime lab and arson guys were finally packing up their gear. Theresa walked over to their van just as they finished loading the last of the equipment, saying, "Well, guys. Did you come up with anything?"

Bob Tackard, the lead investigator, replied, "Not really. But we won't know for sure until we run some tests back at the lab on a few of these samples. We did find some traces of blood under the charred deck boards, but that could have been from an animal crawling under there and dying. I'll check it out and give you a report in a couple of days."

"Thanks for your help on this, Bob. You, too, Nick."

When the van was fully packed, Bob waved to Theresa as he backed out of the driveway so he could return to headquarters. For Theresa, her next move was to call Captain Thiemeyer to fill him in on the phone bill she had discovered in Marco's mailbox.

Paul Marco woke up around six o'clock because he was freezing. It was dark and cold outside as he moved the curtains to look at the effects the gusting wind was having on the bare shrubbery lining the parking lot. He then turned up the thermostat to warm the tiny room and flipped on the TV to listen to the news. In the bathroom, he looked into the mirror, trying to decide whether to shave. After a long stare, he decided another hot shower and a clean shave would probably make him feel better. He was right.

Once Paul was dressed, in the last of his clean clothes, he took his gear out to the Jeep. It was only six forty-five, so he had plenty of time to get something to eat before he needed to call the *Cell Block*. Paul climbed into the Jeep to start it up, then drove off the motel parking lot heading toward Hagerstown. He saw a gas station on the right, so he pulled in to fill his tank and the four one gallon gas cans he had bought from the old mechanic. When Paul went up to the booth to pay for the gas, he bought four quarts of oil, then asked the attendant where he could get a good homecooked meal. The young female attendant said he should stay on the main road for about five miles. The place he should look for was named the Smokehouse. The young woman said they had the best surf and turf anywhere.

Paul thanked the pretty attendant, then loaded the gas cans and oil into the back of the Jeep. He pulled out of the gas station and headed for the restaurant with his mouth already beginning to water in anticipation of a good steak dinner. The town was busy with traffic moving in all directions. Paul kept an eye on the right side of the four-lane road for the Smokehouse restaurant sign. He stopped at a traffic light and spotted the neon sign that advertised *Steak & Lobster Dinner Special* straight ahead. When the light changed to green, Paul made a direct line to the restaurant parking lot. *The food must be good here*, he thought, *because the parking lot is full.* Paul saw an elderly couple leaving the restaurant, so he waited for them to vacate their parking space. Paul pulled into the vacant spot, then locked the Jeep, making sure to leave his weapons behind. He did not see any need to carry a gun in this place, because there was little chance that he would actually need it now. Paul walked to the front of the restaurant fighting the bitter-cold wind, which seemed to go right through his clothes and skin only to stop when it hit the bone. Once he was inside the Smokehouse, a burst of hot air quickly warmed his cheeks as he looked around the small waiting area in front of the dining room. There were three or four couples in front of him waiting for tables. Paul gave the hostess his name as Billy Sharp, then took a seat while he waited to be called.

The Smokehouse atmosphere was purely western. There were wagon wheels hanging from the ceiling with lights attached to give the illusion of chandeliers. The attire for the waitress and waiters was red-and-white checked shirts, tight jeans, and cowboy boots. There were about forty tables in the main dining room, and it appeared that there were more tables in two smaller offshoots. Paul looked to the rear of the restaurant, where he saw the restrooms and a sign that read: *Telephones*. He looked at his watch to see that it was now 7:10. He might have to call the *Cell Block* before dinner, unless he was seated at a table soon.

Slowly the names of those on the waiting list were called and Paul was seated around seven-thirty. A waitress came over to take Paul's order. She was in her twenties and very good-looking, and she must have had her jeans spray-painted on, because they were very tight. Paul gave the waitress his order, then she said that she would bring his beer and salad right away. Paul watched her walk away from his table and smiled to himself, thinking, *Nice butt*. The man at the next table saw Paul following the girl's butt with his eyes and smiled. He was with his wife or girlfriend and must have been looking at the same cute butt while the waitress was taking Paul's order.

Paul ate his salad, then looked at his watch again. It was 7:55.

The waitress came over to take his salad plate, and Paul asked her to hold off on his entree a few more minutes because he had to make a quick telephone call.

Paul used his prepaid phone card to dial the *Cell Block* at exactly eight o'clock.

"Who's this?"

"Is that you, Mikey?" "Hi, Pauly. Yeah, it's me."

"Where's Gary? Selling snowballs to Eskimos?" "No. Listen, Pauly. Gary is at the Angle Inn." "What in the hell is he doing there?"

"Hold your horses, Pauly. Gary and I discussed this before he left. He wants to help you with that business in Virginia."

Mikey went on to tell Paul how Gary didn't want to come to the cabin unannounced for fear of getting his head blown off, etc. When Mikey finished his explanation he said, "Now if you want Gary's help, he is waiting for you at the Angle Inn. If you don't want his help, he will leave the bar at nine o'clock to come home. Do you understand all that?"

Paul looked at his watch to see that it was now 8:15. He would never make it back to the Angle Inn by nine o'clock. Paul said, "I'll meet with Gary, but it's going to take me a while to get there. I'm in Hagerstown right now. I'll call the Angle Inn to see if he will answer a page."

"What are you doing in Hagerstown?"

"It's a long story. The cabin was burned to the ground, and a few stiffs were left behind. None of it could have been helped. Trust me."

"Damn, Pauly. You sure have a way of getting things done. Look. If you page Gary at the Angle Inn, use the name Mikey Roth. He will know something is up and answer the phone. If you ask for Gary Roth, he may figure someone is trying to flush him out as a trick."

Paul hung up the phone and immediately called Information to get the number for the Angle Inn. He asked the bartender if he would page a Mr. Mikey Roth. Paul described him as having dark hair and a mustache, about 180 pounds, and probably drinking tequila. The description didn't mean much to the bartender, but the drinking-tequila part narrowed the field to only one patron.

"Hello."

"Hey, asshole. It's me, Paul."

"Yeah, buddy. How ya doin'? I guess you talked to our mutual friend. So what's it going to be? Are you going to let me help, or are you going to send me packing?"

"Listen, hard head. I'm in Hagerstown right now. It'll take me about an hour or so to get to the Angle Inn. Drink a few Cokes on me, because I need you with all of your wits tonight."

"Hagerstown? OK. I'll be here ordering dinner and cola on you, buddy. See you in an hour or so."

Paul went back to his table to finish eating his dinner. The waitress brought him a plate of food that was enough to feed two adults and a small child. As he ate, Paul kept thinking about how Mikey and Gary must have come up with this little plan of theirs over several drinks. He started to laugh loudly but quickly caught himself before others around him might have figured him to be a nutcase.

Detective McGavin and Captain Thiemeyer were in the commissioner's office telling him about their latest break in the case. Theresa said, "The telephone company matched the cell phone calls' origin to a twenty-mile area east of Hagerstown. The zone includes some parts of the Hagerstown area as well, making it a bit more complicated to pinpoint an exact location. Anyway, I called the local sheriff and told him I was trying to find out if there was anything unusual going on in his town during the past few days. He didn't take a liking to us big-city folks bothering him with stupid questions. So, I called some of the smaller towns in the area, and I think we may have struck pay dirt. There's a place actually named Small Town, just off Interstate 70, about twenty miles east of Hagerstown on Catoctin Mountain. The local sheriff there said he has had more than his fair share of excitement the past few days. Apparently there was a fire at a remote hunting cabin yesterday. When the volunteer fire department arrived on the scene they found four dead bodies lying around the place. They suspect that explosives of some sort were used but have to wait for a lab report to come back from Hagerstown for confirmation. The sheriff said the bodies were hit with what could only be described as multiple double-aught buckshot."

Captain Thiemeyer said, "I'm thinking a mine or several mines at this point, Commissioner."

The commissioner replied, "That could very well be, but we better hold off on the speculation at this point. Did the sheriff have anything else to report?"

Theresa continued, "Yes. He said this morning there were two pickup trucks that blew up in the center of town soon after they left a local diner. At first he thought the explosion was due to one truck hitting the other. Witnesses said that there was no accident. The trucks just blew up, a few seconds apart. He investigated further and found two grenade handles, or spoons as he called them, near the diner where the trucks were originally parked. He sent them to Hagerstown for prints and analysis. The sheriff is a Korean War veteran and is 99 percent sure they were hand grenade handles. At this point, I tend to believe him."

The commissioner was very intently listening to Detective McGavin's report. Finally he said, "Booby traps."

"Excuse me?" asked McGavin.

"I said the grenades may have been used to booby trap the trucks. Listen. Did you run a check on the bodies at the fire with those found at the accident in town?"

Detective McGavin looked at Captain Thiemeyer while responding, "Ah. No, not yet. Do you think we have two related incidents instead of two separate acts?"

"I surely do, Detective. I think we need you in Hagerstown to push the crime lab boys into finding a link between these two crimes. I'm willing to bet they are tied together somehow. Does the sheriff have an ID on the deceased yet?"

Captain Thiemeyer responded, "Yes and no. He has the two deceased at the truck explosion and two of the four from the cabin fire IDd. The last two bodies from the fire scene will take a while longer because they were so badly mangled. Dental records may not even help with this one, according to the sheriff."

The commissioner said, "OK. Theresa, I want you in Hagerstown ASAP. Don't push the locals too hard, but get some answers quick. Call me if you run into any flak."

"What do you want me to do?" asked Thiemeyer.

"I want you to call the FBI so they are involved. Tell them we think military ordnance was used in a couple of crimes on Catoctin Mountain. They will jump all over the Hagerstown cops when they hear that stuff about hand grenades. You may even want to toss in the use of mines as an enticement. The locals out there will be so ticked off that the feds are taking over their investigation that it might lessen the pressure on Theresa, who is going to be playing the good-cop role. In fact, she will look like a savior to them and just might get the quick cooperation we need. The fingerprints on the grenade handles are critical right now. The FBI should be able to run them through their computers in record time. That might tell us if our boy Marco has been around Little Town recently."

John Toby spent the remainder of the morning and most of the afternoon on the phone trying to bring some shooters down from New Jersey. He was assured by his contact that he would only need one man, but he did not come cheap. John was beyond his wits over this Marco incident. He didn't care what it cost if the man could guarantee an end to this nightmare. The contact negotiated a price of $50,000 to be paid up front and another $50,000 when the job was done. John agreed to the terms, then asked, "When does he get here and how will I recognize him?"

"You won't even know he's there. The up-front money is to be put in a single suitcase left in a locker at the Harrisonburg bus station. Put the key into an envelope and overnight it to me. Once I have the key, I'll have my man on the job within a few hours."

John didn't like being told how to do things by anyone, except Billy Sharp, of course. He didn't like Billy telling him what to do much either, but at least Billy paid him well for his services. Anyway, John agreed to the terms, so long as he could finally get this Marco character out of his hair.

Billy Sharp was in the bunker looking over the receipts totals when John entered. Billy was not very happy with the recent 15 percent decline in protection money, and now in D.C. it was hovering around 25 percent in losses. Billy asked, "Did we get a handle on the Jamaicans horning in on our D.C. operations yet?"

"Yeah. The Jamaican gang has been fingered by one of their own. Of course, we had to put a few drill holes in his legs before he talked, but we got what we needed. I have six guys going to their place later tonight to put an end to their venture into the protections business."

"Who do you have heading up the raid?"

"Little Ralph Duffman has the honors. He'll get the job done if you know what I mean."

"Yeah. I know exactly what you mean. Now, tell me where we stand with this Marco business."

John told Billy about the big-time hitter coming down from Jersey to take care of Marco, then told Billy the high price tag for the hit. Billy turned toward John saying, "Now, who do you think is going to pay this 100 grand?"

"I figured you would go for it, Boss. After all, it's you that wants him so badly."

"Well, you figured wrong, Johnny." Billy reached under his jacket and produced a revolver. In one quick motion, he pointed and fired three times into John Toby's chest.

Billy picked up the black phone on the nearby table to call a cleanup crew to come down to the bunker.

Chapter 25

Paul drove past the Angel Inn and parked off to the side of the road. He still had a bone to pick with Lenny and his boys, because he suspected one of them had sold him out. *How else could those six guys know I was at the cabin?* he thought. Paul took one of the 9mm pistols and tucked it into his waistband. He then put on his gloves and wiped down a fragmentation grenade and placed it in his jacket pocket. Paul then looked around to make sure that things were quiet before exiting the Jeep. He walked back to the Angel Inn and went around to the rear of the building. The door that led to the small room where he had spent that first night was in sight. Already Paul could hear the loud jukebox playing through the cinder block walls. Paul quietly walked up to the door and tried turning the doorknob. It was obviously locked, since the knob didn't turn. Paul lightly rapped on the door to see if anyone would answer. Nothing happened, so Paul banged harder this time. Still nothing happened. The sound of the jukebox was so loud that a person would have to be practically standing next to the door to hear Paul knocking.

Paul picked up a heavy metal trash can that was close by and slammed the bottom edge against the cheaply made doorknob. There was a solid loud sound of the metal trash can hitting the knob, then the tinny sound of the knob bouncing on the asphalt covered ground. Paul set the trash can down and pulled out the 9mm in case someone charged out through the door. No one came. Paul used two fingers to turn the spindle protruding through the door, thus releasing the bolt from the doorframe. In a slow, steady motion, Paul opened the door, allowing the loud music out into the night while he slipped, inside pulling the door closed behind him.

There was no one in the small office, so Paul made his way to the door that led to the bar and grill. He opened the door about an inch, so he could look out into the main area and still remain somewhat concealed. The place was really jumping. The music was so loud, Paul could have blown the back door off with dynamite and no one would have heard him.

Suddenly, Paul saw a figure approaching the door. He quietly pushed the door closed and quickly pressed his back against the wall. The door opened and in walked Lenny. Paul slammed the door closed, startling Lenny as he turned to face his intruder. Paul was pointing the pistol at Lenny's head.

Lenny said, "Oh, it's you. You scared the hell out of me, man." Now, as Lenny realized that the gun was still pointed at his head, his facial expression turned to one of fear as he said, "Hey, wait a minute. I had nothing to do with that trouble you had out at Yingling's place."

Paul moved in front of the door that Lenny had used to enter the room so he could set the lock. He then motioned with the gun for Lenny to sit on the couch as he said, "There were only three of you here that night I picked up the keys. So that means one of you sold me out. I want to know who it was, and you're going to tell me."

"I didn't do it, man. And my two regular men would never sell out to anyone. I trust those guys with my life."

"You may very well be doing just that, my scared friend. I want you to call them both in here so I can find out who's lying." Lenny stood up and went to the desk, where he picked up the phone, saying, "Get in here and bring Art with you." Lenny hung up the phone, then returned to the couch while Paul unlocked the door.

Within a few seconds the door opened and the two men hurried inside as Joe asked, "What's up? It's a real madhouse out there tonight and—"

Paul slammed the door closed, startling the two new arrivals, and said, "Sit on the couch next to your boss." Then Paul moved to the door and locked it again.

Joe eyed the pistol, then said, "Hey, you're that Nuncie guy.

Right? The one from the other night—"

"Shut up and listen. Somebody sold me out the other night. I had a few uninvited visitors, and I'm looking for the guy who's responsible. Lenny here says it wasn't him, so that means it had to be one of you two guys."

Joe looked at Art and quickly replied, "Wasn't me, man. We would never turn in somebody unless the boss said to do it."

Art joined in, saying, "That's right. He's telling you the truth. There's no way we would do that. Besides, from what we heard, you wasted all them dudes, so why would we be hanging around here if we ratted you out? Think about it, man."

Paul took a few seconds to think about Art's defensive argument. It did make sense for the real rat to have taken off by now. Paul said, "You make a good point, except only you three knew where I was going. It had to be one of you."

Lenny said, "Hold it. Mary knew. It has to be Mary. You can't hurt her, man. She's an old salt that means well, but sometimes she has a big mouth."

Paul suddenly realized that maybe Lenny was right. It could have been Mary, and she might have said something without even realizing it could have cost him his life. He lowered the gun, then said, "There's a guy out there who was drinking tequila and is now drinking Coke."

Art said, "Yeah. He got a call an hour or so ago. Name of—" "Yeah. Yeah. Look. You two can take off now, but send that guy at the bar back here. Tell him Danny Nuncie wants to see him."

Art and Joe were more than happy to leave the small office. Lenny was more relaxed now, too. He stood up to light a cigarette and offered one to Paul. As they waited for Gary to come to the back room, Lenny stated, "Look, Danny, or whatever your real name is, I'm not crazy about guys ganging up on one guy. If you need some help taking care of business, let me know. I have resources available to me in this area that might be of some help to you."

Paul looked at Lenny, then said, "Thanks, but that won't be necessary. My business is finished in this area. I have to get going soon anyway."

The office door opened and Gary stuck his head in, smiling as he said, "It's about damn time you showed up, partner. My kidneys are floating in a sea of cola."

Paul introduced Gary to Lenny, and the two men talked about the mutual friend they had who had agreed to let Paul use the cabin. When the two were finished reminiscing, Paul said, "We need to get going, Gary."

As Gary and Paul left the office through the back door, Paul turned to Lenny and said, "Sorry about the door and your friend's cabin."

Outside the inn, Paul told Gary about how he suspected someone there of ratting him out. As they walked to the Jeep, Paul asked, "Where did you park your car?"

"I'm on the other side of the parking lot."

Paul told Gary to leave his car at the Angle Inn for now. They could come back for it tomorrow, if things worked out OK.

Gary said, "There is no need for that, Paul. The car is stolen, so the cops can have it."

In the Jeep, Paul told Gary all about the six men who were sent to kill him at the cabin. Gary listened to every word, as Paul pointed the Jeep toward Interstate 81, then headed south. After Paul finished telling Gary about all that had happened to him, he said, "Now, are you sure that you want to be a part of this? These guys are definitely not fooling around."

Gary didn't hesitate when he said, "Count me in, partner. I'm sick of guys like this Billy Sharp ruining the lives of decent folks who are just trying to get along."

Paul drove for about an hour, then asked Gary if he was hungry. It was now almost eleven o'clock. Paul pulled into a truck stop where he gassed up the Jeep and the two men went inside to get something to eat. The weather was turning from bad to worse. The forecast in the mountains was for snow, high winds, and very low temperatures. Just what Paul wanted for his night mission to the *Double C* ranch.

Inside the truck stop, Gary ordered hot coffee, steak and eggs, toast, and more coffee. Paul just had coffee and a large slice of coconut cream pie. The whole time they were eating, Paul was telling Gary how he planned to take Billy Sharp down. Gary would actually be Paul's backup and the diversion that would pull Billy out of the main house and into the open. Once Billy was isolated, Paul had a few ideas as to how he would make Sharp's life miserable.

Detective McGavin arrived in downtown Hagerstown around four o'clock, just as the sun was setting behind the mountains. She took a room at the Embassy Suites, which was located about two blocks from police headquarters. After she checked in and placed her bags in her room, she called headquarters and asked to speak to Sheriff Jefferson. She identified herself, then told the sheriff what she wanted. She asked if she could come over to talk about some evidence pertaining to the two homicide cases over at Small Town. The sheriff was not very pleasant-sounding over the phone. However, he did agree to give the detective thirty minutes of his time, if she could come over right then.

Theresa left the hotel bundled up as if she were going to Alaska. The mountain air with the stiff winds made the wind chill factor zero degrees. Her face was already red and starting to chap to the point that it now hurt. The air was so cold that the gusts hitting her face almost seemed to cause more of a burning sensation, as opposed to freezing.

She managed to make it to headquarters with all of her fingers and toes attached. Inside the small building, the warm, dry heat was very welcome, although it dried her skin terribly. Theresa was knocking the snow off her shoes and rubbing her gloved hands together briskly when she heard a voice saying, "Cold enough for ya, ma'am?"

Theresa looked in the direction the voice came from to see a short man in his forties wearing a cowboy hat. His sideburns were graying and his stomach was hanging over his belt, practically covering the buckle, which looked as if it might weigh five pounds. She smiled at the man as he said, "I'm Sheriff Jefferson. You have got to be the city slicker I talked to on the phone a short while ago."

"Oh. Hi, Sheriff. Yeah, I'm the one who called you." Theresa walked over to the sheriff with her hand extended. As Theresa shook hands with the sheriff, she said, "I'm pleased to meet you, Sheriff. Thanks for taking the time to see me on such short notice."

"Weren't nothin'. Come on into my office. Can I get you some coffee or tea?"

"That would be great. Coffee, with a little cream and sugar, if it's not too much trouble."

The sheriff pointed to the open door of his office and told Theresa to go inside while he fetched the coffee. Inside the sheriff 's' s office, Theresa looked around, somewhat amazed. She had expected to see stuffed deer heads and mounted fish on all the walls. What she saw was a nicely decorated office with certificates, awards, and photographs of the sheriff with political dignitaries. There were several newspaper clippings in glass frames and an entire wall with military decorations, including a silver star. Under the military awards, were several old photographs of the sheriff wearing his green beret.

The sheriff walked into the office carrying two mugs of steaming coffee and saying, "Sorry I took so long, but I had to make a fresh pot. The stuff that was out there would take paint off the walls."

Theresa took the hot mug and wrapped her hands around it to soak up its warmth. As she took a sip of coffee, she said, "Thanks, Sheriff. This is good."

"You're welcome. Now, why don't you have a seat so we can discuss this business about military explosives."

Theresa asked, "Then it was a bomb that killed the men at the cabin fire in Small Town?"

Sheriff Jefferson looked at Theresa over his coffee mug, then said, "Of course, it was. More correctly, it was claymore mines that did those four fellows in. Any damn fool could see that right off the bat."

"But when I talked to the sheriff over at Small Town, he wasn't sure if—"

"Sheriff Belomy is a damn fool. He wouldn't know a claymore mine from his ass. Excuse me, ma'am."

"It's OK, Sheriff. How did you determine the deaths were caused by . . . claymore mines, is it?"

"Look, miss. I saw you eyeing those pictures on the wall over there when I came in with the coffee. I was a Green Beret in Vietnam for almost two years and saw my share of bodies hit with claymore mines. I knew what done it as soon as I saw the photos of the crime scene. Besides, we now have some real proof." The sheriff pulled a folder off the top of a stack in his in basket. He handed it to Detective McGavin as he said, "The lab report shows a high concentration of C-4 explosive residue on the bodies. We even found two charred detonators in the rubble of the cabin after it burned to the ground.

Yep. No doubt about it, lady. Claymore mines were used to kill those four fellows up at the cabin."

"What about the other two men that were killed several hours later in Small Town? I understand that Sheriff Belomy believes that hand grenades were used?"

Sheriff Jefferson took a long drink of coffee and lit a cigarette. He offered Theresa a smoke, but she waved her hand to indicate no thanks. The sheriff said, "Well, at least Belomy isn't a total idiot. The evidence he sent over to our crime lab to check for prints was definitely from fragmentation grenades. There is a number stenciled into each one identifying them as such. It's called an FSN, or federal stock number, to you nonmilitary types. Anyway, there were no prints on either handle."

"Well, Sheriff, I don't know what to say. You have all the answers to my questions right at your fingertips."

"Maybe. Then again, maybe not. I could have given you all this information over the phone. However, you came all the way over here from Baltimore, so there must be more to it than questions about military ordnance. Besides, you haven't asked the big question yet."

"What question is that, Sheriff?"

"Do I know who is behind these six murders."

"Well, Sheriff, if you knew that, you would probably already have them in custody awaiting trial."

"Maybe so, Detective. Maybe so. But I'll bet you must have a pretty good idea who he is or you wouldn't be here."

Theresa was impressed with the sheriff 's wit and keen sense of logic regarding the criminal element. She was not ready to let him know that she suspected Paul Marco, because there simply was no proof of that yet. Theresa asked, "Have the FBI been notified?"

Sheriff Jefferson looked a little surprised when he heard that question. He responded, "They have been here and gone already. Why do you ask?"

"Oh. I thought it was routine for the FBI to investigate crimes that are committed with military ordnance. I could be mistaken, though."

"I see, Detective. Well, those suit-and-tie types came in here and confiscated damn near all of our evidence. Seems that they want to find out where this hardware came from pretty damn quick, if you know what I mean."

Theresa set her empty coffee mug down on the desk as she stood up to leave. The sheriff shook her hand, saying, "Sorry we couldn't have been more help, but so far we have no idea as to who committed the murders or why."

Theresa again thanked the sheriff for his time, then bundled up for her two-block run to the hotel. The wind was now at her back and actually helped propel her down the slippery street to her hotel.

Once she was safely in her room, Theresa called Room Service to order a BLT sandwich and a bottle of wine. While she waited for the food and drink to be delivered, Theresa filled the tub with hot water and called Captain Thiemeyer to bring him up to date. Thiemeyer said they had a preliminary report on the blood found at Marco's house. It was too contaminated to use DNA typing with any degree of accuracy. However, the blood type was AB negative, which matched the blood type for one of the bodies they had fished out of the Gunpowder River.

Thiemeyer said, "It's very thin from an evidence standpoint. Right now we don't have enough to bring Marco in for questioning, much less accuse him of murder."

"Well, it appears that we have a whole lot of nothing. All circumstantial bullshit, if you'll pardon my French."

"You're right, Theresa. Every time I think we have a bead on this case, we come up empty. Do you think that Paul is still in the Small Town area?"

"I doubt it. I told the phone company to let us know if he activated his cell phone, but so far they haven't reported zilch. Damn, this case is frustrating."

"Well, get some rest, Theresa. Tomorrow you can head back to civilization and brief the commissioner on your visit."

Theresa hung up the phone in time to answer the door. Room Service brought her the BLT and a bottle of red wine. While she ate her sandwich, Theresa was trying to think about what Paul could possibly be up to now. *The six bodies that were found in and around Small Town were holding back information*, she thought. *Tomorrow, I'm going to pay a visit to Sheriff Belomy to see what kind of spin he might be able to put on things.*

A man about six feet tall, with graying hair and mustache, was at the Harrisonburg bus station looking for locker number 335.

He inserted a key and opened the door to remove the small suitcase containing $50,000. He then walked across the street to climb into his rented car. He looked at his watch to see that it was almost ten o'clock. The weather was turning colder as the winds came down from the north. He drove out toward the *Double C* ranch using the map he had received by way of fax from Billy Sharp. The man from New Jersey entered Harrisonburg from the south. He had just finished a job in Richmond, Virginia, when he had been contacted to handle the *Double C* job. All he knew about the mark was his name and a brief description that could have fit half the white males over forty living in the U.S. The difference was this man named Paul Marco was trying his best to make Billy Sharp's life miserable. The man from Jersey had to slow down because the roads were starting to become covered by drifting snow. The *Double C* was only a few more miles, so he could actually walk if it became necessary. He looked at his watch and decided that the next cutoff was where he would pull over to catch a few hours' sleep before making another move.

Chapter 26

Paul and Gary drove past the *Double C* ranch driveway checking to see if everything looked normal. Then Paul turned the Jeep around and headed back toward the ranch, stopping about one hundred yards from the beginning of the long driveway leading to the main house. The wind was blowing the falling snow in swirls, making visibility less than a few hundred yards, at best. Paul put the Jeep into four-wheel-drive and pulled off the main road into the woods. The snow was almost six inches deep already, but the drifts were well over two feet in some of the more open areas.

Gary and Paul put on all the clothes that were in the back of the Jeep. It was going to be a cold night, but if things worked as they had planned, it would be over in less than two hours.

Paul looked at his watch and said, "I have 11:10."

Gary looked at his watch saying, "Close enough, partner." "Okay, Gary. You ready to get it?"

"Let's do it. I'll see you back here at the Jeep between one and one-thirty. If I'm not here by then, take off without me. No questions asked. That's our deal, right?"

"I still don't like the way you divvied up the work, but it's your call, Paul. One-thirty is takeoff time."

Paul left the keys in the Jeep under the driver's side floor mat, just as they had agreed to do earlier. They both went to the back of the Jeep to grab the gear that each would need to execute his portion of the plan. Paul shook Gary's hand, then took off into the woods with two of the one-gallon gas cans. Paul set a course that made a direct line to the main house. Gary gathered the two remaining one-gallon gasoline cans and other paraphernalia to begin setting up his part of the diversion and escape plan.

Paul humped through the woods, keeping an eye on the distant lights illuminating from the main house upstairs windows. The snow was not hindering his progress too much, because he was still in the woods. As he approached the open pastures, the snow was deeper and the drifts were a definite nuisance. He had to adjust his course several times to maneuver around some of the deeper snowdrifts. The wind was wiping across the pasture unabated, making it more difficult to see a mere seventy-five yards at times.

Gary already had poured a little more than half of the gasoline from the two gas cans into the Jeep's fuel tank. He then poured two quarts of oil into each can, making a crude giant Molotov cocktail of sorts. The gas and oil mixture filled the cans to within two inches of the top. Gary then walked about twenty feet from the Jeep and buried the empty plastic oil containers in the snow. Before Gary and Paul left the truck stop, Paul had pulled out two long pieces of wire from under his dash that feed the rear speakers for his Jeep's stereo system. Gary took the nine-volt batteries Paul bought at the convenience store and taped the bare portion of the speaker wires around the positive and negative battery contacts to make a small electronic power pack. The other ends of the speaker wires were attached to two flashlight bulbs. Gray broke the glass around each bulb, leaving the filament intact but exposed. When the electric charge from the batteries passed through the exposed bulb filaments, a small red-hot spark would be produced.

Gary had fabricated a detonator from an alligator clip that was in Paul's toolbox. He carried the two gas cans to the driveway entrance, then walked up to the small wooden bridge that crossed the stream running through the *Double C's* property. Gary hung the two gas cans on the side of the bridge with string, then poked a hole into each gas can cap. He fished the wire through the hole so the bulb filament was inside the can just above the oil and gas mixture. Very carefully, he then lightly placed the cap on top of each can. When both fuses were in place, Gary propped open the alligator clip with a matchbook. He then ran a string from the matchbook to the other side of the bridge, where he fastened it to the railing. When a vehicle crossed the bridge, it would pull the string that was attached to the matchbook. After the matchbook was pulled free, an electrical connection would be made, sending the current to the two gas cans simultaneously.

Gary went back to the Jeep to get the one remaining claymore mine from the back cargo area. He went back to the driveway but did not cross the bridge. He set the claymore up on the side of the road so it faced toward the main house, then attached the detonator wire to the mailbox post with electric tape. The detonator was actually placed inside the mailbox to keep it dry. When the two main explosive devices were in place, Gary went back to the Jeep one more time to make sure two fragmentation grenades were placed in the cup holders, for easy access. He then took the M-1 with two extra clips of ammo and slung it over his shoulder.

Gary rubbed his gloved hands together, trying to warm them. He pulled up his collar then checked his watch. It was now 12:15. The long wait was about to begin. Gary picked up the twelve gauge shotgun and headed into the woods on the opposite side of the driveway to wait.

Paul was close enough that he could now see the construction work that was going on around the *Double C* ranch. According to the map that Gary had faxed to him a few days ago, there were three air shafts that serviced the underground bunker. The actual steps leading down to the bunker were camouflaged as a pair of old wooden doors supposedly leading to a storm cellar. Paul could see three cars and a pickup truck parked by the main house as he made his way to the first air shaft. The pipe opening was covered with a sheet metal cap that resembled an upside-down funnel. Paul easily twisted the cap off the pipe, exposing the six-inch diameter air duct. The second and third air ducts were about ten feet apart. Paul moved over to each air duct and twisted off the vent caps. The middle vent was the largest in diameter. It was about twelve inches in diameter and was used for incoming air, while the other two vent pipes were used to exhaust air. Paul laid an incendiary grenade and a gallon can of gasoline next to each of the exhaust vents. He then placed a two-pound C-4 charge with a timer detonator by the incoming air vent. Quickly, Paul moved toward the storm cellar doors. With a piece of string Paul attached a fragmentation grenade to one handle of the double doors. He then attached another piece of string to the grenade pull pin and tied it to the other handle.

Paul looked at his watch to see that it was almost twelve o'clock. He saw the construction trailer next to the new equipment outbuilding, just as the map had indicated. To the left of the trailer was a small building that housed the two backup generators. Paul ran to the small generator shed in a low crouch. He tried the door, but it was locked. Paul used his elbow to smash through one of the small glass panes on the door. With the noise from the gusting wind and the heavy blizzardlike snowfall, the breaking glass could hardly be heard ten feet away.

Inside the generator shed, Paul located the distributor cap on each engine and removed the center coil wire. The converted gasoline generators were actually fueled by liquid propane gas. The propane tank was against the wall and held maybe one hundred pounds of the liquid gas. Paul took another fragmentation grenade and rigged it to the tank using string. He then attached a piece of string to the pull pin and ran it to the shed door. Paul closed the door and reached inside through the broken glass to attach the string to the inside doorknob. When the door was pulled open, the pin would be yanked clear, creating more fireworks.

Paul looked at his watch to see that it was almost twelve-thirty. He left the generator shed to make his way over to the construction trailer. Paul took one more look around, then crawled underneath the trailer to wait and protect himself from the blizzard conditions.

Gary was patiently waiting and freezing his tail off in the woods. He looked at his watch to see that it was now exactly 12:29. Gary then aimed the twelve-gauge shotgun, loaded with double-aught buckshot, at the utility pole across the road. His target was the step-down transformer at the top of the pole that fed electricity to underground lines that powered the *Double C* ranch. Gary took off the safety and fired one round into the transformer, pumped the handle to eject the spent shell, and fired a second and then a third round in rapid succession. The transformer was sparking and flaring as it shorted out. Flames were now blowing in the brisk wind, causing the top of the pole to also catch fire.

Gary picked up the three spent shell casings and placed them inside his coat pocket. As he was about to stand and leave, he was startled by a voice behind him saying, "I've been waiting for you, Mr. Marco."

Gary felt the cold, hard steel of a gun barrel on the back of his head. The man behind him said, "Now why would you want to deny electricity to a nice man like Mr. Sharp? Is this childish prank the best you could come up with to harass my client? And here I thought you were going to be trouble. After all, my information was that you killed several good men that worked for Mr. Sharp. Now why don't you stand up real slow and leave that shotgun and rifle on the ground?"

Gary had no idea who was behind him, but obviously the man thought he was talking to Paul Marco. Gary dropped the shotgun and rifle into the snow and stood as he was instructed. The man behind him moved the gun barrel away from Gary's head to stick it into his back while saying, "I would like to end this here and now. But then my employer said he would pay me a bonus if I delivered you to him personally. I think he wants to do the job himself. Move out."

The man poked Gary in the back so he would walk out of the woods and up the driveway. Gary still had not said one word since the man startled him. Besides, the man never made any attempt to look at Gary's face. Gary moved out, high-stepping the deep snow on the side of the road. The stranger did not have the gun in Gary's back any longer, but he could feel the man's presence a few feet behind. Gary started up the driveway and toward the bridge. He knew he would have the element of surprise, if his plan worked.

Gary reached the bridge and began to cross it as he kept a close eye out for the string. He was having a little trouble seeing with all the swirling snow, so Gary began to drag his feet as he walked. Suddenly, Gary felt the string on his leg and in one swift motion he kicked the string and dived over the bridge railing on the opposite side of where he had placed the gas cans. As Gary was falling into the stream five feet below, he heard the explosion and felt the heat from the huge fireball above. The stream was only two to three feet deep, and Gary landed in the water in a poorly executed bellyflop. The frigid water was more of a shock to his system then the actual fall. Luckily, Gary only ended up with scrapes and bruises. He had just missed several large rocks in the streambed that could have otherwise been lethal.

Gary quickly climbed out of the streambed looking for signs of the man who had been behind him before the explosion occurred. The flames from the burning wooden bridge gave off a good deal of light, but still Gary could not see the man anywhere. As he climbed to the top of the driveway, Gary was shivering terribly. He had to get back to the Jeep, where there was some heat, or risk hypothermia.

When Gary reached the top of the drive, he saw a burning body lying on the bridge deck that was now beginning to be engulfed by oily flames. Gary looked at the man from a safe distance but could not make out who he was. He briefly enjoyed the heat from the flames until it was time to turn away and retrieve his weapons from across the road.

When the transformer was destroyed by Gary, the main house was immediately blanketed in darkness. Paul patiently waited under the construction trailer for the next explosion.

Someone from inside the bunker was by now obviously disturbed that the auxiliary generators did not kick in as they should. A male figure threw open the storm cellar doors to go investigate. The motion of opening the cellar doors pulled the grenade pin, causing a loud explosion that killed the man immediately. Paul continued to focus on the main house, where he spotted what looked like two people holding flashlights heading toward the bunker doors. Suddenly there was an unexpected explosion down the driveway and a huge fireball lit up the sky for a few seconds. Paul's first thought was that maybe some of Sharp's men had been called to the main house and had tripped the Molotov cocktail booby trap set by Gary.

One of the men with a flashlight yelled to the other, "You go check the generators and I'll go see what that explosion was down the driveway!"

One man got into a pickup truck and hurriedly headed down the driveway toward the main road. The other man walked over to the generator shed and pulled open the door. Paul held his gloved hands over his ears as the huge explosion rocked the earth surrounding the ranch. The propane fireball illuminated the entire area around the main house and could be seen for several miles. Paul knew it was time to make a move. When the last of the debris fell to the ground, he crawled out from under the construction trailer. Slowly and quietly, he worked his way to the side of the main house. The man who had gone down the driveway to investigate, was now returning in a big hurry. He pulled the pickup truck up to the main house front door as he repeatedly blew the horn. Two men came out onto the front porch. In the glow of the pickup headlights Paul recognized one of them as Billy Sharp. Paul did not recognize the second man and didn't care.

"What in the hell happened out here, Chris?"

"I don't know, Boss. I sent Wayne to check out the generators and I went down the driveway to check out an explosion. There's a dead man at the end of the driveway and the bridge is on fire."

"Where's Wayne?"

"I don't know! But something big is going down."

Billy ran into the house and came out with a flashlight and machine pistol. The man he called Chris was also following close behind Billy, as was the third man, who had been standing on the porch. They all headed to the bunker entrance, then suddenly stopped to look at the smoldering remains of their coworker.

Billy said, "Jesus Christ. It's happening again. We're under attack. That goddamned Marco has to be behind this."

Chris said, "We'll probably be safer in the bunker, Boss."

Billy, Chris, and the third man scurried down the steel steps that led into the bunker. Billy hurriedly punched in the three digit code to unlock the thick steel door. All three men were quickly inside the confines of the concrete structure that was soon to be their tomb.

Paul watched the three men descend into their underground sanctuary. They would only have a brief false sense of security. Paul quickly ran to the demolished wooden cellar doors and picked up a large piece of debris to jam against the bunker door and the steel steps. He then ran to the exhaust air duct and picked up the can of gasoline. Paul unscrewed the cap and turned the can upside down over the opening to let it drain. He then did the same thing to the second exhaust duct. Paul picked up an incendiary grenade and pulled the pin while he held onto the handle. He placed his ear next to the duct opening and could hear Billy's voice. Paul placed his mouth over the opening and shouted down through the pipe, "Billy Sharp. This is Paul Marco. It has come time for you to pay for murdering my wife. It's your turn to burn in hell!"

Billy looked up at the vent above his head and yelled, "You're a dead man, Marco! Do you hear me? A dead man!"

Paul smiled as he released the handle and dropped the incendiary grenade down the pipe. He then quickly ran to the second exhaust pipe, picked up the incendiary grenade, pulled the pin, and let it drop down the pipe. Paul had about five seconds to clear the area. He took off running for a few seconds, then stopped to turn around and watch. The smoke and fire shooting out from the three air vents were pure satisfaction for Paul. The scene looked like three big Roman candles shooting fire into the sky. The end was finally here. Paul ran back to the center intake pipe and picked up the C-4. He set the detonator to thirty seconds and dropped it down the vent pipe. Paul took off running for about fifteen seconds, then slowed his pace to a nonchalant walk. Several seconds later a tremendous explosion sounded that made the ground rumble like an earthquake was occurring. Billy Sharp and his cronies were no longer in business. *Any business*, thought Paul.

Paul looked at the main house wondering if Billy's widow would like to rebuild or if he should leave it alone. After thinking for a few seconds, Paul decided to let the widow keep the house. He thought, *That's more than her husband allowed me to keep after my wife was murdered.* Paul then started to slowly walk down the long driveway to meet up with Gary.

Gary went back to the Jeep and placed the weapons in the backseat. He started the Jeep to get the heater going. He was shaking so much that it was difficult for him to put the key into the ignition. Once the Jeep was started, Gary pulled out of the woods and drove up the main road until he was positioned at the Sharp mailbox. After a few minutes he saw a figure coming toward him from the direction of the main house. He looked at his watch to see that it was 1:17. Gary smiled as Paul got closer and realized he would have to go down the side of the streambed to cross and come back up the other side, since the bridge was gone.

When Paul finally climbed above the steep streambed wall, Gary said with a big smile, "You're late, partner."

Paul laughed, then said, "What in the hell happened here?"

Gary started to tell Paul about the unidentified man who had mistakenly thought he was Marco. Suddenly two pairs of headlights were racing toward them from the direction of the main house.

Gary asked excitedly, "What in the hell is going on now?" "I don't know buddy, but it's time to vamoose."

Paul went around to the passenger side of the Jeep to climb inside. The two vehicles were clearly pickup trucks with high intensity floodlights mounted on the top roll bars. Paul said, "They must be some of Sharp's men. They probably used the service road that connects the farm next to

Sharp's ranch. They were probably stirred up after seeing and hearing all the fireworks. Now they are coming to see who we are, and they don't look to be very neighborly."

Shots rang out and muzzle flashes were bouncing in the darkness. Gary said, "With the bridge out, we can probably outrun them, Paul."

"Remember the rules of the jungle, Gary. Leave no witnesses.

Get the mine detonator in your hand and wait for my signal."

Paul got out of the Jeep with the M-1 carbine. He took one of the fragmentation grenades from the coffee holder and knelt in the snow right in front of the burned-out bridge. Paul leveled the M1, took aim, and squeezed off ten rapid rounds. The two pickup trucks came to a screeching halt fifteen yards in front of the now missing bridge. Paul fired two more bursts from the M-1, then tossed the grenade at the two pickups. The explosion damaged the two vehicles, but not the men, who had scattered to both sides of the driveway. Paul fired the remaining rounds in the clip, then pulled out his 9mm. He fired rapidly as he ran back to the Jeep, where Gary was holding the detonator for the claymore in one hand and firing a 9mm with the other to cover Paul. Bullets were hitting the side of the Jeep, making Gary very nervous. When Paul and Gary stopped firing, the men on the other side of the burned out bridge took that to mean they were out of ammunition. They stood up to move toward the Jeep. Before they could fire another shot Paul yelled, "Now!"

Gary quickly squeezed the plunger three times, and the resulting explosion made quick work of the pursuing bad guys. Gary took the remaining fragmentation grenade from the cup holder, pulled the pin, and tossed it toward the two trucks, making sure they would not be followed by anyone else. Paul tossed the M-1 into the backseat and climbed into the passenger seat. He looked at Gary for a few seconds, then said, "How in the hell did you get so wet?"

Chapter 27

Detective McGavin received a telephone call from Captain Thiemeyer at 7:00 a.m. He told McGavin that there was no need for her to continue investigating the murders in and around Small Town.

"The FBI was able to tie the men to a known racketeer named William Sharp. He was killed either late last night or early this morning at his ranch near Harrisonburg, Virginia. The commissioner told me to tell you to come home."

"I was going to go talk to the local sheriff in Small Town this morning, but I guess there's no need for that now. Did the FBI say how this Billy Sharp character was murdered?"

"They are going to send a full report to us within the next day or two. One agent described the ranch as something from out of a war zone. They found a mine detonator and grenade handles stamped with the same lot numbers as those found when the two pickup trucks were blown up at that little diner. It appears that the deaths at that remote cabin location, the ones in Small Town, and the murders down in Harrisonburg are all related somehow. I don't suspect you think this is all coincidence; do you?"

Theresa thought a few seconds, then responded, "No. Not unless you can tell me that Mr. Paul Marco was sitting in your office since late last night and didn't leave until five minutes ago." "I know what you mean, Theresa. Unfortunately, there is still no evidence that points to Paul Marco, and the FBI has been all over the three crime scenes with the proverbial fine-toothed comb." "I don't know why I'm not surprised at hearing you say that, Captain. This guy Marco has to have made a mistake someplace, and I'm not going to give up looking for it just yet."

"Well, that may be so, Theresa. But you will be doing it on your own time, because the commissioner has officially closed the case."

Theresa took a shower, got dressed, then ate breakfast before heading back to Baltimore. Her cop gut feeling told her that Paul was as guilty as the day was long. Paul was involved with these murders somehow, but unfortunately, she couldn't prove a thing.

The inclement weather finally subsided after one foot of new snow fell overnight, with two to three more feet of accumulation in the higher elevations. In some places the drifts were five to seven feet high. Most main roads were passable, but caution was the word for the day. Theresa pulled out of town heading back to Baltimore, where the weather was more seasonable.

Paul and Gary drove for almost an hour before stopping at a motel to clean up, eat, and rest. Paul used the laundry room to wash and dry some clothes. Gary, on the other hand, took a long hot shower to warm his still frozen body. After the two showered, shaved and dressed they went to a small restaurant that was within walking distance from the motel. Paul ordered a hearty breakfast and Gary opted for the lunch menu.

As they ate, Paul said, "I checked out the left side of the Jeep and found four bullet holes. I parked the Jeep next to a huge trash dumpster so the holes would not be easily visible to anyone merely walking past."

"I'll make a call when we get back to the room. I have a guy who will take care of the bullet holes in no time. He runs a small chop shop operation in West Baltimore."

"That sounds good, Gary. But what if a cop decides to stop us on our way to the shop? It's going to be very hard to explain those bullet holes. God forbid if he happens to check out the arsenal in the back of the Jeep."

"You worry too much, Pauly. I'll take care of it as soon as we finish eating. Trust me."

Paul and Gary finished their meals, then drank two more cups of coffee while relaxing. The roads would be clear sailing now that they were out of the mountains. Gary's plan was to take a long nap, then travel at night so their vehicle damage was less obvious. Paul didn't like that they would have to lie around for several hours, but he agreed to Gary's plan.

The two men lay on the twin beds and managed to stay awake for almost half an hour. Last night had taken a lot out of them, so they slept soundly until almost four o'clock.

Paul woke up first. He went over to the restaurant to buy two large coffees to go. When he got back to the room, Gary was talking on the telephone. Paul handed Gary a large coffee as he placed the receiver back into the cradle.

"What's up?"

"I set up a rendezvous with a very trusted friend of mine. We're to drive to the rest stop just outside Baltimore on Interstate 95. He'll meet us there with a car. We'll switch vehicles at that point. The Jeep will be taken to the chop shop and repaired. The weapons will also disappear, unless you want to dispose of them yourself?"

"No. I don't think we'll be needing them anymore. We can wipe them clean and use one of these pillowcases to bundle them together. Say, do you think he can fix my rear speakers when he fixes the bullet holes?"

"Yeah. Sure. Do you want me to ask him to wash and wax the damn thing while he's at it?"

They both had a good laugh before finishing their coffee. It was now four forty-five and the sun was almost set. Paul took one of the pillowcases off the bed, and the two men headed for the Jeep. As Paul drove, Gary wiped down the weapons and placed them in the case. He climbed into the back of the Jeep to find all the extra ammunition and spent shell casings, included the three shotgun shells in his jacket pocket. Gary wiped down each casing and dropped them into the pillowcase. When he was finished, Gary wrapped the top of the pillowcase around the long gun barrels and fastened it together with the remaining electric tape.

It was almost seven o'clock when they pulled into the rest stop on I-95. They only had to wait about fifteen minutes for Gary's friend to show. They made the switch of vehicles and took off again. Gary was driving the Dodge

Neon toward Baltimore when he asked, "What are you going to do now that your business with Billy Sharp is concluded?"

"To tell you the truth, I haven't given it much thought. Hell, I don't even know where I'm going to sleep tonight."

The next fifteen minutes passed in silence. Gary finally said, "You can still bunk at my place, if you want. You know, until you figure out where you're going to go and what you're going to do. What do ya say?"

"No. I appreciate the offer, Gary, but I need some time alone to sort things out. How about if you drop me off at the downtown Hilton on your way home and I'll call you in the morning? We can arrange to meet for lunch or something. How long do you think it will take your friend to patch up my Jeep?"

"I'd say it will be ready for paint and rubbing out in less than two hours. I'll have him drop it off at the downtown Hilton and leave the keys under the passenger-side floor mat. But, I sure wish you would change your mind about staying at my place, man. Remember, this dude Sharp has a crazy brother who is probably going to be gunning for your ass."

Gary pulled in front of the Hilton to let Paul out by the lobby. Paul grabbed the small bag with his clothes in it from the back seat, then walked around to Gary's window. Paul stood there for a second before shaking Gary's extended hand. Paul said, "You did really good last night, partner. I'll never forget all you did for me in setting things right for what they did to my Diana."

"Weren't nothin', pal. I'll see you tomorrow."

Paul watched Gary pull out into traffic, then went inside the hotel to register. The clerk looked at him as if he were from Mars or something. The look disappeared, however, when Paul flashed his Gold Card and the clerk ran it through the computer, finding out that it was OK. Paul took his card key and headed for the elevators. As he rode up to the tenth floor he thought, *How long before the police are notified about my credit card being used?*

Paul went into his room and lay on the bed to stare at the ceiling. Gary's words were bouncing around inside his brain: *What are you going to do now?* Paul thought about that question, and then another popped into his mind: *Where are you going to go? There was no home to go back to. No business to run. No means of support. What if Sharp's brother picks up where Billy left off? My*

God, life has certainly been hard lately. Paul drifted off to sleep still not having any answers to the questions that now hounded him.

Captain Thiemeyer called Theresa at home around eight o'clock that night. "Hey, guess who's back in town?"

Theresa was watching a movie on TV and was not in any mood to play games. She snapped, "I give up. Who?"

"Our boy Marco. That's who."

Theresa turned off the TV, then asked, "No kidding? When? Where is he?"

"He used his credit card to get a room at the downtown Hilton. I guess it wouldn't do any good for me to tell you that we have nothing to warrant an official police visit to Mr. Marco?"

"Oh. I wouldn't think of it, Captain. However, there is nothing against two acquaintances getting together for a drink."

"I told you all that I am going to, Detective. I don't want to know what you're up to."

Theresa quickly fixed her face and changed into jeans and a sweater. She was out the door and into her car in record time. As she was driving to the Hilton, she kept thinking about how Mr. Marco has played her for a chump. She wanted to have it out with him right now.

Theresa drove to the parking lot at the Hilton, then went to the front desk. She showed her badge to the clerk and inquired about Mr. Marco's room number. The clerk told her his room number as he pointed to the elevators at the end of the hall.

When the elevator doors opened, Theresa took a few seconds to get her bearings for Room 1014. She then walked around the corner and turned to stand squarely in front of Marco's door. She took a deep breath, then gently knocked on the door. She waited a respectable amount of time, then hammered on the door with her fist as anger started to build.

Paul jumped off the bed and onto the floor trying to think. *Where am I? What is that noise?* He finally got his wits about him, as the sounds of someone banging on the door now had his undivided attention. Paul got up off the floor yelling, "Wait a goddamned minute!"

Paul went to the door to look through the spy hole. He blinked his sleepy eyes to focus better. When he was sure that he was looking at the face of Detective McGavin he unlocked the door. While opening the door he asked, "What are—"

Theresa took a balled-up fist and hit Paul square on the chin with a roundhouse right.

Paul backed up while holding his jaw, saying, "What in the hell did you do that for?"

Theresa walked into the room and shut the door behind her.

She looked at Paul, then said, "I ought to arrest you."

"On what charge? Sleeping alone in a damn hotel?" Paul was still rubbing his jaw. Then he said, "Hey, that punch really hurt." "Good. And the charges would be murder, attempted murder, interfering with a police investigation, and a few more I haven't thought of yet."

"Hold on, Detective." Paul sat on the bed and motioned for Theresa to sit in the chair by the desk. He then said, "Why don't you start from the beginning and tell me why you're so damn angry?"

Theresa sat in the chair, then asked, "Do you want me to get you some ice for that?"

"No. I'll live. Thanks anyway."

"OK. I must tell you that this isn't an official police visit. I don't have a search warrant and I can't technically arrest you for anything, yet. And I do mean, yet."

Paul put up his hand to stop Theresa from saying anything else. He said, "Stop there, Detective. Let me tell you what I know and then you won't have to hit me anymore. Boy, talk about police brutality."

Paul laid out a scenario of how he had gone to visit a friend on his farm down in Culpeper, Virginia. He said he had spent several days backpacking in the area and just got into town several hours ago. The reason he didn't call sooner was that he was tired.

Theresa said, "You know, I'm not buying a word of your story. Yeah, I suppose you have someone who can vouch for you in Culpeper. And you can say you called me from your cell phone on the way there the other night, explaining why the call was generated from around Hagerstown. You may even say that you couldn't possibly be the one involved in over ten killings in that area in the past seventy-two hours. I'm still not going to buy any of it."

"Well, Detective, all I can say is if you have some proof that I'm guilty, then you should arrest me. I won't put up a fight. I'll go peacefully. But if you expect me to give you a last-minute Perry Mason confession to murder one, you have a long wait ahead of you, sweetheart."

"Don't call me sweetheart. And I know that I don't have any proof right now. But I'm going to stay on the case, Mr. Marco. Is that clear?"

"Perfectly clear, Officer. I wouldn't have it any other way. Now, I'm hungry. What do you say we go upstairs to the top-floor restaurant and I'll buy you dinner for old times' sake."

"OK. But I still hate you."

Paul and Theresa had dinner and talked about how screwed up life can be at times. During one of the five after-dinner drinks, Theresa asked, "What will you do now, Paul? I mean with the house. Will you rebuild?"

Paul thought about it for a few seconds, then said, "No. I don't think I could live there now, even if it were a newly built home. Too many memories to haunt me when I get lonely. Know what I mean?"

"Yeah. Maybe I do."

"I guess I'll take some money out of the bank and travel around to see some friends. I don't really know for sure."

It was almost one in the morning when Detective McGavin left the hotel for her apartment. Paul went to his room, took off his clothes, and climbed into bed.

At eight o'clock Paul woke up, took a hot shower, shaved, and got dressed. He went down to the coffee shop to eat breakfast, then took a walk to the small shopping area across the street from the hotel. He bought some new clothes and toiletries as well as a large suitcase. Back at the hotel he removed all the tags and pins from the new purchases and then packed the suitcase.

Paul went down to the lobby to check out. He then walked to the back parking lot looking for his Jeep. There was only one bright red Jeep on the lot, making it very easy for Paul to spot. Paul walked up to his vehicle with a big smile on his face. Not only did Gary have the bullet holes patched, but his men had repainted the entire vehicle. Inside, the driver's seat was new, because the old one had caught a bullet. Gary was not too happy about discovering that, since he was the one sitting in the seat at the time. Paul put his suitcase in the back and started the Jeep. Immediately the stereo was blasting the air waves with some local rap station. Paul tuned the stereo down and changed stations to something mellow. Again he smiled, because the rear speakers were now working again.

Paul drove out Interstate 83 toward his house. He stopped at the post office to retrieve his mail and rented a P.O. Box before leaving. Paul then drove the six or so miles to his house. As he approached the driveway, his eyes filled with tears. The once beautiful home was now reduced to a pile of charred timber and ashes. He climbed out of the Jeep and walked around the grounds one more time, making sure he stopped at the grave sites for all the family pets. He said good-bye to his favorite dog, Auggie, then slowly walked back to the Jeep.

Paul sat there for about twenty minutes just staring at the rubble. Finally, he went across the street into the woods to retrieve the rucksack he had left hidden in the hollowed-out tree. He made sure the .22-caliber Ruger was there, then walked back to the Jeep to toss the rucksack into the back with his suitcase. Paul took another long look around the former homestead, then said, "What does a man do when he has absolutely nothing to lose and no place to go?"

About the Author

Dominic Fino, who resides near his hometown of Baltimore, Maryland, is retired from the computer technology sector. For Dominic, writing is not just a task but a cathartic release, offering him a platform to channel his frustrations and construct a world where clarity reigns. As a Vietnam War veteran, a graduate of Johns Hopkins University, and a seasoned professional in corporate America, Dominic brings a depth of experience and authority to his storytelling.